Why read ... *Black Sun...*

'A **fantastic read**: entertaining, tense, suspenseful, full of comic humour and wit'

'As good as *The Puppet Show*, **if not better**!'

'I would give it **a hundred stars** if I could'

'I am **stunned** by this book'

'Excellently plotted, well thought out, **instantly addictive** and wholly absorbing'

'M.W. Craven is in a **league of his own**'

'Everything I look for in a crime novel . . . A **banquet of delights**'

'M.W. Craven has done it again with the **unlikely, but fantastic, pairing** of Poe and Bradshaw'

'Dark, witty, **grisly**, brilliant!'

'The **one I had been waiting for** . . . it had me guessing right through to the end'

'What a premise! And what **phenomenal execution** too'

More praise from readers for

Black Summer . . .

'An outstanding return for Washington Poe and his colleague Tilly Bradshaw, in a thriller that is as captivating, dazzling and edgy as any crime mystery I've read this year'

'Readers of police procedurals and those who love puzzling, hard-to-solve crimes will not want to miss this one'

'For those who love a crime thriller that's taut and brilliantly twisted, it's a must-read'

'This second Washington Poe book is even more fiendishly twisty than the first'

'It's almost impossible not to fall in love with the fascinating dynamic between Poe and Tilly'

'I read it in two sittings because it was impossible to put down ... Aside from the brilliant story, I was overjoyed to have Poe and Tilly back in my life'

'One of the most unique and interesting murder mysteries I have had the pleasure to read'

'Undoubtedly my favourite crime book of 2019, and it breaks my heart that we have to wait until 2020 for another instalment of Washington Poe and Tilly Bradshaw'

'M.W. Craven proves that his stellar crime debut *The Puppet Show* was no fluke with this sequel featuring the charismatic pairing of D.S. Washington Poe and the unforgettable genius and endearing crime analyst, Matilda "Tilly" Bradshaw'

'I cannot find fault with anything in this book ... the only annoyance is that I now have to wait for book three!'

'The interaction between Poe and Bradshaw is beautifully written ... some real laugh-out-loud moments in an otherwise gruesome tale. This is a partnership that demonstrates absolute trust and loyalty, and it is a joy'

'If you are a fan of slick crime thrillers with fantastic characters, I can't recommend this series enough!'

'*Black Summer* is supremely visceral, expertly delivered, yet laced with a keen humour, and warm in the subtlest of ways. Beyond compelling, and brilliant to the point of outrageous. This will be massive'

'It will keep you gripped and guessing until the very end'

'This is a book to read when you have several hours to devote to it, as you will want to keep reading long beyond bedtime!'

'The twist at the end was amazing, and I for one didn't see it coming at all'

'Tautly written, well plotted with excellent characters, I was drawn into this book from the opening chapter and the tension and excitement never diminished'

'I was overjoyed to have Poe and Bradshaw back in my life … This is by far my favourite book of the year'

'Washington Poe is a superb creation … I was hooked from the very beginning. The story is ingenious, and the twists and turns are breathtaking. Brilliant!'

'[M.W. Craven] has a great way of writing … Very intelligent, knowledgeable, dark, emotional and, dare I say, a little twisted'

'Having crowned *The Puppet Show* the best book I've read this year, I had high hopes for *Black Summer*. But I wasn't disappointed. Not in the slightest … I can't praise this author, this series or this book enough'

'Utterly gripping, this book is a complete page-turner … Poe is a great character, and the plot is brilliant'

'A spectacular follow-up to *The Puppet Show*! Cleverly plotted, excellently written, and darkly funny throughout, I'd recommend this to anyone who loves top-notch crime fiction'

'The twists and turns of this book are so brilliant, some of them so completely unfathomable, that it is super hard to put it down. But what I love even more than the crazy-good plotting are the characters, especially Washington Poe and Tilly Bradshaw, and the atmospheric, beautiful but brutal Cumbrian setting'

Also by M.W. Craven

Washington Poe series
The Puppet Show

Avison Fluke series
Born in a Burial Gown
Body Breaker

BLACK SUMMER

M.W. CRAVEN

CONSTABLE

CONSTABLE

First published in Great Britain in 2019 by Constable

This paperback edition published in Great Britain in 2019 by Constable

Copyright © M.W. Craven, 2019

11 13 15 17 19 20 18 16 14 12

The moral right of the author has been asserted.

*All characters and events in this publication, other than those clearly in the public domain,
are fictitious and any resemblance to real persons, living or dead, is purely coincidental.*

All rights reserved.
No part of this publication may be reproduced, stored in a retrieval system, or
transmitted, in any form, or by any means, without the prior permission in writing of
the publisher, nor be otherwise circulated in any form of binding or cover other than
that in which it is published and without a similar condition including this condition
being imposed on the subsequent purchaser.

A CIP catalogue record for this book is available from the British Library.

ISBN: 978-1-47212-749-5

Typeset in Adobe Caslon Pro by Initial Typesetting Services, Edinburgh
Printed and bound in Great Britain by Clays Ltd, Elcograf S.p.A.

Papers used by Constable are from well-managed forests
and other responsible sources.

Constable
An imprint of
Little, Brown Book Group
Carmelite House
50 Victoria Embankment
London EC4Y 0DZ

The authorised representative
in the EEA is
Hachette Ireland
8 Castlecourt Centre
Dublin 15, D15 XTP3, Ireland
(email: info@hbgi.ie)

An Hachette UK Company
www.hachette.co.uk

www.littlebrown.co.uk

To Jo. My best friend, my soulmate.

My body is eating itself.

I can't stop it.

I'm too weak to move. My muscles have been broken down into the amino acids my body needs to stay alive. My joints stiffen and ache as they are no longer being lubricated. My feet and hands sting with pins and needles as the blood vessels under my skin contract to protect my major organs. My teeth loosen as my gums shrink.

The end is close.

I can feel it.

My breathing is rapid and shallow. I feel dizzy. For the first time in days I want to go to sleep. A sleep from which I'll never wake.

I'm not angry any more.

I was at first. For days I screamed and shouted at the unfairness of it all. That just when I was about to make my mark, everything was taken away from me by the man with the eyes of a shark.

I've accepted it now.

It's my fault, after all. I came down here voluntarily, eager to show off what I'd found.

I should have known that he didn't care about that. My discovery wasn't what he was interested in. He only cared about the other *thing.*

So, I'll lie down and rest my eyes.

For a minute.

Maybe a little bit longer . . .

CHAPTER ONE

In the South of France there is a songbird called the ortolan bunting.

It is six inches long and weighs less than an ounce. Its head is grey, its throat is pale yellow and its plumage a delightful orange. It has a stubby pink beak and its eyes shine like glass peppercorns. Its staccato chirping brings a smile to all who hear it.

It is a thing of remarkable beauty.

Most people, when they see an ortolan bunting, want to keep it as a pet.

Not everyone.

Some people don't see its beauty.

Some people see something else.

Because the *other* remarkable thing about the ortolan bunting is that it's the main ingredient in the most sadistic dish in the world. A dish that demands the tiny songbird is not only killed, it is tortured . . .

The chef had bought two, a month earlier. You can't shoot ortolans without destroying them, so she'd paid a man to net them. He'd charged her one hundred euros each. A steep price but the fines if he'd been caught were far steeper.

She'd taken them home and fattened them up the way the cooks at Roman banquets had done: by stabbing out their eyes. For the two ortolans, day turned into night.

And at night they fed.

For a month they gorged on millet, grapes and figs. They quadrupled in size. Fat enough to eat.

A dish fit for a king.

Or an old friend.

When the call came she'd taken them over the Channel herself.

She'd disembarked at Dover and driven all night to a restaurant in Cumbria called Bullace & Sloe.

Her two diners could not have been more of a contrast.

One man wore a fine suit with a high collar. It looked oriental in design. His shirt was stiff and white and his cufflinks were pure gold. He appeared cultured and at ease. He had an affable smile and would have raised the tone of any dining room in the world.

The other man wore mud-spattered jeans and a wet jacket. His boots dripped dirty water onto the dining room floor. He looked as though he'd been dragged through a gorse bush backwards. Even in the low light of the flickering candles he looked nervous and fidgety. Desperate.

A waiter approached their table and presented the birds in the copper pots they'd been roasted in.

'I think you'll enjoy this dish,' the man in the suit said. 'It's a songbird called the ortolan bunting. Chef Jégado brought them over from Paris herself, and not fifteen minutes ago she drowned them in brandy . . .'

His companion stared at the bird: it was toe-sized and spitting in its own fat. He looked up. 'What do you mean, "drowned"?'

'It's how you get brandy into their lungs.'

'That's barbaric.'

The man in the suit smiled. He'd heard this all before when he'd worked in France. 'We throw live lobsters into boiling water. We rip the claws off living crabs. We force-feed geese for foie gras. There is suffering in every bite of an animal we take, no?'

4

'It's not legal then,' the man in jeans countered.

'We all have legal problems. Yours are more serious than mine, I think? Eat the bird, don't eat the bird, it is all the same to me. But, if you decide to, do as I do. It will create a scent-tent and hide your gluttony from God.'

The man in the suit placed a starched, blood-red napkin over his head and put the bird in his mouth. Only its head remained outside. He bit down and the head fell onto his plate.

The ortolan was scalding hot. For a minute the man in the suit did nothing but rest it on his tongue and take small, rapid breaths to cool it. The delicious fat began to melt down his throat.

He sighed in appreciation. It had been six years since he'd been able to dine like this. He chewed into the bird. An explosion of fat, guts, bones and blood filled his mouth. The sweet flesh and bitter entrails were sublime. The grease that coated the roof of his mouth was breathtaking. Sharp bones pierced his gums and his own blood seasoned the meat.

It was almost overwhelming.

And finally his teeth penetrated the ortolan's lungs. His mouth was flooded with the delicious Armagnac.

The man in the jeans didn't touch his bird. He couldn't see the man in the suit's face – it was still under the napkin – but he heard the crunch of bones and his sighs of pleasure.

It took fifteen minutes for the man in the suit to finish eating the songbird. When he emerged from underneath his napkin, he wiped away the blood that was dribbling down his chin and smiled at his guest.

The man in the wet jeans spoke, and the man in the suit listened. After a while, and for the first time that evening, the man in the suit showed a hint of annoyance. Fear flashed across his perfectly composed face.

'It's an interesting story,' the man in the suit said. 'But alas, one we can't continue, I'm afraid. It seems there are others joining us.'

The man in the wet jeans turned around. There was a figure dressed in an ordinary, workaday suit standing at the door. A uniformed police officer was by his side.

'So close.' The man in the suit shook his head and beckoned the police officers inside.

The plainclothes officer approached the table. 'Sir, could you come with us, please?'

The man in jeans, his eyes darting, searched for a way out. The waiter and the chef were both in the kitchen so they would block his escape.

The uniformed officer extended his baton.

'Don't do anything stupid, sir,' the plainclothes officer said.

'Too late for that,' the man in jeans snarled. He grabbed a half-full wine bottle by the neck and held it in front of him like a club. Its contents sluiced down his still-damp shirt.

It was a Mexican stand-off.

The man in the suit watched it unfold, the smile never leaving his face.

'You have to let me explain!' the man in jeans hissed.

'You'll get your chance tomorrow,' said the plainclothes officer.

The uniformed policeman moved to the man's left.

The kitchen door opened. The waiter walked out. He was holding a platter of oysters. He saw what was happening and dropped the metal dish in surprise. Ice cubes and shellfish scattered across the flagged floor.

It was the distraction they needed. The uniformed officer went low; the plainclothes officer went high. The baton took the man behind the knees and the plainclothes officer's punch caught him on the jaw.

The man in jeans collapsed. The uniformed officer knelt on his back, pushed his head into the flagstone floor and handcuffed him.

'Washington Poe,' the plainclothes officer said, 'I'm arresting you on suspicion of murder. You do not have to say anything, but it may harm your defence if you do not mention when questioned something that you later rely on in court. Anything you do say may be given in evidence.'

Two weeks earlier:

Day 1

CHAPTER TWO

The blue light has gone out in rural England. Grand old Victorian police stations have been consigned to history, reduced in number and replaced by modern, well-equipped and soulless centres of excellence.

And gone too is the local bobby. They now only exist in the minds of those who yearn for a rural idyll. These days, police officers mostly see their patch through the windows of a patrol car.

Tesco has twice as many twenty-four-hour shops as the police have twenty-four-hour stations.

Nowhere has been hit harder than Cumbria. A county of almost three thousand square miles – geographically, the third-largest in England – has just five full-time police stations.

Alston, in the North Pennines, the highest market town in the country, never stood a chance. Its police station, a large and beautiful detached building, was sold in 2012 and replaced with a police *desk*. On the fourth Wednesday of the month, a member of the Eden Rural neighbourhood policing team – designated as 'problem solvers' – would drive all the way up there, sit behind a desk in the library and listen to people complain.

Problem Solver Constable Graham Alsop hated the fourth Wednesday of the month. He also hated being called a problem solver. Some of the gripes he was forced to listen to were so mind-numbingly petty, so headbangingly intractable, he felt the town sometimes had the collective intelligence of fish bait.

He didn't need to go back further than a month to find a

good example of what he had to put up with. An elderly gent had approached him and dumped a full bag of dog turds on his desk. Fucking dog turds. The man had said he was sick of finding them in with his prize-winning Lady Penzance roses. Claimed his neighbour was letting her gimpy dachshund defecate all over them as revenge for beating her in the village show. He'd demanded that Alsop take them to the 'lab' for DNA testing. He'd seemed surprised to find out there was no 'lab', nor was there a dog DNA database that could compare one turd against another. It was a civil matter and the constable accordingly advised him to see a solicitor. And he was to take his bag of shit with him. Of course, if it escalated into an infamous dog-turd murder, Problem Solver Constable Alsop would have some explaining to do, but some risks were worth taking.

That said, it *was* an easy day. The library opened at nine and, until the first reading group arrived an hour later, Alsop and the library staff usually had the place to themselves. Plenty of time for tea and toast before the lunatics arrived.

And that morning he even had a plan. He would read his paper then wander across to the deli for some Alston cheese. One of the librarians was going to teach him how to make a soufflé. And Alsop reckoned baking a cheese soufflé for his long-suffering wife would be the perfect way to soften her up before telling her about his proposed golfing trip to Portugal.

It was a good plan.

But the thing about plans is that they can turn into a bag of turds in the blink of an eye.

At first he thought the girl was doing the walk of shame, sloping back home after a night in someone else's bed. She wore a woollen hat, a plain, long-sleeved T-shirt and black leggings. She was limping, her progress uneven and faltering. Her cheap trainers scuffed on the carpet.

She stood in the middle of the library and looked around. She didn't seem to have any particular book in mind. Her eyes ran over children's fiction, then local history, then autobiographies. Probably a ruse so she could use the toilets. A quick wash, maybe a line of coke, then a taxi back to Carlisle. Alston didn't have a resident student population but parties still happened.

But . . . for most of his career Alsop had been a beat cop in Carlisle city centre and he still had all the right instincts.

Something was a bit off.

His initial assessment had been wrong. The girl didn't look ashamed, she looked scared. Her eyes flitted back and forth, searching for something. She squinted through the dust floating lazily in the air, never settling on any one thing for more than a second. But the books, neatly arranged, spines out and in alphabetical order, weren't holding her interest. She was checking out the library staff, dismissing each one as soon as she laid eyes on them.

When she saw him, Alsop knew his morning was no longer going to be about baking the perfect soufflé. He was the reason she was there. She limped over to his desk, her face contorting with the effort. She stood in front of him, draping her left arm across her skinny frame and grabbing her right elbow. Her head tilted to one side. It would have been cute if it weren't so disturbing.

'Are you the police?' Her voice was flat.

'Not all of them, no,' he replied.

She didn't smile at the flippant remark. Didn't respond at all. Alsop studied her, trying to get a clue, a heads-up as to what was about to happen. Because he was under no illusion: something was about to happen.

The girl was exhausted. Her tired brown eyes were set back in bruised, shrunken sockets. The hair that poked out from underneath her hat was tangled, limp and lifeless. It framed a harsh face. Her pallid cheekbones were pronounced and the grime on her skin was broken by tear tracks. White gunk had formed around a mouth surrounded by spots. And she was skinny. Not skinny in a fashion model kind of way. Gaunt. Malnourished.

Alsop walked round to the other side of his desk, pulled out a seat and offered it to her. She sank into it gratefully. He returned to his own seat, steepled his fingers and rested his chin on them. 'Now, love, what can I do for you?' He was an old-school cop and had no use for the gender-neutral forms of address he was supposed to use.

She didn't answer. Just stared through him. He may as well have not been there.

That was OK, though. He was used to dealing with the public and knew that people gave up things in their own time.

'Tell you what, why don't we start with an easy one? Why don't we start with your name?'

She blinked and seemed to snap out of whatever trance she'd been in, but it looked like the concept of a name was alien to her.

'You know what a name is? Everyone's got one, right?'

She still didn't smile.

But she did tell him what she was called.

And Alsop knew he was in trouble.

They all were.

Day 4

CHAPTER THREE

An old Cherokee said to his grandson who'd come to him filled with hate for someone: 'Let me tell you a story. I too have felt hate for those who have done me wrong. But hate wears you down and does not hurt those who have hurt you. It is like taking poison and wishing your enemy would die. I've struggled with these feelings many times. It is as if there are two wolves inside me, fighting to dominate my spirit. One wolf is good and does no harm. He lives in harmony with everyone around him, and he takes no offence when none is intended.'

'What about the other wolf, Grandfather?'

'Ah,' the old man replied. 'The other wolf is bad. He is filled with anger. The smallest thing sets him off into fits of temper. He cannot think properly because his anger and hate are so great. And it is a helpless anger, for it cannot change anything.'

The boy looked into his grandfather's eyes. 'Which wolf wins, Grandfather?'

The old man smiled. 'The one I feed.'

Detective Sergeant Washington Poe had been thinking about the old Cherokee fable recently. All his life he'd been feeding the bad wolf. He'd thought he'd known why. His mother leaving him when he was an infant had made him an angry child, and the feeling of abandonment had never disappeared. It had occasionally grown fainter, but rarely long enough for him to make it through a whole night without bolting awake, trembling.

And now he knew that his anger had been based on a lie.

Poe had been conceived when his mother was raped at a diplomatic party in Washington, DC. She hadn't abandoned him at all. And, like a warning label, she'd named him Washington so she'd have the courage to leave. She was terrified she wouldn't be able to hide her revulsion when the image of her rapist began to appear on her son's face.

The man who had raised him, the man he'd called Dad for nearly forty years, wasn't his biological father. That honour belonged to someone else.

Since he'd discovered the truth, his anger and resentment had morphed into a white-hot rage, a burning need for retribution. That his mother had died before he'd found out added to his sense of raw injustice. Something inside him had crumbled to dust recently.

For a while, he'd had the distraction of the Immolation Man Inquiry. He'd been a key witness and had spent days giving evidence to committees and at public hearings. But now it was over. Poe's testimony, along with the evidence that he and everyone else involved in the case had uncovered, had ensured the right result: the Immolation Man's story was verified and in the public domain. Poe had won but it was a hollow victory. What he'd learned about his mother had blunted any satisfaction of a job well done.

Someone asked him a question and he jolted back to the present. He tried to focus on what was happening. He was representing the Serious Crime Analysis Section at a departmental budget meeting. It took place every three months and, for reasons long forgotten, it was always on a Saturday. Section heads usually attended it, but when he'd been the temporary detective inspector he'd delegated the duty to his detective sergeant, Stephanie Flynn. When she'd taken over the DI reins on a permanent basis, and their roles had been reversed, she'd taken a perverse delight in doing the same to him. Now *he* had to go to London every

18

quarter, not her. He didn't appreciate the irony, although he did like being a sergeant again. It was the optimum balance between power and responsibility. And being an inspector had never sat well with him. The rank always sounded as though it should be prefaced with 'ticket', or 'lavatory'.

'I'm sorry, what?'

'We're discussing quarterly projections, Sergeant Poe. DI Flynn has asked for a three per cent increase in SCAS's overtime budget. Do you know why?'

Poe did. He usually didn't. Usually he kept his mouth shut and relied on Flynn's paperwork being thorough enough to not warrant further examination. He picked up the document. It fell to pieces. Poe silently cursed the admin assistant who'd prepared it for him. If papers were supposed to be together, then staple them. Paperclips were for hippies and people with commitment issues. He gathered them up but couldn't tell if they were in the right order. The words and page numbers were a blurry mess. He removed his reading glasses from his top pocket. They were a new thing. A reminder that he wasn't a young man any more. Not that he needed reminding – these days he clicked when he walked. When he found himself holding documents farther and farther away from his eyes, he decided to take the plunge and get tested. Now he couldn't drink coffee without his glasses steaming up. He couldn't lie on his side and read in bed. He'd forget they were there and knock them off. He'd forget they *weren't* there and jab himself in the eye when he tried to adjust them. And no matter how hard he tried, he couldn't keep them clean.

He rubbed them on his tie now. He might as well have wiped them on some chips. He squinted through the smudge and familiarised himself with the document.

'It's because of the Immolation Man case. Myself, Analyst Bradshaw and DI Flynn were in Cumbria for some time and most of the OT budget was used up. She wanted to spread the cost rather than hit you with a large deficit at the end of the financial year.'

'Makes sense,' the meeting's chair said. 'Anyone want to add anything? I suppose we could argue that it falls under the LOOB provisions.'

By the time Poe had failed to locate LOOB in his internal database of nonsensical acronyms, the discussion had moved on to an additional funding request from the transnational organised crime unit. They were struggling to cope with the threat of Entity B. Not a lot was known about them. They didn't run bouncers or women. They didn't have dealers on street corners. They *did*, however, control the supply routes the underworld used. If a Chinese illegal was working off debt in a south London brothel, the chances were it was Entity B taking the biggest cut of her takings. If a mid-level heroin supplier in Arbroath was cutting his product with brick dust, then the pure stuff almost certainly came from an Entity B supply chain. If another Russian state-sponsored assassination occurred on British soil, it was likely the killer had been smuggled in and out of the country by Entity B.

But . . . managing Entity B was someone else's job. His was to catch serial killers and help solve apparently motiveless crimes. Something he hadn't spent too much time thinking about lately. He stopped himself subsiding back into thoughts of revenge and retribution. He didn't want to keep feeding the bad wolf. Instead he turned on his phone to see if there were any news alerts about Storm Wendy. It was all the media were talking about. A summer storm was rare. A storm of this supposed magnitude was a once in a generation event.

While he waited for his BlackBerry to power up, he examined his reflection in the blackened screen. A sullen, grizzled face with bleary, bloodshot eyes squinted back – the inevitable by-product of neglect, insomnia and self-pity.

The screen changed from black mirror to colourful apps, most of which he didn't recognise and wouldn't use if he did. He had three missed calls and a text message, all from Flynn. He was on-call so should have had his BlackBerry switched on, but in the National Crime Agency if you got a reputation for answering your phone, it never stopped ringing. He read the text: Call me as soon as you get this.

That didn't sound good. Poe made his excuses and left the room. The office manager directed him towards an empty desk. He dialled Flynn and she answered on the first ring.

'Poe, you need to contact Detective Superintendent Gamble immediately. He's waiting for your call.'

'Gamble? What's he want?'

Gamble worked for Cumbria Constabulary and had been the senior investigating officer on the Immolation Man case. He'd been demoted one rank when the dust settled and the finger-pointing began. Poe knew Gamble considered himself lucky to still have a job. Although they hadn't always seen eye-to-eye, they'd parted on good terms. Their paths had crossed occasionally during the inquiry, but it was over now. There was no obvious reason for them to talk.

'He wouldn't tell me, which makes me think it may not be about the Immolation Man,' Flynn replied.

Poe had left Cumbria Constabulary five years ago. His home was still there but if anything had happened to it, it would be a uniformed constable from the Kendal station calling, not the superintendent from Major Crimes. And anyway, his home was four solid walls of unrendered Lakeland stone, a slate roof and not much else. There wasn't really anything that *could* happen to it.

'OK, I'll call him.'

She gave him Gamble's number. 'Let me know?'

'Will do.'

21

Poe hung up and dialled Gamble. Like Flynn, he answered on the first ring.

'Sir, it's DS Poe. I got a message to ring you.'

'Poe, we have a problem.'

CHAPTER FOUR

Poe, we have a problem. Five words he never tired of hearing.

Flynn had arranged for him to get the first available train to Cumbria. He had an hour before it left. The tickets would be waiting for him at Euston. He had no idea what was up; Gamble wouldn't tell him anything more over the phone.

Poe made his train with fifteen minutes to spare. London to Penrith was just over three hours and he spent the time on his phone, searching for anything in the news that might hint at what he was about to step into. He found nothing out of the ordinary. Storm Wendy continued to dominate the local and national press. It was still a week away but had already wreaked havoc on the other side of the Atlantic.

A uniformed officer waited for him at Penrith and he was whisked off to Carleton Hall – Cumbria Police's headquarters building. Ten minutes later he was taken to Conference Room B. It was a large room, full of character. Poe thought it might have once been the Carleton family's dining room. It had the original, ornate fireplace, a carved mantelpiece and tall, impractical windows. A long conference table dominated the room.

Detective Superintendent Gamble was already there. A detective Poe thought he remembered from his days on the local force sat beside him.

They both looked up. Poe got the impression he'd interrupted something. The detective's expression was flat and neutral. He had a large file in front of him. He closed it and put it face down.

Poe nodded a hello. Gamble returned it, the other man didn't. Gamble stood and shook his hand. Poe noticed him glance down.

'How is it?' Gamble asked.

The skin on Poe's right hand was shiny and scarred. A permanent reminder of what happens when you grab a cast-iron radiator in a house fire. He'd been trying to get the Immolation Man out of a burning farmhouse at the time. He flexed it and said, 'Not bad. Got most of the feeling back.'

'Coffee?'

Poe declined. He'd already had too much and he was feeling jittery.

'I think you already know DC Andrew Rigg,' Gamble said. 'He has some questions about one of your older cases.'

Rigg had been in uniform when Poe was with CID. Tall and gangly, with buck teeth that occasionally earned him the nickname Plug, Poe remembered him as a solid cop.

'What's going on?'

Rigg wouldn't meet his eyes, which was strange. They'd never been friends but there'd never been hostility between them.

'Tell me about the Elizabeth Keaton investigation, Sergeant Poe,' he said.

Elizabeth Keaton . . .

Why wasn't he surprised?

'It was the last major case I worked up here,' Poe said. 'Started as a high-risk missing person. Her father had called 999 from his restaurant. He was in hysterics saying his daughter hadn't returned home.'

Rigg looked at his notes. 'It was a suspected abduction?'

'Not immediately.'

24

'Not what it says here. According to the file, abduction was discussed very early on.'

Poe nodded. 'The file says that because it's what Jared Keaton was saying.'

Gamble's brow furrowed. 'I was attached to the Met back then, and I don't want to second-guess what happened, but might there have been some pandering? We don't usually let relatives dictate our lines of enquiry.'

Shrugging, Poe said, 'Most relatives don't cook for the prime minister.'

At the time of his daughter's disappearance, Jared Keaton was the owner of Cumbria's only three-Michelin-starred restaurant: Bullace & Sloe. He was a celebrity chef who counted film stars, rock icons and ex-presidents as his patrons. He'd cooked for the Queen and he'd cooked for Nelson Mandela. When a chef with three Michelin stars spoke, important people listened.

'So it *was* pandering?'

'No. The file said what Keaton wanted it to say. We investigated Elizabeth Keaton's disappearance the same way we would every other young girl's: seriously and with an open mind.'

Gamble nodded, satisfied with Poe's explanation. 'Go on.'

'She should have called him for a lift back from the restaurant, but he'd fallen asleep watching the television and hadn't woken until the early hours. It was then he noticed that she hadn't returned home.'

'She worked there?'

'Front-of-house and accounts. Dealt with suppliers and the payroll, that type of thing. She was also responsible for closing up at the end of the night.'

'She was still a teenager. Wasn't she a bit young for all that responsibility?'

'You know her mother died in a car crash?'

Rigg nodded.

'She took over from her.'

'So, she never called him for a lift?'

Poe knew the file was thorough. Knew that Rigg was doing what every good cop did: asking questions to which he already knew the answers. It still rankled, though. The investigation might have headed down the wrong road initially, but it quickly about-turned.

'Not according to Keaton. He said the phone would have woken him.'

'Bullace & Sloe was only a short walk from the Keaton family home. Why would she need a lift?'

Poe shrugged. 'Young girl late at night, I suppose.'

'And this was when you got involved?'

'It was. I'm surprised you weren't too. There were hundreds looking for her.'

'I was,' Rigg admitted. 'I was part of the lot that walked the route from the restaurant all the way to the M6, searching for any sign of a struggle.'

The M6 was the spine of Cumbria and it neatly bisected the county in two. Poe remembered seeing cops scanning the verges, stopping passing cars and showing photographs.

'Although the M6 was seen as the abductor's most likely route,' Poe said, 'we did our jobs and considered *every* angle.'

Rigg referred to his notes again. 'It was you who asked for the kitchen to be forensically examined.'

Poe nodded. 'Although the detectives working the case had searched and found nothing, I wanted a crime scene manager to go through it with CSI and double-check Elizabeth hadn't been taken at source. I wanted to at least rule it out.'

'Why were you thinking differently? Nobody else suspected anything other than what it seemed to be.'

'Nearest and dearest until proven otherwise,' Poe said. 'I thought someone should at least ask the question.'

'And that's when CSI found it?'

'It was SOCO back then, but yes, that's when they found it,' Poe confirmed. 'In the kitchens.'

CHAPTER FIVE

The 'it' referred to bloodstaining.

Not a lot, but when CSI found the first traces, the kitchens of Bullace & Sloe went from being a place of award-winning gastronomic excellence to a crime scene. Poe talked them through what had happened next, the details of the case flooding back as he did.

'The early forensic strategy was to find out exactly what had happened in the kitchen. CSI used luminol and found more blood. Lots of it. It was on the ceiling and some of the low-level fixtures. The amount lost was judged to have been incompatible with life.' Poe stopped to take a sip from the glass of water in front of him. 'With blood confirmed, they used 360-degree photography and blood pattern analysis to build up a picture.'

'Which was?'

'There'd been a brutal and sustained assault, there was more than one attack site, and attempts had been made to conceal the crime.'

'A clean-up?'

'And not a particularly sophisticated one. Enough to beat a visual examination but nowhere near good enough to beat a scientific one. Little more than a wipe-down really.'

'The blood matched Elizabeth's?'

Poe nodded.

'And it was then the investigation changed from a high-risk missing person's investigation to a murder?' Rigg asked.

'That's right. Additional resources were found, overtime was preapproved and all leave for Major Crimes staff was cancelled.'

'Working theory?'

'The early lines of enquiry were it was either a drifter who'd come to the back door in search of food or petty cash, or a stalker we didn't yet know about.'

'What did you think?'

'I wasn't sure. I doubted it was a drifter. Not in Cotehill – they'd have stood out like a turd on a cake. Someone would have seen them.'

'A stalker?'

'That was certainly what the senior investigating officer thought. Elizabeth was eighteen years old and looked like a young Audrey Hepburn. She was popular and had an active social life. We examined all her belongings. Phones, computers, diaries. Found nothing. We did passive data searches and reviewed CCTV recordings of the last few times she'd been out in Carlisle. Again, nothing. The SIO expanded the search to include any man she'd had contact with. Old school friends, men in her social group – no matter how fleeting their interaction – staff at Bullace & Sloe. Everyone, basically.'

'What about you?'

'I began looking at Jared Keaton.'

CHAPTER SIX

'Why was that, Sergeant Poe?' Rigg asked.

Poe composed himself. The truth was, Keaton hadn't been a suspect initially. Not even with him. Not really. It had been a sense of unease, a feeling that something wasn't quite right.

'There were discrepancies in his statement.'

'Go on.'

'Someone in the village had driven past the restaurant on their way back from Manchester Airport. They said his car was still there at two in the morning.'

'Eyewitnesses are extremely unreliable,' Rigg said.

Poe nodded. They were. According to the Innocence Project, eyewitness accounts were inaccurate 75 per cent of the time.

'There was more,' he said. 'Keaton said he drove home to watch *Match of the Day* but it was an international weekend: *Match of the Day* wasn't on.'

'Easy mistake to make.'

'Agreed. It's transmitted almost every Saturday night so you can assume it'll be on. But you're hardly likely to forget it wasn't if you go home especially to watch it.'

'That all?'

'He had all night. In fact, he called only twenty minutes before the early shift came in to start prepping the lunch service.'

'He said that was when he woke up.'

'And if that *were* the case, if he had woken up and noticed his daughter was missing seven hours after she was supposed to be home, why would he drive straight to the restaurant? Why would he assume she was there? Why didn't he call her friends first?'

'So you suspected him?'

'Enough to not rule him out.'

'But if he was the killer, where did he hide her?' Gamble asked. 'I know you didn't think he'd buried her.'

Poe shook his head. 'No. We were in the middle of a sustained cold snap. Temperatures hadn't risen above freezing for almost a month. The expert in geoforensics we consulted said that the frost line – that's the depth at which the groundwater in soil is frozen – was down to three and a half feet. He'd have needed mechanical tools to bury her.'

'He couldn't have driven her somewhere for later disposal?'

Again, Poe shook his head. 'We put his Range Rover through a full examination. Not a single trace of blood was found and, believe me, Elizabeth Keaton did not die well; she would have left a mess in whatever she was transported in. Even if he'd wrapped her in bin bags and sealed them with duct tape, there'd have been some forensic transfer. The body would have been far too wet.'

'But you searched anyway?'

Poe nodded. 'We did. A field-based geoscientist came up from Preston. She examined the surrounding area and gave us the most likely deposition sites. She completed an aerial image analysis to see if there were any obvious recent ground disturbances, and she took samples of all surrounding water just in case Elizabeth was buried near some groundwater. None of it came back positive. We searched but found nothing.'

Gamble said, 'I hesitate to bring this up, but if you believed the murder took place in the kitchen, did you consider she might have been processed? Fed into the grinder and disposed of as kitchen waste?'

'We did. Every tool and machine in the kitchen capable of

reducing animals into their component parts was put under a microscope. We turned the kitchen upside down. Checked the meat in the freezers. Found nothing at all to suggest that anything had been used to assist in body disposal.'

'So—'

'So if he couldn't have done it, why did I still think it was him?'

Gamble nodded. The atmosphere was heavy with unspoken words. Poe wondered if Keaton had finally been granted leave to appeal his conviction.

'Because by then I'd stopped focusing on who Jared Keaton was, and began focusing on *what* he was.'

'Which was?' Rigg asked.

There was a long pause before Poe answered. 'Have you ever seen a list of the most popular careers for psychopaths, DC Rigg?'

Rigg shook his head.

'No? Perhaps you should. I can tell you that number three is the media. Bit of a no-brainer, right? You can't turn on the TV or open a newspaper without seeing people who imagine themselves so important that everything they say or do should be exposed to the public. Make sense?'

'I suppose. But what's that got to do with—'

'Can you guess number nine?'

Rigg, not in the mood for guessing games, said nothing.

'Chef,' Poe said. 'Number nine on the list is chef.'

The room stayed silent.

'And Jared Keaton wasn't just a chef; he was a *celebrity* chef. Three *and* nine on the list. Technically he was also the CEO of a business. Number one on the list. A toxic trio. So I looked at the man in depth. Full profile. Spoke to his friends and colleagues, old and new. Took his life to pieces, bit by bit. And I came to this conclusion, gentlemen: he might not have horns but, in every other regard, Jared Keaton is the complete manifestation of evil.'

CHAPTER SEVEN

How on earth did you describe Jared Keaton to someone who didn't know him?

Charming. Charismatic. Highly intelligent. A genius chef. No conscience whatsoever. The most dangerous man Poe had ever met. He'd taken an instant dislike to him. He was too superficial, too well groomed, too polished. He'd reminded Poe of a fake Irish pub. Pretty, but of no real substance.

'I found a different person to the one we've all seen on the Saturday morning cookery programmes,' Poe said. 'The happy, cheeky, playful chef was an act. A part he felt obliged to play. Off camera he was detached, unflinching and manipulative. I don't think he enjoyed the celebrity lifestyle, but as a chef he was the real deal. Every person I interviewed said Jared Keaton was a focused and brilliant man. Intuitive about food trends, ahead of his peers with new techniques, a perfectionist with his wine pairing. His front-of-house hospitality was unmatched. By all accounts he was the best the country has ever produced. He put the UK on the culinary map. Chefs, celebrities and restaurant critics from all over the world still come to eat at Bullace & Sloe.'

'That's what I have here,' Rigg said, reading a page with pink highlighted sections. 'Statements say he was witty, clever, genius, dedicated, gorgeous.'

'No one ever said he was nice, though,' Poe said. 'And that's because he wasn't. He was a cruel man. Found a sadistic joy in causing pain. Capable of holding extraordinary grudges, taking excessive revenge against imagined slights, and punishing chefs who made mistakes.'

'Explain,' Gamble said.

'One chef told me about the time he'd over-seasoned some stock. Keaton made him drink salted water for the rest of the day. He spent three days in hospital with kidney damage.'

Rigg flipped through the file, frowning. 'That's not in here, Sergeant Poe.'

'No. A lot isn't. You have to understand that Jared Keaton was held in awe by almost every chef in the country. A bad word from him could break a career. No one wanted to go on the record.'

'Anything else?' Gamble said.

'Lots, sir, but I'll tell you the one that really demonstrates what type of person he was. I heard this from three separate sources so, as far as I'm concerned, it's credible. Jared Keaton ran a traditional kitchen and that meant it was split into different sections. Hot stations like fish, soup and sauce, and cold stations like hors d'oeuvres, salads and showpiece preparation. Bakery and desserts. Weighing and checking, vegetable prep, pot wash, plating.'

'So?' Rigg said.

'A kitchen is like any other place of work. Certain jobs are more sought after. They have a higher status and they pay more. In other words, chefs and kitchen staff can go for promotions.'

Rigg and Gamble waited for him to explain.

'Now, in the police, we have promotion boards. You take the necessary courses and apply for posts as they come up. Attend interviews. Jared Keaton did it differently. He had the hot-plate challenge. If two or more people wanted a position, he had them hold their hands on the hot plate. The one who left them on the longest – the one who was prepared to endure serious burns for their work – got the promotion.'

'That has urban myth written all over it,' Rigg said.

34

'The three people I spoke to all had hands like mine.' He turned his own hand palm up, showed his scars, and waited for what he'd said to sink in. 'That's who we were dealing with, gents. You will never meet a more intelligent and evil man.'

He paused. Took another drink of water.

'But his intelligence was also his greatest weakness. I don't think he could conceive that someone might not believe him. He'd spent his whole life bending and shaping people to his every whim, so hadn't considered that someone might be immune. When I conducted a forensic check on the business, I found that he'd recently purchased several items.'

'Which were?'

'A butcher's saw, a heavy and a light cleaver, and a boning knife.'

'I assume what you've described are the tools of his trade?'

'They are. And Bullace & Sloe buy whole carcasses to butcher on site. More economical that way. But there are two things you need to be aware of: Jared Keaton wouldn't ordinarily dirty himself with ordering equipment – that was Elizabeth's job – and the make of the knives and cleavers he ordered matched the sets they used in the kitchen.'

'So?'

'I believed he killed Elizabeth with those tools.'

'All of them?'

Poe shrugged. 'We know there was a struggle. He might not have had it all his own way. He had no defence wounds but that doesn't mean Elizabeth didn't pick up something to defend herself with. I think the *original* tools are wherever she is.'

'Yet you still had no idea how he transported her corpse and you have no idea how he disposed of her,' Rigg said. 'Hardly a perfect case, Poe.'

'No case ever is. And anyway, perfection's the enemy of good.'

* * *

35

'Did you ever develop a motive?' Rigg asked. 'Even one you couldn't share?'

'Other than him being a psychopath, I didn't come close,' Poe admitted.

'Best guess?'

'Guessing's dangerous for detectives. I try not to indulge.'

Rigg reddened at the rebuke. He went back to his file. 'You think he planned it?'

Poe waited a beat. 'He's certainly intelligent enough to get away with murder. The fact he didn't makes me think, no, he didn't plan it.'

'Spur of the moment then?'

'Probably. But if you try and apply the thought processes of a normal person when second-guessing what Jared Keaton might have done when he was under pressure, you'll always get it wrong.'

'So, no means, no motive, and only a tenuous window of opportunity,' Rigg said. 'I'm surprised the CPS authorised the charge.'

It wasn't a question so Poe said nothing. The CPS decision to charge Keaton with murder had been based on two things: his absolute refusal to try and explain the discrepancies, and the fact that a murder had almost certainly occurred.

Rigg scowled at Poe's silence.

'I'm amazed he was convicted,' Gamble said. He looked tired.

'I'm not,' Poe said. 'The CPS did a good job persuading the jury, but ultimately Keaton was undone by his own ego.'

'His ego?' Rigg asked.

'His brief didn't want him to take the stand but he insisted. I think he thought all he needed to do was smile and wink at the two women on the jury.'

'There were only two women?' Rigg said. 'That's statistically unlikely.'

36

'One of those quirk of fate things. And his all-powerful charm wasn't as effective on working-class men from Cumbria.'

'Two jurors going not guilty would be enough, though.'

'The foreman was a strong character,' Poe said. 'And they took a long time. Almost two days. When the verdict was read out Keaton was outraged. He couldn't believe he'd been found guilty. It was the right decision, though, and I slept well that night. It's not often you take a true psychopath off the street.'

Rigg didn't reply. Instead, he looked to Gamble for guidance. 'Sir?'

Gamble nodded once.

'So what would you say, Sergeant Poe, if I told you that three days ago Elizabeth Keaton walked into Alston Library alive and well?'

CHAPTER EIGHT

Poe went rigid. The summer tan drained from his face. A sheen of sweat formed at the back of his neck. Conference Room B had descended into silence.

'Impossible,' Poe whispered. The blood in his ears was deafening. He could barely hear himself. It couldn't be true. Elizabeth Keaton was dead. Jared Keaton had killed her. He knew it in his bones. Someone was playing a trick. But . . . Gamble wouldn't have brought him back to Cumbria unless he'd already checked under his bed.

What wasn't he being told?

'Tell me what you know,' he said.

'It was a bad investigation from the start, Sergeant Poe,' Rigg said. 'You had no body, no way Keaton could have disposed of a body, and no motive. But instead of doing what you should have been doing, which was searching for an abducted girl, you fixated on the first solution that fell in your lap.' He jabbed his finger in Poe's direction. 'Just because you didn't like him.'

Poe stared at the tall detective. Rigg's eyes were angry.

Rigg flicked through his file and removed a photograph. He slid it across the table. It was a screenshot of a girl in an interview room. Probably a still from a video recording.

Poe rubbed his reading glasses on the cuff of his shirt and perched them on his nose. He studied the woman in the photograph. His stomach acid began to bite. Her age *did* look right. Elizabeth Keaton was eighteen when she was murdered and the girl in the photograph was in her mid-twenties. And despite being gaunt and unkempt, she *did* look like Elizabeth Keaton might have looked if she'd lived for another six years.

'Elizabeth Keaton was abducted by a man who'd entered the kitchen through the servers' door,' Rigg said. 'She thinks he might have been a customer who'd hidden in the disabled toilet until everyone but her had left for the night.'

Poe couldn't drag his eyes away from the photograph.

'You were right about one thing: there *was* a violent struggle in the kitchen. The man – and after six years we finally have a description – tied her up before nicking one of her larger veins with a knife. According to Elizabeth he filled a sauté pan with her blood and then spilled, sprayed and threw it everywhere. Made it look like an abattoir. He then set about cleaning it up.'

'But . . . but why?'

'Why? I'm keen to ask him that myself. We assume he staged a murder so you . . . sorry, the *investigation* would focus on the wrong thing. Looking for a body is completely different to looking for a person. The media strategy is different, the tech support is different, the experts you call in are different. While you were busy accusing Jared Keaton, Elizabeth Keaton was being raped in a cellar.'

Poe flinched. If it were true then he was responsible for a catastrophic mistake. A mistake he knew he'd never recover from.

'Talk me through how you originally matched the blood found in the kitchen with Elizabeth Keaton,' Rigg said.

'We swabbed it and got a DNA profile. We then took more samples from a variety of sources to check the blood was Elizabeth's. We used hair from her bedroom and from her work clothes. We sourced saliva from her toothbrush and from a can of Coke we found in the bin. Everything matched. The blood in the kitchen *was* Elizabeth Keaton's. No question.'

'You're certain?'

'Absolutely positive.'

'The FME was called when we got her back to Penrith, Sergeant Poe,' Rigg said. 'Elizabeth wouldn't let anyone touch her – who could blame her? – and we needed to know if she required immediate hospital attention. It took a while but Elizabeth finally agreed that Doctor Jakeman could take a blood sample.'

Poe said nothing. Force Medical Examiners were qualified doctors who were forensically trained. Due to large geography and low density, Cumbria operated on an on-call system rather than employing them full time.

'I'm sure you'll want to watch the video, but the chain of custody is flawless. Doctor Jakeman took four samples. We recorded the needle going in, and the Vacutainers were immediately sealed in evidence bags. We sent one sample to our lab.'

Poe knew what Rigg was about to say but he asked anyway. 'And?'

'And the blood matched, Poe. There's no doubt – the woman in the photograph *is* Elizabeth Keaton. Six years ago you convicted an innocent man.'

CHAPTER NINE

'You'll want to see the tapes,' Gamble said, getting to his feet. 'DC Rigg will sort out a computer for you.' He clearly knew that when a man has one of his fundamental beliefs shattered, the transition from non-believer to convert isn't instantaneous. Some things have to be seen to be believed.

The superintendent left Poe on his own while Rigg went to get a laptop. Poe drained the rest of his water. It was tepid and covered in a film of dust, but he didn't care – his mouth was bone dry. His stomach churned and he had a restless leg. All signs he was nervous. It didn't make sense. Elizabeth Keaton *was* dead. He was certain.

But was he?

He had been certain. He could remember that much. But he also remembered feeling an intense and immediate dislike for Jared Keaton. Had known from the moment he'd met him that he was a dishonest and manipulative man. But he also knew that when you expected deceit, you saw it everywhere. Had that happened? Had his dislike for Keaton made him see things that weren't there? Made him interpret the evidence just the one way, build up a narrative that only considered the facts that supported it, dismissing as unimportant anything contradictory. He hadn't thought he had, but that was the point: no one ever thinks they have confirmation bias – that most dependable of mental stumbling blocks.

And the fact Keaton couldn't have disposed of Elizabeth's body had always bothered him. He'd told himself that Keaton had been too clever for them. That one day Elizabeth's corpse would be discovered somewhere. The law allowed no-body murder convictions precisely for situations like Keaton's.

His mind raced. He was a good cop but he wasn't infallible. If it were proven beyond *his* doubt that he was wrong, then he was the main contributor in six years of absolute hell for Elizabeth Keaton. And six years of not much better for Jared.

How could you apologise for something like that? How could that wrong be righted?

Rigg entered the room. He was carrying a laptop. He put it in front of Poe and opened it. It was already in the right place.

'The interviews are set to run in chronological order. The first file is the CCTV from Alston Library. You can watch her make first contact.'

Poe made no move to do anything. 'If I was wrong, I'll say so, Rigg. I won't hide from this.'

Rigg left the room without responding.

The Alston Library file wasn't particularly helpful. The picture was good but there was no sound. It showed the girl entering the library, hesitating as if she were building up the courage to do something, then approaching the police desk where a bored-looking uniformed cop was seated.

He had to be honest – she really did look like Elizabeth Keaton. She was stick-thin and filthy but the resemblance was uncanny.

After taking a seat, she said something. It must have been her name as the cop reacted immediately. He reached for his radio, spoke into it, then raced round his desk to comfort her. He shouted something. Off-screen, a brew had been made as a couple of minutes later a cup of tea and a plate of biscuits arrived via a middle-aged woman. The cop waved her away when she'd set down the tray.

The girl made no move to reach for the cup or the food.

Nothing much happened in the following thirty minutes but Poe wasn't tempted to hit fast forward. The cop and the girl waited without speaking. Poe reached for the case file that had been left for him. He found the notes Problem Solver Constable Alsop had made – and if they were calling cops problem solvers these days then the world truly had gone to shit. They were rushed but provided a sense of what had happened. She'd given her name as Elizabeth Keaton and he'd treated her as a crime scene from that moment on. He had called his sergeant and was told to sit with her, not to ask questions but to record anything she said. He was to wait for assistance.

It arrived in the form of two detectives. One of them was Rigg. No wonder he was so angry; he'd been involved from the very beginning. Rigg and the other detective sat with Elizabeth for a while. They then led her out of the library and out of sight.

Poe opened the file labelled 'Police Interviews'. There were three videos in total.

The video stamp had the location of the interviews as Penrith police station. They were good quality – the type that's admissible in court – and Poe settled down to watch the story unfold.

In the first interview she still had on the clothes she'd been wearing when she'd entered Alston Library. Poe was surprised she hadn't been given a paper evidence suit, although Rigg had mentioned she hadn't wanted to be touched. Getting naked in front of a stranger would have been even more difficult for her. Despite the summer heat, her woollen hat was pulled tight over her head. Her chin was on her chest and her arms hugged her torso. She looked terrified.

Rigg, for all his earlier abrasiveness, knew what he was doing. He was empathetic but focused. When the girl veered off on tangents, he gently brought her back. Over the course of an hour, he put together a full storyboard – from disappearance to

43

reappearance. The details would come later. The first interview was always about the broad strokes.

She talked them through the night of her abduction. The man had entered the kitchen from the restaurant. She'd been surprised but not scared. It wasn't the first time a diner had enthusiastically indulged in their excellent wine list and succumbed to a toilet nap. There'd been a struggle but he'd overcome her before restraining her with butcher's twine. It had then gone exactly how Rigg had described earlier. The man had collected some of her blood, sprayed it around the kitchen, and then spent time cleaning it up.

She was led to a van and bundled into the back. The man had pressed something to her face and she'd woken up in an underground room. She thought it was a cellar but wasn't sure.

It had been an emotionally draining account and Rigg had rightly insisted on everyone taking a break. The camera wasn't turned off and Poe kept watching – he wanted to see everything. The girl sat and stared into space for almost twenty minutes. She didn't touch a thing.

Eventually the interview started again and Rigg moved on to the man who'd taken her. She didn't think he'd eaten at Bullace & Sloe before. She gave a description – which a police artist would no doubt work on later – then talked them through her six years. It was as horrible as expected. When she had woken on her first morning in captivity, she had a craving for something but hadn't known what. When the man entered with some food and a syringe she'd taken the needle first; she'd instinctively known it was what she needed. Within a day she was hooked. It was how the man had controlled her. Made sure she did what he wanted when he visited her.

Do what I want and you get a syringe. Defy me and you get nothing . . .

It was at that point that she broke down in tears. The interview

44

was suspended and the FME was called in. Poe checked the file. The FME was called Felicity Jakeman and she was on-call when the girl had arrived at Penrith police station. She looked to be in her early forties and had the no-nonsense, harried look all doctors have. She checked the girl's vitals: pulse, blood pressure and temperature and declared the interview over. She told the detectives she was sending her to hospital for a full medical. Rigg agreed. He glanced at the camera and his anxiety was palpable. It was clear he believed her story.

To be fair, Poe did too.

The next video was recorded later the same night. Rigg was still doing the interview. The FME wasn't present but the girl was reminded she was outside if needed. For the video, Rigg explained that the girl hadn't gone to hospital in the end. She'd refused to leave the police station. She didn't feel safe enough yet. As a compromise the FME had examined the girl in her suite.

She continued with her story. The six years she'd been imprisoned were described in a flat, lifeless voice. It wasn't pleasant listening. When she finished, Rigg sensibly took another break.

When they returned she talked them through her escape. Like most of her ordeal, it raised more questions than answers. The man's visits had inexplicably stopped, and after four days, when her heroin cravings compelled her into action, she had finally forced the door and escaped. She was in a house in the middle of nowhere. Somewhere hilly.

She'd walked all night, keeping off the roads in case the man had returned and was looking for her. She estimated she'd walked ten miles before it got light enough to see where she was. She saw the signs for the village of Alston and remembered going there as a child. She knew they had a police station. When she asked for directions she'd been told the station had closed years ago. It

45

was now a monthly police desk, but she'd been in luck: it was the fourth Wednesday of the month . . .

Rigg took her back a bit and asked what she thought had happened to her captor. She had no idea.

'Do you think he might have died?'

She didn't think so. He hadn't been an old man and, judging by his sexual appetite, he seemed healthy.

Rigg leant in and whispered something to the female DC. She nodded and left the room. Poe checked the notes and found what he'd said. Rigg was floating the idea that the man had been charged with something serious enough for him to be remanded in custody. A current line of enquiry was checking the residences and hangouts of anyone in the area who'd been remanded or sentenced during the last week.

Poe grunted. It was what he'd have done. He watched the rest of the video but it was little more than housekeeping. He took a break and stretched his legs. Wandered over to the canteen. He had a visitor's ID card but hadn't been told the door code. He flashed his National Crime Agency ID card at a pair of giggling police staff and was let in. He paid for a dry tuna sandwich at the till and grabbed a can of Coke and a packet of Quavers from the vending machines.

As he ate, he pondered what he'd seen so far. Nothing he hadn't already been told, he decided. The girl looked like Elizabeth Keaton – but so what? Lots of girls would. He was yet to watch the last video – the one where Rigg would no doubt gently tease out how she could prove she actually *was* Elizabeth Keaton – but there was really only one thing that mattered. Had the blood been handled correctly? Gamble had said the chain of custody – the way evidence presented at court is demonstrably proved to be the same as that collected at a crime scene; an unbroken chain of custody that offered no opportunity for alteration or substitution – was flawless, but Poe needed to see it for himself.

The first part of the chain of custody was always the weakest; it was where people least familiar with the process were involved.

Rigg was waiting for Poe when he returned.

'Early thoughts?' He seemed a bit less edgy.

'Too early,' Poe replied, sitting back down in front of the laptop. 'I don't remember Elizabeth Keaton being so thin and pale, but if she's been locked in a cellar for six years . . .'

Rigg didn't comment.

Poe pressed play.

Rigg, just as Poe thought he would, went on to question the girl about her identity. He apologised for doing so. Said he appreciated that she'd been through a terrible ordeal but her father had been convicted of her murder and, for the Criminal Cases Review Commission – the organisation that investigates miscarriages of justice – to refer his case to the Court of Appeal, her identity would need to be proven beyond doubt.

The girl nodded. She didn't seem fazed and was under no illusion that her father would not be freed until she did what she was being asked. She provided as much detail as she could about her old life: who her friends were; what her hobbies had been; what her job at Bullace & Sloe had entailed. She told them anecdotes about kitchen life and she told them about the staff there. She told them all about growing up with a famous father and how her mother had died in a car accident.

It was convincing. Some of the things she said were impossible for anyone else to know, and Rigg confirmed they'd since been verified. She was either telling the truth or had been extremely well briefed.

As she spoke, her thin voice captivating her audience, Poe's feelings of self-doubt intensified. He'd always prided himself on his ability to spot a liar and he didn't see it with her. All he saw was a victim.

And then came the blood.
Not circumstantial evidence. Not corroborating evidence.
Definitive evidence.

CHAPTER TEN

Rigg called in Felicity Jakeman, the FME. Drawing blood was a medical procedure and police rules are clear: a doctor has to do it. It wasn't a problem; Jakeman hadn't left the building since the girl had arrived. She wasn't exactly mothering the girl, but it was clear she was her patient and her care came first.

Poe asked Rigg why they'd used a blood sample rather than a mouth swab to get her DNA profile.

'So she could be screened for STDs and blood-borne infections at the same time. As Elizabeth wouldn't go to hospital or the Sexual Assault Referral Centre, the FME wanted to check her out without her *knowing* she was being checked out.'

Clever, Poe thought. *Why worry someone with what might be when you didn't have to?*

'Also to make sure she wasn't pregnant,' Rigg added. 'Carrying their rapist's baby is one of the most traumatic things a victim can go through.'

Poe physically flinched. His mother *was* that victim. He *was* that baby. A baby who in most cultures would have been aborted. Half his genes came from the monster who'd stolen his childhood. He found himself wanting to check his phone to see if his dad – his real dad, the man who'd raised him, the man who'd been married to his mother and kept her secret all these years – had got back to him yet. Poe had emailed him a few weeks earlier but was yet to receive a response.

Poe's jaw hardened. He leaned in and stared as Felicity

49

Jakeman lifted up the girl's right sleeve. As well as track marks, she had thin lines around her lower forearm and wrist. Some were fresh and red, some were faded and pink. Poe pressed pause.

'Self-harm?'

Rigg nodded. 'Her thighs too, according to Flick.'

'Flick?'

'The FME. She doesn't like Felicity. Says it makes her sound old.'

Poe pressed play. The FME, in deference to the marks of self-mutilation, had lifted the girl's sleeve just enough to expose a vein. After disinfecting the entry site, and applying a tourniquet, she sprung a viable vein and filled four Vacutainer blood collection tubes. She placed them on the table.

As soon as she'd loosened the tourniquet and removed her needle, the girl pulled her sleeve down before bringing her knees up and hugging them to her chest. Classic defensive body language. Poe didn't blame her – invasive medical procedures like drawing blood are usually done in private. For obvious reasons blood taken to establish DNA can't be. The female detective made a weak joke about how she was now eligible for some tea and biscuits. The girl didn't laugh. No one did.

Poe stared at the laptop screen. Like a man watching the cup he knows the pea is under, his eyes fixated on the blood samples. At no point did any of the Vacutainer tubes leave the screen. They weren't blocked by anyone's sleeve and they were never out of sight. The FME had simply filled them, then put them on the table. Good forensic practices had been followed. Poe wouldn't have expected anything less. The way blood had been collected was often challenged in court, so procedures were simple and not open to interpretation. If sleight of hand had occurred then it was via micro-magic on David Blaine's level.

But the chain of custody didn't stop there. The FME held up to the camera an A4 sheet of sticky labels. The labels were printed with the girl's name – listed as Jane Doe for now – and were serial numbered. Poe watched as she affixed one to each Vacutainer tube. Again, the tubes never left his sight.

The third and final stage was the samples being sealed in evidence bags. As before, each uniquely numbered bag was held up to the camera before a vial was put in each one. The bags used by Cumbria Police were the standard design used everywhere. Made of tough, clear plastic with a non-tamper seal, they had a chain of custody table on the front. Rigg signed and dated the first row on all four.

One would go to whichever lab Cumbria used these days, one would no doubt go to a lab chosen by Jared Keaton's legal team, and two would be secured in the evidence locker in case they were needed later.

Poe made a note of the four serial numbers.

By the time he got to the end of the tape his mind had drifted. The only thing that mattered was the blood. If the blood *was* Elizabeth Keaton's then the *girl* was Elizabeth Keaton. It was the only viable explanation. And that meant Jared Keaton hadn't murdered her. There was no getting round that fact.

Six years ago he'd secured the conviction of an innocent man.

Poe went back to the beginning and watched the videos again.

After the second viewing, Poe got up and stretched. Being hunched over the laptop had made his neck stiff and his shoulders ache. He'd studied everything until his eyes felt like sandpaper but he'd seen nothing untoward. Nothing at all.

He still wanted to check other links in the chain of custody but he knew he was clutching at straws. Venturing into tin-foil-hat territory. As soon as the blood had been secured it would have taken a conspiracy of epic proportions and complexity to change all four samples. There were too many people involved.

'Well?' Rigg asked.

He had forgotten he was still in the room. Rigg had been quietly reading a file. Or pretending to anyway. Poe reached for his coffee mug but it was cold. He grimaced, then drank it anyway.

'It does seem conclusive,' he replied.

Rigg walked over to Poe's table and, reaching across him, turned off the laptop. 'You were played, Poe. It's as simple as that.' His voice was tight and controlled. 'The perpetrator had the foresight to make the abduction look like a murder and you fell for it. You all did.'

Poe swallowed. The same thought had been going through his mind and the words hit him hard. Rigg walked to the door. Before he left the room, he turned. The anger was back.

'You should all be fucking ashamed of yourselves.'

And with that he killed the lights, plunging the room into darkness.

CHAPTER ELEVEN

Poe sat in the dark for a long time. He found it conducive to thinking.

How could he have been so wrong about someone?

In his entire career, he'd never been as sure about anything as he had about Jared Keaton's guilt. And yet . . . the blood hadn't been falsified. Elizabeth Keaton was alive.

For years, Poe had known an interesting fact about statues of men on horses. If the horse had a foot off the ground, then the rider had been injured in battle and later died of his wounds. If the horse had two legs off the ground, the rider had died during the battle. And if all four feet remained on the ground, the rider had died by other means. It was a bit of trivia and he'd repeated it countless times over the years. His colleague and best friend, civilian analyst Tilly Bradshaw, had recently told him it was total nonsense. Even when he'd read the truth for himself, he still found it hard to move away from his long-held belief. He'd actually gone as far as defending his position to her with absolutely no facts to back him up.

He felt like that now – in need of a serious mental realignment. After all these years, Keaton was innocent.

He considered getting another coffee while he thought about what to do next, but his excessive caffeine intake was bringing on a headache. He rubbed his temples in a futile attempt to move the pain elsewhere. He glanced at his BlackBerry and saw he had another missed call from Flynn. He rang back but got her voicemail. He didn't like leaving voicemails. They made him babble as if English was his second language. He sent her a text instead.

A minute later she replied: I'm not doing this via 200 texts, Poe. She'd also included a videoconference link. He rebooted the laptop Rigg had just turned off and typed in the URL.

A phone icon began pulsing. Someone in Hampshire must have answered it as SCAS's conference room appeared on his screen. Flynn was seated at the table. She didn't look happy.

'Steph.'

'Poe, I can't see you.'

There was a small black rectangle in the top right of the screen. From past experiences of videoconferences, this was where the picture of him was supposed to be.

'I'll try typing the address in again,' he said.

She glared at him through cyberspace. 'Don't touch anything. Tilly's joining us. She'll sort it.'

Two minutes later Bradshaw arrived. She was a slight woman with thin brown hair and skin that never saw sunlight. Thick Harry Potter-style spectacles magnified her grey eyes. She wore a T-shirt with the ampersand symbol and 'Phone Home' underneath it. He'd seen it before. Apparently it was a play on the ampersand being a ligature of 'et', the Latin word for 'and', and a film about a spaceman or something. Or at least that's what he thought she'd said. He'd stopped listening after a while . . .

'Sorry, DI Flynn, I was on the toilet,' she said.

Flynn ignored the over-share.

Poe smiled. Bradshaw had spent most of her working life, and a large part of her childhood, in academia undertaking research in mathematics. As brilliant as she was, until she'd joined the National Crime Agency there'd never been any need to learn the social skills that everyone else took for granted, the skills everyone began learning in the schoolyard.

And, as maths was a binary science with little room for

selective interpretation, she had never grasped how to express an argument. Maths didn't have subtlety. It didn't need discretion and it didn't need empathy. It was either right or wrong. Maths told the truth and therefore so did she. It would never occur to her to do anything else.

Still, she was getting better . . . A few months ago she'd have told them what she had been *doing* on the toilet.

'Where's Poe?' Bradshaw asked.

'He can see us, we can't see him.'

Bradshaw took over. She talked Poe through a series of checks and reboots. Eventually she became exasperated. 'You *have* removed the webcam's cover?'

'Yes, of course I've removed the cover.' Poe checked the top of the laptop. A small plastic clip shielded the camera's lens. He removed it. The small black rectangle disappeared and Conference Room B appeared.

'Doofus,' Bradshaw muttered, unpacking her bag. She glanced at Flynn and copied how she'd laid out her pen and notebook.

Flynn crossed her arms and watched. A smile tugged at the corners of her mouth. A month after the Immolation Man case, Bradshaw had surprised everyone by applying for an internal promotion. As soon as she had, all the other applicants had withdrawn. When she was confirmed in post, she'd asked for Poe's advice on managing a team. He'd told her she could do a lot worse than to use Flynn as her role model. She'd taken it to the extreme and now copied everything Flynn did. If Flynn wrote something down, Bradshaw did too. If Flynn checked her phone for messages, Bradshaw checked hers. She even laid out her pen and notebook the same way.

Poe found it endearing. Flynn found it irritating.

'Ready?' Flynn asked.

Bradshaw compared her part of the desk with Flynn's, then nodded.

'Poe, what's happening?'

'I don't want to upset you, boss.'

'Why don't you try and find the willpower?' she snapped.

Poe bit back a snarky response. Flynn had been misdirecting anger for weeks now. No one knew why. Instead, he brought her up to date. She listened without interrupting.

'Do you need my help, Poe?' Bradshaw asked when he'd finished. She looked anxious. She always did when she thought he was in trouble.

'They're just rerunning the original investigation, Tilly. They won't want me up here getting in the way. I'll be back soon.'

'OK. But send me everything you have. I'll have a look.'

'I can't. We're not officially involved.'

'What do *you* want to do?' Flynn asked. She knew him well enough to know that if he'd made a mistake he'd want to try and fix it.

Poe paused. That was the question, wasn't it? What *could* he do? He was saved from an awkward answer when the conference-room door in Carleton Hall opened and the lights snapped on. Poe blinked and shielded his eyes.

It was Gamble. He didn't look angry. He looked resigned and he looked worried.

'Can you give me five, boss?' Poe asked. 'I think Superintendent Gamble's wanting a word.'

Flynn reached over and pressed something. The screen went blank.

'Was that DI Flynn?' Gamble asked.

'Yes.'

'I'll call her later.'

Gamble walked over to the coffee machine. He poured himself a mug, picked up an empty one and gestured to Poe.

Against his better judgement, Poe nodded. Gamble carried both mugs over. He pulled out a seat, slumped into it and passed the drink over. Poe took a sip. The coffee was stewed and bitter and perfectly matched his mood. The steam fogged Poe's reading glasses. He removed them and put them back in his jacket. For a minute they both blew on their drinks and took tiny sips.

'How's DI Flynn?'

'Doing well, sir. Being the permanent DI suits her.'

Gamble smiled. 'And Tilly?'

'Fine as well. Better than fine, actually. The Immolation Man case brought her into her own but she's pushed on from there. She's learned to drive and has bought a Ford Ka. She has her own section of analysts now, and if you thought she was weird, wait until you see them. They all need hi-vis vests with "Careful, I'm still being taught how to be around people" printed on the front and back. Call themselves the Scooby Gang, which is off some kids' vampire show they all watch. *Buffle the Vampire Killer* or something. Everyone else calls them the Mole People. They know their stuff, though. Did you hear about that man in Scarborough?'

'The supposedly unconnected stabbings?'

Poe nodded. 'They solved that on gait analysis alone. Studied the CCTV footage and realised that all three assaults had been committed by the same person.'

'That was her? Wow, well done, Tilly. The perp was dressing up as a woman, wasn't he?'

'Different women,' Poe confirmed. 'It was extraordinary work. They drew up a profile and North Yorkshire Police picked him up the same day.'

They settled into silence. Poe finished his coffee and took both mugs to refill them. When he returned, Gamble was ready to talk.

'What's your take on this, Poe?' he asked. '*Was* that Elizabeth Keaton?'

Poe studied the ageing detective superintendent. He looked

shattered. Since he'd last seen him the creases around his eyes had lengthened and deepened. His hair was a lighter shade of grey. Poe knew he wasn't far off retirement. Following his demotion after the Immolation Man case, Poe assumed he'd be toeing the party line from now on. But . . . if anything, he looked defiant.

Realisation dawned on Poe. Gamble wanted him for something.

'Why am I really here, sir?'

Gamble said nothing.

Poe continued, 'I could have spoken to Rigg over the phone. I didn't have to come up north.'

Again, Gamble remained silent. He took a sip of his coffee and closed his eyes.

'And other than some of the anecdotal stuff about Keaton himself, everything I told you this afternoon was in the file.'

Gamble opened his eyes and looked at him.

'You're not sure, are you, sir?' Poe said.

Gamble let out a long, low sigh. It sounded like he was deflating. 'I don't know what to think, Poe. I may be tilting at windmills here but I do know that if I'd listened to you during the Immolation Man case, we might have had a different result.'

Poe didn't respond. Gamble was being unfair on himself. The Immolation Man case had been unprecedented in police history. From the moment it had started, Gamble had never stood a chance. No SIO would have.

'I'm calling DI Flynn and asking for assistance from the Serious Crime Analysis Section,' Gamble said. 'Officially, it'll be to assist with the enquiry into the abduction of Elizabeth Keaton, and, as you were heavily involved in the original investigation, I'll be requesting you as my contact.'

'And unofficially?'

'I want to be sure. I want to be sure that girl really is Elizabeth

58

Keaton. I don't want my last act in the police to be helping a murderer go free.'

Gamble stood. Put his mug on the table and offered his hand. Poe took it and they shook. They looked each other in the eye.

'And I'll *only* be sure when you are, Poe.'

CHAPTER TWELVE

Poe reconnected the videoconference. Gamble stayed in the room.

There was a bit of small talk then Gamble got down to business.

'I'm formally requesting SCAS involvement in the enquiry into the abduction and false imprisonment of Elizabeth Keaton. The paperwork will be with you tonight.'

There was a pause at the other end.

Eventually Flynn said, 'Sir, SCAS can't be used to assuage Poe's guilt.'

'It's not about that, DI Flynn. If we've made a mistake then we'll accept whatever's coming. I'm sure Poe will too.'

'What do you mean "if" you've made a mistake?' Flynn asked. 'Is this girl Elizabeth Keaton or isn't she?'

'I think she almost certainly is, boss,' Poe replied. There was no point in lying.

'But?'

'But Jared Keaton's the most intelligent man I've ever met. If anyone can pull this off, it's him.'

He didn't embellish it. Flynn would either agree or she wouldn't. They'd spoken about Keaton a while back – one of those late night "what's the worst case you've ever worked on?" chats – so she knew what he thought about him.

A full thirty seconds passed before she spoke again. As Poe had expected, she'd come to a pragmatic, defensible decision.

'OK, sir. A stranger abduction *does* fall into SCAS's brief. I'll authorise our involvement for as long as you need it. It will only be DS Poe for now, but he can call on our resources as he sees fit.'

They discussed a couple of administrative issues and hung up.

Gamble looked at Poe. 'Where do you want to start?'

'The blood. I want to know if a DNA test is as infallible as we've been led to believe.'

'I'm told it is.'

Poe nodded. That was his understanding as well. You couldn't just 'give' a person someone else's blood to change their DNA. It didn't work like that. But . . . he also knew medical advances were being made all the time. Things might have moved on since his last DNA briefing.

'I'll check anyway,' Poe said. 'I know a pathologist who'll be able to give me the definitive answer.'

'You don't look happy. What's the problem?'

Poe sighed. 'She's weird as fuck.'

Day 5

CHAPTER THIRTEEN

Although biological evidence could be stored in the fridges and freezers of any CID evidence store, they all ended up at Carleton Hall eventually. The girl's blood – drawn at the nearby Penrith police station – was already there. Poe had agreed to meet Gamble outside at nine the next morning.

The day had slipped its leash by the time he left Gamble, but he was still tempted to head back to his croft on Shap Fells. It looked like he was going to be in Cumbria for a while and, as he hadn't been home for a few weeks, there would be some immediate jobs to get it habitable again. The generator would need an oil and filter change, the water pump would need adjusting for the lower summer levels, and everything else would need a good clean.

It would be a lot of work, but the truth was he missed the place. It was his home. He didn't owe a penny on it and he owned the land around it. Before the Immolation Man had dragged him back to SCAS, he'd built a life there. He also missed Edgar, his springer spaniel. Edgar stayed with Thomas Hume, his neighbour, when he was down south, but recently Poe had been exploring ways to have him with him permanently.

In the end sanity had prevailed and he got a room at the North Lakes Hotel and Spa in Penrith. The thought of a double bed, crisp cotton sheets and a late evening meal at the bar had been too tempting.

* * *

Poe was outside the CSI store fifteen minutes before it opened. Gamble arrived five minutes later. He'd come directly from a meeting with the new chief constable – the old one had disappeared into obscurity after the attempted cover-up of the Immolation Man case – and she wasn't happy, and not just because she was working on a Sunday.

'Five minutes away from standing in front of the biggest TV camera she could find and publicly condemning the original investigation,' was how he described her mood.

'Will she do it?' Poe asked. He didn't know the new chief. She'd been a superintendent in the west of the county when he was with Cumbria. She was well respected and took no shit from the police and crime commissioner.

Gamble shook his head. 'I doubt it. She has to be a bit political but she'll back her officers if it comes to the pinch.'

The CSI store manager, a young woman called Angie Morrison, interrupted them. She unlocked the door and ushered them into a cage-type reception area. She let herself into the main store. Gamble explained they were there for one of two remaining blood samples.

After he'd signed for it, Poe said goodbye to Gamble in the car park and got in the hire car SCAS had provided for him – his BMW X1 was still down in Hampshire. Two minutes later he was on the M6, and twenty minutes after that he was on the A69 heading towards Newcastle.

Poe navigated Newcastle with all the ease of a nervous tourist. It was a compact city centre with complex one-way systems and an inexhaustible supply of locals with their hands on their horns. It wasn't until he turned off the radio – because when Poe was lost, that was what he did – that he discovered the hire car had a built-in satnav. He was soon on the right road and going in the right direction.

He entered the car-park lottery of the Royal Victoria Infirmary but got lucky and found a recently departed space. A prowling car honked its horn in anger but Poe ignored it.

The RVI is the University of Newcastle's teaching hospital, and the person Poe had travelled to see split her time between there, the lecture hall and Newcastle Laboratories. As well as being a Home Office pathologist for the North East, Estelle Doyle was *the* senior lecturer in forensic pathology. Pathologists from around the world attended her coveted lectures. When she wasn't lecturing she could usually be found in the bowels of the RVI.

As he paid for his parking, Poe's nerves began to jitter.

Estelle Doyle did that to him.

By all accounts she was brilliant. But . . . there was another side to Estelle Doyle.

Poe knew that people who cut up dead bodies for a living rarely walked down the sunny side of the street, but even by their standards Estelle Doyle was a bit grim. As he made his way to the lower basement, and the mortuary, he thought back to the previous times he'd worked with her.

Once she'd offered him some wine from a bottle that had been chilling in the children's cold-chamber; the one depressingly labelled in Comic Sans typeface. She had said it was the best fridge in the hospital. He'd politely declined. On another occasion she'd asked him to hold the arm of an overweight man she'd been dissecting. 'Pull that tendon,' she'd instructed, pointing in his arm cavity and handing him some surgical tweezers. He'd done as he was asked. The corpse flipped him his middle finger. Poe had fallen over in shock. Estelle Doyle hadn't even cracked a smile.

The door to the mortuary had a piece of A4 paper Sellotaped to the frosted glass. It said: 'Pathologists have the coolest patients'. Poe sighed, took a deep breath, knocked and entered.

Estelle Doyle was bent over a corpse. Without any indication she'd seen him, she said, 'Ah, Poe, I'm glad you're here. What do you think of these?'

Poe opened his mouth in disbelief.

CHAPTER FOURTEEN

The cadaver on the table looked blanched and mottled under the harsh lights. She was an elderly female: thin and withered with crooked, yellowing fingernails. Her face was wrinkled and her eyes were shrunken and cloudy.

Estelle Doyle was painting the woman's toenails.

Each one was a different shade of purple. The juxtaposition of the gothic colours against the colourless flesh was stark.

Poe gawped.

'I have a dinner engagement tonight. I thought I'd try these out. Tell me, Poe, which one goes best with my shoes?'

She lifted the hem of her long, tight skirt to reveal a pair of high heels. They were glossy black with bright red soles. They looked expensive.

'Umm . . . that one,' Poe said, pointing at the nearest toe.

'Ah, Frosted Tulip. Good choice.' A smile ran across her lips. 'Now, what can I do for you this time, Poe? I do so look forward to your little visits.'

She finished painting the last nail, picked up the dead woman's foot and gently blew on her toes. It was both intimate and creepy.

Poe was sure she'd waited so he would catch her doing it.

She turned and faced him. Gave him the up-and-down. Her tongue played across her bottom lip. Poe squirmed under her gaze.

He found Estelle Doyle incredibly sexy and utterly terrifying. Even without her heels she was as tall as him. Her dark blue eyes were framed by black eyeliner and red eyeshadow. Her powdered face contrasted sharply with lips that were painted crimson. Jet-black hair flowed like ink against her long creamy neck. Her cheekbones were high and severe. Her arms were heavily tattooed, full sleeves, all the way to her wrists.

'You've lost weight, Poe. It suits you.'

'I've had a rough year.'

'I read about it in the papers. Your Capra-esque qualities won through in the end, though?'

'Er . . . what?' Each time he stood in front of Estelle Doyle he struggled to form a coherent sentence.

'You're the perennial underdog, Poe. It's what drives you on, what makes you do the things others won't.'

Poe didn't respond. He didn't have a clue what she was talking about.

Doyle sighed. 'The Immolation Man case is sorted, yes?'

He nodded.

'But you're in new trouble?'

Poe nodded again. He needed time to regroup. He pointed at the recently manicured corpse. 'Are you even allowed to do that?'

She shrugged. 'I'll paint them all the same before she leaves here.'

Poe said nothing. On the Estelle Doyle scale of weirdness it barely registered.

She lifted the dead woman's arm so he could see the inside of her wrist. 'See this?'

He warily leaned in. There was a small and old-style tattoo. It was a symbol he didn't recognise – a labyrinth pattern contained by a circle. 'What is it?'

'Hecate's wheel. It represents the three aspects of the goddess: the maiden, the mother and the crone,' Doyle said, affectionately stroking the old woman's hair. 'She was almost certainly a Wiccan. I suspect she'd have approved of her new nails.'

She looked back down at the cadaver. 'Can you imagine the life she led? The trouble that tattoo must have caused her.'

Poe peered at the tattoo closely, his natural inquisitiveness taking over. It looked homemade. At least fifty years old, he reckoned. 'More than a bit of grief.'

'Master of the understatement as always, Poe.' Doyle flipped a sheet over the old woman. 'So, what is it this time?'

'I have a problem. An intractable problem.'

'Ooh, a puzzle.' Her voice was flat and hypnotic. 'I like puzzles. Please, continue.'

He reddened. He couldn't believe he was about to ask this. 'I need to know how the dead can come back to life.'

'Ah, finally something interesting.'

Poe told her what had happened. She asked him to go back further and describe the crime scene at Bullace & Sloe. He explained how the estimated blood loss had been assessed as incompatible with life.

'That's your first mistake right there. You had my number, you should have consulted me. Your forensic scientists always overestimate how much blood there is at a scene. Even a small amount, particularly when spilled on low-absorption surfaces like kitchen tiles, will make a crime scene look like an abattoir. Unless the blood's in situ, there's no way to tell how much was spilled. Anyone who tells you otherwise is either lying or incompetent. I wrote a paper on it a few years ago. You should read it.'

'I will,' Poe replied. He wished he'd had the foresight to bring a copy of the file. Estelle Doyle looking at crime scene photographs was better value than most pathologists actually being there.

'And this girl looks like Elizabeth Keaton?'

'She does.'

'And she isn't a twin? Either identical or non-identical?'

'Not as far as we know.'

She raised a razor-thin eyebrow.

'No, Estelle, she's not a twin.' In his entire police career, he'd not once investigated a crime where a twin had been involved.

'And you saw the blood being collected?'

'Not personally, but I've seen the video and the chain of custody wasn't compromised. The FME and the investigating officers were aware of the significance and, from vein to bag, the blood never left anyone's sight.'

'Tamper-free evidence bags were used?'

Poe nodded.

'And the same bag was received by the lab?'

This time Poe shrugged. 'I'm going to check but it seems implausible that it wouldn't have been. The usual courier firm delivered it and all protocols were followed. It's a cheat-proof system.'

'Which lab are Cumbria using?'

Poe told her. The lab serviced all the police forces in the north-west.

She nodded in approval. 'They're reputable. Know what they're doing. I assume you don't think a bunch of unrelated individuals somehow got together and replaced one sample with another?'

Poe shook his head.

'And the original DNA sample, the one her blood is being matched against, it's reliable?'

'It is. I collected it.'

Doyle nodded. She was good like that. If she trusted you to do your job, you never needed to justify your actions.

'Thank goodness you came to me then.' She gestured to her office. 'I have a couple of things to tie up then I'm all yours, Poe. Why don't you take a seat in there?'

Poe did. He watched her work for as long as he could stand but when she began pulling blood clots out of the old woman's veins he turned away. Doyle's mortuary was used for training so there was a Perspex-protected gallery above the table she was working at but, as it was a Sunday, it was empty. The rest of the mortuary was fairly standard. A bit more modern but essentially the same as every other one he'd been in. The cold-chambers hummed like tuning forks. Some of them would be set to minus 20°C: the temperature at which cadavers could be kept indefinitely. The air conditioning, which could charitably be described as 'eager', chilled the sweat on his forehead. A lemony, chemical smell lingered in the air. It wasn't unpleasant but it pinched the nostrils and watered the eyes. Large sinks, drains and sluices were fitted against tiled walls adorned with laminated health-and-safety notices. It was a room that respected the dead, but not at the cost of the truth. Poe hated mortuaries. Always had. Every time he had to be in one, the police had failed someone.

Eventually Doyle joined him. She didn't waste time on small talk.

'I'm struggling to see what you want from me, Poe. It sounds like you know what happened.'

'I just want to pick your brains, Estelle. I know this is going to sound stupid, but is it possible for someone to have someone else's DNA? To go through a procedure that's good enough to fool a lab?'

To his surprise, she didn't laugh in his face. Or worse, raise an eyebrow.

'Recently a team of scientists in Israel proved it is technically possible to engineer a crime scene. They were able to remove all traces of DNA from a blood sample and replace it with someone else's.'

Poe stared. What she'd said was extraordinary.

'And it was good enough to fool forensic scientists,' she added as a kicker.

His eyes widened further. The National Crime Agency was

73

supposed to be at the cutting edge of law enforcement – why hadn't he heard about this? He made a note to pass this on to Flynn.

Doyle continued. 'And, in a fully equipped molecular biology lab, any halfway-decent biologist can synthesise DNA.'

Poe took a moment. Although science seemed to be fast approaching the world depicted in *Blade Runner*, it didn't seem relevant to the matter in hand. 'I'm assuming it wouldn't work on an actual person, though – you can't synthesise DNA in a living thing presumably?'

'Not yet, no. I was making a point, Poe. I need you to understand blood.'

Doyle never wasted words: if she thought he needed to understand blood, then he needed to understand blood.

'Blood is life. It's the most perfect and specialised fluid that has ever existed. Organic engineering at its absolute finest. Everything we need it to do, it does. It feeds us and it protects us. It takes oxygen around our body and it removes carbon dioxide. It regulates our temperature and it helps us reproduce.'

Poe said nothing.

'Even looking at the colour red makes our heart beat faster. It's because we associate the colour with blood, and when we see blood, something bad has happened.'

Poe didn't know that. Didn't realise that he had so little control over his own body. He said as much.

'Don't worry, Poe. I'm sure there's a point when someone has seen so much they stop getting such a visceral reaction. In fact, I might just offer that as a hypothesis to be proved or disproved next time I'm lecturing.' She picked up a pen and made a note.

'Suppose someone had a load of Elizabeth Keaton's blood – would it be possible to transfuse it into a host body and change the DNA?'

74

Doyle shook her head. 'That's not how it works. DNA comes from the fusion of our parents' gametes.'

Poe sighed. Listening to Doyle was a bit like listening to Bradshaw – she had the same gift for making the complicated sound even more complicated. Doyle was a clinical professor of medicine and he'd failed O level biology. There was no base level of understanding. His confusion must have been obvious.

'Gametes are our reproductive cells, Poe. We inherit . . .' She petered out at his blank expression. 'Look, I can explain it to you but I can't *understand* it for you.'

Scratch that. It was *exactly* like listening to Bradshaw.

'Sorry.' He refocused and did his best to follow what he was being told.

'A person's blood comes from their bone marrow, not the other way around. Even if someone had a full transfusion, their DNA wouldn't change. And, because the body produces one hundred billion red cells and four hundred billion white cells every hour, a blood sample that would fool a sophisticated DNA test would need to be drawn almost simultaneously with the transfusion.'

'So . . . you're saying it's not possible?'

'Not even remotely.'

Strike one.

Poe, picking up on what Doyle had just said, and to show he'd been paying attention, said, 'What about bone marrow transplants? Can they mess with a person's blood?'

'You're talking about a chimera. Where someone has two types of DNA.'

'I am?'

'You are. In the old days of oncology, with some types of leukaemia for example, the patient had all their bone marrow destroyed. It was then completely replaced with a donor's. Theoretically, that had the potential to change the DNA of someone's blood. The rest of their DNA doesn't change, though.

All the other cells in the body would have the person's original DNA.'

Poe's eyes narrowed. Was he getting somewhere?

'But,' she said, curbing his enthusiasm, 'these days oncologists don't need to destroy all a patient's bone marrow. A chimera is therefore someone with a mixture of their own and someone else's DNA.'

Strike two.

'So, the only way this girl could have Elizabeth Keaton's blood is if she *is* Elizabeth Keaton?'

Doyle shrugged. 'I'd never say never. If you gave me a live donor and weren't watching, I *might* be able to fool a test. But only in laboratory conditions.'

Poe sighed. 'And there's another problem. The only live donor that Jared Keaton would have been able to use would be his daughter and—'

'—and if he had her, why bother with the charade?'

'Exactly.'

They descended into silence.

Eventually Doyle broke it, and when she did she showed she was as sharp as she'd ever been. 'You're not here for a chat at all, are you, Poe? All of this could have been done over the phone. Out with it, what is it you really want?'

Poe reached into his bag and removed two things. He put them on her desk.

'And what treats have you brought me?'

'The first is the DNA report on Elizabeth Keaton. It's from the original investigation. It's triple sourced and I am one hundred per cent certain it is hers.'

'And the second?'

'The second is some of the blood drawn at Penrith police station less than a week ago. The lab Cumbria used matched it with Elizabeth Keaton's.'

76

'And you want me to do what with it?'

'I want you to blind test it. I know Newcastle Laboratories do non-NHS work. I want you to test it in your own lab. No name on the evidence bag, just a serial number that only you know. Completely anonymous.'

When Doyle replied, it was in a soft, husky voice. 'And why would I do that, Poe?'

Poe channelled what Gamble had said to him the night before. 'Because until *you're* sure it's Elizabeth Keaton's blood, Estelle, *I* won't be sure it's Elizabeth Keaton's blood.'

CHAPTER FIFTEEN

Poe called Gamble on his way back to Cumbria and told him that
Doyle had agreed to fast-track another DNA test.

'Can you be back at Carleton Hall at three?' Gamble asked.
'There's a strategy meeting. It'll be a chance to meet everyone.'

Poe checked his watch. It was just after midday. He needed
to eat and he didn't fancy the canteen again. Luckily the A69,
one of the main east-west roads, had plenty of places he could
stop for a bite on the way. Hexham had a good chippy and he
fancied a battered sausage, washed down with a can of freezing
cold Sprite.

'I'll be there.'

The pre-meeting – the one where police officers spread rumours
until someone senior tells them to shut up – was in full swing
when Poe walked into Conference Room A. Nobody paid him
any attention. In his suit he could have been anyone.

He made his way to the coffee urn and poured himself a drink.
He took it to the conference table and sat beside a woman he
didn't know. She smiled politely then turned back to the person
she'd been talking to.

'Oh, look,' someone called, 'it's the National Chaos Agency.'

The room went quiet fast. Everyone stared as Poe took a sip of
coffee. He calmly placed his cup back on his saucer and stared at
the person who'd spoken. He was a squat man with hooded eyes
and fat arms.

Rigg was seated beside him. The tall detective had the grace to look embarrassed.

'What the hell are you doing here, Poe?' the squat man said. 'I thought you'd been sent packing?'

Poe picked up his drink and slowly drained his cup. When he finished he said, 'And you are?'

'Just answer the fucking question, Poe! This is a Cumbrian matter. What the hell are you doing in my briefing room?'

'*Your* briefing room, DCI Wardle?' Gamble said. He'd slipped into the room without the squat man noticing. 'And not that it has anything to do with you, but Sergeant Poe's here at my invitation.'

'May I ask why, sir?' Wardle said, his voice flat and annoyed.

'No, you may not.'

Wardle's pallid face flushed red.

Gamble turned to Poe. 'DCI Wardle is one of our direct entry officers, Sergeant Poe. Occasionally he forgets that others earned their rank.'

Wardle scowled. He obviously preferred people to think he was a DCI on merit, rather than because he was a 'brat' – a direct entry officer who'd never served as a uniformed constable. Notorious for being hopelessly underprepared – Poe had never met a good one. By saying it publicly, Gamble was telling Poe to watch his back.

'Shake hands with Sergeant Poe, DCI Wardle,' Gamble said. His tone didn't invite debate.

Wardle reluctantly offered Poe his hand. Poe held it briefly. It was as clammy as a fish. In full view of everyone, he wiped his hand on his trousers.

'Excellent,' Gamble said. 'It looks like we're all going to get on famously. Now, to business. As expected, Jared Keaton's legal team have referred his case to the Criminal Cases Review Commission.'

Poe's stomach flipped. The CCRC, the independent organisation with the power to investigate cases if a miscarriage of justice was suspected, didn't have the power to overturn convictions, but if they sent a case back to the Court of Appeal they were legally obliged to hear it.

'They can't,' Rigg said. 'The CCRC only accept cases that have lost appeals. Keaton hasn't had one yet.'

'They can if they claim exceptional circumstances,' Poe said.

Gamble nodded. 'And that's exactly what they've done. The submission states that exceptional circumstances are justified as the murder victim has been demonstrably proven to be alive. I've just got off the phone with the CCRC caseworker and they've accepted it. They'll do their own checks but I can't see any other outcome than them referring it for immediate appeal.'

Poe agreed. The CCRC had no choice.

'As things stand now, the CPS will offer no evidence at any appeal hearing.' Gamble paused to allow them to digest what he'd just said. His gaze rested on Poe for a moment. 'The caseworker at the CCRC said they are treating Keaton's application as urgent and we can expect it to be dealt with within a fortnight. If the CPS don't object, the Court of Appeal could sit the week after.'

Rigg and Poe shared a glance. Rigg nodded slightly. Poe returned it.

'So there we have it, ladies and gents,' Gamble said. 'In as little as three weeks, Jared Keaton will be back out on the streets.'

CHAPTER SIXTEEN

Poe thought three weeks was optimistic. Keaton's legal team would almost certainly go for judge-in-chambers – an application for bail that a judge considers in private.

Keaton could be back behind the pass at Bullace & Sloe in a few days.

Poe had a lot to get through before then. He wanted to speak to the cop at Alston Library. Sometimes cops kept things out of their pocketbooks in case they looked stupid later. Poe needed to know if Problem Solver Alsop had anything he hadn't reported. He would meet with the FME as well. She'd been on-call when the girl had been brought in and he wanted to hear her medical opinions first hand. He'd also speak to the person who signed the sample over to the couriers and, if necessary, drive down to the lab and interview the scientist and anyone else involved in handling the sample.

Every link in the chain of custody needed to be vigorously stress-tested.

But first he needed to go home. The day was pressing on and he had things to do.

Other than some remote areas of Scotland, Herdwick Croft was as isolated as it was possible to be in mainland Britain. It was on the ancient moorland of Shap Fell, and Poe couldn't actually drive there. His nearest neighbour – a hotel once used as a German POW camp – was over two miles away and he had an arrangement with them to park his car there. Ordinarily, his quad – the only vehicle rugged enough to manage the rough terrain – would have been waiting for him in the hotel's car park, but he'd been away for a few weeks and hadn't wanted to impose. His quad was back at Herdwick Croft.

He'd have to walk.

It wasn't usually a problem, in fact it was usually a pleasure, but he'd had to buy some provisions. The croft's electricity ran off a generator and, if he was going to be away for any length of time, he turned everything off. As perishable food would spoil, he always emptied his fridge – usually into Edgar – before he left.

Carrying bags of meat, assorted root vegetables and other essentials, over two miles of moorland was an arm-stretching endurance march and by the time he arrived at Herdwick Croft – an ugly building that looked as though it had forced its way out of the ground rather than being built on top of it – he was drenched in sweat. He dumped his groceries on his outdoor table and spent five minutes getting the kinks out of his muscles. When he was finished, he unlocked the door and stepped inside.

He was home. At last.

Despite it being dusk the air in Herdwick Croft was still and hot. A pristine layer of dust coated everything. Poe opened the shutters and let the evening breeze in. He'd clean everything tomorrow.

After sinking a warm bottle of Spun Gold, Poe put on a pair of old shorts and tackled his generator. Before long, he had it stripped to its component parts. One of the seals was showing early signs of corrosion. It probably wouldn't start leaking for a few weeks but he had a spare so he replaced it. The filter also needed changing but that was routine. He smiled as he worked. Two years earlier his technical abilities started and ended with folding up a wad of paper to fix a wobbly table leg. He could

82

have no more serviced a generator than he could have licked his own elbow. Now he didn't even need to think about what he was doing.

As soon as the generator was back together he pressed the ignition button. It started first time. He turned on the DAB radio that Bradshaw had bought him. The news would be on soon and, like the rest of the country, he wanted to hear what Storm Wendy was doing. He restocked his fridge while he listened. There was no new information. Storm Wendy *was* coming but they weren't sure when. He flicked over to BBC Radio 6 Music. They had a pot-luck playlist – from punk to Mongolian throat-singing – but he usually found something to enjoy.

With the electricity on, Poe moved to the water pump. The only real issue at Herdwick Croft had been clean water but he'd got lucky. The company he'd hired to drill a borehole had found water immediately. It wasn't even that deep so he hadn't needed an expensive pump to get it to the surface. Poe examined the pump's motor. He hand-turned it a few times and saw nothing that needed urgent attention. He attached the power lead to the generator and fired it up. Before long he had running water again.

The last thing he did was light his wood-burning stove. It was a warm and balmy evening but his stove also heated his water. And Poe needed a shower.

He decided to get Edgar the following day. Two hours later he was at the bar in the Shap Wells Hotel enjoying a pie and a pint. He had his laptop with him and, after he'd eaten, he emailed Bradshaw an update.

She replied immediately.

It wasn't good news. Jared Keaton's legal team had already made their judge-in-chambers bail application. Bradshaw sent a link. Poe read it. Phrases like 'incompetent', 'flawed investigation' and 'unparalleled miscarriage of justice' were used interchangeably and with little regard for accuracy. It was sensationalist but it was supposed to be. The message was clear: we have you over a barrel and we'll go to the press if you don't play ball. Poe was right: Gamble's three-week deadline had been far too optimistic. They had days now, not weeks.

Bradshaw must have had a read-receipt on her emails as she sent another one ten minutes after he'd read the first: Are you OK, Poe?

He hunted for and stabbed the keys as he composed an answer. He chose his words carefully – if he didn't, she'd grow more and more anxious the longer he was up here. She'd only been in the field once and she'd ended up saving his life. She worried when he was on his own or she couldn't contact him. He settled for telling her it was annoying but expected. As soon as he'd pressed send, his BlackBerry rang. It was a number he didn't recognise.

'Detective Sergeant Washington Poe?' It was a man's voice. He had a high-pitched, androgynous Scottish accent.

'Speaking.'

'Mr Poe, this is Graham Smith. I'm a journalist and I was wondering if you could shed light on this new evidence that has come to light?'

Poe remained silent.

'Is it true that you got it badly wrong six years ago, Mr Poe?'

'Piss off.' He threw his phone down on the table. It clattered into his half-empty pint glass.

Bollocks. They'd already leaked something to the press and he hadn't even dipped his toes in the investigation yet.

He wondered how Smith had got his number.

Day 6

CHAPTER SEVENTEEN

Gamble had arranged for Problem Solver Alsop to be at Kendal police station at eight in the morning. It was the closest one to Herdwick Croft and the last time Poe was there, he'd been told to fuck off. A combination of the trouble he'd been causing and some long-clung-to animosity – a legacy from his time with Cumbria Police.

It wasn't much better this time. A week ago he might have been welcomed. He was the man who'd made sure the truth about the Immolation Man got out – a truth welcomed by every man, woman and police dog on the force.

But if a week is a long time in politics, it's even longer in Cumbria. While no one explicitly said that they blamed him for Keaton's botched investigation, it was obvious why his reception was so frosty. Eventually someone went off message and made him a coffee.

Alsop arrived a few minutes later.

Poe took an immediate liking to the man. He was a solid, no-frills cop. Rough-edged and prepared to do whatever was asked of him. Poe asked if there was anything he hadn't deemed important enough to put in his official notebook, no matter how trivial it had seemed at the time.

He needn't have bothered. Alsop was a veteran and wise enough to know that just because he didn't find something important, it didn't mean someone else wouldn't. He went through the morning again, referred to his notebook only once, and told Poe nothing he didn't already know.

Poe gave him one of his NCA business cards and thanked him for coming in.

He planned to interview everyone involved in the order they spoke to the girl. The next person on his list was the FME.

Previously referred to as police surgeons, force medical examiners have been part of the police service for over a hundred years. Their role is varied, but the most common reasons for call-outs are certifying deaths, examining and providing care for injured persons in police custody, and taking blood samples from drunk drivers. FME training is comprehensive. It includes forensic and legal medicine, the Police and Criminal Evidence Act, consent and confidentiality, and how to give evidence in court and to the coroner.

It is a specialised role and Cumbria, like all small police forces, employs several on a freelance basis. So, instead of meeting Felicity Jakeman at a police station, Poe had to travel to the south of the county and her practice in Ulverston.

Poe liked Ulverston. It was the birthplace of Stan Laurel and also the self-designated festival capital of Cumbria. From massive food events to quirky folk concerts, people travelled far and wide to get there. Famous for having the world's shortest, widest and deepest canal, it is a myriad of old buildings and a labyrinth of twisting cobbled streets.

Felicity Jakeman was one of eight doctors in her practice. Poe had told her he was coming and they'd arranged to meet at the end of her morning surgery. Bar any urgent house calls, she expected to be free around midday.

Poe had an hour to kill so he grabbed a coffee in a nearby deli-café. As soon as he entered, the smell of cinnamon, warm caramel and freshly baked cookies assaulted his nostrils. His stomach growled but he resisted the temptation. He found a window table and ordered an Americano from a teenager wearing an old-fashioned lace apron. The coffee was served in a bone china cup and was delicious. He traced circles in some spilled water and idly watched Ulverston go about its business.

He reviewed what he knew. It wasn't much and ultimately it would all come down to the blood sample he'd left with Estelle Doyle. If her lab confirmed Cumbria's result, it was game over. Jared Keaton hadn't killed his daughter. Poe would apologise to him personally.

The door jangler jingled and Poe's vision was filled with orange and maroon. Some nuns from the town's Buddhist temple, the internationally renowned meditation centre, had come for an early lunch. Anywhere else in Cumbria, a bunch of women with bald heads and brightly coloured robes would have attracted stares and suspicion, but in Ulverston the Buddhists had been there that long they were part of the town's flavour.

Buddhism seemed a peaceful religion. Poe didn't know the actual definition of Zen, but at Herdwick Croft without a television, and as in tune with nature and the land as he'd ever been, there were times when he must have been close to achieving it.

One of the nuns caught him watching her. She smiled. Poe returned it. He glanced at his watch. He had ten minutes to get across to Felicity Jakeman's surgery. He drained the dregs of coffee – dark and syrupy and like a shot of Pro Plus – put a two-pound coin on the table as a tip and left the café.

Ulverston was a prosperous town – certainly in comparison to its nearest neighbour, the much larger Barrow-in-Furness – and this was reflected in the waiting room's decor: muted colours, live plants and up-to-date magazines. Comfortable chairs instead of moulded plastic back-breakers. There was even a water dispenser.

Poe let the receptionist know he'd arrived and took a seat. As the morning surgery was nearing its end, the number of people waiting to be seen was minimal. An old lady a few seats away coughed delicately into her handkerchief.

'Doctor Jakeman will see you now, Sergeant Poe,' the receptionist called over. 'She's in surgery number three. Just over by the water cooler.'

Poe thanked her.

Felicity Jakeman was casually dressed in jeans and a faded sweatshirt with the logo of London's University College Hospital on the front. She wore light make-up and her shoulder-length auburn hair was pulled into a low ponytail.

She'd already started her lunch and, through a mouthful of Asian salad, she told Poe she could give him a maximum of twenty minutes. She didn't look impressed to see him. She was probably in the 'It's all Poe's fault' camp. He'd no doubt be getting a lot of that over the coming days . . .

It was a typical GP's surgery: functional furniture, a couple of anatomy posters, a computer attached to a prescription printer, and an examination bed covered in blue roll. On her desk was a photo of her walking up Cat Bells. The distinctive shape of the fell couldn't be mistaken. Cat Bells was near Keswick and Poe didn't like it. Even during the off-season it was packed.

Poe took the seat beside her desk. Jakeman leaned forwards and looked at him like he'd just asked for a two-week sick note.

She was an attractive woman, probably three or four years older than Estelle Doyle, but whereas the Pathologist Grimm worked with patients who couldn't get any worse, the stress of working with patients who could was evident. She had the ingrained fatigue all doctors seemed to have. Her eyes were lined with crow's feet and her hair was flecked with grey.

She swallowed whatever it was she was chewing and continued to appraise him. After a moment she shrugged and offered him a half-smile. Probably decided he wasn't the enemy after all.

'You don't mind if I eat, do you? After a twelve-hour shift it's sometimes hard to resist the takeaway menu drawer so I try to eat healthily during the day.'

'Of course. Doctor Jakeman, could you—'

'Please, call me Flick. Doctor Jakeman reminds me of my ex.'

Poe had never liked nicknames – they conferred a level of intimacy he wasn't comfortable with – but he could hardly say no. He glanced down at her left hand. He couldn't stop himself; he was paid to be a nosy bastard. The wedding band indentation was visible but the same colour as her finger. It didn't look as though she'd worn one for a while. At least a year, he reckoned.

'I'm sorry,' he said automatically.

She shrugged and put down her salad bowl. 'Sometimes it's not Mr Right you find in high school, it's Mr Wrong.'

'Is that why you moved up here?'

'You've been checking up on me.' Her eyes twinkled in amusement.

'I haven't actually, but you're wearing a London hospital sweatshirt and your accent's not local.'

'I was a hospital doctor in London but fancied a change when we split up. We used to come to the Lakes on our holidays so I decided to take the plunge and move up permanently. I've been here a couple of years now and I love it. I love the people and I love the landscape.'

Poe wouldn't have minded more of a chat – she was an interesting woman – but he was aware that the clock on his twenty minutes had already started. 'Tell me about the day Elizabeth Keaton was brought in.'

She folded her arms. 'Hasn't she been through enough?'

'She has. And I'm extremely sorry for the part I played in it all. But now my focus is on catching the man who took her.'

Flick sighed. 'What do you want to know?'

'Everything,' Poe replied.

* * *

Flick had been called around ten-thirty in the morning. She hadn't known the significance of who the girl was claiming to be and, during her first examination at least, hadn't cared. She'd have given the same level of care to anyone – victim, witness, criminal or cop. Her primary role was medical.

The girl had refused to go to hospital and, when it became apparent to Flick that her police colleagues would be questioning her for a sustained period of time, she examined her in the force medical suite.

'She was fragile. Malnourished but not in immediate danger. And, although the worst was behind her, she was suffering from opiate withdrawal. As you'll have seen from her self-harm scars, she has psychological scars that will require years of therapy.'

'Any fresh injuries?'

She nodded. 'Cuts and abrasions to her ankles, hands and face. A couple of torn fingernails. All consistent with running through woods, unprotected. I removed a couple of thorns and dressed her wounds. Fixed her to a drip and fed a bag of saline into her.'

'Did you believe her story?'

'Not my job. I was only there to offer medical support.'

'Why did you take a blood sample?'

'Instead of a swab?'

Poe nodded.

'It was agreed with the officer in charge as being the least traumatic option.'

'To check if she was pregnant?' That was what Rigg had told him.

'That is correct. Blood tests are ninety-nine per cent accurate and can detect the pregnancy hormone hCG as early as seven days after conception.'

'She wasn't pregnant, though?'

'No.'

'And there were no STDs, or viruses associated with intravenous heroin use?'

Flick shook her head. 'No.'

'And there was no irregularity with the evidence bags?'

'There wasn't a person in that room who didn't know what was at stake, Sergeant Poe. I'm assuming you've seen the tape? The chain of custody was unimpeachable. If I have to stand in court and say so, I will.'

'Why didn't she want to go to a hospital? Or a Sexual Assault Referral Centre?'

'Point blank refused both. Told me later that she just wanted to be on her own. Didn't even want to go to the restaurant until her dad was released. The only reason she stayed as long as she did was to make sure the police had everything they needed.'

'Did you ask for the blood to be tested for opiates?'

'We did, although it was predictably pointless.'

'Why's that?'

'Heroin only stays in the system for a few hours. Elizabeth hadn't taken anything in the four days before she escaped and the test came back negative. All the tests did. She wasn't pregnant, she didn't have any infections and there were no drugs in her system.'

Poe made a mental note to call Estelle Doyle. He wanted to rerun everything. He didn't doubt that Flick was right, and he was sure a second testing would only confirm the results of the first, but he wanted every angle covered.

He asked a few follow-up questions but got nothing he hadn't been able to get from the file. He thanked Flick and left her his card. By the time he'd reached the door, she'd pressed her intercom and called for her next patient.

And he thought police officers had busy jobs . . .

CHAPTER EIGHTEEN

Poe called Estelle Doyle on the way back to his hire car. She answered on the fourth ring.

'Not even the living get DNA profiles back this quickly, Poe. I'll call you when we have it. It won't be today, though.'

'That's not why I'm ringing. Did you use all the blood?'

'Of course not.'

'Can you run some more tests for me then, please?'

'And Cumbria are happy to pay, are they?'

'Good point. Can you bill the NCA directly? If you put DI Stephanie Flynn on the invoice, I'll email you where to send it.'

'What do you need?'

He rattled off the same tests Flick Jakeman had requested.

'STDs, pregnancy and opiates,' Doyle repeated. 'Is that all?'

'What are my options?'

'Expensive or very expensive.'

'What's the very expensive?'

'Liquid chromatography-mass spectrometry.'

Poe had always been a need-to-know-what-it-can-do rather than a need-to-know-how-it-works kind of guy and, anyway, he suspected Doyle was purposely talking in scientific riddles just to annoy him. He settled for, 'And that's good, is it?'

'Gold standard. It'll analyse every chemical in the sample.'

'How much?'

She told him. Poe winced. It was an awful lot of money. He

would have to run it by Flynn – SCAS's sergeant wasn't author-ised to sign off purchases that big. But . . . she'd almost certainly say no. Screw it. He'd pretend there'd been a misunderstanding with Cumbria when the invoice landed on her desk.

'Do it,' he said.

'You sure?'

'No. But do it anyway.'

'What are you up to, Poe?'

'Clutching at straws, Estelle. Clutching at straws.'

Poe called Gamble and told him what he needed next: the name of the police officer who'd signed the blood sample over to the courier service. Gamble said he'd arrange for him to be at Kendal police station. Poe appreciated the gesture, but as he was going to be speaking to the couriers in Penrith, he would see him at headquarters.

Poe threaded his way to the M6. When he finally reached the motorway, he called Thomas Hume, the farmer who looked after Edgar when he was away. He planned to collect Edgar later that afternoon.

A woman answered the phone, which was a first. Hume was an irascible fell farmer and Poe assumed that he lived the same monastic existence he did.

'Can I speak to Thomas, please?'

'Who is this?'

Poe told her. There was a pause. Eventually she said, 'May I ask what this is about?'

'I want to collect my dog. Thomas looks after Edgar when I'm away.'

'Oh, of course. Yes, that's fine. Any time after five?'

'After five is great.' Poe hung up. That was odd. The woman had sounded worried when he'd told her his name. When he'd said he only wanted his dog back she'd seemed relieved. He put it to the back of his mind – he had more important things to worry about.

The evidence room cop was called John Langley. He was a fat man with a crooked knee. Watching him get out of his seat was to witness an exercise in fulcrums and counterpoints. He rocked himself backwards and forwards until he had enough momentum to tip himself out of his reinforced chair. He limped to the door and let Poe in.

'Old rugby injury,' he said.

Poe doubted it. The human knee is essentially a load-bearing hinge and Langley was carrying quite a load. Gamble had said he was on restricted duties until either his knee recovered or he was let go. He'd been in the evidence room for over a year and knew what he was doing. Unsurprisingly, he resented being questioned.

Poe wasn't bothered. The blood being transferred to the courier firm was a link in the chain of custody. He was testing it; he didn't care who he upset along the way.

'Elizabeth Keaton. You packaged her blood for the courier?'

Langley didn't reply.

Poe waited.

Langley cracked. 'I'll need to check.'

'Please do that.'

He shuffled across to a sleeping computer and touched the mouse. The screen burst into life. Miraculously it was already on the right page.

I'll need to check my arse, Poe thought. Langley had probably been worrying since Gamble had told him that Poe was on his way to see him.

'Yes, it was me.' He printed the page and handed it across. Poe checked the serial number with the one in his notebook. It matched.

'Talk me through the process. Start to finish, leave nothing out.'

Langley began tapping the keyboard. For a few moments Poe was forced to put up with the solitary clack of the one-fingered typist. Eventually the force policy on handling, packaging, labelling and transporting biological forensic evidence appeared on the computer screen.

For thirty minutes Langley talked him through each step.

An order was generated by an authorised investigating officer – in this case, DC Rigg – when samples needed to be sent to the lab. Langley had emailed the courier and arranged a pick-up time. He had also emailed the lab to let them know what to expect and the serial number of the evidence bag. Fifteen minutes before the courier was due, he had signed out the blood from the CSI store. He then brought it back to the evidence store and had a second member of staff sign to confirm it was the correct serial number and the bag hadn't been tampered with. Because they were sending biological material, Langley had then put the evidence bag in secondary packaging – a watertight, clear plastic bag supplied by the lab. This was sealed and a biohazard sign was attached.

When the courier had arrived, the driver had checked the serial number and watched Langley place it in a polystyrene box. This was sealed and biohazard signs were attached to every side. The courier had then signed for the package and taken it away.

'Very good,' Poe said, when he'd finished. 'Now you've told me what's *supposed* to have happened, how about you tell me what *actually* happened?' It was an aggressive question and was taken as such.

Langley growled, 'I'm going to pretend you didn't say that, son.'

Poe didn't respond.

'I work in an evidence room, dickhead. Look up.'

He did. There were three cameras. Including one right above the hatch.

'Now look over there.' Langley pointed to the far wall.

There was another camera.

'You're not the first cop to try and blame the evidence room for his own fuck-up. These tapes are kept for five years and Superintendent Gamble has authorised you to view the time in question. We're like a Vegas casino in here: every transaction is done under a camera. If there was a balls-up, we didn't make it.'

Poe apologised. Cumbria was a high-performing police force – of course they wouldn't put an idiot in charge of their main evidence room.

Langley opened a different screen and sat back as Poe watched the collection of the blood sample by the courier. It was exactly as Langley had described.

Another link crossed off.

Next stop, ANL Parcels in Carlisle.

Kingmoor Park, an ex-MoD storage facility with over two million square-feet of offices and warehouses, was, according to its website, Cumbria's premier business park. It was at the north of the city and Poe left the M6 at junction 44 before joining the Carlisle Northern Development Route, otherwise known as the A689 (W). The business park had over one hundred tenants, one of which was a local courier service called ANL Parcels.

Poe found them easily enough. He'd deliberately not told them he was coming. He intended to come in under the guise of a random audit, and knew that his NCA ID card would be enough to get a sit-down with the driver and see their parcel-tracking systems.

He parked in the bay reserved for the deputy manager and entered the reception area. A tall woman looked up from her computer. She wore a hands-free telephone headset and a dark blazer with a golden ANL Parcels logo on the breast pocket. Poe's first impression was that ANL was a professional outfit.

The woman gave him a two-minutes hand signal and went back to her phone call. It sounded like she was taking an order. He took a seat and leafed through a glossy brochure. According to what he was reading, ANL was a dedicated local courier service, and had contracts with the local authority, North Cumbria University Hospitals, Cumbria Police and any number of smaller businesses.

The receptionist called him over. Poe showed her his warrant card and asked to speak to the operations manager.

Within a short time he was in a control room with a woman who was a bit too enthusiastic about the courier business for Poe's liking. She was called Rosie and she was keen to help with his 'audit'.

Three minutes later Poe was ready to cross the courier off his list. He couldn't see how the package could have been tampered with. Rosie explained that, because they were a responsive and flexible business, drivers were randomly assigned routes each day. Poe asked if a package could be sidelined for half an hour while someone accessed it.

'It's possible,' she admitted. 'But as they don't get assigned collection or delivery routes until they arrive at work, I don't see how. No driver can just "arrange" to be the one to pick up a specific package. The system's designed to avoid that exact problem.'

Poe removed his phone and read out the ANL tracking number that Langley had recorded on the evidence log. 'Can you tell me who delivered this parcel?'

'This isn't an audit, is it?' Rosie asked.

'No, it is not.'

She tapped the keyboard and played with the ergonomic mouse.

'Martin Evans. He was on a nice little half-shift. A collection from Furness General Hospital in Barrow, a delivery in Lancaster and he finished with your parcel at Combined Science Services.'

'And he's been with you a while?'

'At least ten years.'

'Do you think he's capable of tampering with a parcel?'

'Martin Evans? Good heavens no,' she laughed. 'How can I put it? We don't exactly employ geniuses here, Sergeant Poe. If you're of good character and have a clean driving licence, you're in. Martin doesn't really have the guile to be involved in anything more elaborate than ordering chips.'

Poe sighed inwardly and crossed ANL Parcels off his internal list.

Next stop, Combined Science Services. The final stop.

But not now.

Now it was time to get his dog.

CHAPTER NINETEEN

Poe had a dog when he was a child – an arthritic ex-sheepdog his dad had been suckered into taking. Poe would take Tess with him when he and his friends were searching for conkers. The effort of walking the five hundred yards to the local park usually saw her collapse in front of the fire for the rest of the day.

Owning a springer spaniel was an entirely different experience.

Poe had never seen such concentrated energy before. For his first year, Edgar only had three states of being: eating, sleeping and sprinting. Whenever they left Herdwick Croft, Poe's journey was five times longer than it needed to be as Edgar seemed incapable of running in straight lines. Instead, they took jaggy detours, sometimes miles in the opposite direction of where they were supposed to be going.

For twelve months, Edgar did Poe's head in.

Eventually, and not before time, he calmed down and Poe finally understood why springer spaniel owners were addicted to them. He was an absolute joy to be with. He chewed on Poe's sleeves, followed him everywhere and barked at the slightest noise. He'd fearlessly dive into ice-covered becks but would refuse to get in the bath. Poe had yet to find something he wouldn't eat, although he seemed to have a particular fondness for cheese and sheep shit. He'd spend two minutes getting filthy then lick himself clean for ten hours. He'd drink from the toilet then dribble on Poe's face. He'd steal food from his plate and growl if Poe dared try to take it back.

Poe wouldn't have it any other way.

As the crow flies, Thomas Hume's farm was a little over three miles from Herdwick Croft, farther by road. Ordinarily, Poe would have driven his BMW X1 right into the yard and collected Edgar without bothering the grumpy old farmer. The Shap grapevine would have already let him know that Poe was back in Cumbria. This time, though, he was in a natty little hire car, and he didn't want to get a windscreen full of buckshot – Hume spooked easily and carried his twelve-gauge everywhere.

Poe parked on the verge of the tractor-wide lane and walked the rest of the way. As soon as he rounded the bend he knew something was up.

The farmyard, normally chaotic with barking dogs and screeching chickens, was deathly still. Hume's battered Mercedes was in its usual place, but beside it there were three other cars, all of them small and all of them clean. Town cars, not country cars. Cars in rural Cumbria tended to be dirty, and powerful enough to cope with light off-roading.

Poe recalled the woman who'd answered the phone earlier. She hadn't introduced herself and she'd been wary when he'd told her his name. In fact, she'd seemed relieved when Poe had explained why he was calling. He wondered if Hume was in trouble. Probably financial given the pittance hill farmers made these days. Perhaps the woman was one of Hume's daughters and she'd mistaken Poe for a creditor.

Sneaking in and taking Edgar didn't seem like the right move this time. Poe hesitated, not sure what to do for the best. *Sod it*, he thought. He wasn't doing anything he hadn't done countless times before. He approached the front door.

The farm and outbuildings had been constructed using the same mottled grey stone as Herdwick Croft – buildings around this part of Cumbria were tied together by the limited choice of construction materials. It was only the farm's newer structures – the shearing shed, the sorting pens and the sheep dip – that were made from more modern materials such as steel and corrugated iron.

The front door had no bell and Poe made his knock as un-aggressive as he could. No one answered and he couldn't hear anything. He put his ear to the warm wood and knocked again, louder. This time he heard whispering, muted crying and foot-steps. He took a step back and waited.

A woman opened the door. She studied him silently. She was about Poe's age and her face was wet and blotchy. Her make-up was streaked with track marks and her eyes were puffy. She'd been crying, although she wasn't now.

'Can I help you?' Her voice was cracked and raw, like she'd been chain-smoking Russian cigarettes.

'Er . . . hi.' Poe was never at his best when others showed emotion. 'My name's Washington Poe, I called earlier. Thomas looks after my dog when I'm away. Was it you I spoke to before?'

The woman nodded.

'Is Thomas in? Would it be possible to speak to him?'

She shook her head but didn't elaborate.

'He's not in trouble, is he?'

Poe had seen actors cry on television but they never got it right. People rarely 'burst into tears'. It is almost always a slow build-up. Something happens and they move from the 'just about managing to hold it together' stage into the 'can't hold it in any more' stage.

Like now.

The woman's nose grew red at the tip. Her mouth twitched. Her eyes swelled. A solitary tear rolled down her cheek. Two more followed. Before long, her body was racked with tremors and noiseless sobs.

Poe averted his eyes. Grief wasn't a voyeuristic pastime. After a minute the sobbing abated and he felt confident enough to look up. Red, tear-rimmed eyes defiantly stared back at him. He already knew what she was going to say.

'My father's dead, Mr Poe.'

He nodded. 'I'm so sorry, Mrs . . .'

'Hume. Victoria Hume. I'm his eldest daughter.'

There was an awkward pause.

Poe broke it. 'I had no idea. Had he been ill?'

'A stroke.'

'I'm so sorry,' he repeated. He couldn't really demand his dog back but hanging around making small talk was an imposition. He wished Bradshaw was there – she'd have just come out and said it. Probably added statistics on how many people die of strokes each year. He was saved from further awkwardness by the sound of barking. Edgar skidded round the corner of a small barn, immediately followed by two border collies. A Jack Russell, its feet moving twice as fast as the other dogs, brought up the rear. When Edgar saw Poe, his excited barks turned into ear-splitting yelps of unadulterated joy.

He really had no sense of occasion.

Victoria Hume managed a weak smile. 'Someone's happy to see you.'

Poe caught the unspoken 'at least'. There was something else going on. He was reminded how cagey she'd been when he'd called the day before. There was something he wasn't being told and it had nothing to do with the death of her father.

'Look,' he said, deciding now wasn't the time to dig for information, 'I'm going to get out of your hair. I'm truly sorry for your loss. I always got on well with Thomas and he was a huge help with Edgar.'

She gave him a tight smile but didn't respond. She certainly didn't offer to continue the tradition. It would put Poe in a bind later, but now was hardly the time to ask for a favour.

Because he hadn't immediately turned and left, Victoria Hume must have thought he wanted something else. She clenched her jaw and crossed her arms. They locked eyes. 'I'm sorry, Mr Poe, but I can't discuss anything else with you now.'

Poe held her gaze. He didn't have a clue what she was talking about.

'I have to go,' she said, stepping back inside and shutting the door.

Poe stared at the closed oak door for a moment before reaching down and stroking Edgar's ears. 'Well, matey, that was a bit weird. You ready for your tea?'

The spaniel looked up, his eyes liquid brown. Happy just to hear Poe's voice. He let out a gentle whine.

'Come on then, let's get you home.'

Day 7

CHAPTER TWENTY

Combined Science Services was based in Preston. They opened at eight and Poe intended to be first through the door. They had large grounds so Poe took Edgar with him. He didn't really have a choice; he could hardly impose on Victoria.

His appointment with the CEO wasn't until nine but Poe wanted to have a root around before then. See if he could spot any weak points in their process.

The M6 was no busier than normal and he arrived at CSS fifteen minutes earlier than he'd intended. He took Edgar for a short walk around their grounds. It gave him a chance to scope the complex. He saw nothing unusual.

He ran through his interview strategy for the CEO. She'd almost certainly be on the defensive. Police contracts accounted for over 30 per cent of CSS's business and a process flaw that had allowed contamination of evidence would be disastrous for them. The CEO couldn't clam up and hide behind a legal team either – a hint of a cover-up would have the same impact as an actual cover-up. Every police contract would be cancelled. No, today Poe was expecting the CEO to be on a charm offensive. She'd play up their strengths and play down their weaknesses. Poe wasn't worried. He'd investigated corporations before.

His phone rang. It was Estelle Doyle.

'Your profile came in late last night, Poe,' she said.

'And?'

She paused. Nobody paused when they were about to give good news. His mouth went dry.

'I've emailed you the full analysis but I'm sorry, Poe, it's bad news. The sample you gave me is the same as the control sample. The blood *does* belong to Elizabeth Keaton.'

Gamble ushered Poe into his office. The superintendent was bleary-eyed and unshaven. He leaned back in his seat and rolled his neck and shoulders.

'There's no doubt?'

'None. I was at Combined Science Services when Estelle Doyle called, but I boxed it off anyway.'

Doyle's news had made the CSS chain-of-custody visit redundant but he'd gone ahead with it nonetheless. His visit only confirmed what Estelle Doyle had told him: CSS were reputable and professional. He told Gamble.

'And even if they weren't, the whole thing's moot now,' Gamble said. 'The girl *is* Elizabeth Keaton, and Jared Keaton *was* wrongly convicted.'

Poe nodded. There was no other explanation.

'You can't blame yourself, Poe. Things like this are never down to one person. The police, the CPS, Keaton's defence team – everyone fucked up.'

Gamble was right, of course. Poe had been a small cog in a big machine, but that wouldn't be how the media would see it. It wouldn't be how the rank and file of Cumbria would see it. It certainly wasn't how he saw it.

'I'll tell Keaton, sir. I owe him that much.'

Gamble nodded. His focus seemed to be elsewhere. Like he was listening to music that only he could hear. 'The prison service have already transferred him to Durham. They must be expecting his imminent release.'

That made sense. Whenever possible, HMPS transferred

inmates to the prison closest to their release address during the last few days of a sentence.

'You're booked to see Keaton tomorrow,' Gamble continued. 'DC Rigg will be accompanying you.'

'You knew I'd ask?'

'Not really, no.'

'Then . . . then why?'

Gamble's eyes regained focus. They bore into Poe's. 'Because, Poe, for reasons that are beyond me, Jared Keaton has asked to see you.'

Day 8

CHAPTER TWENTY-ONE

Poe slept strangely. Asleep, but aware he was asleep. Keaton wanting to see him played on a loop in his conscious and unconscious mind. If it were just about gloating, then why do it in the privacy of a prison interview room? Keaton was a publicity whore – embarrassing Poe in front of the world's media would be much more his style.

It made no sense. And that made him nervous.

Because Jared Keaton never did anything without a reason.

Poe had risen early and eaten his breakfast over the sink and directly from the frying pan. Edgar licked it clean. With Hume dead, and Hume's daughter not his greatest fan, Poe had been forced to do something he'd sworn he'd never do: put Edgar in kennels. He knew he needed a long-term solution going forward but, for now at least, he was out of options.

Officially it was a Cumbria Police visit so Rigg drove. He picked up Poe outside the main doors of Carleton Hall at seven o'clock. He didn't turn off the engine and was moving before Poe had shut the door.

HMP Durham was a straight run across the mountainous A66 and a short drive up the A1. Rigg didn't speak, didn't even turn his head in Poe's direction, until they'd passed the Warcop army ranges, a good thirty minutes into their journey. And even then it was only to crudely respond to something Poe asked.

'So, why do you think Keaton wants to see me?'

Rigg said nothing. His jaw hardened and developed a tic.

'Because I've got to be honest, this is worrying me a bit,' Poe continued.

This time Rigg muttered something under his breath.

'Sorry, I didn't catch that.'

'I *said*, my heart bleeds purple piss.'

Poe ignored the insubordination. The anger ultimately came from a good place and, although he couldn't explain why, he wanted Rigg onside.

Probably because he reminded Poe a little bit of himself.

As one of the few remaining great nineteenth-century prisons, HMP Durham is old. Over the years it has housed some of Britain's most notorious prisoners. Murderers Rose West, Myra Hindley and Ian Brady, and gangsters Ronnie Kray, John McVicar – who managed to escape – and Frankie Fraser all spent time behind Durham's bleak walls. It's two hundred years old and holds over a thousand inmates. It's overcrowded and underfunded, unbearably hot in summer and dangerously cold in winter, and should have been demolished fifty years ago. Poe had always thought HMP Durham was symbolic of the UK's broken criminal justice system.

The prison had recently been part of the high-risk estate, however, and that meant it had state-of-the-art gate facilities. After having their IDs checked, passes printed off and going through the meticulously thorough search, they made their way to the official visitors' suite. 'Suite' was a grandiose term for what was little more than a corridor with eight dirty boxes on each side. It looked like a Third World call centre. The kind that sold knockoff prescription drugs. The walls were clear Perspex, the decor was drab and the smell of bleach was overpowering.

They were allocated room number three, second on the left. The bleach mingled with the BO of the room's last occupant. Poe and Rigg both winced at the smell. There were four chairs and one table, all fixed to the painted concrete floor. The only other furnishing was a cheap tin ashtray.

The suite's corridor had entrances at both ends. Poe and Rigg had come through the visitors' entrance. The other entrance led into the bowels of the prison. Poe couldn't take his eyes off the silent, metal door. As the other interview rooms were empty, the next person to step through would be Jared Keaton.

With a solid clunk, the metal door opened, and Poe saw the man who'd haunted last night's dreams.

Keaton walked to room three and entered without waiting to be asked. He took one of the two remaining seats. For several moments, Poe and Keaton stared at each other. Rigg might as well not have been there.

Poe hadn't seen Keaton since the day of his conviction. Although he wasn't as clean-cut or as well polished as he'd been during his trial, six years in prison hadn't made Keaton any less striking. His teeth weren't as dazzlingly white, and a prison barber instead of a celebrity stylist had been cutting his blond hair, but the matinee-idol looks were still there. His perfectly symmetrical face. The distinct cheekbones and the angular jaw. The designer stubble. His famous baby-blue eyes. Rugged enough to not look effeminate, but sensitive enough to appeal to everyone. It was no wonder the TV production companies and publishing houses had fawned over him.

Before his arrest, Jared Keaton would run five miles and spend an hour in the gym before breakfast and, although his muscular definition had worn off due to the lack of facilities, his prison-issue sweatshirt still clung to his chest and biceps. He smelled of cigarettes even though Poe knew he didn't smoke. That was no surprise, everyone smelled of cigarettes in prison.

Rigg cleared his throat but Keaton raised his hand and

stopped him from speaking. He flashed the detective a mischievous grin. The same grin he'd aim at the cameras when he was explaining a complicated technique to one of the sycophantic celebrity guests on his weekly cooking show. Simultaneously disarming and smug. The one that had graced numerous magazine covers and centre spreads. 'An award-winning smile' as one newspaper had described it.

He faced Poe.

'Before we begin, do you have something to tell me, Mr Poe?' His affected French accent had somehow survived the harsh prison system.

Poe didn't respond. He'd planned to open with an apology and take whatever came afterwards. Keaton was a man he'd wronged and he had a right to be angry. On little more than a hunch, Poe had stolen six years from him, and six years from his daughter.

But the vibe wasn't right.

Keaton should have been purple with fury. A seething wrath, impossible to hide. But he wasn't. He was looking at Poe like a rattlesnake about to strike.

For several moments they stared and appraised each other.

When it was clear neither of them was going to speak, Rigg started talking. For thirty minutes he laid out what was happening in the search for Elizabeth Keaton's abductor, where the police were in investigating a potential miscarriage of justice, and when the Criminal Cases Review Commission might refer his case to the Court of Appeal.

Keaton's eyes didn't leave Poe's.

Eventually, Rigg's information dump – all of which Keaton undoubtedly knew from his legal team – dried up. Rigg looked at Keaton expectantly but got nothing back to show he'd even been listening.

'Do you have any questions, Mr Keaton?' he asked.

Without glancing in Rigg's direction, Keaton repeated the

question he'd asked thirty minutes earlier: 'Do you have something to tell me, Mr Poe?'

Poe had to say something.

'You've had quite the experience, Mr Keaton.' Something was telling him not to apologise.

Keaton raised his eyebrows and broadened his smile.

Rigg grimaced. 'I'm sure what my colleague meant to say was—'

Keaton dismissed him with a flick of his hand. He continued to stare at Poe and said, 'Your colleague is correct, Constable Rigg. I have had quite the experience.'

Rigg swallowed.

'Can you imagine what it's like to be accused of murder? For your friends to think the worst of you? To have your reputation ruined? To lose what you've spent your whole life working towards. Can you imagine what that's like, Constable Rigg?'

Rigg shook his head.

Poe watched, fascinated. The way Keaton could control people was extraordinary. Rigg, a battle-scarred veteran of countless interviews, had been stopped dead in his tracks. His mouth hung open. It looked like he couldn't quite believe what was happening.

Rigg finally found his voice. 'You're smiling, though, Mr Keaton.'

Keaton turned to face him. 'I am?'

'You are.'

'I suppose it must be because I'm happy, DC Rigg. Vindication, even after six years, is still vindication.'

Rigg was silent.

Keaton turned to Poe and, making no attempt to conceal it, winked at him.

'Or maybe it's because I know what happens next.'

CHAPTER TWENTY-TWO

'You're being uncharacteristically quiet, Sergeant Poe.'

Poe could have said the same thing. They were halfway back and it was the first time Rigg had spoken. He'd been glancing across at Poe for nearly half an hour, as if he were after some reassurance. His fingers had been tapping the steering wheel since they'd joined the A1. Keaton's alpha-male display had clearly upset him. The earlier surliness had disappeared, replaced with what looked like reflection. Poe knew it well – he'd felt the same after meeting Keaton for the first time. He had the weird ability to dominate any room he was in. It didn't matter where he was, or what he was doing. It hadn't mattered that he was a convicted murderer and Rigg was an experienced and tough police officer – with a flick of his wrist he'd made him irrelevant. Emasculated him.

'You can't let him get to you, Andrew.'

Rigg's grip on the steering wheel tightened. His knuckles turned white. 'Let who get to me, Poe?'

'Keaton. You can't let him inside your head. If you do you'll never get rid of him. Trust me on this.'

Rigg turned to face him. His eyes were narrow.

'Who the fuck do you think you are, Poe?'

Poe didn't answer.

Rigg jabbed a finger in his direction. 'Jared Keaton is not inside my head. Are we fucking clear about that?'

'Crystal, DC Rigg.'

'And neither are you.' Rigg put his hands back on the steering wheel and stared ahead. A muscle twitched in his jaw.

'Suit yourself.' If Rigg needed to save face then Poe didn't mind being his punchbag for now. He opened his notebook and jotted down his thoughts. When he was finished, he read them. Something wasn't quite right but he couldn't place it. It nibbled at the edge of his brain. He read his notes again, looking for what was missing. And there it was. He was surprised he'd overlooked it. Keaton had made no effort to hide it. He glanced at Rigg. He was still angry but this couldn't wait.

'Do you remember Keaton asking after his daughter?'

Rigg's head turned. But instead of barking at him, the policeman in him took over. 'Actually, I don't.'

Poe was sure Keaton hadn't. Not in any meaningful way. He hadn't asked how she was coping. Rigg had told him how the search for her abductor was progressing but Keaton hadn't asked any follow-up questions. He'd seemed bored by it all.

'And that doesn't seem strange to you?'

'They spoke on the phone a few days ago,' Rigg said. 'Perhaps that was all he needed.'

'Perhaps.'

Poe had told Rigg and Gamble that celebrity chef combined the third and ninth most popular career choices for psychopaths, but it had only been a flippant way to demonstrate Keaton's unusual psyche. To the best of his knowledge, Keaton didn't have a formal diagnosis. He'd refused all pre-sentence reports before the judge had given him life with a twenty-five-year tariff.

Maybe he'd refused the tests because he knew what they'd show.

But so what? As an SCAS officer, Poe was aware that almost 1 per cent of the population met the accepted criteria but, because Hollywood had taken ownership of the label and used a mental health diagnosis as a marketing strategy, most people assume all

121

psychopaths are serial killers. The truth is different. The majority are law-abiding citizens, living and working in the community the same as everyone else.

That Keaton was the psychopath among us, Poe took as a given. Everything pointed towards it. It was probably why he was so successful – he had that ruthless edge he needed to rise above his competitors.

But . . . to get everything he wanted, Keaton would have needed to hide his condition. He would have had to become an expert at mimicking emotions he was incapable of feeling. Like the colour-blind man who doesn't understand what red is, but knows the top traffic light means stop, Keaton would have practised emotions until they were second nature. He might not have understood empathy but he'd have recognised when he was expected to show it. He'd have learned to laugh at the same time as others, and he'd listen when you told him about your kids. He'd discuss the weather and your holiday plans with you. He'd listen to your dull chattering without you ever realising that he viewed you as little more than cattle. Irrelevant unless he needed something from you. If he cared about you at all it was because you were a means to an end.

Keaton was exceptional at it, as good as anyone Poe had seen. He understood what people wanted to see and hear, and he gave it to them.

It made forgetting to fake empathy for his daughter's horrific experience all the more implausible. Where was the faux-rage? The hollow vows of revenge against her abductor. And where was his anger at the police for their catastrophic failures?

Why hadn't he been wearing his mask?

The answer was obvious: he hadn't wanted to.

But why?

Poe's thoughts were interrupted by a muffled buzzing coming from the glove box. He'd forgotten to retrieve his mobile – even the NCA weren't allowed to take phones into prisons – and it was vibrating.

He checked the number. It was Estelle Doyle.

'Poe,' he said.

'I have your drug tests back, Poe,' Doyle said in a smoky voice.

'Thanks, boss.' He didn't want Rigg to know that Gamble had asked him to double-check his findings. He was angry enough with him as it was.

'You can't talk?'

'That's right.'

'What are you up to, Poe?'

He could tell she was smiling. 'What have you got for me, boss?'

'The test was negative for heroin. It only stays in the body for a few hours so no surprises there.'

'It's what we expected. Thanks any—'

'Poe, darling, can I just stop you there? We didn't find heroin but we did find an anomaly with your account of the victim's ordeal.'

Poe's stomach tightened. 'Go on.'

'If we'd been using any process other than the liquid chromatography-mass spectrometry technique, we wouldn't have caught it. But, as the NCA were willing to pay the four thousand pounds fee,' – Poe gulped, he'd forgotten how expensive it was – 'we found something that didn't add up. At first, we thought it looked like tetrahydrocannabinol, which would have at least been consistent with what you told me.'

'It would?'

'Tetrahydrocannabinol indicates trace elements of cannabis, and obviously cannabis stays in the system far longer than heroin. If we were going to detect any drug, it would be that.'

'But it wasn't . . . that?'

'It was not, Poe. A lesser pathologist might not have noticed, but, as has been said before, I am *not* a lesser pathologist. It wasn't THC, it was something else entirely. When we separated the proteins and reran the test we found it was actually a chemical only found in *Tuber aestivum*.'

'*Tuber aestivum?*' He didn't care that Rigg was listening. It wouldn't mean anything to him anyway.

'Black summer truffles, Poe. Pound for pound, they're worth more than gold.'

'So, you're saying—'

'You know what I'm saying, Poe. Before Elizabeth Keaton turned up at Alston Library, she had been eating one of the most expensive ingredients in the world.'

CHAPTER TWENTY-THREE

Poe had managed to hold it together in front of Rigg. He'd also managed to keep the conversation one-sided. He wasn't sure how to play this.

If Elizabeth Keaton had eaten truffles before presenting herself at Alston Library, there were only two plausible explanations: she'd either been held captive by the most eccentric foodie in the world or . . . she hadn't been held captive at all.

Poe didn't think a foodie had held her captive.

The reason Keaton hadn't asked about his daughter was obvious now: he knew where she'd been all along.

Like father like daughter . . .

But, if she hadn't been abducted, what on earth were the pair of them up to? Why had they sacrificed six years of their lives? What possible motive could they have?

And where did he fit in? For some reason Keaton was making it personal. He'd asked to see him and he'd given him a cryptic warning. What was he missing? Which piece of the puzzle couldn't he see?

He needed to speak to Elizabeth Keaton. He said as much to Rigg.

'Why?'

Poe had prepared a lie in advance. 'To apologise for what she's been through. And also to see if I can get an angle on why Keaton didn't ask about her.'

He expected Rigg to refuse and come out with something like Elizabeth being too vulnerable to speak to the man responsible for her six years of hell.

But Rigg didn't refuse.

He couldn't.

'She's missing.'

'What do you mean, "missing"?'

'We haven't been able to contact Elizabeth Keaton. She dismissed her family liaison officer after her final interview and she's missed all subsequent appointments with Victim Support. She hasn't shown up at the family accommodation at Bullace & Sloe either. I'm sorry, Poe, but we have no idea where she is.'

Rigg carried on talking but Poe tuned him out. It didn't make sense. Why would Elizabeth disappear again? Unless . . . unless this was also part of what Keaton had alluded to. Which didn't make sense either. Then again, this was a plan at least six years in the making – why did he think he would be able to figure out what was going on?

Poe knew one thing, though: whatever they were up to, he doubted it would end well for him personally. The threat, like a crocodile submerged in muddy water, was there – he just couldn't see it yet.

Discovering Elizabeth had consumed truffles before reappearing in Alston had been a lucky break. He suspected she'd made a mistake. But it was a small one and, legally speaking, irrelevant. Keaton had been convicted of her murder and she was demonstrably alive. That she hadn't actually been abducted made no difference. He clearly hadn't murdered her.

Keaton *would* be released. And when he was, Poe was in trouble. He was certain of it.

He knew what he had to do. It was time to stop messing about. He needed to play his wild card. His nuclear option. He unlocked his BlackBerry, typed out a four-word text message, and sent it into the ether.

Four words Keaton couldn't have planned for: Tilly, I'm in trouble.

CHAPTER TWENTY-FOUR

Poe needed to go back to the beginning. He'd investigated Jared Keaton before, but this time he would do a SCAS number on him. Go deeper. Work up a complete psychological profile. Find out exactly who he was. What drove him. Who he'd hurt on his rise to culinary stardom. Get them to tell him the things no one else would.

And he'd do the same for his daughter. Elizabeth had been investigated as a victim last time, not as a co-conspirator. One of Poe's mantras was 'everyone has secrets' and Elizabeth obviously had several.

He wondered what he'd uncover.

On the journey to Herdwick Croft he calculated what time Bradshaw might arrive. He didn't doubt for a second that she'd come. It was two o'clock now and he'd sent the text thirty minutes ago. He figured that if she read it as soon as she received it – which was a fair bet as her phone was permanently attached to her – then she'd probably arrive some time the following evening. She couldn't simply 'up sticks' any more; she'd have to reallocate her work first. The earliest she'd be able to get away would be lunchtime tomorrow – plenty of time for him to stock up on weird bread and funky smelling tea.

He collected Edgar from the kennels and made his way back to the croft. Before he'd left Carleton Hall, he'd made a copy of the original file – the one Rigg had referred to during their first meeting. Gamble had given him his own code for the photocopier. He wasn't sure if it was one of those that recorded everything on their hard drives. He didn't care. If the worst that happened was that he got busted for a data security breach, he'd be a happy man. He'd spend the time until Bradshaw arrived familiarising himself with the original investigation.

Poe arrived at Herdwick Croft just after four. He made himself a fried egg sandwich and scrambled the rest of the carton for Edgar. They were on the turn anyway.

There was still no sign of Storm Wendy. The sunny afternoon was bleeding into a glorious evening and the air was heady with the scent of summer. Evenings like this didn't come along often and Poe decided to work outside. He arranged his table and chairs to catch the best light, and sat down. When he bought his heavy, pressure-treated outdoor furniture, it was a natural pale green – now, after almost two years of exposure to the sun and the elements, it was the colour of driftwood: a beautiful silver-grey.

Picking up the stones he used as paperweights, he spread out the file's contents on his table. Edgar wandered off and began roaming. The nearby sheep watched him warily.

Poe polished his reading glasses on his sleeve and began triaging the file's contents. The crime scene photographs were interesting but, now he knew they'd been staged, he resisted the temptation to spend too much time on them. He looked at them once to refresh his memory and then put them aside.

The pathologist's report on the blood found at the scene, he ignored. When it was an abduction case the pathologist had said there wasn't enough to have caused death through blood loss, but when the high-risk missing person's case had turned into a murder, he'd flip-flopped and said there *had* been. Poe didn't have time for a pathologist who simply told the police what they wanted to hear. If Estelle Doyle had attended the scene, she'd have told them the facts as she saw them and wouldn't have cared if it had fitted any emerging narratives.

He skimmed through the weather report for the week leading up to Elizabeth's disappearance. He'd get Bradshaw to double-check it. Whatever they'd been planning, Poe suspected it hadn't gone exactly as they'd wanted that night, and it was possible that the severe cold snap had played a part.

He added two more documents to the 'to-be-checked pile': Keaton's requisition order for the boning knife, cleavers and butcher's saw, and the discrepancy in his timeline. It was possible that Keaton had made those mistakes deliberately but Poe would get Bradshaw to check them too. New eyes on old evidence never hurt a case.

What he was really interested in was the witness statements. That's where the gold would be. Who had they spoken to? Who *hadn't* been spoken to? Who'd been asked the wrong questions? Who'd given the wrong answers to the right questions?

He didn't expect to gain anything tangible from the file – if there'd been anything he'd have picked up on it six years ago – but he did expect to develop a list of people to whom he wanted to speak.

After he'd sorted the file into documents he could ignore for now, documents he wanted to read again and documents he was already familiar with, he began reading the final pile: documents he hadn't seen before.

They were mainly post-sentence. The minutes of the Multi-Agency (Lifer) Risk Assessment Panel, usually shortened to MALRAP, he read immediately. This was the meeting that had taken place immediately after Keaton's life sentence had been handed down. It had taken place at HMP Durham, and had been attended by people who had been, and who would be, involved in the case. Some names Poe recognised, others he didn't. He added the name of Keaton's personal officer to the list of people to whom he wanted to speak. Although Durham was a dispersal prison, and Keaton hadn't been there for long, his personal officer would be able to tell him how his first few days as a convicted prisoner had progressed. He made a note to get Keaton's prison record. It would be useful to know who'd been visiting him these last six years.

Poe read for as long as he could but eventually his eyes tired. He needed to take a break. Leaving the deconstructed file where it was, he walked inside Herdwick Croft, filled Edgar's bowl with kibble and poured himself a glass of beer.

He sat outside and watched the sunset. As the sun got lower, and the light of day drained away, the sky gradually turned pomegranate pink. Poe lit a cigar. This was what he loved about Herdwick Croft: the peace and the sense of place. Evenings like this were medicine for the soul. As the perfect circle of the sun was bisected by the horizon of the ancient moorland he called home, Poe made a vow to stop feeding the bad wolf. Feeling sorry for himself wasn't what his mother would have wanted and it was a poor way to honour the sacrifice she'd made.

As his cigar burned down, and the sky changed from the colours found in the heart of his wood-burning stove to a darkness that hid everything but the silhouette of the rolling moors, Poe gathered the file and moved inside.

After a quick supper of cheese on toast, Poe stretched out on the sofa and reread some of the documents he'd marked as key. Edgar jumped up beside him, turned round three times then flopped on a cushion. Before long the spaniel was snoring.

'All right for some,' Poe muttered. He didn't blame Edgar, though. His own eyes were getting heavy. As midnight approached he began nodding off. He turned off his reading lamp. He didn't want to unsettle Edgar and he couldn't be bothered going upstairs. Brushing his teeth would have to wait until morning.

The sleeping conditions were sublime: a gentle breeze blowing through the open shutters, the sound of Edgar's soft snores, and a comfy sofa. Poe shut his eyes and, despite his tangled thoughts, he was asleep in seconds.

Three hours later, Edgar started to growl.

Burgling houses in rural Cumbria isn't easy. In theory it should be. Properties are isolated. Some are more than an hour from a police station. You can approach under cover. Very few have modern security. Some aren't even locked.

There are two problems, though.

The first is dogs.

Most rural households have at least one and, with sound in the countryside travelling farther than it does in towns and cities, by the time you're near enough to jemmy a window, someone could be waiting with a loaded gun.

That's the second problem with burgling houses in rural Cumbria: many owners are registered shotgun users.

Break into the wrong house in Cumbria and you might end up with an arse full of buckshot and a border collie gnawing on your ankles.

Edgar wasn't a good guard dog, though. Springer spaniels seldom are. While dogs like Dobermanns and German shepherds were originally bred to attack and drive away predators, spaniels were bred to flush and retrieve game. They are small and nimble and, to a wolf or a bear, not in the least threatening. But that didn't matter – what Edgar lacked in guarding instincts, he more than made up for by being a nosy bastard.

Poe had lost count of the times he'd woken to the sound of him growling. It was usually a sheep. He'd bark a few warnings but would rarely leave the sofa or the bed. He'd do enough to make it clear that this was his turf, not theirs.

But when Poe woke this time, Edgar was standing upright

and rigid. He was staring at the door, his growling low-pitched and continuous. Edgar's ears were erect and his tail ramrod high. His hackles were raised and his teeth exposed. Poe had never seen him like this before. He quivered with unspent energy.

Someone was outside.

'Who is it, Edgar?'

The spaniel turned briefly but quickly went back to staring at the door.

Quietly, Poe stood. He didn't want to advertise that he was awake so he made his way to the kitchen area by touch. In the sink was the knife he'd used to slice the cheese he'd eaten earlier. He softly made his way to the door. He dropped his spare hand and rested it on Edgar's head. The spaniel stopped growling immediately.

Poe tried to regulate his breathing. He had no idea how near the person on the other side of the door was – Edgar's hearing was almost as sensitive as his nose. They could be standing outside, they could be half a mile away.

Without warning, Edgar cocked his head and let out a gentle whine. He lifted his nose and cast about for scent. His tail began wagging. It was someone he knew.

Poe checked his watch. Who the hell visited at three o'clock in the morning? Now that Thomas Hume was dead, the only other person Edgar was familiar with in Cumbria was Gamble. Or Hume's daughter, Victoria. Poe doubted it would be either of them.

There was a sudden clatter. It sounded like one of his paperweight stones had been knocked onto one of his chairs. Whoever was outside had walked into his table.

'Oof.'

You have *to be kidding* . . . ?

Poe smiled. Edgar went crazy in the way only springers can. He whirled in a circle and began barking like a lunatic.

'Poe? Poe? Are you awake, Poe?'

Edgar barked even louder.

A pause.

'Hi, Edgar. I've brought you some treats.'

Bradshaw was fifteen hours early.

CHAPTER TWENTY-FIVE

'Hi, Poe. I got your message.' Bradshaw's face was timid yet hopeful.

Poe hit the light switch beside the door. Bradshaw shielded her eyes. She was wearing her usual cargo pants and trainers combo. A new-looking fleece covered the inevitable superhero T-shirt. When she'd started with the NCA, Flynn had told her about the dress code. Bradshaw had thought it was silly and told her so.

Flynn had wisely decided that there were some arguments not worth having. You didn't employ Bradshaw for her people skills or for her sartorial elegance – you employed her because she was the best profiler in the country and could do things no one else could.

Some assets had to be managed differently.

Bradshaw was holding a torch and carrying a map in a clear plastic case. A large rucksack was on her back and she wore a woollen hat. Her hair was in pigtails.

While Poe stared in confusion, Edgar launched himself at her.

Bradshaw screeched with joy, dropped to her knees, grabbed him by the neck and bear-hugged him. She reached into her fleece pocket and handed him a rawhide chew. 'I've missed you, Edgar!'

'What the hell are you doing here, Tilly . . . ?'

Her smile dipped. 'Did you not want me to come?'

'Of course I wanted you to come! But not at three in the

morning. It's pitch black. What were you thinking of, walking around here in the dark?' Poe had a feel for the landscape. He'd formed a mental map and knew every dip, every pratfall, the shape of individual rocks. And the moors had an edge to them during the day – at night they were treacherous. 'Even I don't walk around here when it's dark, Tilly.'

'You're such a liar, Poe,' she giggled. 'You're always walking home in the dark. And you're drunk half the time.'

Damn her perfect memory.

'I know the way, though, you don't,' he countered. 'What if you got lost?'

She gave him a look he knew well. Holding up her torch and her map, she reached into her pocket and retrieved a compass. 'I'm not stupid, Poe.'

She had to be kidding. A map and a compass? The Cumbrian fells had killed hundreds of people kitted out with maps and compasses. The weather turned, they had falls, they got lost . . . Something dawned on him. 'How long have you been able to read a map, Tilly?'

She smiled. 'Since this afternoon. I googled what to do and bought a compass on the way up. I already had a torch; it came with my new car.'

He sighed and silently cursed all outdoor survival shops and the shameless chancers who sent every Tom, Dick and Harriet out into one of the most hostile environments in the UK with just a compass and a sense of invincibility.

'You did, did you?' Bradshaw's IQ was higher than the late Stephen Hawking's, so if anyone could learn map-reading from the internet, it would be her. Her absolute loyalty to him meant she sometimes put herself in unnecessarily dangerous situations.

'I did, Poe. And before you start moaning, I learned to map read just in case I needed a backup. I geotagged Herdwick Croft ages ago so it was my phone that directed me here, not the map.'

'Your phone?'

'Yes, Poe, my phone. I geotag everywhere I go. Don't you?'

He shook his head. Even if he knew what a geotag was, he doubted he'd have the technical skills to manage it.

'So why are you holding your map if you didn't need it?'

Her expression turned shifty. 'Just because.'

Poe reckoned there was something she wasn't telling him, but he decided to leave it. There was no point arguing – Bradshaw was so logical she won every time, even when she was wrong.

'You're not angry, are you? I came as soon as I could. I checked in at the hotel then walked straight here.'

Poe wasn't angry. How could he be? He'd asked for her help and she'd dropped everything. However, he knew someone who *would* be angry. It looked like Bradshaw had upped and left. Flynn was going to go spare and he knew she'd blame him. He said as much.

'DI Stephanie Flynn was on a course today so I left her a message to say that you needed my help.'

'But you can't just . . .'

'She's OK with it, Poe. She called me when I was shopping for a hat.'

'Really?' He was surprised. Bradshaw was one of Flynn's main assets – integral to most of the cases the unit was working on.

'Well, what she actually said was, "Please go up to Cumbria and bail my detective sergeant out of the S.H.I.T., Tilly." Except she didn't spell out the swear word like I did.'

That sounded more like it. He suspected Bradshaw hadn't given Flynn much of a choice and, like the dress code, some battles weren't worth fighting. Not if Bradshaw had something in her head. She'd only ignore you, and then you had the problem of deciding how to discipline her. He realised they'd been standing outside for almost five minutes.

'Get yourself in, you daft thing. I'll put the kettle on. I hope you've brought your own tea; I wasn't expecting you until tomorrow and I've not had a chance to get to the shops yet.'

'Why ever not, Poe?'

'Well . . . because I haven't. I'm sure there's something here from the last time you visited, though. It might take a bit of find—'

'No. Why weren't you expecting me until tomorrow? I got your text this afternoon.'

'I assumed you'd have things to tie up in the office first.'

Her lips flattened and she blew a raspberry through them. 'If I'd sent that text, would you have waited?'

She was right. If the situation had been reversed, at best he'd have called Flynn after he'd set off. Bradshaw was Poe's best friend – he sometimes forgot that he was also hers.

'Well?' he asked.

'Well what?'

'Do you have one of your smelly teabags with you?'

Bradshaw grinned. 'I do, Poe. You can tell me what's happened while the kettle boils.'

Poe told Bradshaw about the prison meeting and about Jared Keaton's cryptic comment. He told her about Estelle Doyle and the anomaly with the drug test. And he told her that Elizabeth Keaton was missing again.

Bradshaw didn't interrupt. She listened and made notes on a laptop she'd pulled out of her rucksack. She didn't challenge him on anything. Poe knew it was the first part of her process: gathering all the available data.

After they'd recharged their mugs and, working on the basis that only bad decisions are made at four in the morning, they agreed that the time was best used setting up Bradshaw's equipment.

'What have you got in there, Tilly? It looks heavy.'

She looked pleased with herself as she opened her rucksack. She removed two more laptops, several cables of different colours and thicknesses, and what looked like a miniature projector. She placed them on the kitchen bench, then reached back into the rucksack. 'Aha! Found it.'

She put a small, flat, deep-blue box on the table beside the sofa. She turned on his reading lamp so he could see it properly. Her eyes shone with excitement. 'Ta-da!'

Poe didn't respond.

'Well, what do you think?'

He looked at it in bemusement. It had steel fittings for cables to be attached and the top was ribbed with inch-deep cooling vents. Poe suspected he could have spent the rest of the day guessing and still wouldn't get close to the box's purpose. If it had been khaki-green, he'd have said it looked a bit like the spare batteries he'd had to carry for the Clansman – the combat radio the section signaller had used – when he was in the Black Watch. When she showed him a pair of aerials – one large, one a whip – he was even more confused. The best he could do was shrug.

Her face dropped. 'You don't know what this is?'

'I don't.'

Bradshaw giggled and Poe realised she was teasing him. She knew he didn't have a clue.

'What was the big problem working here last time?'

'We didn't have a blue box?'

Bradshaw nodded. 'Exactly right! This is a mobile phone signal booster. When I place it on the outside of the building nearest the local mobile phone mast, it will capture and send a signal to this repeater amplifier here' – she held up another bit of equipment – 'which, in turn, will boost my mobile phone signal when I'm here.'

'It will?' Poe appreciated technical know-how in others; it meant he didn't have to have any of his own.

'It will, Poe.'

'And how much did this all cost?'

'I got it all for under six hundred pounds.'

'That's a sweet deal.'

'I know, right!'

'And we need this why?'

She shook her head. 'You didn't bring me up here for my people skills, Poe.'

The blue box was to do with access to the internet then. The last time they'd worked at Herdwick Croft she'd done something called 'tethering' – a baffling process that had somehow turned her mobile phone into the internet for her computer. However, it had been quite slow – Herdwick Croft had 'low bandwidth' apparently – and, whenever they'd needed anything larger than a plain text file, she'd had to go to the Shap Wells Hotel to use their free Wi-Fi.

'It means I can work here, Poe. I have a printer back at the hotel, as well as some other stuff, but this is enough to get started. I know you said we should wait until the morning but, Earth to Poe, it *is* morning now.' She checked her phone. 'Four twenty-two.'

She'd got the call at two in the afternoon. Thirteen hours later she was at Herdwick Croft. During that time she'd passed off her active cases, bought some electrical bullshit and survival gear, learned how to read a map, and driven three hundred and fifty miles north. She'd then loaded a rucksack and hiked across two miles of rugged and dangerous moorland.

At night.

And she wanted to get to work immediately.

It was incredible.

The Keatons didn't know what was about to fucking hit them.

Day 9

CHAPTER TWENTY-SIX

'Poe . . . Poe . . . Poe . . .'

The voice pierced his dreams. It was insistent and repetitive. He got the feeling he'd been hearing it for some time. He opened sleep-caked eyes and stared at the blurry figure leaning over him.

Bradshaw's face was fewer than six inches from his. He jerked back in surprise and so did she.

'What the bloody hell . . . ?'

'Wake up, lazy bones,' she said. She plonked herself beside him on the sofa. He bunched his legs to give her more room. Edgar hopped on and nuzzled into her neck.

'Tilly . . . what time is it?' He remembered sitting down on the sofa while she ran diagnostics and accessibility tests on the databases she planned to use. Before long they were having one of their one-sided conversations where his only contribution was staying awake. Evidently he'd failed. He wondered how long he'd been asleep. Blades of sunlight cut through the narrow gaps in the wooden window shutters. Half the croft was lit up like a stage. It was the height of summer, and at this altitude the sun rose early.

'It's five thirty-six, Poe.'

Poe groaned. He'd slept for less than an hour.

Bradshaw looked fresh. 'I've been thinking about definable patterns and rules.'

'Who hasn't?'

'The problem we have is, although we have data, we have the wrong kind of data.'

'For God's sake, Tilly. Let me wake up and get a coffee.'

Her eyes widened and he apologised. It was hardly her fault he'd fallen asleep.

'It's OK, Poe. This must be very stressful for you.' She reached over and awkwardly patted him on the head.

'Er . . . I suppose so, yes.'

'And I knew you'd want a coffee so I've made one for you.'

She handed him a mug. It was filled to the brim and steaming-hot.

'That's grand, Tilly.' She didn't drink coffee so had no way of gauging its strength, but she'd got this one perfect. As he sipped the scalding drink, he mentally translated what Bradshaw had just said. Something about having the wrong kind of data. He was about to ask her what she meant, when she said something that gave him a nasty turn.

'I've arranged a videoconference with DI Stephanie Flynn at eleven o'clock, Poe.'

'You did what?'

'I said I've arranged a vid—'

'Why on earth would you do that?' He'd intended to call Flynn first thing to explain what had happened. Now it would look as though he'd been avoiding her.

'It was DI Stephanie Flynn's condition. We have to report back every day. She said that she needs to monitor the parameters of the investigation to ensure we stay within SCAS protocols.'

Poe paused. They sounded awfully like Bradshaw's words, not Flynn's. 'What did she actually say, Tilly?'

Bradshaw reddened.

'If Poe thinks he's operating up there without adult supervision he can effing well think again.'

'She said that?'

'She did. Except she said the F-word, not effing.'

'How rude of her.'

'Can we start now?'

'We can, Tilly. Let's turn over some rocks and find what doesn't want to be found.'

Bradshaw nodded. 'Cool saying, Poe.'

When they were sitting down to tea and toast, Poe asked the one question he'd been dreading since Bradshaw had turned up.

'Does your mother know where you are?' He felt a bit silly but he had no choice – Mrs Bradshaw had his telephone number. Bradshaw was only a few years younger than he was but, as far as her mother was concerned, she should never have left the world of academia and taken a job with the NCA.

'She does, Poe.'

He noticed she didn't say that her mother was OK with her only daughter blasting up north on another open-ended job. The last time they'd worked in Cumbria it had been . . . unnecessarily exciting. Bradshaw had ended up pulling him out of a burning building. They both carried the scars.

'And?'

'She wasn't happy, Poe.'

'What did she say, exactly?'

'She said that you had no right to ask, and that no doubt you'd be putting me in danger again.'

'And what did your dad say?'

'Bloo . . . blinking good for Washington Poe,' Bradshaw replied. 'Mum then told him off for swearing.'

Poe smiled. He'd only met Bradshaw's father once. He was a welder. Working class through and through. Nice man. Loved his wife and daughter. Had no idea how his and Mrs Bradshaw's genetics had spliced to make someone like the person now in Herdwick Croft.

Bradshaw had changed, though. When he'd first met her, there was an instant dislike between them: he was the Luddite and she was the overeducated idiot. But . . . it kind of worked. And because it did, both their attitudes softened. Bradshaw no longer got frustrated with his indifference towards anything mathematical or scientific, and he stopped correcting her every social faux pas. Instead, he began to enjoy them. From endearing to embarrassing, she was who she was. Poe wouldn't have her any other way now.

And some of her awkwardness had gone. She no longer kept up intense eye contact when they were talking, she didn't talk about her bowel movements so much and she'd stopped prefacing everything with 'Riddle me this, Poe'. She had even come to recognise the point during one of her monologues when his eyes glazed over.

In the past he'd sometimes fallen asleep only to find her still talking to him when he woke.

CHAPTER TWENTY-SEVEN

Bradshaw had all three of her laptops open. One was logged into the NCA intranet, one was split between Google's homepage and some notes she'd made, and the last one displayed an obscure search engine that Poe didn't recognise. Probably one used to search the dark web. He made a note to refill his generator. Bradshaw was using all his spare sockets and Storm Wendy was coming.

'Before we speak to DI Stephanie Flynn, can we summarise what we think we know, Poe?'

'Good idea.' Much better they disagree now than in front of the boss.

'You think Jared and Elizabeth Keaton are planning something?'

'I do, but I've been wrong before.'

'And as part of this plan, they faked Elizabeth's death.'

Poe nodded.

'But something went wrong and Jared Keaton was convicted of her murder.'

Poe shrugged. 'I was at the trial. He definitely wasn't expecting to go to prison.'

'But for reasons unknown, they have to wait six years before Elizabeth can return to prove she hasn't been murdered.'

Poe said nothing. Hearing it said out loud made it sound even more implausible.

'And now she's disappeared again,' Bradshaw said.

'Apparently.'

'And this was before you found out about the blood anomaly?'

He nodded.

She stared at him. 'We'd best get started then. We have lots to get through.'

'We do?'

'Questions, Poe. We have lots of questions.'

Bradshaw was right. And with questions came data searches. And with the correct data, Bradshaw could find the answer to almost anything you asked.

'The way I see it there are five main questions and a number of subsidiary ones. Each has a direct and indirect route to getting the information we need. Some I can get now, some we'll need permission for, and some we'll need to go out and find.'

Poe settled back with a notebook. 'Fire away.'

Bradshaw held up one finger. 'We want to know where Elizabeth Keaton has been for six years.'

'Agreed.'

She held up a second. 'We want to know where she is now. Is it the same place or has she moved on?'

Poe suspected if a hidey-hole was good enough for six years, it'd be good enough for a few more days, but he said nothing.

'Three: did Keaton have a pre-existing grudge against you? In other words, had you crossed paths before the investigation?'

Poe hadn't considered that. He didn't think they had but he couldn't discount it. Over the years he'd upset a lot of people. It was possible one of them had indirectly been Jared Keaton.

Bradshaw held up four fingers. 'What could possibly be so important that they'd voluntarily give up twelve collective years?'

'And five?'

'Is anyone else involved?'

Poe nodded. He already believed that the conspiracy was wider than the Keatons. Elizabeth passing messages to her father in prison carried a high risk factor. Phone calls were recorded and mail was intercepted. Far better if a third party acted as liaison.

'We need his prison records,' he said. 'Who visited him. Who he spoke to. Who he was padded up with.'

'And I can't access them,' Bradshaw said. 'Not from here, not without permission.'

'Hence the videoconference with Steph.'

Bradshaw nodded.

He was willing to bet that within minutes of getting his 'Tilly, I'm in trouble' text, she'd have collated what she already knew from their videoconference, emails and texts, and put it through that brilliant mind of hers. She'd have come up with a number of scenarios and each one would have an action plan attached to it.

That was why Bradshaw needed the early videoconference: her action plans would necessarily include accessing Keaton's prison records. And as a source of data to be mined, they would be huge. Her Majesty's Prison Service was a behemoth. Each prison that Keaton had been in would have generated several sets of records. Wing officers, personal officers, discipline, the secretive security unit, education, training, work, prisoner finances, offender management, medical – the list was endless. That was a lot of information to process.

Bradshaw revelled in large amounts of data, though. The bigger the data sample, the more accurate the analysis. She'd said it before: give her enough of the right data and she could find the pattern in anything. It wasn't idle bragging; he'd seen it first-hand.

And, as no one else had had reason to go through it, it would be fresh. Everyone else was still buying whatever Keaton was selling. That was fine: it meant that if usable intelligence were to be found, they could act on it before anyone else had a chance to screw it up.

Poe wondered what else Bradshaw had done before she'd left Hampshire. She'd already achieved more than he had.

Something occurred to him, something of which Bradshaw would be unaware. 'We need to factor in one more thing, Tilly.'

She pushed her glasses up her nose, and waited expectantly.

'The enormous drag factor of Jared Keaton's ego,' he said.

He watched as she opened up a new file and typed in 'Ego'.

'Keaton isn't wired the same way as everyone else. As far as he's concerned, for him to win, someone else has to know they've lost. I have no doubt that was why he couldn't resist dropping in those hints. His ego is how we'll beat him.'

Bradshaw typed a series of numbers and letters into whatever software she was using. Poe could see the lines of code reflected in her glasses.

'We'll call that an outlier, Poe.'

'Exactly what I was about to say.'

Bradshaw grinned.

One of the advantages of Bradshaw's early morning call was that he could do his afternoon jobs – namely getting in provisions for Storm Wendy and a weird vegetarian house guest – in the morning.

They'd made a decent start. Or Bradshaw thought so. She had a suspicious amount of data already logged in a programme of her own design. Bradshaw refused to use HOLMES 2 – the second incarnation of the Home Office Large Major Enquiry System – the software every police force used to manage complex cases. 'What's the point of having a massive database if it can't analyse and predict?' she'd said. Poe had been in the room when it had been pointed out to her that HOLMES 2 *did* have analytical and predictive capabilities. Her resulting sneer had reduced the HOLMES 2 tech-head to tears.

She told Poe her programme would run for about ninety minutes, and then they would need Keaton's prison records. Poe decided he had enough time to get the shopping in and be back before the videoconference with Flynn. He showed Bradshaw what he was buying and asked her to jot down anything she wanted that wasn't on the list.

She did. And she took a suspiciously long time to do it.

Poe took his quad to Shap Wells, jumped in the hire car and drove to Booths in Kendal. He normally used greengrocers and butchers in Shap village but he'd looked at what Bradshaw had asked for and realised he needed somewhere a bit more middle class. Plus, he didn't fancy handing his usual green-grocer a list containing pretentious fruits like pomegranates and kumquats.

The fruit and veg section of Booths was set out like a market stall and Poe had to ask a tattooed store assistant where everything was. When Bradshaw's fruit had been located, Poe asked him if they stocked such things as Puy lentils, organic wholegrain pasta and tofu. In the end Poe simply tore the list in two, gave the store assistant Bradshaw's half, and told him to meet him back at the butcher's counter.

The store assistant read it and smirked. 'Someone's being spoiled tonight.'

'Just fucking get it, will you?' Poe grunted. He wasn't enjoying himself and everything on Bradshaw's list sounded bowel-scour-ingly healthy. He already knew he wouldn't like it.

His mood improved at the excellent butcher's counter. He treated himself to a beautifully marbled ribeye steak, and restocked on bacon, black pudding and Cumberland sausage. When the tattooed assistant returned with a wicker basket overflowing with food he didn't recognise, Poe gave him a two-pound coin and apologised for being rude.

'Don't worry about it, mate.' He looked at the basket full of fibre-rich food then back up at Poe. 'And the bog roll's over there . . .'

By the time he got back to Herdwick Croft, Bradshaw had stopped typing and was sitting with her feet up having a cup of green tea. She was watching cookery shows on YouTube.

Jared Keaton's cookery shows to be precise.

CHAPTER TWENTY-EIGHT

Bullace & Sloe opened in 2008 to critical acclaim, but Jared Keaton had been culinary royalty long before then. He won a major award when he was a teenager and shortly afterwards a respected magazine called him one of the most naturally gifted chefs the UK had ever produced. Instead of accepting one of the many offers from the kitchens of London, he surprised everyone and relocated to Lyon, France. There he continued his culinary apprenticeship under the tutelage of the famous chef Gilles Garnier. French cooking came easily to the young Jared Keaton and he was soon working as Garnier's *sous-chef de cuisine*. Two of the mainstays of the restaurant's menu were soon replaced by dishes that Keaton developed. He learned to speak French fluently and he rented a flat on the banks of the River Saône.

And then he quit.

The first of his two autobiographies stated that he'd woken up one morning and found he wasn't excited about cooking any more. Whatever the real reason, the next time Jared Keaton was seen, he was married with a young daughter, and in a Parisian restaurant belonging to celebrated fusion chef Hélène Jégado. It was there he rediscovered his love of food. In ten years, the restaurant went from having no Michelin stars to getting the coveted three. He and Hélène Jégado became great friends. From Paris he moved to London but didn't stay long. In a television interview he claimed the food in the capital was too conservative.

He wanted to get out of the stifling London culinary scene and do his own thing.

And that thing was Bullace & Sloe. With a loan from Hélène Jégado, he bought a dilapidated watermill a mile outside the small village of Cotehill in Cumbria.

When he was awarded his first Michelin star, he became a mainstay on the Saturday morning cooking shows. When he was awarded his second he was given his own television series. And when Bullace & Sloe joined the list of the world's elite three-starred restaurants, he'd been able to name his price, travelling the globe as a guest chef.

He could have retired. He had the money. Even if Bullace & Sloe hadn't been as successful, the TV deals were bringing in an annual seven-figure income. The books brought in the same again.

But Jared Keaton loved to cook.

In the days when a two-hundred-pound taster menu might actually be cooked by someone who'd been shown how to cook it by someone who'd been shown how to cook it by the chef named above the door, at Bullace & Sloe the chances were better than even that: if Jared Keaton hadn't personally cooked it, he had at least stood at the pass and checked your dish as it went out.

'Anything?'

Bradshaw held a finger to her mouth. She wanted silence. She had created a little nest for herself. Moved furniture around so the banks of computer monitors weren't being hit by the morning sunlight. Her workspace was laid out in a crescent shape. She sat in the middle like Kirk on the bridge of the *Enterprise*. As she watched YouTube she typed on a portable keyboard that she had balanced on her stomach. What she was writing was appearing on the laptop to her left. She didn't look at it once.

Poe read part of it and saw it was free of errors and correctly formatted. The laptop to her right was filled with the brightly coloured, bouncing lines of an audio programme's graphic equaliser. The kind that top-of-the-range hi-fi systems had in the late 1980s.

She pressed pause and everything stopped.

'You're right, Poe. He's a textbook psychopath. A psychopathic narcissist would be more accurate. It's all "I", "me" and "my" phraseology. Very little engagement with his guests. When they're talking he's not listening, he's waiting for his turn to speak again.'

'It's just a cooking show. I suppose you have to factor in an element of one-upmanship. There'll have been some pretty big egos on set for him to manage.' Poe wasn't defending Keaton but he needed to be fair.

Bradshaw had already factored that in.

'The text analysis tool I'm using is able to focus on what the linguists call "function words": the natural language we use without thinking. Excluding all scripted segments, Jared Keaton's word-pattern phrases show a higher use of the "I", "me" and "my" pronouns than any of the other chefs', and far higher than the general population's.'

'At least I was right about something then,' he grunted. Up until now, he'd been the only one who'd diagnosed Keaton as a psychopath. 'Did you find anything new?'

'We can't really start until we get his prison records, but . . . there was one interesting section.' Bradshaw went back to YouTube and selected a different video. She pressed play. A young Elizabeth Keaton appeared on the screen. She was around fifteen and on Jared's show. The other chef had his daughter with him as well. They were blind-tasting their fathers' food in some sort of cook-off.

Poe had only seen photographs of Elizabeth Keaton up until

then. He noticed the audio programme was running on the other laptop. The bar at the bottom of the YouTube video said it was a twenty-seven minute programme. Bradshaw paused it.

'We can watch it properly later, but I want you to hear how she talks.'

After they had listened for a few moments Bradshaw paused it again.

'Her speech pattern doesn't portray the same narcissistic characteristics as her father,' she said.

'It doesn't?'

'No evidence of it at all.'

'She's young. Doesn't this type of thing develop over time?'

'With speech it's the opposite. Children haven't yet learned how to hide what they are, so their speech pattern is natural with very little deception.'

Before Poe could respond, the middle laptop began to shrill noisily. Bradshaw pressed a button and Stephanie Flynn's face appeared on the screen.

There's a tired that comes from a late night and a few too many drinks. It hurts to get up in the morning but, once you have, it soon fades. It can be sorted by getting in a full eight hours the following night – your body's way of reminding you that you're not twenty-one any more.

Then there's the other kind of tired. The kind you wear like a heavy coat, that makes your bones ache. It doesn't matter how much sleep you get, it feels like you're constantly leaking energy. That you're always going to feel tired.

Flynn seemed to be that kind of tired. The whites of her eyes were the colour of a hangover piss and her shoulders were round and slumped. She was dishevelled and looked like she'd slept in her car. She'd been like that for at least a month.

'Good morning, DI Stephanie Flynn,' Bradshaw said.

Flynn dived straight in with a question. And she aimed it at Bradshaw.

'How much shit is he in?'

Bradshaw reddened.

'I'm not sure, DI Stephanie Flynn. On paper, and after reviewing what Cumbria sent us, I would have said that their assessment was accurate. Poe's report on the blood's chain of custody is thorough and he's correct: it was gathered, transported and tested safely. Elizabeth Keaton is therefore alive and Mr Keaton couldn't have murdered her.'

'But . . . ?'

'But there is an issue Poe hasn't told you about yet.' She turned to Poe.

Poe told Flynn about the traces of truffle found in Elizabeth's blood. He didn't mention that the bill would shortly be landing on her desk.

'Is it possible that her abductor fed her truffles? You've told us many times that second-guessing what criminals will do under pressure is an exercise in futility.'

'It's possible,' Poe admitted. He doubted it, though. The most likely explanation was that Elizabeth Keaton had, unsurprisingly given her upbringing, developed a taste for fine food and hadn't denied herself during her time in exile.

Flynn said nothing. Poe could tell she wasn't convinced.

'Is that all you have?'

Before Poe could admit it was, Bradshaw got in first.

'It isn't all he has, DI Stephanie Flynn. There's a problem with where Elizabeth Keaton claims to have been these last six years. It supports Poe's theory.'

'You're not buying the abduction?' Flynn asked.

'I think there are issues with it.'

'Which are?'

'Forget the odds of her turning up at the police desk when it's

157

only at Alston Library 3.29 per cent of the time, the main problem is that she claims to have walked there. I timed how long it took me to get to Poe's house last night and then correlated that to Elizabeth Keaton's version of events.'

Poe stared at her. He knew there'd been something else. As well as making an immediate start, she'd wanted to work out how quickly Elizabeth Keaton could walk at night.

'I carried a nine-kilogram rucksack to make up for the fact that she said she hadn't eaten for four days. Using a variation of the asymptotic expansion theory, I made the necessary adjustments.'

Flynn folded her arms and glared.

Sometimes what was in Bradshaw's head didn't easily translate into words either of them could understand. Prior to joining the NCA she had only ever worked with people whose IQ was in the highest percentile, the type of people who understood and *expected* scientifically pure explanations. She didn't have the tact to brief a different type of colleague simply without appearing rude or condescending, and although Poe had been gently coaching her in diplomacy – hardly his strongest trait – it was proving to be an uphill task.

'Can we have my version, Tilly?' he prompted.

She sighed. 'I calculated how far she could have walked then drew a circle on a map.'

'Ah, like they did in *The Fugitive*,' Poe nodded.

'This is basic statistics. I really don't know how you guys manage,' Bradshaw muttered.

'And?' Flynn said.

'I plotted my calculations on a satellite photograph of Alston and the surrounding area,' Bradshaw said. 'It's very rural and there isn't much else nearby. If she *did* escape from a building then the police would have found it by now.'

Flynn steepled her fingers. 'Could it be that we have this the wrong way round? Is Elizabeth punishing her father for some reason? Might she have faked her own death and then sat back and enjoyed what was happening to him?'

Poe had considered that. In theory it made more sense. It certainly left fewer unanswered questions.

'Certainly possible, boss,' he said.

'But you don't think so though, do you?'

'I don't, no.'

'Why?'

'Because Keaton wasn't angry. He barely mentioned Elizabeth. If she'd been behind it all, he wouldn't have been able to conceal the rage he felt for her. All I got was hostility towards me.'

'OK,' Flynn said. 'You were in the room, we weren't.'

One of the things that made Flynn such a good DI was that she never micromanaged or second-guessed. She had a team she could trust so she trusted them.

'One at a time, what do you think happened?'

'They planned this together,' Poe said.

'I concur, DI Stephanie Flynn.'

Flynn looked thoughtful. 'What a fucking mess,' she said eventually.

'I agree, DI Stephanie Flynn, it is a . . . flipping mess.'

'What do you need?' Flynn asked.

'Full SCAS profiles on Jared and Elizabeth Keaton,' Poe replied.

'Was Keaton not profiled six years ago?'

'Not by anyone who knew what they were doing.'

'Fair enough.'

'And there'll be information to analyse onsite.'

'So . . . ?'

'I need Tilly to stay up here.'

To his surprise Flynn agreed. To his even greater surprise she didn't offer to come up and help. He was her friend and he was in trouble – he'd have expected her to get the first train up. *Just what the hell was going on with her . . . ?*

'We'll also need Keaton's prison records,' he said. 'There's very little on what he's been up to since he was sent down. We don't know who's been visiting him. We don't know who his brief is. Other than Durham, we don't even know which prisons he's been in.'

Flynn made a note. 'I'll sort that this morning. Anything else?'

'I'll need ad-hoc permission to access certain databases, DI Stephanie Flynn,' Bradshaw said.

'Send me a list when you have one,' Flynn said. 'What's your next move?'

'Basic police work, boss,' Poe said. 'Develop a TIE strategy and start putting some useable intel together.'

There was little else they could do at this point. TIE – Trace, Interview, Eliminate – was at the heart of everything detectives did. Identifying and locating those you needed to speak to, getting as much out of them as you could, then deciding if it was useful. Like the rings of a rippling pool, TIE enquiries inevitably generated further TIE enquiries.

Flynn nodded in approval. 'Tilly, anything you need at this point other than prison records and database access?'

Bradshaw shook her head. 'I trust Poe, DI Stephanie Flynn. He'll know what to do when we get started.'

'I think that as well, Tilly. Right, you two, listen. I can't get away from Hampshire just now so you're going to be on your own. Please, please, pleeeease, do not do anything that will embarrass me or the NCA.'

For a moment neither of them responded.

Eventually Poe said, 'Why did you look at me when you said that?'

Flynn snorted. 'You fucking know why, Poe.' She leaned forwards, jabbed a button, and Bradshaw's laptop screen flipped back to the NCA logo.

CHAPTER TWENTY-NINE

Flynn was as good as her word. Within thirty minutes, compressed files began coming through on Bradshaw's email. Records from every department in the prison service, from every prison to which Keaton had been sent. There was also a link to some computer programme called P-NOMIS. Apparently it stood for National Offender Management Information System. It was a live database shared by both the prison and probation services. According to Bradshaw, who seemed to know every acronym in the criminal justice system, the P stood for Prison.

She set the printer running and fed it ream after ream of paper. Poe made lunch. He didn't know much about Puy lentils but assumed they'd make a decent dahl. He set them to boil, dry-fried a few spices and added them to the thickening stew. While he waited for it to cook through, he gathered two bits of white bread for him, two bits of something called spelt bread for Bradshaw, and a jug of chilled water. He carried them outside and took in a lungful of fresh air.

He squinted and looked up. The sun was corn-yellow and the only blemish in the flinty-blue sky was the solitary scar of an aeroplane's vapour trail. Despite the warnings, it didn't look like Storm Wendy was coming any time soon.

And it was hot. Too hot for the sheep. Herdwicks were a Nordic breed, dating back thousands of years, and they'd all retreated to somewhere cooler. There was nothing for them to eat this high up anyway: the grass was pale and stunted, the heather grey and brittle. It wouldn't put flesh on a goat.

The moors were hauntingly beautiful, though. Beautiful but endless. Edgar could run away for a week without Poe losing sight of him. A granite net of drystone walls was the only sign humans had ever lived there.

Poe noticed something moving. He grabbed the binoculars he kept with his quad and took a closer look but it was only a flatbed truck leaving the quarry. It was fully loaded and Poe wondered where the stone would end up. He turned and looked at Herdwick Croft. The stones used to build his home were the same stones that had been used to build St Pancras station and the Albert Memorial. This personal link with his country's heritage made him puff out his chest in pride.

For the first time, home was now more than just a physical place; it was a feeling. He wouldn't be able to explain why any more than he could explain why certain pieces of music made him happy and others made him melancholic. Each time he came back it was harder to leave. When he was in Hampshire he missed the fells and he missed the fog. He missed the sheep and he missed the silence. Missed the rhythm of the place when he wasn't there. City life wasn't for him any more. He didn't want to live in a place that wasn't changed by the seasons. Where you didn't know where you were in the cycle of life.

He'd once been helping Thomas Hume repair a wall when the old farmer had asked if he knew what hefting was. Poe didn't. Hefting, Hume had explained, was an ancient shepherding technique where the sheep were persuaded to stay on the same part of the fell without the need for dry stone walls. He told Poe that the trick was to put food down in the same area each night, thereby encouraging the flock to congregate there at dusk. During the night and the following day they wouldn't stray too far. When this understanding became intergenerational, the flock could be considered hefted. And that was how Poe felt now. He'd become hefted to Herdwick Croft. He never wanted to leave again.

'Are you OK, Poe?'

Bradshaw had joined him outside. She was clutching a sheaf of papers.

'I'm fine, Tilly.'

'What were you looking at?'

'Nothing in particular. I just miss this place when I'm not here.'

Bradshaw, who'd spent her entire life indoors, looked to where he was facing. She frowned and craned her neck as if she was missing something good. Eventually she gave up. 'I have Mr Keaton's visitor printouts. I don't know if you're going to be happy or sad.'

Bradshaw had separated the list into two columns: official visits and social visits. The official visitors' list – people who had lawful business with the prisoner – contained no surprises. His legal team saw him many times at the beginning of his sentence, presumably to discuss possible appeals against conviction, and also when Elizabeth Keaton reappeared and they were filing their brief with the CCRC. Poe dismissed them. It wasn't unheard of for solicitors to be a conduit for illegal activities but Poe knew the legal firm, and they were far too big and respectable to get involved in something shady. They'd have little to gain and everything to lose. Keaton also had yearly visits from his probation officer. Nothing surprising about that – she had annual lifer reviews to complete. Poe made a note to check her out but he doubted she'd be involved. There were a few others but they were inconsequential. He noted that Graham Smith, the journalist who'd called him the other day, had tried and failed to get an official visit. Probably the first time in his life Keaton had ever refused free publicity.

When Poe saw the size of the social visits list – those who needed a visiting order from the prisoner – he discovered it was possible to be both shocked and unsurprised at the same time. It was small.

One name small.

Keaton's conviction for filicide inevitably made him toxic, but Poe hadn't realised just how much. At the height of his pomp, everyone had courted him. A-list movie stars dined and took selfies with him, government ministers held away-days nearby so they could eat at Bullace & Sloe, even members of the royal family weren't above stopping off in Cumbria on their journey to Balmoral Castle. Although Poe knew that Jared Keaton only had to issue visiting orders to those people he wanted to see, and he didn't doubt that a great number of the chefs who'd supported him pre-conviction had secretly been delighted by the jury's guilty verdict, he'd assumed one or two might have stood by him. Evidently not.

It was the curse of the psychopath, he supposed. They didn't have friends.

So, there was only one name on the list: Crawford Bunney.

Bradshaw had googled him and there were some documents attached. As they ate their curried lentils, Poe skimmed them.

A native of Edinburgh, Crawford Bunney had been with Bullace & Sloe since the early days. He started at the vegetable station then moved on to sauces. Keaton must have seen something in him because within three years, Crawford Bunney was appointed sous chef – effectively his number two. In an interview with *Carlisle Living*, Bunney had described his dismay at Keaton's conviction, his belief that the truth would come out some day, and the arrangements Bullace & Sloe had made until that day came.

Poe made a note to find out exactly what those 'arrangements' were. As far as Bradshaw had been able to tell, Keaton was still the sole owner of Bullace & Sloe.

He turned to a new sheaf of documents. Keaton's phone records. These were less reliable because illegal phones were prevalent in UK prisons. They listed the same legal firm, although without names, just numbers. Keaton seemed to have regularly scheduled calls with Crawford Bunney, and some of these had been recorded and transcribed. Poe was reading one conversation about problems with Bullace & Sloe's fish supplier when he was interrupted by a beep.

Bradshaw checked her watch. It was one of those smart watches. He assumed it was linked to her phone. She picked up her glass of water and noisily gulped it down. When she'd finished she tapped something on her phone.

'What?' she said, when she noticed him watching her.

'Nothing. I can stir some cream through the lentils if they're too hot for you?' He couldn't. He hadn't bought cream. In fact, he couldn't remember ever buying cream.

'I drink six glasses of water a day, Poe. You should too.'

'I drink plenty of water.'

'I don't believe that you do. Since I arrived yesterday you've had four cups of tea, seven cups of coffee and two pints of beer. And I saw how much meat you bought. That's a catering pack of sausages in the fridge. It isn't good for you, Poe.'

He felt the heat grow in his cheeks. He knew his diet left a lot to be desired, and that he was only stacking up health problems for later, but the thing was . . . a good Cumberland sausage was a thing of perfection. He'd rather croak it than give them up.

'When I'm near a chemist we're buying a cholesterol test for you,' Bradshaw said, hammering what was no doubt the first nail in the coffin of his meat-only diet.

'Oh goody,' he replied. There was no point arguing.

'You sit here, mister,' she said. 'I'll go and make us both a fruit salad for pudding.'

Poe sighed, picked up another sheaf of papers, and started

reading again. After a while a smile spread across his face. It was nice to be fussed over occasionally.

They worked into the early evening. Poe read outside but, despite the glorious weather, Bradshaw refused to join him – the glare was too harsh on her laptop screens. He read the additional research she'd brought him about Crawford Bunney but it didn't add much. When he'd read everything twice and filled a notebook with questions, observations and tasks, he joined Bradshaw inside. She hadn't yet found a link between him and Jared Keaton. She wasn't giving up, though, and had sent Flynn another list of databases to which she wanted access.

Poe called a halt and they had a quick tea of brown pasta in a pre-made tomato and basil sauce. He added bacon to his but it was still horrible.

'I'll get started on Elizabeth Keaton's profile,' Bradshaw said.

Poe nodded. A SCAS profile would examine the areas of Elizabeth's life that hadn't been considered during the original investigation. Bradshaw would also take information from the victim file and interrogate it from another angle.

Bradshaw made an immediate start. In stark contrast to Poe's patented hunt-and-stab typing technique, her fingers flew over the keyboard in a blur, her eyes not once leaving the screen. 'This is going to take a while, Poe. It may be better for us to call it a night now, and for me to continue at the hotel. The booster and repeater are good, but I need better bandwidth to do this properly. If we leave now, I can have something for us to work on tomorrow.'

It made sense. Also, he was tired. He hadn't wanted to say anything as he'd had more sleep than Bradshaw, but his eyes were gritty again. An early night would do them both the world of good.

'Come on then. Grab what you need and I'll run you across.'

* * *

The hotel bar was full, and although Poe's attitude to tourists was the same as William Wordsworth's – 'Let then the beauty be undisfigured' – he didn't mind the ones at Shap Wells so much. Even in the height of summer, the fells in this part of Cumbria only attracted serious walkers. The area didn't have the picture-postcard beauty of the National Park. There were no lakes or towering mountains, no cutesy villages and no small-gauge steam trains – nothing to keep the twenty-first-century tourist entertained. Shap Fell was an unrelenting and barren landscape of treeless slopes, granite-capped hills and boggy hollows. Populated with tens of thousands of sheep and tens of people, they were stunning in the way a pit viper was: beautiful to look at but dangerous to the unwary. The weather was nice now but it could turn in a matter of minutes, even at this time of year.

He bought a pint of Spun Gold, a malty and hoppy beer brewed by the Carlisle Brewing Company, a soft drink for Bradshaw and a packet of crisps for Edgar.

Poe drained half his drink in one go and was contemplating another before heading back when Bradshaw asked: 'Why don't you have a girlfriend, Poe?'

Uh-oh . . .

Bradshaw's seclusion from the outside world explained a lot of her personality, but it couldn't account for everything. It couldn't account for how direct she could be. Sometimes they'd be working in silence and she'd blurt out something like 'I like you, Poe', then go back to whatever she'd been doing as if she hadn't just been weird. If she *were* developing feelings that went beyond their friendship, then she'd have already told him.

So why did she want to know?

And how was he supposed to answer?

He couldn't tell her the truth. He couldn't tell anyone the

truth, couldn't explain that his mother's supposed abandonment had soured all his relationships. That from the moment he met a woman he began collating reasons why it wouldn't work. That every flaw became something to obsess over and dwell on until the inevitable happened, and he stopped calling them. His longest relationship had lasted six months and that was only because he'd been undercover for four of them.

And now he knew that his mother hadn't abandoned him, had in fact sacrificed everything *for* him, how was he supposed to tell Bradshaw that he'd started to think about women again. The terrifying Estelle Doyle, the sexy divorcee Flick Jakeman and, to his eternal discredit, the grieving Victoria Hume – had all been in his mind over the last couple of days.

'Tilly?'

'Yes, Poe?'

'Do you remember that discussion we had about tact?'

'I do, Poe. I made notes on my iPad. Am I to fetch it? It's in my room.'

Poe smiled and shook his head. He drained the rest of his pint and said, 'Just read it again sometime.'

'I'll read it tonight.' Realisation dawned on her. 'Oh. I'm sorry, Poe.'

'Tilly, you never have to apologise to me, remember? Now, do you want another drink? I'm having one.'

She checked her watch. 'No, thank you, Poe. I'll drink some water when I brush my teeth but I don't want to urina . . .' She faded out. 'No, thank you, Poe.'

Poe smiled. Impressed at her restraint. A year ago she'd have told him that she didn't want to go to bed on a full bladder. He, however, was at the age where making it through the night without having to get up at least once was a distant memory and he figured he may as well make it worth his while. He walked to the bar and ordered another pint.

'I think you should ask DI Stephanie Flynn out on a date, Poe,' Bradshaw said after he'd returned.

'And why do you think that, Tilly?'

'Because she's sad.'

Poe nodded. Flynn was sad about something. He was also glad someone else had noticed. And because Bradshaw – whose grasp of non-verbal communication could best be described as a work in progress – had, it meant others would too. When the time was right he'd ask her. If it was the other way round, he knew Flynn would ask him.

'And you're sad too, Poe. You pretend you're not but I can tell. Ever since the Immolation Man case.'

Poe didn't like keeping secrets from Bradshaw but this was one he couldn't share yet. Not until he'd figured out what he wanted to do about it. He didn't even know if there was anything he *could* do about it.

'I'm fine,' he said.

'You and DI Stephanie Flynn like each other. You should go to the pictures sometime.'

Poe drained his pint.

'You do know DI Flynn's gay, Tilly?' It wasn't a secret so he wasn't betraying Flynn's confidence. 'She's been with her partner for nearly fifteen years and they're very happy together. And even if she weren't, I hardly think going out with me is the right way to cheer her up.'

'Oh,' Bradshaw replied, a flush reddening her cheeks.

He'd never seen her really blush before. Embarrassing incidents bothered her about as much as waves bothered seagulls.

'But you're right – she does seem sad about something.'

Bradshaw said nothing for several moments. 'It's bound to be something you've done, Poe.'

'Bound to be.'

They fist bumped.

'Anyway, you have work to do on Elizabeth Keaton and I need some sleep. I'll pick you up here at seven sharp.'

'I'm not coming across to you?'

'Not tomorrow, Tilly. Tomorrow we're going on a field trip.'

She raised her eyebrows. 'Wherever are we going, Poe?'

He didn't immediately answer even though he'd known for a while. Ever since he'd left HMP Durham. Like a moth to a flame, there was an inevitability to it.

'We're going to Bullace & Sloe.'

Day 10

CHAPTER THIRTY

Poe woke to a mackerel sky: rows of rippling clouds that resembled fish scales. He was no shepherd, he didn't have a magical ability to predict the weather, but he'd lived on the fells for a while and he could tell when things were about to change. It wouldn't rain yet but the clouds were the start of the early skirmishes. Storm Wendy was on her way. He ate a bit of toast over the sink, showered then got dressed. With no Thomas Hume to look after Edgar during the day, he was taking the spaniel with him. Bullace & Sloe was out in the north Cumbria boondocks; there'd be somewhere for him to run around when they'd finished.

He took the quad to Shap Wells. Bradshaw was waiting by the hire car. She had a small rucksack with her and was wearing what looked like a Wonder Woman T-shirt, one of the few superheroes Poe recognised from his youth. He couldn't recall any of the stories, although he did remember having a thing for Lynda Carter . . .

Poe left the M6 at junction 42 and took the Wetheral road, turning right when he reached the village of Cumwhinton. Before long he was caught behind a Mercedes-towed caravan. He cursed at the stuttering driving of the distracted tourist.

'Welcome to Cumbria,' he muttered. 'Please drive at twenty miles an hour and don't forget to stop for photographs every hundred yards.' He tailgated the caravan and beeped his horn.

173

Eventually it pulled in at a passing place and let him by. He put his foot down and the sluggish hire car picked up its pace.

'Are you OK, Poe?' Bradshaw asked. She was gripping the passenger-door handle.

Poe tapped the brakes and slowed down. He was nervous and he couldn't explain why. It wasn't that he was going back to Bullace & Sloe – he'd only been there once and the place held no fear for him.

And it wasn't because this was the strangest case he'd ever been involved in.

It was something he couldn't put his finger on, and that was what worried him.

As they rounded a bend and entered Cotehill – a small hamlet where the white-washed houses all leaned into one another – he gave himself a mental shake. Worrying would have to wait. They'd arrived.

Bullace & Sloe was just outside the village. A converted water-mill, it was a Grade II-listed building. And it was very old. According to Bullace & Sloe's website, there'd been a watermill on the edge of Cotehill going back to the Domesday Book. And it *did* look like a piece of England's rich history – a monument to the days when buildings were built to last. It sat on the bank of one of the River Eden's subsidiary becks. The stretch adjacent to the mill had been widened and deepened so the water could turn the wheel, although these days the waterwheel was ornamental.

It had started life as a rectangular two-storey building – a ground floor to work the mill and a first floor to store the corn – but over the years its many extensions had seen it grow into a large and ungainly-looking complex. It was made of the same flecked, grey stone as Poe's croft. The external beams had been weathered by countless winters and baked by relentless summers. The unfinished wood was cracked and warped and as hard as frosted iron.

While the Keatons had used the first floor as their living quarters, the kitchen, developmental kitchen, larders and stores were on the ground floor. The restaurant was in the old mill room and, because the Grade II-listed status meant Keaton had been limited in what he could change, the original wooden shafts, spur wheel, gears and runner stones were still there.

The car park was on the opposite side of the road. Poe got out and stretched. He took Edgar to a nearby field and let him roam and do his thing for five minutes before putting him back in the car. Although he'd parked under a tree he opened all four windows.

'You ready?' he asked Bradshaw.

'I am,' she replied, pushing her glasses up her nose, tightening the bands on her pigtails and hoisting up her daysack. He hadn't seen what was inside it but his first ten guesses would all have been 'computer'.

Poe crossed the road and, ignoring the enormous entrance door, walked to the back of the building. There was a small patch of hardstanding. A van was parked there. Its doors were open and it was full of vegetables. A man in green overalls carried a wooden box of carrots towards the back door. Poe jogged over and opened it for him. The deliveryman nodded his thanks and disappeared inside.

Poe held the door and beckoned for Bradshaw to join him. He readied his warrant and identification card, and together they entered the bowels of Bullace & Sloe.

CHAPTER THIRTY-ONE

'Where are those fucking potatoes?' a loud and fast Scottish voice yelled.

Poe and Bradshaw worked their way into the kitchens unchallenged. The vegetable deliveryman had passed them on his way out but otherwise they hadn't seen anyone. They headed towards the voice, passing store cupboards, rooms containing nothing but white linen, and a door with 'Wine Cellar' etched into it. Finally, they saw a modern-looking door with a stamped plastic sign that said 'Main Kitchen'.

Poe opened it and stepped inside.

Although the watermill was centuries old, Bullace & Sloe's kitchen was modern, sleek and spacious. Stainless steel benches were loaded with a bewildering array of equipment. Knife blocks and chopping boards were scattered throughout in organised chaos. Plastic containers filled with vegetables, herbs and a hundred other ingredients lined rows and rows of metal shelves. Six stoves, in two rows of three like a domino, were loaded with spitting frying pans and steaming copper pots. Utensils on hooks hung from the ceiling. The walls were tiled white. Everything was spotless.

Although it had been six years since Poe had set foot in the kitchen, it was exactly as he remembered.

Except the heat. Last time it had been the dead of winter and nobody had been cooking. Unlike now. It had barely passed 8 a.m. but the kitchen was already bustling. Poe had assumed that the busiest time for the restaurant would be when it was full of paying customers, but it looked as though he was wrong. He counted ten chefs working flat out.

Poe watched as one expertly scaled and filleted a salmon, before wrapping lemon halves in muslin and tying them off with ribbons. Another put meat – duck or pigeon breasts by the look of it – into clear plastic bags before placing them under a machine that looked like a boxy trouser press. There was a hiss of air and she removed it. The bag was now sealed and vacuum-packed. Poe watched her ease it into a water bath. She checked the temperature and set the timer before repeating the process.

'Gosh,' said Bradshaw.

'Indeed,' Poe agreed. The kitchen was like a Swiss clock. Efficient. Effortless. Streamlined. He ran his fingers round his collar. It was damp already. He wondered how anyone could work in this environment day in, day out. The jungles of Belize weren't as humid.

'Who the fuck are you two, and what the fuck are you doing in my kitchen?'

It was the Scottish voice again. The one who'd asked for potatoes.

Poe turned. He recognised Crawford Bunney from the magazine article. He was dressed in jeans and a T-shirt. Tall and gangly, his simian arms were pale, hairy and disproportionately long. His nose was beak-like with large, visible pores. His shaved head highlighted his male-pattern baldness – shiny on top, stubbly on the sides – and his cheeks were crossed with broken veins. His eyes were bright, alert and wary.

'Crawford Bunney?' Poe asked.

Bunney gave Poe a chin up, reverse nod. 'Who's asking?'

Poe handed him his ID card.

Bunney studied it and shrugged. 'What you wanting with me?'

'Just a chat.'

177

'Am I under arrest?'

'You're not.'

'Well, then, you couldn't have picked a worse day.' He turned back to his counter. 'I said, where are my fucking potatoes?'

'Coming, chef,' came a distant reply.

'Look, we're down two chefs so I'm having to do sauces *and* vegetable prep today. I can't afford to take a break so either you talk while I work or you come back tomorrow.'

Now suited Poe. Busy people were less guarded.

A young woman ran up with a crate of mud-caked potatoes. She was wearing chef's whites and blue-and-white-checked trousers. Her blonde hair was plastered to her forehead with sweat. She glanced at Poe and Bradshaw and smiled in the way people do when they haven't got time for introductions.

'What are these?' Bunney snapped. 'Fucking wash them, will you? I'm the executive chef not a fucking *plongeur*!'

Poe sensed Bradshaw stir beside him. She was typing into her phone.

'You won't get a signal in here, love,' Bunney said to her. 'You'll have to go outside.'

'What's a *plongeur* then, Chef Bunney? I read up on kitchen terminology last night and it's not a word I'm familiar with.'

'Pot washer.' His mouth became thinner and tighter as he watched the blonde chef scuttle over to a sink and begin scrubbing the potatoes. While he waited, he barked out a series of instructions. They were all in French and Poe didn't understand them. Each one was met with a loud '*Oui*, chef!'

'Sorry about that,' he said, turning back to face them. 'The younger chefs aren't interested in mastering the basics these days. All they want is a fucking TV deal.' As he spoke he pulled his T-shirt over his head, threw it in a laundry basket, and put on his whites. By the time he'd buttoned up his jacket the blonde chef had returned. The potatoes were now clean. Bunney picked up

178

one and, in the time it would have taken Poe to peel a carrot, he'd cut it into a perfect seven-sided barrel shape. He threw it in a bowl of water and picked up the next. Before long the bowl was loaded with potatoes, all precisely shaped, all the same size. Although every cut of his knife was exact and machine-like, his eyes continuously prowled the kitchen.

He caught Poe looking and scowled. 'I have one chef who can turn vegetables properly and quickly. Fucking one. When I started here Chef Keaton had me whittling away at sacks of these things until my fingers bled.'

Poe watched, baffled. As far as he could tell, most of the potato ended up as shavings in the sink. It was a good opener, though, and he asked: 'So why bother?'

Bunney snorted. 'You want the official reason or the unofficial one?'

'Official.'

'It produces a uniform size. Means they'll cook evenly and the shape allows them to be tossed and rolled in a sauté pan so they get colour on all sides.'

'And the unofficial?'

'Because we've always fucking done it. You give a Michelin inspector an unturned potato and they'll take a star off you.'

'You've kept your three stars, though,' Poe said. 'After Keaton got sent down I bet people expected standards to drop.'

Bunney grunted something unintelligible.

'I didn't catch that,' Poe said.

'I said, I owed the man.'

'Keaton?'

'*Chef* Keaton, yes.' Bunney sighed, put down his knife, picked up a towel and wiped the sweat off the back of his neck. 'Look, this business takes everything from you. I worked seventy hours a week as Chef Keaton's sous chef. Now I'm acting exec I work even longer, and I didn't think that would be possible. I take a

179

fifty grand salary, and if you divide it by the hours I work I doubt I make minimum wage.'

He picked up his knife and turned another potato. 'Most days start at seven in the morning and don't finish until after midnight. Today we're expecting a delivery of crabs so they need to be sorted through and picked apart. Later on I have a meeting to discuss the development of Chef Keaton's new autumnal menu, and I've just found out that we've lost one of our meat suppliers, so at some point today, and fuck knows when I'll have time, I'm going to have to find a new one.'

Another potato splashed into the already overflowing bowl. A chef rushed over and took it away. Bunney started the whole process again. Poe wanted to ask about the new menu, and why Keaton was still involved, but he thought it best to let Bunney vent for now.

Bradshaw took advantage of the pause. 'I wouldn't like to work that hard, Chef Bunney. Why do you still do it?'

Bunney smiled quickly. 'It's an addiction. You either love it or hate it, and I love what I do. I have a passion for fresh local ingredients and I'm lucky enough to work with them every day.' He waved his arms around. 'And I get to work with these guys. Unless you've worked in a professional kitchen it's hard to explain how close you get to your colleagues. Because of the crazy hours and the intensity of what we do, they become your surrogate family. I see more of them than I do my wife.'

Bradshaw nodded enthusiastically. Statistics were about to make an appearance.

'Yes, the average working parent spends only thirty-four minutes a day with their children. If you assume that the average person works between thirty to thirty-eight hours a week, then by extrapolating your excessive hours, particularly in the context of how unsocial they are, I calculate that you'll have less than half of the national average.'

She stared in expectation. Poe knew she only cared about the maths. Although she was more empathetic than she'd been a few months ago, the human aspect would always take second place to the science.

Bunney looked bewildered.

Poe translated for him. 'She has a unique thought process. Don't worry about it.'

He shrugged. 'Aye well, she's not wrong. I see my wife for breakfast and on the odd day I have off. Thank fuck we don't have kids.'

'So why take on the extra responsibilities?' Poe asked. 'You've worked in a Michelin-starred kitchen for years. Surely you could get a job somewhere else, where the pressure isn't so great.'

'I told you. I owe Chef Keaton.'

'Why?'

'When I first knocked on his restaurant door I was a pimply-faced seventeen-year-old. Didn't have a fucking clue what I wanted to do with my life. Chef Keaton took me in, gave me a job as a *plongeur*, and put me in the staff accommodation. I assume you've done background searches on me so you'll know that he mentored me from washing dishes to prepping veg all the way up to being his sous chef. It's not just burn scars I've accumulated over the years – it's a sense of identity. You go in any decent restaurant and ask who Chef Keaton's sous chef is and they'll say my name.'

'Still—'

'How could I not keep Bullace & Sloe going for him? And I knew he'd be back at the pass one day, terrifying the guys. No one here believed he killed Elizabeth.'

Poe paused. Up until then, everything Bunney had said sounded genuine. That last part had sounded glib. As if he'd practised the words. Poe wondered what he really thought.

Bunney finished his potatoes and walked over to the water

bath. He took a bag of meat out with some metal tongs and prod-, ded it with his index finger. Now he was up close, Poe could see that it wasn't duck or pigeon in the vacuumed bags – it was pork belly. Bunney grunted and put the bag back in the water.

'Boil-in-the-bag?' Poe wanted to keep Bunney talking.

'Sous-vide. It cooks the meat evenly without overcooking the outside. Keeps it moist. We'll keep these in here until before service then we'll caramelise them on the hob with burnt apple vinegar and some cane sugar. It's served with one of those pota- toes I turned.' He gestured to the water baths. There were six of them. 'We use these more than any other machine in the kitchen. They're a godsend. This one here' – he pointed at the largest one – 'is our workhorse. It holds fifty-six litres, has a circulating pro- peller inside and it's plumbed directly into the drainage so we never have to move it.'

Poe nodded, unimpressed. He remembered the big water bath from last time. CSI had checked it but found nothing.

Bunney nodded at the chef preparing the pork belly before moving along to a giant pot. He took a spoon out of his jacket and tasted what was in it. He reached for a tub and threw in more salt than Poe used in a week. Bunney saw him staring and smiled.

'I'll let you into a secret, shall I? If you want a long and healthy life, reduce your salt intake. If you want one that involves good food, use more. Salt is the main difference between home cook- ing and restaurant cooking, Sergeant Poe. We use as much as we can without the food tasting salty. It brings out the real flavour of ingredients.'

Poe turned to Bradshaw. 'Told you.'

Bunney's mobile rang. He listened, then shouted, 'Bullace & Sloe uses local fucking lamb! We can't get it from fucking Scotland.' He paused. 'No, you dickhead! It's got to be fucking Cumbrian and it's got to be fucking Herdwick!'

He hung up. 'Will you excuse me for one minute. I need to

go and find my little black book. If we don't get this sorted the entire menu will have to be changed.'

'Don't mind us,' Poe said. 'OK if we stay where we are?'

Bunney nodded. 'Just don't bother my team. They have enough to do.'

Bunney returned in a better mood. He'd sorted a new supplier, and was now darting around the kitchen giving instructions and words of encouragement. He never stopped tasting things. At every station he'd dip his spoon into whatever the chef was preparing. Twice. 'It's how you check seasoning,' he explained. After a taste he'd usually add something, occasionally he just gave a nod of approval. Poe noticed that the chefs tensed up while Bunney checked their food. The kitchen was working well, though, and now that his vegetable prep was over, Bunney had relaxed slightly.

Poe asked him about Jared Keaton.

Bunney's eyes narrowed. 'I'm hearing he'll be out next week. Why don't you ask him yourself?'

'Humour me.'

'I don't think I will. He's my boss and if the police are sniffing round trying to save face that'll only end badly for me.'

'We're not sniffing round, Mr Bunney,' Poe lied. 'We're trying to build up a picture so mistakes like this aren't repeated in the future.'

Bunney said nothing for several moments. 'You'll have heard the saying that the easiest way to make a small fortune in the restaurant business is to start off with a *large* fortune?'

'I have,' said Poe. He hadn't.

'It's why ninety-nine per cent of restaurants fail. They don't impress their diners enough for them to want to rebook a table. They cook the same dishes as everyone else but expect different results. Chef Keaton knew that to succeed in this business you had to know the difference between cooking and *creating*. Cooking is following a recipe, and although it does take some skill to recognise what's happening in the pan, when to add salt, when to add acidity, that type of thing, essentially anyone can be trained to do it.'

Poe seriously doubted that. He'd tried and failed many times to follow simple recipes. These days, if he couldn't fry it in a pan, squeeze it between slices of white bread or cook it for ten hours in a hotpot dish, he didn't want to know.

Bunney continued. 'Creating is imagining a dish in your head then combining different flavours, textures, temperatures and techniques to form something that is more than the sum of its parts.'

'And Keaton could do this?' Poe couldn't bring himself to prefix his name with 'chef'.

'*Chef* Keaton could. He was also the first to forage for his own ingredients, the first to use molecular gastronomy, and the first to set the menu each day depending on what had been brought in that morning. We were also the first to offer the no-menu experience.'

Poe knew that Bullace & Sloe didn't have menus. All diners, apart from those with specific dietary requirements, were fed the same meal. Sometimes there were nine courses, sometimes there were more than twenty. Poe didn't know if it was innovative or pretentious. Probably the latter although he accepted he was a bit of a troglodyte in this area.

'For a long time Bullace & Sloe was the most exciting place to eat in the UK. Chef Keaton ignored the models that the continent had adopted and London had followed, where the diner's pleasure was secondary to the creative genius of the chef. He wanted the diner to relax into the meal. To that end we only have one sitting per night. If you come at six you can stay until eleven. The table's yours regardless. None of that "the chef sets the rules and the diner obeys" pish that happens everywhere else. And that's why Bullace & Sloe is still the leader in its field.'

Poe had heard Bunney wax lyrical about Keaton the chef. But he was yet to hear him talk about Keaton the boss, about Keaton the *person*. He asked the question.

'Tough,' Bunney admitted.

'But fair,' Bradshaw finished. She looked happy to contribute.

Bunney smiled. 'Nope. Just tough.' He lifted up his trouser leg and showed them a silver scar on his shin. 'That was a ladle. We were trying to keep our second star and the pressure was enormous. Tempers were fraying. I'd fucked up a pistachio crumb – used the wrong nuts and no one noticed until the lamb got to the pass. Chef Keaton lost his temper.'

'Ouch,' Poe said.

'I've never used the wrong nuts again, though.'

'Still . . .'

'Still nothing. Our second star was at risk and we couldn't afford any more mistakes.'

'What happened to put your star at risk?'

'Schoolboy error,' Bunney replied. 'We had a mackerel gravlax as dish number four and the inspector got a fragment of bone.'

'That not a bit fussy?' Poe had never eaten a fish that didn't have a bone in it.

'Not at this level.'

'You didn't lose your star, though, did you?' Poe turned to Bradshaw for confirmation.

She shook her head. 'They didn't, Poe.'

Bunney looked evasive all of a sudden. His eyes scanned the kitchen like he wanted a reason to leave the conversation.

'Chef Bunney,' Poe said. He waited until the tall Scotsman looked at him. 'What happened? How did Bullace & Sloe keep its star?'

Bunney mumbled something.

'I'm sorry, I didn't catch that,' Poe said.

'I *said*, when his wife died in the car crash we got a three-month extension.'

He looked defiant.

And embarrassed.

CHAPTER THIRTY-TWO

'He was given a sympathy-extension?' Poe asked. He made a mental note to ask Flynn for a copy of the accident report. Other than her being in a car crash, he didn't know anything else about how Lauren Keaton had died.

'Something like that,' Bunney admitted. 'There was no way they could remove a star when his wife had just died. It was only a temporary reprieve, though. Chef Keaton knew they'd be back and that was why we were under so much pressure.'

'And you kept it,' Poe said. Keaton taking advantage of his wife's death didn't surprise him. It was cold, opportunistic and in keeping with what he knew of the man.

'No, Sergeant Poe, we added to it. Lauren's death hit everyone hard but it drove Chef Keaton to even greater heights. He revamped the menu, brought in new suppliers and put his daughter in charge of front-of-house.'

Poe asked Bunney if anyone had spoken to Elizabeth since she'd returned.

'She never came back here. I think she's staying at some hotel the police got for her. Her room upstairs is untouched, though, so when she does come back she can settle straight in. I've changed the linen and let in some fresh air.'

'The staff must be excited, though?'

Bunney shook his head. 'They don't know yet. They have enough on their plates as it is with Chef Keaton's imminent return. All they know is that some new evidence has exonerated him. I'll leave it up to him to tell them.'

Bradshaw wanted to move things along. She flipped her notebook over and said, 'You visited Chef Keaton in prison thirty-six times, Chef Bunney. Why was that?'

He frowned. 'I'm contractually obliged to. Part of assuming the executive chef position meant I had to visit him each time I wanted a major menu change other than seasonal ones agreed in advance. I also had to do a full report on the state of the business every quarter.'

'It says here you visited him three times one month,' Bradshaw said. She didn't refer to her notes. 'In HMP Pentonville. Why was that?'

It was a good question. The Carlisle to London trip was a pain in the arse. Poe didn't care how grateful Bunney was to Keaton, three times in one month was excessive.

Bunney considered this for a moment. 'That'll have been after he was stabbed.'

Poe and Bradshaw looked at each other. There was nothing about a stabbing in his prison file.

'Are you sure?' Poe asked.

'He was in hospital for over a month.'

Poe said, 'Excuse me a moment.'

He leaned in and whispered in Bradshaw's ear. 'Get a video-conference set up with DI Flynn for tonight. Ask her to find out about this stabbing, and why it's not in his prison records. And while you're at it, see if she can get the accident report on his wife.'

'I'll go outside to make sure I have a signal, Poe. If you give me the car keys I'll let Edgar out while I'm there.'

When she'd gone, Poe turned back to Bunney. 'Go on.'

'Nothing more to it, really. He was stabbed and while he was in hospital I thought he might have had time to consider his legacy. Thought he could be persuaded to alter my contract and allow me some autonomy. Maybe even give me the location to that fucking truffle wood.'

Poe raised his eyebrows. It was the second time that truffles had come up.

'They're on every other dish and it's costing me a fucking fortune. Really eats into my profit margins. Chef Keaton used to forage his own but he wouldn't say where from. Not surprising, really, those kind of locations are rarer than rocking-horse shit.'

'You have to buy them?'

'And they're incredibly expensive. By weight, they're more expensive than gold.'

'So I've been told.'

Bunney cocked his head in interest but Poe didn't elaborate. He wanted to ask how a city boy like Keaton had discovered a truffle wood but he needed to stay with the stabbing for now. It was new information and he wanted to push it.

'Being in hospital must have slowed him down a bit?'

'Quite the opposite actually. He was full of beans. I'd visited him at HMP Altcourse the month before and he'd been really down. Another application to appeal against his conviction had been denied, and I think he'd resigned himself to doing the full twenty-five years if not longer. He'd even signed off on a new dish without asking what the unit profit was.'

'The stabbing cheered him up?' That seemed unlikely.

'No, his mood had improved before the stabbing. The first time I visited him in HMP Pentonville actually. He was lively. Revisiting his plans to open a new restaurant in the heart of the Lakes, maybe even a pop-up in London. Wanted me to head them both up. He was laughing and joking, full of it actually. Very strange.'

'And then he was stabbed?'

'And then he was stabbed,' Bunney confirmed.

'And that didn't alter his mood?'

'Not at all. I visited him twice in hospital and both times he was happy.'

Poe would ask Flynn if she could look at the period between Bunney's last HMP Altcourse visit and his first at HMP Pentonville. Find out what had happened to put Keaton in such a good mood that being stabbed hadn't been able to dampen it.

Bradshaw returned. 'The videoconference is set for seven o'clock tonight, Poe.'

Bunney took advantage of the break in conversation to begin barking instructions again. Poe knew his time was almost up. In a kitchen this busy, they'd been lucky to get as much as they had. He tried one more question.

'Tell me about Elizabeth. I expect you knew her well?'

Bunney shook his head. 'Not as much as you'd expect. She was front-of-house and I'm kitchen. In a restaurant like this, the two don't have that much contact.'

'But after service, surely . . . ?'

'Chef Keaton was very protective of his daughter. And you can't blame him really. He's been in the business long enough to know that the team, particularly the ones in the staff accommodation, will inevitably end up partying hard in their downtime.'

'Sex?'

'And drugs. It's a high-pressure environment and Chef Keaton knew when to turn a blind eye. As long as it didn't spill over into work, he didn't care what they got up to after service.'

'And did anything ever spill over?'

For the first time since they'd arrived, Bunney looked uneasy. 'I didn't see anything.'

It was a cunning answer. Not a yes, not a no. Bunney wasn't telling him something.

'Is there anyone else you think I should talk to?'

'I'm sorry,' he replied, 'but we're entering the service stage. I really need to get on.'

Poe shook his hand. 'Don't suppose you could fit us in for an early lunch?'

Bunney looked over his shoulder. 'Jen!' he yelled.

'*Oui*, chef?'

'How we doing for lunch covers? We full?'

'*Oui*, chef.'

'We couldn't fit two more in?'

A small pause. '*Oui*, chef. I can turn a four into two twos.'

'Jen must have two diners on a table that can seat four,' Bunney said. 'She'll separate them and fit you in.'

Poe nodded, pleased he didn't have to leave Bullace & Sloe just yet. He'd got a vibe from Bunney. He thought the big chef had wanted to tell him something but hadn't felt able to. Not in a busy kitchen. Poe would try and get him on his own after the lunch service had ended.

'Can you be here by twelve? You have a lot of courses to get through.'

Poe checked his watch. They had an hour and a half to kill. They were near some Forestry Commission land and could take Edgar for a walk in the woods. Let the spaniel see what normal trees looked like. The few that were on Shap Fell were small and stunted and leaned at right angles.

CHAPTER THIRTY-THREE

They returned to Bullace & Sloe, entering via the front door this time. A woman stood behind a tall, thin desk; her face bathed in the glow of her computer. They gave their names and were directed to a small seating area.

A man in a stiff white shirt, black jacket and Bullace & Sloe tie sat down and joined them. He was carrying a leather folder.

'I'm Joe Douglass, the maître d'. Have you dined with us before?'

They told him they hadn't and Douglass explained how things worked. 'Today's sitting is a fourteen-course tasting menu. Dishes will come every twelve minutes and the meal will take approximately three hours to experience.'

That was a new one on Poe. *Experiencing* a meal instead of eating it. And taking three hours over one – that was new too. Meals were to be eaten at your desk, in your car or over the sink. Still, he had wanted to get inside Keaton's mind: eating his food wasn't the worst idea in the world.

'Will sir want to speak to the sommelier, or will you be allowing us the honour of pairing the wine for you?'

Poe didn't know what 'pairing' meant. It didn't matter, though – he didn't like wine. 'I'll have a pint of bitter.'

'And I'd like a sparkling water, please,' Bradshaw said.

Douglass bowed stiffly and removed an iPad mini from his leather folder. He tapped the screen and placed the drinks order. 'Are there any dietary requirements Chef Bunney needs to be aware of?'

Bradshaw said she was vegetarian.

Douglass tapped his iPad again. 'That all seems to be fine. If you'd like to follow me, I'll take you to your table.'

The dining room at Bullace & Sloe was stripped back. The floor was the original flagstone and the brickwork on the walls was exposed. The milling machinery had been preserved but there was nothing else to distract the diner. No pictures, no photographs, not even curtains.

The minimalist ethos didn't end when they sat down. Crisp red napkins on bare wood, bespoke cutlery, and a single white rose in a patina-stained brass vase were all they had on their table. There were no salt and pepper pots. Poe looked to see if it was just their table, but it seemed no one was trusted to season their own food.

It had just turned midday and the dining room was full. The atmosphere was quiet and reverent. Waiters and waitresses in neatly ironed black uniforms and white ties moved noiselessly in packs of three: one to carry the tray, another to serve the dish and the third to explain what it was that the diner was about to eat. A sommelier watched, eagle-eyed, waiting to top up wine glasses.

Although Bullace & Sloe was roomy, and Poe didn't feel squeezed in, he wondered why the gangly man from Edinburgh had been so accommodating. He hadn't needed to be. Bullace & Sloe had been full – saying no would have been perfectly OK. But Bunney hadn't said no. Was this an example of the excellent service Bullace & Sloe supposedly always strived for, or was it something else?

A ginger-haired waitress brought over a basket of bread. She placed a bun on each of their plates with an ornate pair of tongs. Another waitress placed a stone pot filled with creamy butter in the middle of the table.

A third launched into a rehearsed speech. 'Today's artisan

bread is Chef Bunney's organic sourdough with foraged thyme. The butter is made on-site and the milk is from a Cumbrian farm.' She said it as if Jesus Himself had churned it.

Despite his scepticism, the smell of warm bread was one of life's simple pleasures and Poe inhaled deeply. Bradshaw did the same. He tore the bun in two, applied a liberal coating of butter and took a bite. He sighed in pleasure. It was delicious.

A different trio of waiters delivered the first course. It was everything Poe had expected. Tiny, beautiful to look at and unbelievably complex.

'What you have in front of you is Chef Bunney's take on *salade niçoise*,' the third waiter said. 'It is sashimi blue fin tuna, dehydrated egg yolk, tomato sorbet and an olive reduction.'

A slightly different dish was placed in front of Bradshaw. By the time the waiter had explained that her tuna had been replaced with poached tofu, Poe had eaten his. Two small mouthfuls or one medium one, he reckoned. It was nice but he was clearly missing the point. He wouldn't put himself on a two-month waiting list to eat it again. It certainly wasn't as nice as a Cumberland sausage.

Bradshaw made an effort to savour hers. She nibbled each piece individually, and then had a forkful with everything on. 'Yumbles,' she said when she'd finished.

The next course was a vegetarian dish so they both had the same. It was a white, sombrero-sized bowl with a single raviolo in the middle. It was about the size of a business card and had crimped edges. It was covered in what looked like spit.

'Here we have a wild mushroom raviolo. It is served with garlic foam, aged Parmesan shavings and finished with powdered truffle.'

The rich aroma of the dish wafted up and Poe made an effort to take his time. He found that when he did, he could appreciate the wonderfully fresh white parcel. The foam, as off-putting as it looked, complemented the pasta extremely well, and the earthy tones of the truffle balanced the salty cheese beautifully.

'OK . . . that was quite nice,' he admitted. This was his first experience of fine dining and he was feeling a bit out of place. Bradshaw, who didn't have an embarrassment threshold, was oblivious to his discomfort.

A succession of small but delicate dishes followed, each one more complex than the previous. A sea urchin that Poe felt sorry for was served in its own shell. It had the texture of set custard with the briny taste of fresh oyster. Every time he took a bite, Bradshaw said, 'Yuk'. Essence of carrots – which included carrot purée, carrot snow and carrot granita – was a textbook example of the adage 'just because you can, doesn't mean you should'. The raw piece was by far the tastiest. The carrot dish was succeeded by venison tartare on top of a skid mark of something salty.

The next dish looked like chicken nuggets. Poe looked up quizzically. 'Lamb fries served with foraged wild garlic aioli and a bitter lemon syrup,' the waiter explained.

Poe looked over at what Bradshaw had been given and said, 'Ha ha.' She had another 'essence of' course. Borlotti beans this time. It was a pretty dish – the beans were pinkish with red streaks – but *he* had fried lamb.

And it was stunning. Delicately flavoured, it lingered on the palate long after he'd swallowed. It seemed to have been soaked in milk before being breadcrumbed and fried. It was a bit chewier than he'd have expected from a three-star restaurant, but the flavour more than made up for it. Lamb was his favourite meat and frying was his favourite cooking technique so he wasn't exactly surprised.

Bradshaw had finished before him. She watched as he cleared his plate. A strange smile was playing across her lips. It looked like she wanted to say something.

'What's up, Tilly?' He ran his finger around the plate and scooped up the last of the sauce.

'You do know what lamb fries are, don't you, Poe?'

'Fried lamb, I presume.' Bradshaw's smile broadened and all of a sudden he wasn't so sure. 'Isn't it?'

'Technically, yes.' She opened her phone and waited for a signal. Eventually she typed something and handed it across.

He read the Wikipedia article on lamb fries then looked at his clean finger and his even cleaner plate. 'Please tell me this is a joke.'

'It's not. They're testicles.' Her grin was wider than the M6.

Poe said, 'I'm getting a menu.' He raised his hand and the maître d' approached their table.

'Is everything OK, sir?' he said stiffly.

'I want a menu,' Poe said. 'I'm not eating anything else until I know exactly what it is.'

'Diners get a signed menu after the third dessert course, sir.'

Poe stared at him.

'But I'll ask Chef Bunney if he's prepared to make an exception.'

'Please do that.'

'The food's a little bit ostentatious here, isn't it, Poe?' Bradshaw said after the maître d' had disappeared.

Poe grunted. The food at Bullace & Sloe was a little bit ostentatious in the same way sea urchins tasted a little bit fishy.

The maître d' returned. He carried two cardboard menus. He handed them one each.

'Thank you,' said Poe.

The maître d' bowed and left them.

Poe opened his menu. A small envelope dropped onto the table. They looked at each other. Poe glanced round to make sure no one was watching and, using his butter knife, slit it open.

Inside was an index card. Poe read what was written on it to Bradshaw. '"This man was let go for 'deeply flawed time management'. I suspect he has a different take on it."'

Poe flipped the card over. On the reverse was a name: Jefferson Black. He slid the card across to Bradshaw. She read it and immediately began searching on her phone.

Jefferson Black? The name wasn't in the murder file. He wondered why not. Ex-employees, although sometimes bitter, were good sources of information as long as you ran everything they told you through a bias-sieve.

'Signal's gone,' Bradshaw said, waving her phone in the air. She raised her hand. A waiter approached their table. 'Do you have the Wi-Fi code, please?'

'Madam, this is a Michelin-starred restaurant.'

She began typing. 'Is that all lower-case?'

Poe smiled. 'We'll ask DI Flynn to find him, Tilly. You can call her on the way back. Let's just enjoy the rest of the meal.'

'OK, Poe,' she said, putting her phone back in her pocket. The waiter wandered off in a daze.

While they waited for the next course, Poe wondered why Bunney thought Jefferson Black could help them – what was so mysteriously important that he hadn't felt able to tell him in an open kitchen? Nothing obvious sprang to mind.

He idly picked up his menu and looked to see what was coming next. It was another venison dish: braised roe deer cheeks with foraged blackberry compote. Poe found the menu irritating. Unnecessarily complicated cooking techniques, meat from the wrong parts of the animal and grandiose descriptions like 'farm fresh', 'locally harvested' and 'deconstructed'. The word 'foraged' appeared in the description of almost every dish.

And Bunney was right: truffles *did* feature heavily on the menu – out of the fourteen dishes, six of them included the ridiculously expensive fungus. No wonder he'd been keen to find out where Keaton was foraging them.

'Tilly, when you get five minutes can you do me a briefing paper on truffles? What varieties restaurants use, which types

197

are native to the UK, where they can be found – that type of thing.'

'OK, Poe,' she said, looking up from the menu. 'I'll do it tonight.'

Poe thanked her. How Keaton had found his truffle wood was niggling.

Bradshaw slid her menu across the table. She pointed to the small print at the bottom. Poe frowned, put on his reading glasses and read where her finger was.

It was a list of the suppliers used by the restaurant. It was in a smaller and lighter font than the main menu. It looked like they were pre-printed on the Bullace & Sloe stationery, whereas the menu itself changed daily.

Poe ran his fingers down the list until he saw what Bradshaw had found. His heart skipped a beat. It had been in his face all morning. Bunney had even been screaming about it.

Thomas Hume had been Bullace & Sloe's lamb supplier.

CHAPTER THIRTY-FOUR

The rest of the meal passed in a blur. Poe didn't even moan when the bill came. Ordinarily, if he'd been charged almost four hundred pounds for lunch, he'd have been furious. Instead he paid without comment.

His nearest neighbour had supplied meat to the very restaurant he was investigating. And while Thomas was dead, his daughter Victoria wasn't. And she'd been evasive around him twice now. Once when he'd phoned, and again when he'd collected Edgar. He remembered the sound of her voice when he'd told her he was only there to collect his dog. She'd seemed . . . relieved. Was she involved in this? He didn't know for sure but something was going on. Something he needed to get to the bottom of.

They made good time back to Shap Wells but it was still almost six when they climbed onto the quad and headed to Herdwick Croft. Edgar ran beside them the whole way. Poe needed an alternative solution for his day care; he'd only just got away with it today.

Poe put his espresso pot on the stove and brewed some strong coffee. He popped a bag of herbal tea in a mug and covered it with boiling water. While he waited for it to infuse, Bradshaw set up the videoconference.

Bang on seven, the laptop screen flickered into life, and a still tired-looking Flynn glowered at them. 'Director van Zyl will be joining us. He's on a call to the chief constable of Cumbria at the minute.'

'Oh,' said Poe. 'Do you know what it's about?'

Flynn shrugged. 'Honestly, I don't. I'm not even sure he knew what the call was about. He just asked if he could piggyback this meeting after he'd finished.'

'Poe ate testicles!' Bradshaw yelled without warning. She'd obviously been dying to tell her.

'Did he now?'

'Yes, he did, DI Stephanie Flynn. He even licked his plate. And then I laughed and Poe complained to the waiter because he wanted to see a menu.'

Flynn covered her mouth and stifled a smile. It was the first genuine one he'd seen for weeks. Oh well, it looked like he'd taken one for the team.

'You asked for this conference, Poe,' Flynn said. 'What do you have for me?'

Poe told her about Bullace & Sloe and how Crawford Bunney had surreptitiously passed him the name of Jefferson Black, and although Bradshaw had searched the databases at her disposal, they still didn't have a last known address. Flynn made a note and said she'd get onto it.

He told her how Thomas Hume had been supplying Bullace & Sloe with lamb and hogget, and how his daughter, Victoria, had been acting suspiciously.

'Tell me, what do you know about them?' she asked.

Poe didn't immediately answer. What *did* he know about Thomas Hume? Next to nothing really. He hadn't even known he had children. On the day he met Hume, the man had sold him Herdwick Croft. Told Poe that the local authority wanted to charge him council tax for a building in the middle of nowhere. Poe hadn't received his own council tax demand yet, but he knew that it was just a matter of time – they'd catch up with him eventually.

'Not much,' he admitted.

'I'll look into it,' she said. 'Anything else?'

Poe was about to say no, but he remembered that the car accident that had killed Keaton's wife had come at a fortuitous time. Not only had it saved Bullace & Sloe a star, it had allowed him the time to gain another. He asked her if she could get the accident report.

'That it?'

'For now.'

'What about him being stabbed, Poe?' Bradshaw asked.

Damn. With trying to find Jefferson Black's address and the link with Hume, he'd completely forgotten the actual purpose of the videoconference. He told Flynn about Bunney's claim that Keaton had been stabbed and that it hadn't dampened his elevated mood.

'I have a contact at the Ministry of Justice,' she replied, writing it down. 'I'll ask him to look into it.'

The door behind her opened and the huge frame of Edward van Zyl, Director of Intelligence, National Crime Agency, filled the space next to Flynn. His expression was as grim as a cancer diagnosis.

'We have a problem, Poe,' he said.

Why am I not surprised? he thought. *It's the soundtrack to my life . . .*

CHAPTER THIRTY-FIVE

'I've just finished with the chief constable of Cumbria,' van Zyl said, 'but before I get into that, can you bring me up to speed?'

Flynn relayed an accurate portrayal of events. She referred to her notes only once and when she was unsure she called on Poe and Bradshaw.

When she'd finished, van Zyl remained silent.

'Poe,' he said eventually, 'tomorrow afternoon at three o'clock you are to report to Durranhill police station where you will be formally interviewed.' He checked a piece of paper in his hand. 'Because of your rank, a Detective Chief Inspector Wardle will be lead officer. Do you know him?'

Poe nodded. He'd been expecting something like this since Keaton's veiled threat at HMP Durham, but it was still a shock. 'Did the chief constable say why, sir?'

'She didn't. I can buy you some time if you need it? I'll say your fed rep won't be able to get up for a couple of days. I've a good mind to call her back anyway and say she doesn't get to interview one of my officers without first telling me what it's about. It's bad form.'

'No, sir, I'll go. This is good.'

'Explain.'

'Even if I "no comment" the whole thing, they'll have to show me what they have. Intelligence gathering goes both ways so we should get more of an idea of what Keaton's planning.'

'Good man.'

Poe realised van Zyl had already reached the same conclusion.

If he'd really wanted to stop the interview, he'd have already done so.

'But a word of warning, Poe,' he said. 'I need you to do this properly. No kicking off, no being too clever. Get in, find out what they have, then get out. The chief constable has assured me that you will not be arrested tomorrow, but the less you say, the less they can take out of context later.'

'I'll behave, sir.'

'Good. And who is this DCI Wardle anyway? He seems to have a right hard-on for you.'

'Someone I had a small misunderstanding with, sir.'

Van Zyl rubbed his eyes, stretched his arms behind his neck, and yawned. 'I really don't know how you manage to have enemies like this.'

'This is Poe we're talking about, sir,' Flynn said. 'He probably has friends like this.'

With the videoconference finished, and because neither of them fancied an early night, Poe and Bradshaw got to work. Poe perched his reading glasses on the end of his nose and hit the prison records again.

This time he was looking for something to support Bunney's claim that Keaton had been stabbed. It wasn't long before he found it: a three-week period where there was no mention of Jared Keaton on P-NOMIS. Up until then, Keaton's personal officer had been conscientious with his record-keeping, but, as they mainly dealt with issues occurring on the wing, if Keaton wasn't actually *at* the prison – say, if he was in hospital – there'd be nothing to record. And if he had been stabbed, Keaton would have been wise enough to know not to make a formal complaint – being labelled a grass in prison was worse than being labelled a nonce. The whole thing would have been handled quietly, hence there was nothing on the records to which they had access. It would be on his medical record, but Flynn hadn't been able to get those – quite rightly, patient confidentiality stretched to those incarcerated. Keaton's personal officer had made numerous entries to say when Keaton had been on the prison hospital wing but not what for. Poe got the impression he thought he was making illnesses up to get off general population. It was a common thing with nervous or scared prisoners. The hospital wing was safer, and while Keaton might have been top dog at Bullace & Sloe, in an adult prison he was just a man who'd dusted things with icing sugar for a living. That, his wealth and his offence would have made him a target.

Poe thumbed a text to Flynn letting her know what he'd discovered about the blank spot in Keaton's records. The dates when the personal officer had been mute on P-NOMIS might help in her search for whatever it was that had put Keaton in a good mood.

He glanced at Bradshaw. She was being uncharacteristically quiet. Usually when they worked there was a constant, one-way flow of random chatter. Over the last couple of days he'd learned that the actor Michael J. Fox's middle name was Andrew, a piece of paper folded forty-two times would reach the moon, and 70 per cent of jungle animals rely on figs for survival. Things he didn't need to know, but knew he'd never be able to forget.

But not this time.

She was scowling at her laptop. As he watched, she removed her glasses and buffed them on the special rag she always kept handy. Suddenly she leaned forwards and said, 'Flipping heck.'

She studied the page she was on for a few more moments, nodded once, then turned in her chair. She seemed surprised to find he was watching her.

'What's up, Tilly?'

'I have something to tell you, Poe.'

'Is it something other people would keep private?'

'Funny, but this is important.'

204

He took the seat beside her. The website she was on was some sort of property register. She had an address in Kendal displayed.

'Jared Keaton tried to buy this shop, Poe. They wanted a satellite restaurant in the middle of the Lakes.'

'What website is this?'

Bradshaw didn't answer and he decided not to press it. There were some things he was probably better off not knowing. He turned back to the laptop. He recognised the street. It was in a nice part of Kendal. Suburban but close to the town centre.

'What of it?' he asked.

'The sale almost went through but the owner backed out at the last minute. According to the comments box, it was due to a conflict of beliefs. Apparently the owner had been told that the Keatons were opening a social enterprise restaurant but, when he found out that they weren't, and that they'd misrepresented their offer, he took it off the market.'

'Okaaaay . . . But what does that have to do with me?'

'The shop's owner is your father, Poe.'

Poe's mind did a backflip. Before he realised what he was doing, he'd asked himself which father: the one who'd lovingly raised him or the one who'd raped his mother? He gave himself a mental shake – very few people knew about his mother, and Bradshaw wasn't one of them.

'That's not possible, Tilly,' he said. 'My dad doesn't own a shop. He's the world's biggest hippy – he doesn't believe in ownership. Or deodorant for that matter.'

She printed off a one-page document and handed it to him. Poe read it in disbelief. His dad didn't own just one shop. He owned *several* shops. And houses. He counted them. Fourteen in total. Two in Keswick, three in Windermere and one in Ambleside. The rest were in Kendal. The portfolio was worth millions. The rent he collected each year went into six figures.

He looked at Bradshaw. 'But how?'

She shrugged. 'The rent money received goes into an ethically managed fund. That's all I can get.'

Poe didn't know what to say. That his beatnik dad was a shrewd and wealthy businessman who'd had a property dispute with the Keatons was almost unbelievable. Although he sometimes wondered how his father financed his lifestyle, he'd assumed he hitched everywhere, taking paying berths on ships and working his way across the globe. He'd never once considered he might have travelled business class.

An hour later and Poe hadn't achieved a thing. All he could think about was his dad. He was a millionaire. On paper, at least. He wondered if his mother had known. Probably. Probably hadn't cared either.

Eventually he returned from his past. Something had changed. He listened, but other than the fans of three laptops, the croft was silent. He realised that was it: for the last hour the printer had been permanently on. Now it wasn't.

Without asking, he put the kettle on the stove and made some tea. When it had been steeped long enough, he carried two mugs over.

'Thank you, Poe,' Bradshaw said gratefully, blowing off the steam and taking a sip.

He flicked through the first few sheets of what she'd printed. They were all social media profiles. Page after page of photographs, comments and posts. Most of them were accounts belonging to young women. Poe looked up in confusion.

'Seventy-six per cent of females and eighty-two per cent of eighteen-to-twenty-nine-year-olds use social media every day, Poe. Twenty-four per cent use it almost constantly. If Elizabeth Keaton has been alive all this time, it would be statistically improbable that she could ignore social media completely.'

'Her profiles are all inactive, though,' Poe said. 'It was the first thing you checked.'

'She is, but her friends aren't. I've researched who they are and, based on what school most of them went to, I reverse engineered an identity and sent out some friend requests.'

'Have any of them accepted?'

'All of them, Poe.'

He frowned. Although modern teenagers didn't seem to do anything without vomiting it onto social media, and although they were the age where getting likes and shares was more important than protecting their identity, it seemed implausible that they'd all accepted Bradshaw's friend request. That said, she was an expert at this so maybe it wasn't that implausible. She had a genius-level intellect, a knack for computers and a collection of ready-to-use profiles. Legends really. She had built them up over time. They had hobbies and friends. They posted things. Joined groups. Interacted with real people. In short they did everything a person would do if they really existed. Using social media as an investigative tool was now a core part of what she and her team did.

The documents she'd printed included more than just her new friends' profiles, though. Some were private messages and closed groups. Stuff she shouldn't have been able to access.

'How did you get all this, Tilly?'

She looked cagey.

'Tiiiilly?' he said, drawing her name out. 'What have you done?'

'Promise you won't be cross, Poe?'

He folded his arms.

'I created an "If I was a Harraby School teacher" personality quiz.'

'And what's that?'

'It's a quiz I wrote. They all attended Harraby so I sent it from an account that *may* have looked like I used to be a student there.'

Poe suspected what she actually meant was that she'd sent it from an account that definitely *had* looked like she used to be a student there.

'I'm assuming you had a good reason to do that?'

She nodded vigorously.

'Show me.'

She opened a computer file. It was heavily coded although he could make out some plain text. It was the quiz questions. It was infantile but the type of thing to which young people on social media responded.

THE NAME OF YOUR FIRST PET IS YOUR SCHOOL
NICKNAME:
YOUR MOTHER'S MAIDEN NAME IS WHAT THE CLASS
GERBIL IS CALLED:
YOUR FAVOURITE FOOD IS THE STAIN ON YOUR SCARF:
YOUR BIRTHPLACE IS WHERE YOU TAKE THE CLASS ON
FIELD TRIPS:

And so on.

Poe grabbed a blank bit of paper and wrote down his own answers. He frowned. They were all familiar. 'These are—'

'The answers to the most common security questions needed to retrieve a user's password, yes.'

'And this is legal?'

She ignored him.

'Tilly,' he said, louder this time. 'Is this legal?' He didn't see how it could be. Bradshaw had harvested their security questions then hacked into their accounts.

'It's a grey area,' she conceded.

He considered this for a moment. Decided that if it were a grey area, it was an extremely dark shade of grey. So dark in fact, a cynical person might imagine it was black.

He said as much.

'Poe, you're in trouble,' she said, her voice steady. 'Please understand that there isn't a thing I won't do to protect you. Now, can we please move on? Do you want to hear what I found or not?'

He relented. No one would ever know anyway. Bradshaw would have been in and out without leaving a trace.

'What did you find?'

'It's weird, Poe. There's nothing there. She's not posted on any of the major platforms since she disappeared. Not only that, she's not even been on to see what her friends have been doing. Didn't even visit the condolence page her friends set up.'

'That's . . . disciplined.'

'Extremely, Poe. All available research suggests that social media is so ingrained into the lives of Elizabeth's catchment group, it is almost impossible to withdraw from it completely.'

'How did she behave on social media before she disappeared? Anything stand out?'

'Nothing, Poe. Everything was there that should have been. A lot of engagement with her friends, a lot of posts about Bullace & Sloe. No obvious political leaning.'

Poe scanned the photos Bradshaw had printed out. Elizabeth Keaton was smiling in all of them and appeared to be what everyone had described her as: a gregarious, happy teenager. Some had been taken at parties, and some in clubs and pubs. Others were of her at work. She must have gone on holiday with her friends at some point. Madeira, Portugal, if the tags were accurate. Poe knew Madeira was a volcanic island, which was why all the bikini shots had been taken on concrete lidos rather than beaches.

He frowned. Something wasn't quite right. He checked the photographs twice to be sure.

'Tilly, what would you wear to the beach?'

She looked blank. He might as well have asked what she'd wear to the gym.

'Never mind,' he said. 'Have a look at these. Tell me what you see.'

Bradshaw studied the Madeira photographs. It didn't take long for understanding to dawn on her face. 'She's not wearing a bikini top, Poe. All her friends are but she's always wearing long-sleeved T-shirts or blouses.'

'Exactly. I think she's concealing her self-harm scars.'

He showed Bradshaw photographs taken when Elizabeth was fifteen. On another holiday. There were no tags this time but it looked like Allonby in west Cumbria. Taken on a rare sunny day. Sure enough, in these photographs she *was* wearing a bikini.

'The self-harm must have started between those two holidays,' he said.

He wondered what had caused it. Probably the death of her mother. Did Jared Keaton know about it? If he did he'd have no doubt told her to cover up her scars when she was out in public. A daughter who self-harmed didn't fit with the image he liked to project.

Poe put down the pictures. If he stared at young girls in bikinis for much longer, Bradshaw would say something and make it awkward.

One of her laptops beeped an alert. She swivelled to read the new email.

'It's from DI Stephanie Flynn, Poe. She doesn't have an address for Jefferson Black yet but she knows where he'll be tomorrow.'

'Where?'

She told him.

He wished she hadn't.

Day 11

CHAPTER THIRTY-SIX

There's an area like Botchergate in every city. If Carlisle ever applied to host the Olympics, the competing cities would only need to show the selection committee a video of the centre of Carlisle's night-time economy. The street was door-to-door fun-pubs, nightclubs, takeaways and pay-to-use ATMs. It was the part of town that catered for those not looking for anything subtler than pound shots, 8 per cent proof lager and thumping dance music. On Friday and Saturday evenings Botchergate had a permanent police presence.

And nestled in the middle, like a king turd, was a grubby pub called the Coyote. The little organised crime that Cumbria had operated from there. Prostitutes paid their pimps, dealers re-upped and fences hawked their wares. It was the type of place that lowered the average life expectancy of the whole country.

In Carlisle the Coyote was known as the Dog. Even the hard-cases avoided it.

Poe stood at the door and faced up Botchergate, in the direction of the train station. He removed his warrant card from his jacket and held it in the air.

'What are you doing, Poe?'

'You see that tall white pole at the top of the road?'

'I do, Poe.'

'That's the new CCTV, Tilly. I want an operator to see me going in.'

'But it's got to be two hundred metres away.'

Poe smiled. It *was* two hundred metres away. It didn't matter – the cameras were so good, the operator would be able to read the time on his watch. Despite the early hour Poe knew someone would be keeping a weather-eye on the Dog's entrance. It was the cameras' default setting. He waited with his hand in the air for two minutes. More than enough time for the operator to understand that a cop was going in the Dog. Long enough to make sure a patrol car was nearby.

A heavy-set man with a monobrow pushed past them and stumbled inside. *Good.* He'd warn everyone that a cop was about to enter. It meant Poe wouldn't have to overlook any obvious crimes. Drugs and stolen goods would be moved out of sight. He hoped. You could never tell what you were going to find in the Dog.

They were about to enter when the door burst open and a woman in a mini-dress lurched out. She vomited noisily on the pavement. Bradshaw jumped back to avoid the splatter. The woman turned to her and half-smiled an apology. Wiping her mouth with the back of her hand, she said, 'Bastard said he'd pull it out.'

Bradshaw smiled politely but luckily didn't ask what she meant. The woman staggered back inside.

'You ready?' Poe asked.

Bradshaw hesitated then said, 'Yes, Poe.'

'It'll be fine,' he said. 'Just think what you'll be able to tell the Mole People when you get back.'

'You mean the Scooby Gang, Poe.'

'That's what I said.'

Poe pushed open the door and stepped inside. His nose went into shock. The Dog smelled worse than a toilet. He didn't want to know what the actual toilets smelled like. The air was hot and smoky and perfumed with the cloying scent of cannabis. The windows and ceiling were stained yellow with nicotine. Fat bluebottles feasted on something wet and organic on the worn, frayed carpet. Poe's money was on blood. Probably from the bare-chested man using his own T-shirt to stem the flow coming from what looked like a recent head wound. Despite his injury, he continued to drink and chat with the man sitting next to him.

It was that kind of place.

'Oh my,' whispered Bradshaw.

Poe walked to the bar, avoiding the Band-Aids and dog ends on the sticky floor. The barmaid was dealing – literally – with a gaunt man at the opposite end. Poe turned and surveyed the crowd while he waited.

It had only just gone 10 a.m. but the Dog was already filling up with the tracksuit and tank-top community, none of whom were strangers to bad luck. The type of social group most likely to have 'burned to death in a bin fire' printed on their death certificate.

A woman was bawling her eyes out complaining that the 'bastards at the social' were stopping her benefits and she was 'fucked if she would scrub bogs for a living'. A man wearing sunglasses surreptitiously checked his phone like he was working for MI5. Another man, a fat one who looked like he'd been drinking through the night, had clearly pissed himself. Two kids were playing darts. Poe couldn't see a dartboard. He suspected there wasn't one. There was a pool table but a man was asleep on the dirty green felt. For reasons that weren't obvious, someone had covered him in crisps.

Two pit bulls, both illegal variants, growled at each other and strained their leashes. The woman in the mini-dress walked too close to one and it bit her on the ankle. Everyone stopped what they were doing to laugh.

The barmaid finished dealing and Poe caught her attention. She ignored him. He flashed his badge and she skulked over. She was wearing shorts and a filthy T-shirt. She was so skinny, her

215

elbows were the biggest things on her arms. Her left hand was bandaged. She was a well-preserved sixty or a hard-ridden forty.

She waited for him to speak.

'Jefferson Black. Where is he?'

Bradshaw had found an old photograph of Black so Poe had a rough idea of what he looked like and he was confident that he wasn't in the Dog yet.

'Got to buy a drink first,' she mumbled.

The Dog was full of wannabe-alphas and bowing down to the orders of a barmaid was the quickest way to get glassed. He ignored her and turned to face the regulars.

'My name's Washington Poe,' he said. 'And if you don't tell me where Jefferson Black is, I'm coming back every day until I find him. Every. Fucking. Day.'

That caught their attention. Already someone wearing a suit and carrying a briefcase had spun around and left when he saw Poe standing at the bar. The surest way of getting what he wanted was to threaten their business.

He heard the door open behind him. A collective sigh of relief swept over the Dog.

Poe turned.

Problem solved. Jefferson Black had arrived.

CHAPTER THIRTY-SEVEN

Before he'd become a chef, Jefferson Black was a paratrooper. He still walked like one. Back ramrod straight, long strides, complete confidence. In his early thirties, he had cropped sandy hair, a boxer's nose and a jaw like an anvil. He was wearing a pair of loose flannel shorts, a 1 PARA hoodie and a grim expression.

He strode across the sticky carpet to an empty corner and sat down. People either side shuffled to give him space. The Dog regulars did their best to avoid catching his eye. He hadn't asked for anything but the barmaid walked over with a pint of lager and what looked like a brandy chaser. He accepted them without thanks. Black checked his surroundings like the elite soldier he'd been and saw Poe immediately.

Poe held his gaze. Black looked mildly curious. Poe walked over and took the seat next to him. Bradshaw perched on the stool opposite them both and looked round nervously.

'I was told I'd find you here,' Poe said.

Black looked at him. A light smile played on his lips.

Poe reached in his pocket. Black stiffened slightly. Poe withdrew his warrant card and laid it open on the table. Black glanced down briefly.

'And here I am,' he said.

Poe checked his watch. 'You hungry?' he asked. 'I'll buy you brunch if you don't mind leaving your pint. By the looks of things, no one will touch it.'

'I've eaten,' Black replied. 'I try to start each day with some proper food. There's a place I go to on Bank Street. An old-fashioned coffee house. The chef there knows how to cook eggs properly.'

Poe knew it. It was called John Watts and they sold coffee beans from all over the world. Poe shopped there often.

'I eat there before starting the business of the day,' Black continued.

'Which is?'

'Bending my arm.'

Poe didn't reply. The comment hadn't seemed frivolous. He noticed Black was sweating. Everyone was to a certain extent – it was a hot day and the Dog was a Petri dish at the best of times – but Black was dripping. The back of his neck glistened and sweat rolled off his nose. Black saw him stare but offered no explanation.

'So, Detective Sergeant Poe of the National Crime Agency, how can I help you?'

Poe debated whether it would be worthwhile telling Black that he'd also served. Try and get a bit of bonding going. He realised it would be pointless. Black had been a Para, and if you hadn't worn their maroon beret you were dismissed as a crap-hat. That Poe had been in the Black Watch, one of the most feared Scottish infantry regiments, wouldn't matter. Black would either help them or he wouldn't. Better just to ask him outright.

'I'm investigating Jared Keaton.'

Black's nostrils flared and his jaw clenched. The hand holding the pint went white at the knuckles. His breathing quickened.

'What's this about?' he growled. 'What's that bastard done now?'

Poe's brow creased. Keaton's looming release on bail was in the public domain but it appeared Black didn't know. Until he had found out what happened between them, he decided to keep quiet.

'We just want background,' Poe said carefully. He got the impression that Black was one word away from exploding.

'You see this?' Black spat, wiping his brow with the back of his hand and showing them the sweat. 'Jared fucking Keaton did this to me.'

How Jared Keaton became the cause of Jefferson Black's excessive sweating was easily explained but harder to understand. On the one-year anniversary of Keaton's conviction for murder, Black had washed down three packets of paracetamol with a bottle of vodka. His suicide attempt not only failed, it left him with an acquired brain injury. One of the physical manifestations was secondary hyperhidrosis: the inability to regulate body temperature, caused by lesions on the hypothalamus. Other symptoms included severely reduced impulse control – and, as an ex-Para, he probably hadn't had much to begin with – and the return of his post-traumatic stress disorder.

It explained why even the headcases in the Dog were giving him a wide berth. An ex-Para with a brain injury that made him even more aggressive was a scary combination.

The reason he had tried to end his life wasn't what Poe was expecting. He'd wrongly assumed he was going to hear tales of maltreatment in the kitchen, of a sadistic chef who made the lives of his staff a misery. Of split shifts and long hours. Of drug abuse and sex.

And there was a bit of that. Black also told them about some of the tricks Keaton had used to increase his profit margins. Some of these were stomach churning, particularly for two people who'd eaten there a day earlier. Mouldy food used in staff meals. Seafood past its best rinsed in salt and lemon water to hide the smell. Leftovers being recycled.

'Never eat the fucking soup in a restaurant is my advice,' he'd told them. 'It's like eating the black jelly babies: all you're getting is the factory floor sweepings. Anything that's off goes in it.'

Poe had expected to hear all that.

But what he hadn't expected to hear was a love story. He hadn't expected Black to tell him that he'd endured it all to be near Elizabeth Keaton.

CHAPTER THIRTY-EIGHT

'Jared Keaton held grudges over the smallest of imagined slights,' Black explained. 'And my slight wasn't imagined.'

'What did you do?' Bradshaw asked.

Black turned to face her. 'I fell in love with his daughter.'

Poe breathed out heavily. The Para and the psychopath's daughter. That was never going to end well. 'And was it reciprocated?'

Black drew a circle in the condensation on his pint glass. Stabbed it in the middle and said, 'I think it was.' He took a deep breath. 'I *know* it was.'

Bradshaw leaned forwards. She'd been quiet since entering the Dog – the pub was sensory overload – but this had caught her attention. 'That can't have been easy, Mr Black.'

'We kept it quiet,' he replied. 'As quiet as we could anyway. Elizabeth was terrified of what Keaton would say and I didn't need the inevitable grief from my sous chef.'

'Crawford Bunney?' Poe said.

'That's him. Decent bloke. Typical joy-phobic Scot but he was a fair man. Pushed us hard but only because he wanted the last cover to be just as good as the first.'

Black finished his pint and signalled for another. Poe hadn't seen him pay for the first one yet.

'We only met when we were sure no one would see us,' Black continued. 'It was difficult, though. Elizabeth was front-of-house and when her mother died she also took over the accounts so her time off was limited. And even when our downtime matched, more often than not, something would come up: a new technique Keaton wanted the chefs to learn or a media event he needed Elizabeth by his side for.'

'Was she ambitious?' Poe asked.

Black hesitated. 'She wanted her father to succeed and knew she'd have to make sacrifices of her own for that to happen. Managing front-of-house can be challenging. You have the lowest-paid staff with the highest-profile jobs. Keeping them happy isn't always easy but she never seemed to have any issues.'

'Strict?'

Black shook his head. 'No. Just a sweet girl. Impossible to dislike.'

Not that sweet . . . Poe thought. She'd been faking her own abduction for six years. 'When did it end?'

'It didn't,' he replied simply.

'But you were sacked,' Poe said. He checked his notebook, more to show Black that this was coming from someone else rather than to jog his memory. 'For "deeply flawed time management".'

Black snorted. 'Yeah, that's what I was told as well. I'm an ex-Para, Mr Poe.'

It was all the explanation he needed.

'Five minutes before every parade,' Poe muttered.

'You've served?'

'Black Watch. Long time ago now.'

'You know then.'

Poe nodded. Being five minutes early for appointments was second nature for squaddies. To this day he still set his watch five minutes ahead of the actual time.

'You think your dismissal was contrived?' he asked.

Their discussion was temporarily halted when the barmaid brought Black's fresh pint over. They waited until he'd taken a long drink. Less than half of it remained when he set it down on the sticky table. He lit a cigarette and blew out a thick plume of smoke. It twisted and twirled and merged with the nicotine cloud hovering near the ceiling. Poe put his hand on Bradshaw's forearm: now wasn't the time to start reeling off the smoking law.

'Being a chef in a Michelin-starred kitchen is a cut-throat business,' Black said finally, his eyes back in a different time and place. 'Because every chef wants to work in one, opportunities for promotion are rare and highly competitive.'

He took another drink. Dragged on his cigarette.

'There was a snake,' he said through gritted teeth. 'A fucking coward called Scotty. We joined Bullace & Sloe about the same time and, although we were on different stations, we were sort of rivals. One night he saw Elizabeth and me share a goodnight kiss. A spur of the moment decision I'll always regret. I reckon he must have fancied a bit of competition elimination.'

'He told Keaton?'

Black nodded. 'He denied it initially but when I ruptured his spleen . . .'

That cleared up Crawford Bunney's reluctance to say Black's name out loud. Pound to a penny, this Scotty was in the kitchen when they'd been talking. Bunney had already been two chefs down that morning – he wouldn't have wanted to spook another one.

'You were fired,' Poe said.

'That's one way of fucking putting it,' Black spat back. 'You'd be hard-pressed to find a more humiliating display from one human being towards another. Keaton called a staff meeting. Everyone: front-of-house, kitchens, even a delivery guy who happened to be there. We thought he was going to announce that the restaurant had finally got that third star. Instead, for almost fifteen minutes he publicly shamed me. Screamed at me. Said I was the worst chef they'd ever had. Accused me of stealing produce, of stealing the guys' tips. Didn't mention time management once.'

'Harsh,' Poe said.

'And after I'd packed my bags and left, he spoke to every restaurant in the north of England and the south of Scotland and made me a pariah in the culinary world. I reckon he thought I'd have no choice but to head south.'

That explained why Jefferson Black's name hadn't come up in the original investigation. Keaton had probably assumed he'd headed for London and was out of his daughter's life. And, by the sound of things, Black wasn't someone you'd casually try and drop in the shit either. Scotty's spleen was testament to that. When it came to the ex-Para, the staff group had probably decided collective amnesia was the safest option.

'You kept seeing each other, I take it,' Poe said.

For the first time since he'd sat down, Black smiled. 'We did. I loved her more than my career so I stayed up here. Got work where I could. It didn't matter as long as we were together.'

'And how did Elizabeth take this?'

'She loved her dad but she was furious at what he'd done. Absolutely livid. She didn't speak to him for three months.'

'Seeing each other must've been even harder,' Poe said.

'Easier actually. I didn't have regular work so could fit in with Elizabeth's time off. We saw each other at least twice a week. Did all the way up until . . .'

'Until she disappeared,' Poe finished.

Black nodded. He stared into the dregs of his pint. Swirled it round the bottom of the glass before necking it in one. He raised his hand less than an inch. The barmaid began pouring another.

'What happened next?'

'This,' he replied, banging himself violently on the side of his head. 'I started reliving Helmand. While no one was sure what happened to Elizabeth, it was manageable. A few night terrors.

Reliving some of the worst parts. Dead mates, lost limbs. Never knowing if the interpreter who helped you yesterday would blow himself up tomorrow.'

Poe grimaced. His service hadn't included Afghanistan. He couldn't begin to imagine what the soldiers of today were going through.

Black continued, 'But after Keaton was found guilty of her murder, I lost it. Couldn't see a way out. Tried to end it all. Couldn't even get that right. Woke up with a brain that's more fucked up now than it ever was. Can't even control my own body any more.' He lifted the arm of his maroon hoodie to show the dark sweat marks underneath.

How do you respond to that? Poe didn't know. Bradshaw didn't either. Her eyes were moist. Black's story had got to her. It had got to Poe too but he had a job to do.

He was considering how to tactfully ask him if Elizabeth might have had any reason to disappear for six years. He didn't know how to do it without letting Black know that she wasn't dead.

He was saved from making an immediate decision by the arrival of two lambs to the slaughter.

CHAPTER THIRTY-NINE

Poe had been watching them in his peripheral vision. They were part of a group huddled in the opposite corner. If he'd had to guess, he'd have said they were fences and he was ruining their morning's business. The two men had broken away from the pack and were standing at the bar downing shots. It looked like they'd been press-ganged to deliver the group's decision, and were building up liquid courage.

After what seemed like an age they decided it was time to reclaim their pub.

They fake-swaggered over, both nervous as hell, both wishing they were anywhere but where they were now. One was fat, one was thin. They both wore tank tops, grey sweatpants and trainers that looked like shoes. It wasn't a good look, but for some reason Carlisle's underclass had bought into it. Fatty had a neck tattoo, Skinny's was on the back of his hand.

'And what have you two hens been clucking about?' Black asked without looking up.

Fatty nervously looked to Skinny for support. Skinny nodded in encouragement.

'No fucker speaks to the filth in here, Black,' Fatty said. The impact of his words somewhat lessened by the tremble in his voice.

Poe sighed. He was past the age when running was an option. He moved in his seat to shield Bradshaw. If it kicked off he'd drag her out as quickly as he could then go back in and help Black.

Black slowly put down his pint glass. Removed a cigarette from his pack and lit it. He blew the smoke in Fatty's face but said nothing.

Other than the hum of flies, the Dog was silent. Everyone waited to see what was going to happen next.

Black stared at the two men. He was calm. Frighteningly calm.

Fatty and Skinny were losing their bottle fast. Skinny hadn't said a word but his Adam's apple was bobbing up and down like a fishing float. Fatty's eyes were flitting between Black and the group he'd been press-ganged by, all of whom seemed to have taken a great interest in their drinks.

If they'd walked away then, Poe didn't think Black would have followed them. But they didn't walk away. They were too stupid for that.

Fatty sealed their fate.

In an accent so thick and guttural Poe knew Bradshaw wouldn't understand a word, Fatty said, 'And who's this specky bitch? She ain't no fucking cop.'

It was at that point that Black decided he'd had enough – he seized the initiative and did what the Parachute Regiment had spent tens of thousands of pounds training him to do.

He brought violence to the enemy.

What happened next couldn't technically be called a fight: a fight implies more than one participant. It couldn't even be called a melee as that implies confusion and chaos.

What the Dog's punters were treated to was a display of what Anthony Burgess had called 'ultraviolence'.

Black didn't threaten them and he didn't warn them. He launched himself off his seat and struck. Skinny was nearest and he bore the first attack. Black grabbed him by the hair and pushed his lit cigarette into his eye. Before Skinny had a chance to scream Black pulled his head down to meet his rapidly rising knee. There was a sickening crunch. Skinny gurgled once then went quiet. He slumped to the floor, unconscious.

Fatty tried to run but he moved about as fast as smell did. Black swept his legs out from underneath him and Fatty fell to the filthy carpet. He tried to get up but Black kept him down with a kick to his meaty ribs. With him floundering on his back, Black stepped between his legs and stamped on his crotch. Poe winced. Black stood astride the crying man, lifted him by his tank top, and smashed his forehead against the bridge of his nose. Twin jets of blood spurted from Fatty's nostrils. Black let him fall onto the floor. The middle of his face was flat.

It had been brutal and it had been shocking. It was over in seconds. Even if Poe wanted to intervene he wouldn't have had time.

The Dog, whose punters had, not half an hour earlier, laughed when a woman had been bitten by a dog, remained silent. Pale faces stared down at their tables.

Black positioned Fatty and Skinny on their sides then sat back down as if nothing had happened. He lit another cigarette.

'Sorry about that,' he said. 'Now, what was I saying?'

CHAPTER FORTY

'Ah, yes, I was telling you how I had it all: a new career and a girl who loved me. Now fucking look at me. I only ever feel alive when something like this happens.' Black gestured towards the two unconscious men.

'Oh my God!' Bradshaw exclaimed. She couldn't tear her eyes away from the scene of devastation on the floor. She got to her feet and yelled, 'Is anyone in here a doctor?'

Poe didn't know much about what was going on, but he knew one thing: no one in the Dog was a doctor.

'Sit down, Tilly,' he said gently. 'They'll be all right, Mr Black has put them in the recovery position.'

'But—'

'They'll be fine,' Black confirmed.

At least Bradshaw had released the tension that had been building. A couple of punters sniggered at her doctor remark. Before long there was laughter coming from all parts of the bar.

To raucous cheers, the man holding his T-shirt to his head wound shouted, 'If there is, I'm next!'

The Dog went back to normal. Fatty and Skinny were dragged away by members of the posse who'd sent them. One of them caught Black's eye and nodded an apology.

Bradshaw still looked worried. She was probably in shock and needed a distraction.

'Tilly, can you show Mr Black the documents you pulled off social media, please?'

After a pause, she said, 'OK, Poe.' She opened her bag and removed her iPad. The familiar actions seemed to settle her. She swiped through a few screens until she found the one she wanted. She handed it to Black who studied the pictures. He looked at them both quizzically.

'What's this about?'

Poe pretended not to hear. 'None of her recent photos show her dressed the same way as her friends.' He thought it best not to tell Black he'd been looking at a fifteen-year-old Elizabeth in her bikini. 'I reckon she was about seventeen when she began to cover her arms – I assume it was to hide her self-harm scars.'

Black was staring at the photographs on Bradshaw's iPad. 'Elizabeth didn't self-harm.'

Poe was about to say that he knew different, but stopped himself. Black hadn't taken his eyes from the iPad, his voice hadn't wavered. He'd simply stated a fact.

'You're sure?'

Black nodded. 'Why do you think she did?'

Poe didn't answer. If Black was right, then Elizabeth's self-harming started after she disappeared. But if that was the case, why had she been wearing long-sleeved T-shirts in bikini weather?

'Have you found her?' Black asked.

Poe didn't answer.

'HAVE YOU FOUND HER?'

Bradshaw flinched. So did Poe. The Dog slid into silence again. Poe held Black's gaze. Knew that the best way to diffuse the situation was to be open. He also suspected Black was asking about Elizabeth's remains, rather than whether she'd been found alive.

'No, Jefferson, we haven't found her,' Poe said. It wasn't an outright lie. Despite what had just happened, he quite liked Jefferson Black.

'Then why . . . ?' Black's eyes misted over. 'What aren't you telling me? Why do you think she self-harmed?'

'I can't tell you,' Poe said. 'Not yet anyway, but I promise you, as soon as I can, I will.'

Black considered what Poe had said. 'Is this T-shirt thing important?'

Poe shrugged. 'It might be.'

They waited for Black to come to a decision. Without warning he pulled off his hoodie. His fatless torso glistened with sweat. On the top of his shoulder he had an airborne tattoo. It was a screaming eagle, talons open, bearing down on some poor soul. The words '1 Para: Death from Above' were tattooed above it.

Black shifted round so Poe could see his other shoulder.

On it was another, simpler tattoo: a single jigsaw piece. It was about an inch and a half square. It was outlined in red, but instead of being a segment of a much larger picture, there was a word contained within it: Elizabeth.

Poe stared, his heart racing. He took a few moments to let it sink in. *Did that mean what he thought it did?* If it did, it potentially changed everything.

Everything.

He kept his voice as calm as possible and asked the only question that mattered: 'Did Elizabeth have the matching one, Jefferson?'

Black let slip a single tear. 'We had them done together. The pieces interlock. My name was in the middle of hers. Keaton would have gone mental if he'd found out and, because she wore strappy dresses when she attended events with him, she had to get it somewhere more discreet – hers was above her right hip.'

Bradshaw grabbed the iPad and searched for what Poe already knew. Flick Jakeman hadn't mentioned a tattoo when she performed the medical. After a couple of minutes Bradshaw looked up, confused.

'What does that mean, Poe?' she asked.

He almost replied that he didn't know but the words dried in his throat.

Because he was beginning to think he did . . .

They thanked Black and left him to his drinking. As soon as Poe was outside he rang Flick Jakeman. Although the doctor had seemed competent, he wanted to double-check.

'Hello?'

'Doctor Jakeman, it's Sergeant Poe. Sorry to spring this on you, but do you happen to remember if Elizabeth Keaton had a tattoo?'

There was a pause. 'I don't think so but I'd have to check my notes. Why do you ask?'

'It's come up,' Poe said, without offering anything further. He didn't want to tell her what he was looking for in case some lawyer said he'd led a witness. 'Do you have your notes to hand?'

'I'm in my surgery just now, Sergeant Poe. I have a copy on my home computer but you'll have to wait until later, I'm afraid. Is it important?'

'It might be.'

'Will you be on this number?'

'I will.'

'I'll call you as soon as I get back then.'

He told Bradshaw what Jakeman had said.

'You like her, don't you, Poe?'

He shrugged. 'She's nice.'

Bradshaw smiled but didn't add anything.

Poe drove to a cellar restaurant he knew. Although it did smoked and barbecued meat, he ordered the same salad as Bradshaw – not because her noise about eating healthier was getting through, but because he didn't want to feel sluggish when Wardle interviewed him.

While they waited, Bradshaw opened her emails and smiled. 'DI Stephanie Flynn has sent us all the information we asked for, Poe.'

She passed her iPad over. There were two emails. The subject line of the top one read: Lauren Keaton: Accident report. The other one said: Jared Keaton: Stabbing. He opened it first.

It was short and to the point. Jared Keaton *had* been stabbed but, as he hadn't made a complaint against his assailant, it had been recorded as an accident on his medical records. Assaults damaged prison performance figures so whenever they could be recorded as something else, they were. The blade had nicked his bladder and he'd spent almost a month in hospital.

Poe searched for information about the person who'd stabbed him but there was nothing on record. Keaton didn't know the man, was too scared of him or was wise enough to know that snitches got stitches.

Crawford Bunney had said that Keaton's good mood predated the stabbing and that his injury hadn't dampened it. Poe needed to find out what had happened to lift his spirits. He had the feeling it was important.

He sent Flynn a text message and asked if she could do some more digging. He didn't mention the tattoo. He got an immediate, although curt, reply, agreeing to his request. She also reminded him of his scheduled meeting with DCI Wardle.

Their salads arrived and Poe stopped reading while they ate. After they'd finished, he opened the other email. Flynn's summary was more interesting than the technical reports she'd attached. On a wet night, Keaton had lost control of his car on a bend and hit a tree head-on. There'd been mud on the road – a not uncommon phenomenon in Cumbria. Although Keaton's chest had hit the steering column, the driver's airbag had saved him from serious injury. Lauren Keaton wasn't so lucky: her airbag hadn't deployed. The investigation concluded that she'd turned it off the day before when she'd taken a carload of children to a local theatre's performance of *Aladdin*. The child in the passenger seat had been in a car seat, and the accepted practice then was that airbags did more harm than good to young children. The report concluded that Lauren had forgotten to turn it back on. The coroner agreed and recorded an accidental death. Poe went through the technical reports but decided that the right conclusion had been reached: Lauren Keaton's death might have been beneficial to Jared but it had been an accident.

They ordered teas and drank them in silence.

Poe had a lot to dwell on. He had the awful feeling he'd ignored his own golden rule: thinking you know what's happening is the surest sign you don't. Although the tattoo only added to the chaos of the case, Poe suspected he probably had most of the answers – now all he had to do was reframe the questions. And to do that he had to get back to Herdwick Croft.

But first he had to sit down with an arsehole.

CHAPTER FORTY-ONE

'You're late, Sergeant Poe,' Wardle snapped.

Poe ignored him.

'What have you been doing?'

'Police work.' Poe didn't elaborate.

The interview started badly and went downhill from there. Poe suspected that Wardle had wanted to arrest him but hadn't been given the authorisation. Cumbria had autonomy in the Elizabeth Keaton investigation but no one wanted to pick a fight with the NCA.

Instead he'd made Poe wait outside the interview room for fifteen minutes.

Wardle was wearing a suit and a smirk. His suit wasn't custom made and it bunched at the bottom of his short legs. His hooded eyes were drooping even more than the last time he'd seen him; Poe suspected he'd been up all night preparing for the interview. It was clearly a big deal for him. Poe knew he had to be careful. Wardle was an idiot but he was also a careerist, and that was a dangerous combination.

He gestured to the seat opposite and pressed record on the machine. DC Rigg was with him but, other than to witness the interview, it looked like he had no role. Technically he couldn't ask questions anyway; Poe was a sergeant, Rigg was a constable.

'Am I under arrest?' Poe asked when they were settled.

'You know you aren't, Sergeant Poe,' Wardle replied.

'Well, turn your fucking machine off.'

'I won't,' Wardle replied.

'See you later then.'

And that was about as good as it got.

After Wardle had turned off the tape, he asked a series of questions to which he must have known he wasn't going to get a sensible answer.

'Why were you in the Dog this morning?'

'It's a hot day. I fancied a drink.'

'In the Dog?'

'I like it in there. It's a nice pub.' He'd had every intention of taking van Zyl's advice and 'no commenting' all the way through, but he needed to knock Wardle off his script first.

Angry people made mistakes.

Wardle waited for him to expand. It wouldn't work. Poe had been interviewing criminals for years and knew every trick Wardle did. Unfortunately for Wardle, he didn't know every trick that Poe knew.

If he were reading Wardle's playbook correctly, the next thing would be to try to make him angry. Sure enough, the DCI turned to Rigg and said, 'What about that simpleton he was with? How about we bring her in and see what she has to say?'

Rigg said nothing. Poe smiled at the thought of Wardle bringing in Bradshaw. If Wardle really thought that was a good idea then he truly didn't have a clue what he was doing. Bradshaw would run rings round him. She knew the PACE Act back to front – he'd be lucky to come out of it with his job.

'Why don't you just tell me why I'm here, Wardle?' Poe said.

Wardle frowned, as Poe knew he would. Status was everything to him.

'That's *Detective Chief Inspector* Wardle.'

'Yep, that,' Poe said. 'Why don't you tell me what you have?'

Wardle said, 'You know, Sergeant Poe, I do wonder why

someone with such an obvious anti-authoritarian streak has only chosen careers that absolutely insist on respecting rank.'

Poe said nothing. He'd been wondering the same thing for years.

'And if you're not going to honour my rank, I'm not going to honour yours,' Wardle said.

Oh, no, Poe thought.

Wardle reached into a manila folder and retrieved a single-page document. He passed it to Poe. 'Do you know what this is?'

It was a cell site analysis report. Poe recognised the tower from last year's Immolation Man enquiry. It was the one nearest to Herdwick Croft. The telephone number didn't leap out at him but he'd have been surprised if it had – he didn't even know what his own was. Before anyone could stop him, he'd turned on his phone and taken a photo of the page.

Wardle went pale with anger but there was nothing he could do – Poe had an NCA-encrypted BlackBerry and was part of the investigation team. Wardle snatched the document back and held on to it like a holiday souvenir. Poe left his phone on the table and made it clear that anything else he was shown would be photographed.

'Do you recognise the cell tower, Poe?' he said, pointing to the reference number.

Poe didn't answer. He didn't know where this was going yet.

'No?' Wardle continued. He gestured at the mobile number. 'Well, allow me to enlighten you then. It's the tower that proves this mobile telephone was in the vicinity of your home seven days ago. Do you know whose number that is?'

Poe folded his arms and waited.

Wardle smirked at Poe's continued silence. 'That, my smug friend, is the phone victim support gave to Elizabeth Keaton.'

And all of a sudden things became crystal clear.

Although he'd been expecting something, the audacity of what Keaton was planning still hit him like a body blow. His gut tightened and his spine stiffened.

Wardle smiled, enjoying his first success.

Poe didn't care. He knew what was happening now and Wardle wasn't part of it. Time for a bit of offence. Demonstrate that he wasn't going to bend over and take whatever was coming.

'I notice you didn't say triangulate,' Poe said.

'Excuse me?'

'You said the mobile "was in the vicinity" of Herdwick Croft seven days ago. Why didn't you say triangulate?'

Wardle shifted in his seat.

'I'll tell you why,' Poe said. 'It's because you need at least three masts to triangulate a location, more if you want to get it down to a few yards, and I happen to know that where I live there's just the one. It covers a massive area. So when you say "vicinity", what you really mean is that the phone was in a seven-mile radius of the mast.'

Wardle said nothing.

'Now, I'm no Matilda Bradshaw but even I know the area of a circle is the radius squared multiplied by pi. Seven times seven is forty-nine. I'm not sure what pi is but we'll round down to three. Have either of you got a calculator?'

'One hundred and forty-seven,' Rigg said.

Wardle glared at his colleague.

Rigg shrugged. 'He's right, boss.'

'So let me get this right,' Poe said. 'This phone pings in the same one hundred and forty-seven square-mile area that I live in, and you think you've proved something? Good police work, Wardle. Did they teach you that on your accelerated promotion course? Do you want to cuff me, or shall I do it myself?' Poe held out his hands, wrist up.

The look of anger on Wardle's face was priceless, but ultimately hollow. Elizabeth Keaton had disappeared seven days ago and the police were now looking in his direction for an answer.

And Poe knew the cell site analysis report would only be the start. Keaton was planning to have him charged with the no-body murder of his daughter.

And he couldn't think of a way to stop him.

Wardle began detailing the last known movements of Elizabeth Keaton. He'd learned from his earlier mistake and didn't let Poe near the document from which he read. Poe tried to concentrate. He needed to remember this.

It was as Rigg had said on the way back from HMP Durham. Elizabeth had reported for the required police interviews, then she'd disappeared. They didn't know where she was and they didn't know where she'd been. The last time her phone had pinged a cell tower was when it had been near Herdwick Croft. It had then either been switched off or destroyed.

'Can you tell me where you were that night, Poe?'

Poe was in trouble. It was the night he'd arrived in Cumbria – the night he'd stayed at the North Lakes Hotel and Spa. He'd had a drink in the bar and then gone to bed. No one had seen him until the morning. To an unimaginative mind it might sound like he'd been preparing an alibi. Being away from home with no apparent reason was the type of thing that pushed a jury beyond the reasonable doubt threshold.

That's how the prosecuting barrister would present it anyway.

The net was closing. His time was about to become very limited. He couldn't afford to waste it on things outside his control. He needed to get back to Herdwick Croft and start investigating the missing tattoo.

Without another word, Poe left the room.

CHAPTER FORTY-TWO

In an ideal world Poe would have headed back to Herdwick Croft and hit Elizabeth Keaton's video interviews immediately. He needed to be ready if Flick Jakeman confirmed his burgeoning suspicions.

But Poe had a job to do first.

Victoria Hume.

The case was throwing up strange bedfellows: Jared Keaton's connection to his dad, and Thomas Hume's connection to Bullace & Sloe. While his dad's connection could wait, Victoria's could not. If she was involved, he needed to know now.

They agreed that Bradshaw would wait at Herdwick Croft while Poe travelled on to Hume's farm. They were five hundred yards away when she tapped him on the shoulder. Poe brought the quad to a halt. Edgar jumped off and began casting for scent. Before long a small game bird squawked and took to the air.

Poe turned in his seat. 'What's up, Tilly?'

She pointed at Herdwick Croft. 'Someone's waiting for you, Poe.'

He squinted in the sun but could only just make out a shape. He reached into the quad's side container and lifted his binoculars to his eyes.

What the hell . . . ?

It was Victoria Hume.

Bold as brass, sitting at the same table they'd been working at yesterday. She'd even rearranged his paperweight stones.

She'd come to see him.

But why?

Despite the heat and humidity Victoria was wearing jeans and a scratchy cardigan. She wore no make-up and her hair was pulled back into a harsh ponytail. She'd driven to Herdwick Croft on one of her father's quads.

Poe jumped off his own.

'Mrs Hume, what can I help you with?'

His tone seemed to startle her.

She stumbled on her first words. 'It's Miss actually. Victoria if you want. I – I wanted to apologise for my earlier rudeness. It was—'

'What do you want? What's your connection to Keaton?' Things were too serious to faff about.

'Keaton . . . ?' she replied, a confused look on her face. 'You don't mean . . . you don't mean that chef who killed his daughter?'

He held her gaze. 'What's your connection?' he repeated.

Her confusion changed to anger.

'What the hell are you talking about?' she snapped. 'I have no connection to—'

'Your father, *Miss* Hume, was Bullace & Sloe's sole supplier of lamb.'

'I don't have the first clue what Bullace & Sloe is, you stupid man!'

Poe snorted. 'Really? You haven't heard of Cumbria's only three-star restaurant? I find that hard to believe.'

Hume balled her fists and crossed her arms tightly. Through clenched teeth she said, 'I don't bloody care what you do or don't believe. But in case you're interested, I've lived in Devon for the last twelve years.'

Poe remained tight-lipped.

'Oh, you arrogant man!' she yelled. 'I have no idea if he

241

supplied this Bullace & Sloe, but I will say this: my father was Cumbria's premier breeder of Herdwicks. If you say he supplied this place, then yes, he probably did. He had a deal with the abattoir and supplied restaurants and butchers direct. He bred over a thousand lambs a year and sold every single one of them. I'd be surprised if there was a restaurant in Cumbria he hadn't supplied!'

Poe faltered. He didn't think she was lying, and if what she said about her father was true then the Bullace & Sloe connection could have been nothing more than a coincidence. Yet . . . there was definitely something she wasn't telling him.

'If you're not connected to Jared Keaton, then what are you doing here?'

Her face crumpled and she began to sob. Bradshaw handed him a paper handkerchief. He passed it across but Victoria let it fall to the ground. The breeze sent it swirling through the air. Edgar assumed it was the start of a game and chased it, yelping in excitement.

'Why don't you tell me why you're here?' Poe said, gentler this time.

When she looked up, the grief was gone. Her eyes were narrow and hard. 'Fuck you.'

Without a backwards glance she got on her quad and left.

The moor descended into silence. The only noise was Victoria's revving engine and the plinking of his own as it cooled.

Poe turned to Bradshaw. 'That went well.'

She nodded.

Edgar returned. He had the tissue in his mouth. He growled when Poe tried to take it off him. Poe gave up.

'Come on, let's have a look at these interviews,' he said.

Before they could move inside, Poe's phone rang. It was an unrecognised number but the area code was 01229: Barrow-in-Furness and Ulverston. Almost certainly the FME, Flick Jakeman.

It was. He put her on speakerphone.

'Sergeant Poe,' she said without preamble, 'I've been through my notes twice and I didn't write down anything about a tattoo.'

'It would have been on or above her hip,' he said.

'Definitely not then. I gave Elizabeth's genital area a thorough examination. I'd have noticed anything on her hip.'

Poe thanked Flick and hung up.

'Why would Jefferson Black say Elizabeth has a tattoo when she doesn't, Poe?' Bradshaw asked. 'Do you think he was lying? Gosh, I hope he wasn't.'

Poe paused. 'No, Tilly, I don't think Jefferson was lying.'

'Then what does it mean?'

'It means we need to look at those videos.'

CHAPTER FORTY-THREE

The Elizabeth Keaton interviews were all accessible via a link that Gamble had provided when they became officially involved. Bradshaw set them up and they settled in front of a monitor. She pressed play and Elizabeth Keaton appeared on the screen.

The last time Poe had seen these, he'd been intently listening to what Elizabeth was saying. How she'd been attacked in the Bullace & Sloe kitchen. How she'd been bundled into a van and taken to a cellar somewhere. He'd listened as she'd described her escape.

He'd made countless notes. None of it was contradictory, all of it was plausible.

This time, however, he wasn't interested in what she said. He muted the sound and watched what she *did*.

By the time they'd watched the final tape he knew he was right.

The whole thing was extraordinary. Endlessly complex but utterly simple. Breathtaking.

He asked Bradshaw if she were able to set up a videoconference where Flynn could see on her computer what they could see on theirs.

She snorted. 'I could do that when I was eight, Poe.'

Flynn was in the conference room in Hampshire. Director of Intelligence van Zyl had joined her. They'd opened up a video-conference screen and were also watching a mirrored computer.

Whatever Poe and Bradshaw did at Herdwick Croft, Flynn and van Zyl would see at their end.

Poe had explained to Bradshaw how he wanted everything shown. As soon as she gave him the nod, he began his briefing.

He explained in the order that made the most sense to him.

Bradshaw loaded the video of Elizabeth Keaton walking into Alston Library.

'She wore leggings, a woollen hat and a long-sleeved T-shirt,' he said, pointing at the screen. Bradshaw moved the cursor to where his finger was aimed. She had enlarged the area so it could easily be seen on the mirrored screen down south.

He then showed camera stills and photographs of Problem Solver Alsop's pocketbook. Poe had spoken to him an hour earlier and he'd been happy to help.

'It was a hot day and she'd been trapped in a cellar for six years, and for the best part of a week she'd probably been without food or water,' Poe said. 'Yet when she was offered a drink she refused it. Didn't even touch it.'

Neither Flynn nor van Zyl asked anything.

Next he brought up the interviews that Rigg had conducted with Elizabeth Keaton. 'I don't expect you to sit through all four recordings, but you can take it from me and Tilly that at no point does she touch anything in these either. Not her drink. Not the Mars Bar that was brought in for her. She doesn't even push them away, just leaves them where they are.'

Flynn and van Zyl shared a quick glance but kept their counsel.

'And it's hot in there. If you look at the glass of water in front of her you can see the condensation running down the sides. But . . .' – he pointed at the screen and waited for Bradshaw to aim the cursor – 'look at what she's wearing: a baseball cap, hoodie and jeans. She must have been close to passing out.'

He let that sink in for a moment.

'We're going back in time now,' Poe said. 'Six years back in time. Tilly, can you tell the boss and Director of Intelligence van Zyl what you found on Elizabeth's social media pages?'

Bradshaw talked for fifteen minutes about how she'd built up a profile of Elizabeth, and how she'd managed to infiltrate her online social circle. She then gave them a Bradshaw-style briefing on the social media habits of young girls. After ten minutes Poe stopped her.

'What Tilly is saying is that young girls who are active on social media rarely become inactive. And what we have found is that from the night Jared Keaton reported her missing there has been nothing from her on social media. Nothing. She hasn't logged on to any of her accounts and she hasn't commented on, or even looked at, her friends'. She hasn't sent or read any emails, and she hasn't made any phone calls. None of her friends reported any contact with her and neither did her boyfriend.'

'You realise this undermines the theory that she faked her abduction, Poe?' van Zyl said. 'Miss Bradshaw's right. I have two teenage girls and I'll tell you this: if they were playing hide and seek for six years there's no way they'd stay away from their social media accounts.'

'I no longer believe she faked her abduction, sir,' Poe replied. 'But please bear with me a while longer. Let me take you back even further.'

Bradshaw brought up the before and after photographs taken from Facebook and Twitter. The ones with Elizabeth wearing bikinis and crop tops, and the ones where she'd begun to dress more conservatively. Poe talked them through the date they had for the change, and the explanation Jefferson Black had given them.

'She had a tattoo,' Poe said simply, 'and she kept it covered up in all her photographs.'

Van Zyl was frowning. 'I'm not seeing what you're seeing, Poe. I'm not happy my daughters wear make-up; I'd hit the bloody roof if either of them got a tattoo.'

Poe nodded. 'Couldn't agree more, sir. Elizabeth and Jefferson Black got matching tattoos and, fearing a reaction like you've just described, she hid hers from her father.'

'So . . . ?'

Poe leaned back and rolled his neck. 'This case has been a nightmare from the beginning. We've not stopped chasing our tails. I confirmed that the blood sample's chain of custody hadn't been tampered with, which supported Elizabeth's explanation of where she'd been for six years. Everyone accepted that at face value. Then we found traces of truffle in her blood. That suggested she'd actually faked her abduction. But which version of events was true? Had she been abducted or was she part of something far more insidious?'

'And you know now, I take it?'

Poe nodded. 'When Jefferson Black told Tilly and me about the tattoo, everything changed. We had all the answers, but the reason they weren't making sense was that we were asking the wrong questions.'

He wasn't kidding. He'd never had so much evidence all pointing the same way before. It was only when he viewed everything like a Rorschach test – turning it this way and that, looking at it all with a new perspective – that he finally figured out what was happening.

'There are two questions that count, sir,' Poe continued. 'One I can answer now, the other I can't.'

'Start with the one you *can* answer, Poe,' van Zyl instructed. He leaned in to the camera so much that he blocked out Flynn.

'Certainly, sir. My question is this: why didn't the FME see Elizabeth's tattoo when she conducted her examination?'

Both rooms descended into silence.

'Why, Poe?' Bradshaw asked eventually. 'Why didn't Doctor Jakeman see her tattoo?'

Flynn cleared her throat and said, 'She didn't see a tattoo, because Jared Keaton didn't know Elizabeth *had* a tattoo.'

'I don't understa—'

'Elizabeth's dead, Tilly. Jared Keaton murdered her six years ago. The girl on the screen is an imposter.'

CHAPTER FORTY-FOUR

'She didn't touch or drink anything during the interviews to avoid DNA or fingerprint transfer,' Poe explained.

'And she wore long clothes and a hat so she didn't leave any hair or skin behind,' Flynn added.

'Obviously she couldn't go and see anyone who had really known Elizabeth, which was why she didn't go back to Bullace & Sloe. She simply appeared at Alston Library, did what she wanted to do at the police station, then disappeared again.'

'That explains why she didn't contact anyone on social media,' Bradshaw said. 'It was because she's . . . oh golly, that's awful, Poe.'

Van Zyl had left the room. He'd received a text message and wanted to make a call. Flynn stayed behind to coordinate what needed to happen next. They didn't have enough proof to stop Keaton's release.

'Theories, Poe?'

'Several, boss. None that work all the way through, though. They all stop at the blood.'

It was the one thing that still didn't make sense. The blood *was* Elizabeth Keaton's, and yet it couldn't be. Every single person he'd spoken to, and all the research he'd done, told him that one person simply couldn't have someone else's blood in their body. Scientifically it was impossible. And he'd personally tested every link in the blood's chain of custody. It hadn't been swapped.

For the first time in his life Poe understood 'doublethink', the phrase first coined in one of his favourite books: George Orwell's *Nineteen Eighty-Four*. It meant holding two contradictory opinions but believing both. Elizabeth Keaton was alive – the blood proved it; yet Elizabeth Keaton was also dead – he was sure of it.

'We have to find out who this imposter is,' Flynn said. 'If we find her then everything else, including the unexplainable blood, becomes moot.'

It would also put a stop to the 'Elizabeth disappeared again while at Herdwick Croft' trail of breadcrumbs that Wardle seemed determined to follow.

Flynn continued, 'We have to assume Keaton's behind all this, and that means his elevated mood in prison becomes even more important. I'll look into the period between the last time we know he was depressed and the first time we know he was all giddy. Keaton's met this girl somehow and, now we know what we're looking for, it could be that we've missed something. A visitor who wasn't logged properly, something like that.'

'Or the daughter of a con. He could have met her while she visited someone else,' Poe suggested.

Flynn nodded but didn't make a note. Poe knew she'd already reached the same conclusion.

Van Zyl re-entered the room. His face was grim. 'That was Superintendent Gamble. He's been put on gardening leave and he thinks it'll move into forced retirement. He was due to finish at the end of the year anyway. DCI Wardle's been promoted to an Acting Super role and is now in charge of investigating Elizabeth Keaton's abduction, reappearance and disappearance. He thought we ought to know.'

'Does he know why he's been forced out?' Flynn asked.

'He can't be sure, but he was getting pressure to bring Poe in on a more formal basis. Maybe arrest him. I called the chief constable but she's keeping things close to her chest. And although they realise the cell tower intel is weak, and circumstantial at best, I've been asked to ensure that I know where you are at all times, Poe.'

Bollocks. They were already on a tight schedule and there was no way Wardle would accept there was an Elizabeth Keaton lookalike out there pulling his strings.

'That's not all, I'm afraid,' van Zyl went on. 'The request for SCAS involvement has formally been rescinded. We are no longer involved in the case.'

That actually didn't matter as much. Wardle was looking for the body of the girl he knew as Elizabeth Keaton. At some point Keaton would arrange for more manufactured evidence that pointed Poe's way. He'd eventually get permission to arrest him. Meanwhile, Poe would be looking for the girl he knew *wasn't* Elizabeth Keaton so he could disprove everything Wardle was being drip-fed. It was probably for the best that they weren't swapping notes any more.

Bradshaw had been quiet. There was nothing obvious for her to do. The search for the girl had to start with Flynn. Keaton's plan had been conceived in a prison cell and it was there that the answers would be found.

'What can I do to help, Poe?' she asked.

'The blood, Tilly. I can't explain the blood. Everyone says it can't be altered.'

Bradshaw's stare was even more intense than usual.

'Find out how they did it, Tilly. Prove the experts wrong and find out how this girl had Elizabeth Keaton's blood in her system. Do that, and I promise I'll start eating fruit.'

Her jaw hardened. A look came over her face that he hadn't seen for a while. He recognised it for what it was. Everything she'd done so far had been comfortably within her limits. Almost routine. Finding the connection between the Keatons and his own father, hacking the social media accounts of teenage girls – none of this was difficult for her.

But . . . finding out how someone can be both alive and dead at the same time . . . well, that was different. That was a real challenge.

Day 12

CHAPTER FORTY-FIVE

Although he lived in one of the wettest places in the UK, Poe was no pluviophile: he didn't find joy and peace of mind in the rain. But he was Cumbrian and that meant wet weather bothered him about as much as it did ducks. Skin was waterproof and clothes dried.

The morning after the videoconference began with the pitter-patter of rain against his slate roof, and progressed all the way up to the rat-a-tat-tat of a downpour. It wasn't the destructive weather that had been promised but it sounded like the meteorologists were getting this one right. He turned on his radio and found that the Met Office had issued a red, severe weather warning for Dumfries & Galloway, Cumbria and Lancashire. In the next forty-eight hours they expected localised flooding and disruption to power networks. The red warning meant action was required to keep yourself and others safe. Poe paid it scant attention. Herdwick Croft had been on Shap Fell long before the Met Office existed, and it would be there long after the quango had fallen to austerity cuts.

He opened the door to see fast-moving clouds. They were low, dark and swollen. It was probably time to shutter up and hunker down for the day. There was nothing case-related for him to do anyway. Everything that could be done was being done. Flynn was searching prison records to see if Keaton had met the girl there, and Bradshaw had been up all night researching blood anomalies. She'd called him after midnight to say she hadn't found anything.

'Negative results aren't failure, though, Poe. It's scientific discovery, and that means I've already been able to prove thirteen ways it can't be done.'

That sounded like failure to him but what did he know? She'd been attracting research grants in her teens and he'd once set fire to his own hand during a chemistry lesson.

He didn't want to sit around doing nothing, though. Bad weather or not, he needed to keep moving. He put on a thick waterproof jacket and stepped outside. It was like standing under a power-shower. He put his hand out and watched as it dissolved into the rain. The parched earth soaked up the water like a sponge. The stunted grass was already getting its green tinge back. No doubt the Herdwicks would soon be up to nibble on the fresh shoots. He whistled for Edgar. The dog was sodden. He was wagging his tail and whining in excitement; Edgar loved the rain. Poe mounted the quad and Edgar jumped on behind him.

Despite visibility being down to a few yards, Poe got to Shap Wells in short order. He and Edgar jumped in the hire car and headed towards Kendal.

There was something he needed to do today.

The last time Poe had been to Parkside Cemetery he'd discovered another victim of a serial killer. Today it was where Thomas Hume was being interred. Despite the suspicions he had about his daughter, he wanted to say goodbye to the old man. He'd been good to Poe, always ready to lend a hand or offer advice, always happy to take Edgar.

The graveside service had already started when Poe arrived. He stood at the back and paid his respects. He saw Victoria Hume. She was dressed in a black trouser suit and was standing beside two similar-looking women. The other Hume sisters, no doubt.

As the vicar committed Thomas's body into the ground, Victoria glanced up and caught Poe looking. She stiffened but rallied. Instead of sending him a filthy look she clenched and unclenched her fist three times then raised her hand to her mouth in the universal sign language for drinking. She wanted to meet him in fifteen minutes for a drink.

Interesting . . .

Poe pointed at the nearby Bluebell Inn and she nodded. She then went back to burying her father. Poe waited until the first sodden clumps of earth landed against the bare wood of the coffin then left for the pub.

It was closer to forty-five minutes before she turned up. Poe had thought quarter of an hour had been optimistic – there would have been people she had to see after the service had ended – so he'd factored in more time anyway. He met her at the bar and offered to buy her a drink.

'Gin and slim, please,' she said.

Poe ordered her a double and got himself a pint. They carried their drinks back to his table. Victoria took a sip and thanked him. Her hands were shaking.

'Look, I want—' he tried to say.

'I'm sorry—'

Poe let her speak first. He got the feeling she had something to tell him.

'My dad was a good man, Mr Poe,' she said. 'He was a great farmer and an even better father. But . . . he wasn't a very good businessman.'

Few farmers are, Poe thought. And with EU subsidies about to disappear it was only going to get worse. That's why the government was constantly encouraging them to diversify. He'd assumed that Hume had been doing OK, though. Thousands of sheep and few overheads – compared to cattle, with which farmers were lucky to realise 30 per cent profit, sheep brought in close to 100.

'And he found himself in terrible debt,' Victoria continued. 'When I last visited him he told me something terrible. Something that involved you.'

Poe braced himself for bad news.

'Can I ask you something?' she asked.

'Of course.'

'Did you ever receive a council tax demand?'

Poe frowned. He hadn't. Thomas Hume had sold him Herdwick Croft as the council had decided that because it had been a dwelling a hundred years ago, it was still a dwelling now. The fact it was uninhabitable was irrelevant. Poe had taken it off his hands, and the surrounding land, at a price with which they were both happy. He'd spent money making it comfortable and self-sustaining, but he'd never received a council tax bill. It wasn't as if they didn't know he was there as he received the forms to vote in local elections and suchlike.

He confirmed he hadn't. 'I'll get stung for arrears one day no doubt.'

Victoria sighed and shook her head. 'No, Mr Poe, you won't.'

Poe swallowed.

'Did you know Herdwick Croft is now in the southern extension to the Lake District National Park boundary line?'

Poe didn't. For commercial reasons, the National Park boundary had been drawn to specifically exclude the Kendal area. He said as much.

'It's been extended and Herdwick Croft now falls into it,' she said. She looked distraught. 'Dad lied when he told you he'd received a council tax demand, Mr Poe. A couple of years ago he needed to raise some capital so he applied through the council's planning portal for a change of use for the croft. Pre-approved planning permission would make it far easier to sell. The response he got was "Developing Shap and the surrounding area wasn't in the council's current business plan". If he'd applied before the National Park was extended he'd have been fine.'

'So . . . ?' Poe had a horrible feeling in his stomach.

'So, he did an awful thing, Mr Poe. While he was at the council complaining about their decision, he bumped into you and told you a tale. He tricked you into buying the land. You *can* apply for retrospective planning permission, of course. I'll even write a letter of support explaining my father's actions, but now the National Park has been awarded UNESCO World Heritage Status the chances of you being successful are less than zero.'

Poe's stomach lurched. During all the turmoil he'd been through the last eighteen months, Herdwick Croft had been the one constant in his life. He'd made it into a home that he never wanted to leave. He'd eschewed modern comforts, embraced the simpler life and, despite what had happened with his mother, he'd found a semblance of peace.

And now Victoria was telling him it had all been a fantasy. Buildings like Herdwick Croft weren't there for the likes of him. They were there for the tourists. If it didn't 'preserve the character of the area' – which basically meant keeping everything looking like it had in Beatrix Potter's time – it was no longer required.

'What will happen next?'

'Herdwick Croft and the land belong to you,' she said. 'That won't change. You bought it legally.'

'But . . . ?'

'But at some point the council will instruct you to restore it to the condition it was in before you modernised it. You won't be able to live there.'

'And this is why you've been evasive around me?'

She nodded again. 'I thought you must have found out, that someone from planning had already been to see you. I knew I'd have to speak to you one day but Dad had just died and I wasn't ready.'

'So you really don't have anything to do with Bullace & Sloe?'

'I don't know what it is you're working on, Mr Poe, but I can assure you I don't have anything to do with it.'

Poe breathed in and focused on one of his most annoying sayings. The one he used to bend reluctant staff to his will. It seemed apt now, though. *Don't let the urgent get in the way of the important . . .*

As desperate as his housing situation had just become, Herdwick Croft would have to wait. The unfortunate news may even have presented an opportunity. Over the next few days, as Keaton's net closed around him, he would need to be flexible. The damp and smelly dog in his hire car, barking at anyone who fancied a lunchtime drink, was going to become a liability. Offloading Edgar for a few days would be one less thing to worry about.

He asked Victoria if she'd mind and she breathed out in relief. 'I'd be happy to, Mr Poe.'

'Please, call me Washington. Everyone does.'

They finished their drinks in a congenial silence. Neither of them could stay long: Victoria had a wake to get to and Poe needed to get back and see if Bradshaw had found anything. They said their goodbyes in the car park. Poe transferred Edgar to Victoria's smaller car and promised to collect him as soon as he could.

On the way to Shap Wells he stopped off at the post office and bought some insurance: a book of stamps and a padded envelope. He hoped he wouldn't need them.

When he got back to the hotel there was a car in his usual spot.

A BMW X1.

His car.

Which had still been in Hampshire yesterday.

That meant only one thing.

Stephanie Flynn was here.

CHAPTER FORTY-SIX

Flynn and Bradshaw were in the green room; a plush bar area with tall seats covered in dark green leather. The bar was rarely staffed so was usually quiet. Bradshaw didn't like using it as the Wi-Fi wasn't very good there. They were watching a video and Poe could tell it wasn't being streamed – there was a memory stick in the side of Bradshaw's laptop. Flynn must have brought it up.

Both of them looked up. Flynn stood and smiled. 'Poe,' she said.

She still looked exhausted but her black mood seemed to have lifted. As neither of them had ever been part of the 'contact culture', Poe was so surprised when she gave him a quick hug that he left his arms dangling.

'Wanker,' she said, punching his arm.

'Feeling better, then?'

She nodded but didn't elaborate.

'Thanks for bringing my car back.'

She threw him his keys. 'I wanted to come earlier but . . . there was something I needed to take care of in Hampshire. Something time-sensitive. Tilly's brought me up to speed on everything.'

He and Flynn weren't just boss and subordinate – they were mates. He should take the time to find out what had happened to make her so coffin-faced. He'd known her a long time and she didn't succumb to stress easily.

But he needed to see what she'd brought up first. He nodded towards the laptop. 'Found anything?'

'Nothing really,' she admitted. 'I've been through his prison records in the time period Crawford Bunney gave you, and there's no obvious reason for Keaton's mood to have been elevated.'

Poe leaned in and watched the screen for a moment.

'So, what's that?' He could see it was paused footage of a prison-wing's CCTV. It was clear and in colour. Poe assumed it was from a period of association as half the wing looked to be out of their cells. Two prisoners played pool. The rest stood and talked and smoked.

'Do you remember the riot they had in Pentonville a couple of years ago?' Flynn asked.

Poe did. Vaguely. It had made the national news and, because prisoners had managed to get to the roof, there was live footage for viewers to watch. It was a bit of a media event for a few hours. Eventually a 'Tornado' squad – trained guards with specialist equipment – had assembled from around the region and retaken the prison in an hour.

'This is the wing Keaton was on at the time,' Flynn said. 'The riot happened in a different part of the prison, but' – she leaned across Bradshaw and clicked play – 'watch what happens here.'

Poe stared at the screen. The camera showed the long view of the wing. Everyone was in shot and no one was close enough to be identified. That wasn't what she wanted to show him, though.

There was no sound so Poe could only guess what happened next. As one, all the prisoners turned and looked in the same direction. A period of confusion followed. Some prisoners began to look uneasy, others looked excited. Most of them made their way back to their cells. A few stood and waited.

'That was the warning to get back to their cells,' Flynn explained. 'And because it came during their free time, the more experienced cons knew something had happened.'

Poe watched as prison officers rushed on to the wing and began locking up the stragglers. Eventually the wing was secure and the prison officers left, presumably to go to where the trouble was. He frowned. He didn't see how a riot in a different part of the prison was relevant.

Flynn saw his confusion. She shrugged. 'You asked for anomalies. That's it. That's the only one.'

'And where's Keaton during all this?'

Bradshaw did something to the laptop. The footage zoomed in until they could see Keaton. He was standing on his own. Even through the medium of prison CCTV, Poe could tell he was miserable. His head drooped like a month-old daffodil. When the announcement to get back in their cells was made, he looked to be in the group of prisoners who were scared. He looked around wildly. He tried to walk in the direction of what was presumably his cell, but a rush of other prisoners pushed him against the wall. By the time he was free, the guards were on the wing and he was shoved into the cell he was standing next to.

'Whose cell is that, Tilly?'

Bradshaw zoomed in on the ID above the door: B2 – 42. She then cross-referenced it with a list she brought up.

'That's a single cell belonging to someone called Richard Bloxwich, Poe. Jared Keaton's is B2 – 14. He's in a shared cell.'

'We have anything on Bloxwich?'

She shook her head but her fingers blurred over the keyboard. Her brow furrowed. 'Strange . . . there's nothing in the media about him.'

'Reporting restrictions?'

She half nodded, half shrugged. 'Maybe. We can access his prison records, though.' She printed a document and passed it over. It was the summary sheet. Poe handed it to Flynn without looking at it. Now she was here he was no longer in charge.

She read it out. 'Richard Bloxwich. Sentenced to seven years for false accounting practices.'

'What the hell's that?' Poe asked. 'Is he a bent accountant?'

Flynn looked over his shoulder. Without warning she forced the document into the back of her jeans. 'Kill the computer, Tilly.'

Bradshaw pressed something and the screen went black.

Poe turned.

A posse of uniformed and plainclothed police officers were gathered in the hotel lobby. One of them peered into the green room and shouted, 'Found them, sir.'

Wardle marched in. He held a piece of paper in the air like it was the Olympic torch.

'Washington Poe,' he said, with a triumphant grin, 'I have a warrant here to search your vehicle and your home.'

CHAPTER FORTY-SEVEN

'Poe, you do know you gave him the keys to your BMW?' Bradshaw said. 'DCI Wardle probably wanted the keys to the car you've been using up here.'

'Oopsy.'

'Oh,' she said, suppressing a smile. 'You gave him the wrong ones on purpose.'

'That doesn't really sound like something I'd do, Tilly.' It was a small victory but an important one. If anything was found in the BMW, they could prove it had been planted. Poe didn't think for a second that Wardle was bent but Keaton had had years to plan this. Who knew what his next move would be?

It also meant Poe still had a vehicle to get around in.

Flynn had accompanied Wardle to Herdwick Croft to ensure nothing went on that shouldn't. She didn't trust Poe to come with her.

'Tilly, can you do me a favour?'

'Of course.'

That was typical of her. She didn't even know what she was saying yes to.

He handed over some money. 'Can you go and buy three unregistered pay-as-you-go phones?'

'Burners?'

'Yep. I think we're entering the end game now and I need to be able to communicate for as long as possible.'

'Where shall I get them from, Poe?'

Poe considered it for a moment. It needed to be somewhere too small to have saturation CCTV coverage but big enough to have a shop that sold mobile phones. And she needed to be able to get there via a route that wouldn't trigger too many Automatic Number Plate Recognition cameras.

'Sedbergh,' he said eventually. 'It's not far from here and if you stay off the M6 you'll miss most of the ANPR cameras.'

'Shall I go now?'

'Please, Tilly,' he replied. He had no idea what, if anything, Wardle would find at Herdwick Croft, but the fact they were searching meant things were drawing in.

'And use that map of yours, not a satnav,' he added. Satnav destinations could be recovered and he wanted to conceal her movements for as long as he could. Eventually they'd find the shop and get the numbers of the burner phones but there was no point giving them clues. In the meantime, he opened his shopping bag and removed the padded envelope and book of stamps he'd bought earlier. He left his BlackBerry switched on and placed it inside. He loaded it with more stamps than needed, then addressed it to a house on Stornoway in the Outer Hebrides. Poe knew it was unoccupied as it belonged to a woman in the NCA who used it as a holiday home.

Poe wasn't sure how the mail network operated at the top of Scotland but he doubted it was speedy. If Wardle tracked him via his mobile it would look as though he was heading north. It might buy him a few more hours.

He had the feeling time was about to become very precious.

With everyone busy, and with Flynn not wanting him at Herdwick Croft, he settled down to watch the video again. This time he was looking for Richard Bloxwich. He hadn't seen him on the earlier loop so assumed he hadn't left his cell for association. For the duration of the emergency, he and Keaton must have had to share.

Poe watched the part of the video he was interested in again but Flynn was right: nothing stood out. He was about to press rewind and have another look when Wardle entered the green room. He didn't look happy.

'Where's your dog, Poe?' he snapped.

'What dog?'

'This fucking dog!' Wardle shouted, holding Poe's only photograph of Edgar.

Poe smiled politely. 'Is that all you have, Wardle? A frame I haven't yet got round to removing the stock photograph from?'

'You're in it as well, man!'

Poe made a point of looking at what he was holding. 'Nope. Looks nothing like me.' He leaned back and smiled. He didn't want Wardle knowing where Edgar was. Victoria had enough on her plate without a visit from this buffoon.

'Actually, Poe, it's not all I have.'

Poe gave him a withering glance. 'Do tell.'

'Your trailer. It's wet. Looks like it's been cleaned recently.'

Poe stood. Wardle took a step back.

'You see those big grey *cloudy* things in the sky, Wardle?' Poe pointed towards the window. 'It's been pissing down all night and all morning. Did you see a double-garage at Herdwick Croft? No? That's because my trailer's kept outside. Of course it's fucking wet!'

'We'll see about that,' Wardle said stiffly. 'You've heard about my promotion?'

'It's literally all no one's talking about.'

Behind Wardle's back, Rigg stifled a grin.

'My rise through the ranks may have been meteoric, Poe,' Wardle said, 'but don't for one second think I don't know what I'm doing. If there's anything at that place you call home that connects you to Elizabeth's disappearance then you'll spend the rest of your life in prison.'

Poe yawned and stretched his arms. 'Asteroids rise, Wardle, not meteors. Meteors enter our atmosphere then crash to earth in a fiery ball. Foreshadowing perhaps?' As far as he could remember, that was the first time he'd ever used some of Bradshaw's trivia.

Wardle inflated like a pufferfish. A vein throbbed on his rapidly reddening forehead.

'Just be contactable at all times, Poe. I might call you in again.'

'I'll run all the way.'

'Arsehole,' Wardle muttered, as he stalked out of the bar.

Rigg, who'd been hovering, stayed behind. He didn't look happy.

'Is there anything you want to tell me, Sergeant Poe?' It wasn't an aggressive question. He seemed to be offering an olive branch. Well, that was too bad. Wardle had an agenda: securing his promotion. Anyone working with him couldn't be trusted.

'No, there isn't. Now, run along.'

Rigg didn't move. He had the grace to look embarrassed. Poe relented. Slightly.

'I'll tell you what, DC Rigg. If you want to get in the game, start by asking yourself why the girl you interviewed didn't have a tattoo.'

Rigg's eyes narrowed. 'Are you saying she should have?'

'No, I'm saying that instead of being Wardle's lickspittle, you should try being a copper.'

Poe turned back to the laptop. After a while he heard Rigg leave the bar.

He'd forgotten to press pause when Wardle had stormed in and the video had moved on further than he'd watched with Bradshaw and Flynn. The wing's recreation area was empty. The prisoners were still in their cells and the guards were still deployed elsewhere. Out of curiosity, Poe fast-forwarded to see how long they had been locked up for. Presumably they had to be let out to eat at some point, ongoing riot or not.

It was 11.15 a.m. when the alarm had sounded. It was another seven hours before the cells were unlocked. Prisoners gradually emerged and began making their way out of the wing. It must have been time for their evening meal. Poe waited for Keaton and Bloxwich to leave their cell. Keaton stayed where he was until a prison officer walked past. Poe then watched him stick to the guard until he was out of sight of all the cameras.

His earlier despondency had gone. He was smiling.

Poe still hadn't seen Bloxwich yet. He watched the video until the wing emptied and the prison officers secured it. Bloxwich hadn't been in his cell. Mildly curious as to where the missing accountant was, Poe fast-forwarded until the inmates returned. This time Bloxwich was with them. He must have been off the wing when the alarm sounded. He went straight to his cell and shut the door behind him. Keaton returned to his own cell and did the same.

His newfound swagger was still there.

Something had happened in Bloxwich's cell. Poe was sure of it.

He had been alone in it for seven hours.

And when he left it he was smiling.

CHAPTER FORTY-EIGHT

Poe wanted to see if that was the first time Keaton had been in Bloxwich's cell. Luckily the footage on the memory stick wasn't just for the day of the riot. Poe went back a week and checked.

In that period alone it had happened three times, and while the two of them didn't appear to be friends, they did know each other. It seemed they swapped books from time to time.

Poe wandered into the main bar and ordered a pot of coffee. He took it back to his table. This time he went forwards on the video, to the days and weeks after the riot lockdown.

He'd get Bradshaw to check, but just on the visuals alone it was clear that Keaton was going into Bloxwich's cell far more after the riot than before it. There wasn't a reciprocal increase in their social interaction, though. Whereas before, Bloxwich would occasionally drop off a book in Keaton's cell, Keaton's increased visits didn't elicit the same response. He seemed to be forcing himself on Bloxwich.

This happened until Keaton disappeared.

Poe checked his notes and it coincided with the dates he'd been in hospital. Had Bloxwich stabbed Keaton to stop him harassing him? He didn't look the type. Truth be told he looked like a stereotypical accountant. Spectacles, slight frame and a shiny bald spot. He could have paid someone to do it, Poe supposed. It wouldn't have been difficult to get a volunteer. With his boyish looks, haughty arrogance and an eight-figure bank account,

Keaton would have been disliked from the moment he stepped inside. It was probably why he'd tried to spend as much time as he could hiding on the hospital wing.

A quick check with the SCAS office confirmed Bloxwich was still in Pentonville. Poe called Special Visits and arranged for a slot the following afternoon. It would be a long and probably fruitless trip but he didn't have a choice – it was where the case had taken him.

He was deciding the best way to travel south when Flynn walked back into the bar.

'Fucking idiots,' she said as she took a seat beside him.

'Where's Wardle?' he asked.

'Where's Tilly?' she countered.

'Doing a small job for me.'

She glared at him.

Now wasn't the time to be holding things back from his DI. He told her what he'd sent Bradshaw off to buy, and what he was doing with his BlackBerry.

To his surprise she nodded in approval.

'I don't pretend to know what's happening, Poe, but they're doing a full forensic search up there. CSI were swabbing everything and if someone is setting you up, and they've left something that puts Elizabeth Keaton in your croft, there's nothing van Zyl will be able to do to stop them charging you with her abduction.'

'And eventually her murder,' Poe added.

Flynn nodded. 'And eventually her murder.' She stood, a determined look on her face. 'Right, I'm getting some drinks in, and we're not leaving this place until we have something solid to work on.'

'Tell me again why we can't tell DCI Wardle what we've found?' Bradshaw asked.

271

Poe gave her a fond smile. Bradshaw was struggling with the concept that honesty would be counterproductive.

'We have no evidence, Tilly,' he explained. 'From Wardle's perspective – and remember he has no motivation to see it our way, as it would mean Superintendent Gamble being reinstated – it will look as though we're trying to muddy the waters. To begin an early defence should I get charged.'

'An early defence?'

'Another version of events. Juries are far more likely to have reasonable doubt if there's a plausible alternative to the prosecution's story.'

'And because we still can't explain how this girl has Elizabeth Keaton's blood, it's an argument we can't win at the moment,' Flynn added. 'We have conjecture, they have facts.'

Bradshaw looked hurt. Despite her assurances that scientific discovery was simply the process of logging the things that didn't work until you found the thing that did, she'd become despondent. Poe needed her help and so far she'd struggled. She pushed up her glasses, opened her laptop and dived into her work.

Flynn and Poe continued to discuss the case in low voices.

'If we can't explain the blood we only have one play left,' Flynn said.

Poe nodded. 'We need the girl. If we find her, Keaton's plan unravels.'

Even her name didn't help them that much. More trickery, Keaton's team would claim as they waved the DNA profile proving that Elizabeth Keaton had been in that interview room. They needed the girl and they needed her to explain how the blood had been falsified. Anything less than that would be a win for Keaton.

'I'm going to Pentonville tomorrow,' Poe said.

Flynn frowned. 'Why?'

Poe explained what he'd found when the prison CCTV footage had run on. Flynn watched it, then nodded.

'There's definitely a change in his mood,' she agreed. 'Do you want me to come with—'

Her phone cut her off. She showed him the screen. An unrecognised number.

'DI Flynn,' she answered.

Poe could only hear one side of the conversation but it was clear Flynn wasn't happy. She asked permission to put the caller on speakerphone. Poe identified himself. Bradshaw didn't look up from her computer.

'This is Detective Chief Inspector Barbara Stephens,' a tinny voice said. She had a tinge of a Geordie accent. One of those soft ones that Newcastle denizens assumed after they'd been forced to leave their beloved city for any length of time. 'I'm NCA as well. Sergeant Poe, you've booked a prison visit with Richard Bloxwich. Can I ask why you're interested in him?'

'His name's come up in a Cumbrian case.'

'I find that unlikely. Richard has no links up there that I know of.'

'He's had contact with Jared Keaton,' Poe said.

'Ah. The chef who killed his daughter. I heard there was something happening with that. I didn't realise we were involved, though. I assumed it was a local mess to clean up.'

Poe explained where they were up to.

After what seemed like an age, Stephens said, 'While I'm not unsympathetic to your needs, Sergeant Poe, I'm afraid I cannot authorise a visit.'

She told them which part of the NCA she was with. It explained why Bloxwich's case had reporting restrictions. Poe couldn't even claim they had a higher priority – they almost certainly didn't. Every case the NCA worked was big.

Some were huge.

'But if you tell me what you need,' Stephens said, 'I'll go and see him personally. See if there's anything he can help you with.'

Poe's black mood lifted. This was actually a better result. Stephens already had a relationship with Bloxwich so she'd be better placed to find something. Poe told her what they'd seen on the prison CCTV. Stephens said she would get back to them after she'd watched it.

Bradshaw sent her the footage via a compressed file email. They had a nervous thirty-minute wait. As no one was speaking, when Flynn's phone eventually rang, they all jumped. Flynn put it on speakerphone again.

'I agree,' Stephens said. 'It does look as though your target saw something in Bloxwich's cell. It's strange, though, since I know there's no contraband in there.'

'How can you be so sure?' Poe asked. Prisoners were savant-like in their ability to hide things. It was why mobile phones were such a problem.

'Because I am.' Her tone didn't invite discussion.

Poe wondered what he wasn't being told. Stephens had downplayed Bloxwich's importance. Just another crooked accountant, she'd said. Something didn't add up, though. Bent accountants weren't routinely flagged on the prison system. And neither did they get single cells in overcrowded prisons. Perhaps he was part of a bigger fraud case. Perhaps he was *testifying* in a bigger fraud case.

There was no point overthinking it, though. The NCA worked in siloes and with different security clearances. In the grand scheme of things SCAS ranked somewhere near the bottom. Not even van Zyl would know what Stephens's unit was doing.

'I'm meeting my husband, Trevor, in London later on today,' she continued. 'I'll see Richard tonight and get back to you tomorrow.'

'Tonight,' Flynn said. 'None of us are sleeping.'

'Tonight then,' she agreed.

CHAPTER FORTY-NINE

Stephens was as good as her word. It was close to 11 p.m. when she rang but they were still awake. They'd eaten at eight and carried on working.

Bradshaw was getting more and more irate. She'd been given a problem and it didn't look as though she'd be able to solve it. She was muttering like someone who'd lost their car keys.

'I just don't see how it could have been done,' she scowled. 'Even the most advanced synthetic blood wouldn't fool a forensic scientist, Poe.'

Damn. Although everyone had said the same thing, he'd assumed Bradshaw would crack it. Now it seemed she agreed with them. He hadn't really believed the others, but he did believe her.

But he also knew he was right.

Doublethink.

So Stephens's phone call, when it came, was a relief. A time-out from their most singular problem.

'Nothing helpful, I'm afraid. Richard knew Keaton but they weren't friends. They were both readers and, although they had different tastes, the prison library was limited. They shared the books they had.'

'Did he say that Keaton visited him more often after the lockdown?'

'He did. He has no idea why.'

'And there was nothing illegal in his cell that Keaton might have found?'

'Definitely not.'

Another loose end . . .

Unless . . . unless they were looking at this from the wrong angle. They were looking for a girl and Poe knew of one bit of non-contraband that prisoners hid nonetheless.

Family photographs. Sometimes they were hidden away so other prisoners couldn't see them. Especially if they were of children or young women. No one wanted to think of their nearest and dearest being lodged in someone else's wank-bank.

'You've been in his cell?' Poe asked.

'I have.'

'Were his family photos hidden or on display?'

A lengthy pause followed.

'Oh,' she said.

'Exactly,' Poe said.

'And he *does* have a daughter. Chloe. She'll be in her early twenties by now.'

'How long to confirm he has hidden photographs, ma'am?' Flynn said. 'It's incredibly important.'

'It shouldn't take long. His hiding place will be low-tech as he'll need easy access to them.'

Stephens promised she would search as soon as the prison opened the next day. If there was a photograph, she'd send them a copy first thing in the morning. Poe thanked her although he didn't think it would be necessary. Now Bradshaw had a name, she'd find Chloe Bloxwich on social media.

There'd be a few of them but they had an advantage: potentially, they already knew what she looked like. It could have been her who'd been up in Cumbria impersonating a dead girl . . .

* * *

276

While they waited for Bradshaw to do her thing, Poe and Flynn programmed the three burners that she'd bought. They were cheap and nasty and exactly what they needed. If Poe had to disappear, they'd be able to talk without anyone listening in or tracking their location via cell-mast technology.

As she worked, Bradshaw told them what else they needed to do to stay secure.

'We won't leave voicemails and we won't text each other. Both can be retrieved,' she said, without looking away from her screen. 'As they don't know about these phones there is no reason to keep them switched off with the battery removed but . . . if you do get a text, assume one or all of them are compromised. Remove the battery and destroy it.'

'And we speak into this part here?' Poe asked, pointing at the burner's microphone.

'Are you kidding me . . .!' She saw his face. 'Oh, you're teasing me. Ha-de-ha-ha.'

'Behave yourself,' Flynn said, grabbing the phone he was fiddling with as he failed to locate the voicemail function. She disabled anything they wouldn't need and plugged all three into the nearby wall sockets.

'Do you have somewhere you can go if we get the call?' she asked. 'Nothing complicated, Poe. I know from my days tracking down missing sex offenders that simple is best. Somewhere you haven't been before. Stay there. Keep off the roads.'

Poe said nothing. Flynn's 'simple is best' remark had resonated with something Stephens had said: 'low-tech' when she'd described Bloxwich's likely solution for hiding his family photographs.

Low-tech . . .

Every attempt at solving the blood conundrum had been high-tech. All spliced genes and synthetic blood. He'd persisted with the idea but perhaps it was time to listen to the experts

– there *was* no high-tech way of swapping one person's blood for another.

And why should there be?

Keaton had conceived this plan in prison and he was no scientist. He was a cook. Intelligent, yes, but not 'can rewrite the human genome from a prison cell' intelligent.

They should have been looking for a *low*-tech solution.

He was about to give the new search parameters to Bradshaw when she did something unusual. She swore.

'Oh bloody hell.'

Flynn and Poe both leaned in to look at her screen. Bradshaw had been on Facebook and Pinterest but it was on Instagram that she'd found her. Chloe Bloxwich had taken steps to reduce her own online footprint, but she couldn't delete things that others had on their accounts.

It had been taken at night and in a pub. Everyone's eyes were devil-red. A drunken night. It didn't matter. The image was as clear as a passport photograph.

Chloe was front and centre with her arms draped around a boy of about the same age. He was called Ned and it was his account the photograph had been posted on. Underneath was a brief description: 'I f*****g love this girl!'

Poe had spent hours studying the girl who'd walked into Alston Library and he recognised her immediately. There was absolutely no doubt in his mind. Her head was tilted the same way it had been during the police interviews. Even her hair was tucked behind her left ear.

He stared at the laptop – at the girl who was impersonating Elizabeth Keaton.

The girl who was trying to free Jared Keaton and destroy Poe's life in the process.

She looked like an angel.

Day 13

CHAPTER FIFTY

One step forward, two kicks in the gut back. That's how it felt when they were eating breakfast and Flynn got the call they'd been dreading.

It was Gamble. He had tried to call Poe but his phone was switched to silent and inside a padded envelope.

Flynn listened without interruption, her face hardening. Eventually she said, 'Thank you, Ian.'

She ended the call and turned to face Poe and Bradshaw. 'Superintendent Gamble still has friends on the force apparently. CSI found traces of blood in your quad's trailer. They're fast-tracking the DNA but Wardle's going to Kendal Magistrates' Court this morning to apply for a warrant without bail.'

'*Without* bail?' Poe asked. 'That seems unlikely. They'd have to have more than that. Almost everything has blood on it if you look hard enough.'

'Wardle's claiming that efforts had been made to clean it up.'

'It's been raining and I keep it outside! I fucking told him that.'

Flynn held up her hand and Poe's anger fizzled and died. It wasn't her fault. And Wardle was doing exactly what he'd have done: front-loading the warrant to ensure he got what he wanted.

Shit.

He'd been hoping for more time. Cops were usually arrested by appointment. They attended a police station at a specific time, and with their brief. No drama, no fuss and, more importantly, no applying for warrants without bail in a public court where bored court reporters twiddled their collective thumbs hoping for scandal. A WWOB being issued on a cop would hit the internet within the hour, and the front pages of every local rag that afternoon.

Which was of course what Wardle intended.

Poe didn't know who the blood belonged to, and although it was probably Edgar's – the scrappy spaniel was always cutting himself – he couldn't discount it being Elizabeth Keaton's. It had impossibly appeared in the veins of Chloe Bloxwich so he'd be naive to think it couldn't also appear in his trailer.

And he couldn't risk waiting to find out.

Flynn had no choice. Van Zyl had to be told. Bradshaw set up another videoconference.

'What do you have?' he said without preamble.

Flynn told him.

The director lapsed into silence. Poe knew van Zyl had a lot to consider. The NCA were at their most effective when the public and other agencies trusted them. Van Zyl wouldn't throw him under the bus but he'd be limited in what he could do.

'I take it you don't think DCI Wardle will change his mind if you present your findings?' he said finally.

'I don't, sir,' Flynn replied. 'And it might tip our hand if we do anyway. If Keaton finds out we know about Chloe Bloxwich, we'll never locate her.'

Van Zyl stroked his chin. He hadn't had time to shave and the sandpapery sound of day-old stubble came over the speakers.

'And Wardle's going all in on this,' Flynn added. 'He's aiming for Gamble's job and any backpedalling on Poe's involvement will be disastrous for him.'

'And the chief constable has the media camped on her doorstep,' van Zyl said. 'When the news comes out about the warrant without bail she won't be in a position to rescind it. It's probably why Wardle did this so publicly. He's tying the chief constable's fate to his own.'

'Exactly, sir,' Flynn said. 'Wardle might be playing all his cards at once but he does have a strong hand.'

'What would you suggest, DI Flynn? This isn't a scale I feel I can put my thumb on.'

'Officially, we haven't been informed about this, sir. Superintendent Gamble only told us because he believes in Poe's innocence. As far as Wardle is concerned the warrant without bail is still a big secret. I think we just carry on as if we are none the wiser. Because officially we aren't.'

'And you think you can find this girl?'

'I do, sir,' Flynn nodded. 'She's connected to a case one of our other units is working on so there's already intelligence we can mine.'

Van Zyl didn't ask who the other NCA unit was. He clearly knew about DCI Barbara Stephens. Poe wasn't surprised – you didn't get to van Zyl's position by luck.

'What about the blood?' van Zyl asked. 'If you can't find Chloe Bloxwich then we'll have to explain how it was switched.' He faced Bradshaw and said, 'Miss Bradshaw, I understand it is scientifically impossible.'

Bradshaw didn't understand the concept of respecting rank. Not when science was being disputed.

She blew a derisive raspberry. 'Science is more than simply the outcome, Director Edward van Zyl. It's also the endeavour. The discovery is only the end result – science is the process, the theories, the hypotheses.'

Van Zyl didn't answer. The raspberry combined with the scientific gobbledegook would have shut anyone up.

She continued, 'The meta-data *does* suggest that it is scientifically impossible but, as we know, the meta-data doesn't include all the available information.'

'It doesn't?' van Zyl said.

Bradshaw shook her head enthusiastically. 'It doesn't. Because Chloe Bloxwich *did* have Elizabeth Keaton's blood in her; not only is it scientifically possible, it is discoverable. It has to be – it is a fact that it happened. I will find out how it was done, Director Edward van Zyl. I won't let Poe down.'

'Well . . . good then. Keep at it.' Van Zyl had the same bemused look everyone had after they'd been 'Bradshawed'.

Poe smiled and gave her a double thumbs-up. There wasn't anyone else he'd want watching his back at the moment.

Van Zyl came to a decision. 'When I'm officially informed there's a warrant out for DS Poe's arrest the NCA will of course do everything to assist our colleagues in Cumbria. Until then we haven't spoken.'

Flynn nodded.

'And Poe sits this one out, DI Flynn,' van Zyl added. 'You and young Bradshaw need to see this through without him. Poe, your only job is to be wherever DCI Wardle isn't. I know this isn't what you want to hear but it's not the start of a negotiation.'

Poe glowered at the screen.

'That isn't going to be a problem is it, Poe?'

He didn't answer.

Flynn gave the director a tired smile. 'If it is, sir, I'm sure he'll keep it to himself.'

'Ha-fucking-ha, Steph,' Poe muttered.

'Are we in agreement, Poe?' van Zyl asked.

Poe remained silent.

'Poe?' van Zyl pressed.

'We are, sir.'

'Are what?'

'In agreement that I will let DI Flynn and Tilly do their jobs.'

'Good man.'

CHAPTER FIFTY-ONE

Ten minutes later, Poe was on the road. The rain had stopped but the clouds were, if anything, lower. He'd driven his little hire car – the one Wardle didn't know about – to the first post box he knew wasn't covered by CCTV where he posted his packaged-up BlackBerry. He may as well start laying the false trail now. He then U-turned and headed back towards Herdwick Croft. He wasn't going home, though. He needed somewhere local to base himself and he knew someone who owed him a favour . . .

Flynn waited by the side of the road. She wanted reassurance about his new location's seclusion. She also needed to know how to get there in a hurry should the need arise. She was carrying her burner but had left her work mobile with Bradshaw. It felt like they were in a Jason Bourne movie. It would have been fun if it weren't so serious.

Poe passed her and led her down the muddy farm track. He parked and got out. Flynn did the same.

The last time he'd been in the yard there were four cars. Now there were only two: Thomas Hume's Mercedes and a red Ford Focus.

Poe knocked on the door. Flynn stood to his side.

Victoria Hume answered. She looked to be in the middle of cleaning. Her hair was tied in a knot, her sleeves were rolled up and she had yellow rubber gloves on.

'Washington,' she said. 'Have you come for Edgar?'

Flynn turned to Poe with raised eyebrows. 'Washington?'

He shrugged and reddened slightly. Flynn didn't know he'd discovered his name's provenance. As far as she was concerned, he still hated it.

Victoria glanced nervously in Flynn's direction. Poe understood why: her father had wronged him and here he was with a woman in a pinstripe suit who looked every inch a solicitor.

'I need your help,' he said.

After introductions were made, Poe explained that he needed a place to stay that no one knew about. She wouldn't be doing anything illegal and she could ask him to leave at any time.

She waved them inside and brought them into the kitchen. It was large and warmed by an Aga. A garage door-sized oak table dominated the room. A pot of tea was already brewing and she poured three cups.

Victoria asked half a dozen insightful questions, some of which they answered, some of which they couldn't. Poe finished by saying that she shouldn't feel obliged to help if she felt uncomfortable doing so.

'Considering the circumstances, it seems the least I can do,' she said.

Again, Flynn looked at Poe in confusion – she didn't know about his recent housing problems either.

'Thank you,' Flynn said.

'He can stay as long as he likes. He seems a decent sort.'

'Ah well, you haven't known him for long.'

Poe muted his response when Flynn's phone rang. He tensed until he realised it was her burner and therefore had to be Bradshaw.

Flynn listened. Before long she was frowning.

'It's Tilly,' she said, lowering the phone slightly. 'She says she's emailed you the report you asked for.'

'What report?' Poe asked. He couldn't remember asking for something he hadn't already received.

'What report, Tilly?' Flynn said. She looked back at Poe. 'Something to do with truffles?'

Of course. How Keaton found his truffle wood had bugged him until more urgent things had pushed it aside.

'Tell her I'll read it when I get time.'

Flynn repeated what he'd said. She frowned and flashed him a 'why-me' look. 'Yes, Tilly,' she sighed, 'you can hang up now.'

When Flynn left, Victoria insisted on showing Poe to his room. It was in an old annex. It was basic but comfortable. A double bed, a bedside table and a wardrobe. It was attached to the main farmhouse but only accessible through a separate entrance. Probably built for farm labourers, Poe guessed. It was a room for sleeping in and not much else.

'I'll get Edgar for you.'

When she returned with the over-excited spaniel, she also handed him a bit of paper.

'Wi-Fi code,' she explained. She touched the adjoining wall. 'I think the signal's strong enough to get through this.'

Poe thanked her.

He opened the tablet that Bradshaw had loaned him. It was already set up for him to use. He entered the Wi-Fi code. The signal was strong and Bradshaw's email quickly downloaded.

He had a problem.

Poe had been a detective long enough to know that straight-forward call-outs sometimes stretched to seventy-two-hour shifts away from home. Although the pace in SCAS was more measured, he'd never lost the habit of having a 'go-bag' perma-nently ready. As soon as he'd got to Cumbria he'd packed one and put it in the boot of his hire car. The problem was that he'd packed it on autopilot: bottled water, non-perishable food, spare clothing, torch and batteries, forensic gloves; things he might need for a lengthy stay at a crime scene. The same things he'd been packing for years.

But he hadn't packed reading glasses. He hadn't needed them long enough for it to be second nature yet. He checked his jacket's top pocket but he knew they weren't there. He remembered seeing them on the table as he was leaving the green room at Shap Wells.

Bollocks.

The text was too small to read and when he tried the 'pinch out' thing Bradshaw did with her fingers, nothing happened. He threw the tablet on the bed in frustration.

A faint noise from the other side of the wall reminded him that he wasn't the only person in the building. If he could get Victoria to print Bradshaw's email, he was sure he could squint his way through an A4 document.

But first a shower.

Victoria smiled when he knocked and entered the kitchen. She'd progressed from cleaning to baking.

'I was just coming to see if you wanted to join me for an early lunch, Washington. I've got last night's tatie pot in the oven.'

Poe was about to say he'd not long had breakfast but his stomach overruled his brain. It had been a while since he'd had tatie pot.

'I'd love to, Victoria. Thank you.'

He took a seat at the table and she spooned him a generous portion. He leaned in and inhaled the heady aroma. It was heavenly. He raised a spoonful of glistening lamb, rich black pudding and golden sliced potato to his mouth. He closed his eyes and sighed. It was delicious – far nicer than anything he'd eaten at Bullace & Sloe. Before long, Poe had demolished the bowl and Victoria had refilled it.

After his third helping, Poe was done. Victoria passed him a cup of tea and poured one for herself. They drank in a companionable silence.

Eventually Poe said, 'Did your dad have a printer, Victoria? I have a document on my tablet I need to read.'

'No, he didn't. He only had Wi-Fi so he could manage the farm accounts.'

Damn.

She saw his disappointment. 'But I'm going into Kendal later on. I can get it printed there.'

Poe shook his head and thanked her. It was a report on truffles. How important could it be?

They lapsed into silence. After a while Poe said, 'You know a lot about me – well, about my impending accommodation issues at least – but I know next to nothing about you.'

'Not much to tell really.'

Poe settled into the comfy chair as Victoria told him about her childhood on the farm. About how disappointed Thomas had been when neither she nor her sisters had wanted to carry on the family tradition of fell farming. She was the last to leave home but she'd gone the farthest: Chudleigh in Devon where she'd taken a teaching position.

'I love it there, but now I'm back I'm not sure I want to leave. Fell farming didn't appeal to me then, but I'm older now. Perhaps this is something I could do. Carry on Dad's legacy.'

Poe knew what she meant: Cumbria got in your blood the way other counties couldn't. Particularly when the spring of youth was over and life's priorities changed.

'Anyway,' she said, 'what's this document you need printing?'

Poe told her about the report and the issue with his reading glasses.

'I'll pick some up this afternoon. But Dad had a desktop computer. If you email me the document you can read it on the bigger screen.'

Poe hesitated. He doubted there'd be anything confidential on a report on subterranean fungus, but he wasn't allowed to send encrypted files to unsecure networks. Bradshaw had told him why once. Apparently it was something to do with Trojan horses. He'd drifted off long before she'd finished so he never found out why military tactics from Greek mythology meant he couldn't forward emails, but he presumed she knew what she was talking about.

'I can't, I'm afraid.' A thought occurred to him and he brightened up. 'But I can let you read it.'

CHAPTER FIFTY-TWO

Victoria read the document and looked up, puzzled. 'It's a report on truffles.'

Poe knew it was a report on truffles. He'd commissioned it. 'What does it say?'

She swiped through the pages on his tablet. 'You want the David Attenborough version?'

'Why not?' Poe grinned. Victoria Hume was an interesting woman . . .

'*Tuber aestivum*, otherwise known as the summer truffle, or black summer truffle, is native to the UK. It forms a symbiotic, mycorrhizal relationship with the roots of host trees.'

Poe frowned. 'Mycorrhizal?'

'You know those fish that sucker themselves to the sides of sharks and keep them clean?'

Poe nodded.

'Mycorrhizal is basically that, but for plants. According to . . .' she swiped to the end '. . . Miss Matilda Bradshaw . . . gosh, she's got a lot of PhDs . . . the truffle feeds on sloughed-off plant cells.' She read a bit more. 'They basically condition the soil and the roots, which keeps the tree healthy. A tree with truffles is able to absorb more water and nutrients than trees without them.'

'And you know this how?'

'I teach biology.'

Poe felt like slapping his forehead. She'd told him she was a teacher and he hadn't asked what subject or grade she taught. It had been a long time since he'd had a normal conversation with a woman . . .

'I should have asked,' he said.

'And my dad should have told you the truth about Herdwick Croft,' she countered. She went back to the report. 'Apparently, black summer truffles prefer south-facing beech, birch or oak woods. They need dry and free-draining soil and an elevation of at least one hundred feet above sea level. They're more common down south than up here.'

For a while, he chased around the half-formed thoughts he'd had when he commissioned the report. There was no scenario he could come up with that had Keaton finding a truffle wood all on his own. Yet, Bunney said he had. Something didn't add up.

In the grand scheme of things, did it really matter though?

Finding Chloe Bloxwich was important.

Finding out how the blood was switched was important.

Not going to prison for the rest of his life was important.

Where Keaton got his truffles from wasn't.

'Are they valuable?' he asked.

'According to this, anywhere between two thousand and two and a half thousand pounds per kilo.'

Poe whistled. That wasn't something you gave up easily. No wonder Keaton hadn't shared the location with Crawford Bunney. It was worth a fortune.

'This is what the National Crime Agency does, is it – investigate truffle theft?'

Poe said, 'I'm just trying to figure out how someone who grew up in Carlisle might discover a wood with truffles.'

Her smile disappeared. 'This is a serious investigation?'

Poe nodded. 'Very.'

Victoria leaned back in her chair and drained her mug. She pointed at his. 'Another?'

'Please.'

While she was at the kettle she said, 'Is this something to do with that restaurant you mentioned the other day?'

Poe grimaced at the memory. That hadn't been his finest hour. 'It is.'

'You know, when Dad was just getting started he sold his lambs to the auctions like all the other farmers, and because the abattoirs were pretty much the sole purchasers of meat, they controlled the price. Dad's lamb, as good as it was, was simply lumped in with all the rest. He may not have been much of a businessman, but eventually he realised that he'd get a better price if he cut out the middlemen. He took his lambs to get slaughtered properly but sold the meat himself. He didn't have a client list at the time, though, so do you know what he did?'

Poe shook his head.

'He took samples to every decent restaurant and butcher in Cumbria. Gave them a price list and told them what he could and couldn't supply. Before long he was selling everything he produced and demand soon outstripped supply.'

The penny dropped.

'So . . . you're saying that Keaton probably *didn't* find the truffle wood himself. Someone else did, and then either sold him the location or provided him with truffles that he passed off as his own?'

She shrugged. 'If my dad had a product worth selling direct to restaurants, why can't someone else?'

'And if they offered it to one restaurant, they might have offered it to others,' Poe said.

It made sense. Of course Keaton hadn't found the wood himself. He'd been shown where it was and then taken credit for it. How typically self-aggrandising of the man.

Poe didn't see how the information was useful, though. It had answered the question he'd asked, but it didn't matter one way or the other. Keeping a truffle wood's location secret was financially prudent.

Only it wasn't.

Not really.

Keaton was still the sole owner of Bullace & Sloe and additional money spent on truffles came out of his pocket. Of course, he might have kept the location secret so no one could leave for a new restaurant and take the valuable information with them.

But what if there was another reason . . . ?

CHAPTER FIFTY-THREE

Fuck it.

The small but liberating phrase that gave Poe permission to do the things he knew he shouldn't. In this case he'd been expressly forbidden to leave Hume's farm, and although he respected van Zyl and Flynn enormously, they were nuts if they thought he wasn't going to ignore them completely. He might not be able to help Flynn run Chloe Bloxwich to ground but he now had his own loose end to tug on.

He told Victoria he planned to visit some likely restaurants and see if there was anything to her theory about someone going door-to-door selling truffles. She insisted that he take her dad's old Land Rover. It was in one of the barns but perfectly serviceable.

'If people are looking for you, they won't be looking for you in a tatty thing covered in sheep clart,' she said. 'In any case, this weather's going to come down all at once and that stupid hire car will get swept away if there are flash floods.'

Poe couldn't argue. The sky was the colour of a day-old bruise and the wind had stiffened. The air was no longer sticky. Storm Wendy was about to hit the west coast and when it did it was going to be like monsoon season. You could keep your fancy 4x4s, he thought. If the Met Office was right, a tough, no frills Land Rover would be exactly what he needed.

Poe could have done with Bradshaw's assistance. She would have bashed some data together and come up with a prioritised list.

He couldn't involve her, though – she'd worry he wasn't doing as he was told, maybe even enough to tell Flynn.

He drew a circle around Bullace & Sloe on his map – similar to the one Bradshaw had drawn when she'd calculated how far Elizabeth Keaton/Chloe Bloxwich could have travelled when she'd escaped from her imaginary basement. She'd used equations and a computer – Poe used a red felt-tip pen. He would start with the restaurants nearest to Bullace & Sloe and then work outwards. If that didn't work, he'd increase the search radius.

He counted out how many fell into his first catchment area. Nine. Three restaurants and six pubs. He feared that all the pubs would turn out to be gastropubs – those half-pub/half-restaurant characterless hybrids that had risen from the ashes of the doomed village boozer. Unfortunately they probably all reckoned their food was top-notch, so every single one of them had to be visited.

He bought a new pair of reading glasses at a petrol station then hit the first pub on the list.

It was a bust.

'Any food that's not fried don't get sold, mate,' the greasy-looking owner told him.

'And you've never been offered truffles before?'

'What's them?'

Poe told him.

He thrust Poe a menu. The healthiest option was the Scotch egg. Quite an achievement for something that was essentially deep-fried sausage meat.

The next two pubs offered food but it was basic: burgers, fish and chips, lasagne, steak and ale pies – the usual fare. Decent quality but truffle-less.

The first restaurant he tried was more promising. They *did* have truffle on the menu and they *did* consider themselves a fine-dining establishment. The timing didn't match, though. The Salted Pig hadn't existed when Keaton was allegedly foraging for his

296

own truffles. The head chef asked Poe if he knew where to get some, and if he did he'd be interested.

As Poe stepped outside a rainstorm exploded. He stood under the Salted Pig's awning for a moment and marvelled at its ferocity. The sound of rain on canvas was exhilarating. He stood for five minutes and enjoyed the air being cleansed. He breathed in deeply, absorbed the smell of wet mud.

He took advantage of a small lull and ran to the Land Rover. He considered going back to Victoria's – being out in weather like this was reckless – but he was only halfway through his list. The sturdiness of the Land Rover was reassuring, though, and the rainwater wasn't at the stage where it was coming over the riverbanks and on to the roads. He'd carry on while he could.

The next two pubs offered nothing different. One didn't serve food back then and the second's menu was the same as the others: reasonably priced pub grub. None of them had been offered truffles as far as any of the chefs or landlords could remember. He tried two more restaurants but found similar stories. One was an Italian and the other catered for the nearby campsite and caravan park. When tourists had been on the fells all day they wanted something filling, not something fancy.

The last pub was near the village of Wetheral, a couple of miles from Bullace & Sloe. Poe decided he'd have a drink there, then widen his circle another mile. The pub was called the Gamekeeper's Kitchen and it claimed to be a specialist game eatery. The car park was round the back and Poe got drenched on his short walk to the front entrance. The place was empty.

He sat at the bar and ordered half a pint of Spun Gold. The barmaid looked happy to have something to do. While he waited, he used a bar towel to dry his hair. He wasn't hungry but decided to have something to eat anyway. He didn't know what time he'd get back and he didn't want to impose on Victoria. He asked the barmaid for a menu. It featured a lot of game. She told him someone would be out to take his order. A few seconds later, a man with a fine moustache appeared and asked if he'd come to a decision. Poe ordered the rabbit pie with buttered parsnip mash, showed the man his NCA ID card and asked if he could have a word with the chef. He was shown into the kitchen.

It was a miniature version of Bullace & Sloe: similar equipment, only smaller and not as much of it. The head chef was a woman called Gayle Kidmister. She was in her early forties and had been there over a decade.

Poe asked her the same question he'd been asking all afternoon and was surprised when she said yes.

'You *did* have someone round here offering you truffles?'

Gayle nodded. 'Be a few years ago now. At least eight. A strange-looking fella. Looked more like a trainspotter than a forager if I'm being honest. The truffles were fresh out of the ground, though, judging by the amount of dirt underneath his fingernails.'

'And you declined?'

'I did,' she replied. 'We had no need for them. Back then we were an American-style smokehouse. Low and slow BBQ meats, specialist burgers, that type of thing. I did consider it for the House Burger but it would have pushed the price up almost seventy per cent. In the end I told him to go to a restaurant called Bullace & Sloe. Have you heard of it?'

'I've heard of it.'

'They were starting to get a decent rep and I knew they used truffles. He thanked me and that's the last I saw of him.'

'One rabbit pie!' another chef called from the back.

'That's mine,' Poe said. 'I'll go and eat it. If I have any more questions can I pop back in when I've finished?'

'Of course,' she said.

Poe wasn't usually a fan of rabbit – he found the meat too lean for his taste – but the pie was delicious. The subtlety of the rabbit was matched with bacon and leek. It was held in a thick egg custard. The buttered parsnip mash was rich and warming. Ironically, the only thing that could have improved the meal would have been some shaved truffle.

While he ate, Poe thought about what he'd been told. A man had approached Gayle Kidmister eight years earlier. He'd offered to sell her truffles and she'd referred him to Bullace & Sloe. She'd also said he didn't look like a typical forager. Perhaps he wasn't. Perhaps he'd stumbled upon them by accident but had enough nous to know what they were and how much they were worth.

Poe was jerked from his thoughts and back into the present – Gayle, still in her chef's whites, had taken the stool beside him. The barmaid poured her a lemonade.

'One of my chefs overheard us talking,' she explained. 'She reckons that the man ate in the restaurant. She knows because it was the first cover of the day and, because the waiting staff hadn't arrived yet, she had to serve him herself.'

'So he tried to sell you truffles at the back then walked round the front for a cheeseburger and a pint?'

'Seems so. And that's not all. When she brought him his food, he was sitting with one of our regulars: a postman called Brian Wratten. Seemed they were having a right good crack.'

'And this Brian Wratten, he's still a regular?'

'If you can wait half an hour he'll be in.'

Poe peered behind her. The rain was so heavy it looked like someone was hosing down the windows. 'Even in this?'

She snorted. 'When we were flooded he sat in the beer garden in a pair of waders and a waterproof hat. If he doesn't come in, he's dead.'

'I'll wait then.'

By the time he'd finished his meal, Brian Wratten had arrived. Poe didn't need to be told; he just knew. Pubs have locals and the man who entered was a local. The barmaid began pulling a pint as soon as he entered, and before he'd hung up his Barbour jacket, it was on a beer mat in front of a stool at the end of the bar.

Poe waited until he'd taken his first sip before approaching him.

'Brian Wratten?'

'That's me.' He extended a meaty, hairy hand.

Poe shook it then showed him his ID card.

'I'd like to buy you a pint.'

'You would?'

'And in exchange perhaps you could tell me about a man you spoke to a few years ago. The one who'd been round the back, trying to sell truffles . . .'

Brian Wratten had a memory like a filing cabinet. Poe suspected this wasn't an uncommon trait among postal workers, especially in Cumbria where the system for numbering houses could charitably be described as informal.

Wratten remembered the day and the man well.

Poe asked him what they had talked about.

'Truffles,' he replied. 'He showed me one. Offered me some to go with my lunch but I said no. Looked too much like dry dog shit. Still not convinced it wasn't.'

Poe smiled. He knew what Wratten meant. The pictures on Bradshaw's report had looked a bit turd-like. Whoever it was that had tried one first was a brave man.

'Did he tell you how he came by them?'

Wratten shook his head. 'He didn't. He was evasive about that, actually.'

Poe's ears pricked. Words like 'evasive' did that to cops. 'How so?'

'Well, there we were chatting about truffles. What they were, where they grow, how they live, that type of thing. It was only

300

natural that I asked if foraging was a hobby or if he did it for a living.'

'And he said?'

'He said neither, Mr Poe. Nothing strange about that. When I'm out walking the dog I'll often pick up mushrooms, or wild garlic when it's in season, but I'd never describe myself as a forager.'

'But he was evasive when you asked him how he came about them?'

'He was.'

'Might he have been walking *his* dog?' Poe suggested.

'I asked him but he said no.'

'But he wouldn't tell you what he was doing?'

'He would not.'

That was curious. Evasiveness suggested concealment. It didn't necessarily mean criminality but it hardly ruled it out. 'I don't suppose he gave you his name?'

'Les Morris. He was a nice man, Mr Poe. Bought me a drink and we talked for a good forty minutes. Apart from not telling me how or where he'd found the truffles, he was very chatty.'

'He local?'

'Yes.'

Good. He'd ask Bradshaw to compile him a list of Les, Leslies, Lesleys and L. Morris's living in the area. He was trying to think how he could convince her that he was still taking the 'keeping a low profile' thing seriously, when Wratten made the whole thing irrelevant.

'You don't want his address, do you?'

'You have it?'

'He left his scarf behind and I'm a postman. I asked around at the sorting office until a colleague recognised which Les Morris I was after. She returned his scarf on her next round. That's a service you don't get in your fancy cities, Mr Poe.'

'I'm from Shap.'

Wratten smiled and apologised. He gave Poe the address. It was five miles from where he was now.

He thanked Wratten and put a pint on tap for him. He was about to brave the rain when his burner rang.

Uh-oh. Bradshaw had insisted on only communicating when they absolutely had to. *This wasn't going to be good* . . .

He was right, it wasn't.

'Poe, we have a problem,' Flynn said as soon as he answered.

CHAPTER FIFTY-FOUR

Poe, we have a problem . . .

He was hearing the words so often he should probably have them set as his ringtone. Last time it was van Zyl telling him he was to be interviewed under caution, the time before that it was Gamble telling him Elizabeth Keaton had returned from the dead.

This time it was worse.

Keaton's judge-in-chamber application had been successful and he'd been released on bail. The CPS had already hinted they weren't going to submit evidence at his retrial.

And that wasn't the worst thing she had to tell him.

The blood found in Poe's trailer had been confirmed as belonging to Elizabeth Keaton. Poe was now officially a suspect in a murder investigation. Van Zyl had said Flynn was to take him in personally. He had arranged a solicitor for him.

Poe said he wasn't going anywhere.

Flynn asked where he was.

Poe hung up. He heeded Bradshaw's advice about the burners being compromised and removed the battery.

Technically it didn't make any difference. Every cop in Cumbria was already looking for him. Wardle's warrant without bail had seen to that.

Nothing had changed.

They either found Chloe Bloxwich or they explained the blood.

* * *

Les Morris lived in Armathwaite. It was not dissimilar to Cotehill, the village where Bullace & Sloe was located. Small, pretty, stunning surroundings. All meadows and pastures. Horse boxes and 4×4s were parked in drives. They even had a red telephone box.

It was idyllic, like a Rupert Brooke poem.

Cricket on the village green and honey for tea . . .

Morris lived in a double-fronted bungalow. The lawn was trimmed short and the borders bloomed with brightly coloured perennials. A bird feeder hung in an apple tree.

A woman answered the door. Poe showed his ID. 'Can I speak to Mr Morris, please?'

'I'm *Mrs* Morris,' she replied. She didn't offer a first name. She sounded angry and he hadn't even told her why he was there yet. She was tall and waspish, in her late forties, early fifties, and looked like the type of woman who smiled at roadkill. The grey bun on the top of her head was pulled so tight her face was taut.

Despite the continued deluge of rain, it wasn't until she'd closely examined his ID card that she invited him inside. She muttered all the way through to the kitchen, letting him know in no uncertain terms that he was making a mess. To be fair, he was.

She took the only seat and didn't ask him if he wanted a hot drink.

'I was hoping to see Mr Morris. Is he at work?'

She snorted. 'How the hell would I know? I haven't seen that no-good scoundrel for nearly eight years.'

Poe tried to blink the rainwater out of his eyes. Eventually he gave up and asked if it would be possible to use a towel. He might as well have asked to piss in her kettle. She grumbled to her feet and threw him a damp tea towel. Poe thanked her anyway. He set to getting the worst of the water out of his hair.

'What do you want with that worthless man anyway?' she said while he dried himself.

'His name's come up in an investigation,' he said.

She brightened slightly. 'Is he in trouble?'

Poe was about to reply that he wasn't but realised that Mrs Morris didn't want to hear that. The German word *Schaden-freude* sprang to mind: deriving pleasure from someone else's misfortune.

'He might be,' he said carefully.

It was the right decision. A twisted smile tugged at the corners of her mouth.

'I'll stick the kettle on then,' she said.

'You say you haven't seen Mr Morris for eight years,' Poe said, as she made a pot of tea.

'No. He went out one afternoon and never returned. Police weren't interested. Thought he was probably shacked up with a floozy somewhere. One of those stuck-up sorts from that club of his.'

Poe added 'club' to his list of questions.

'And you think he ran off?'

She turned and put her hands on her bony hips. 'And he'll come scurrying back one day when she sickens of him. Tail between his legs, you mark my words.'

Poe doubted it. If Morris had run off, Poe doubted he'd return. Mrs Morris was the type of woman who, if you found yourself chained to her, you'd gnaw your own arm off to get away.

He changed the subject.

'Did Mr Morris ever go truffle hunting?'

'What's that?' she replied, effectively answering his question.

Poe explained what truffles were and where they were found.

'And they're only found in woods?' she snickered. 'My Les was more of a sit at the club and drink home-brewed beer kind of man, Sergeant Poe. I'd be surprised if he even knew what they were.'

At least that tied in with what he'd been told earlier. Neither the chef nor the postman had thought he'd been a forager.

Mrs Morris returned to her seat and poured them both weak-looking tea. She added milk until the tea was the same colour as the milk. Even Bradshaw made better brews. Poe thanked her anyway and took a sip of the insipid, lukewarm drink. He tried not to grimace.

'Did he have a dog?'

Mrs Morris smirked. 'Our Les? With a dog? I don't think so. Fur set off his asthma.'

'Was he friends with someone who had a dog then?'

She shrugged. 'Everyone round here has a dog.'

Fair point. A thought occurred to him. Mrs Morris had said her husband might have been having an affair with some 'floozy'. He wondered if it was the floozy who had the dog. Men would put up with most things when their dick was running the show. That undoubtedly included wheezy chests. An affair with a married woman would also explain his reticence in telling Wratten how he'd come by the truffles.

Poe couldn't ask Mrs Morris that, though. If he did, he'd get nothing else out of her.

'Did he have a favourite walk? Perhaps one that took in a wood?'

Mrs Morris snorted again. 'My Les had no interest in woods and he had no interest in walking, Sergeant Poe.'

This was rapidly turning into a dead end.

'Of course if it was a field . . .'

She left him hanging.

Poe accepted the bait. 'A field?'

'Well, because of that club I told you about.'

She'd mentioned a club but hadn't said what it was. He knew

it and she knew it. She was basically an arsehole. But he was a cop and cops dealt with arseholes all the time.

'Remind me.'

She smirked, happy with her little victory.

'He was a member of the Cumbria branch of ROCA.'

'Rocker?'

'Not rocker as in punk rocker. ROCA as in the Royal Observer Corps Association. ROCA.'

Poe was nonplussed. He had no idea what the Royal Observer Corps Association was. He asked Mrs Morris but, as it had become apparent that her husband wasn't in trouble, her mood had soured again.

'I don't want to talk about that stupid club of his. It's bad enough that he spent all his time there without a nosy policeman wanting me to relive it all.'

Poe stood. He was about to take his leave when he saw a shed in the back garden. The garden was well kept but he doubted Mrs Morris was responsible. She was too . . . fussy. Too prim. She probably had a gardener.

And gardeners have their own equipment.

Whereas the great British shed was a haven for hen-pecked middle-aged men. And fussy women never entered sheds. They were too dirty. Too full of spiders.

'Was that his shed?'

'What of it?'

'Would there be some of that Royal Observer Corps Association stuff in there?'

She let out an exasperated sigh. 'I can't even get in to throw it all out it's so full of that nonsense.'

'Don't suppose I could get inside and have a quick look?'

'What's it worth?' she said slyly.

Not getting bloody arrested, he almost said. Instead he reached into his wallet and handed her three twenty-pound notes. She slipped them in her cardigan pocket and handed him the shed key.

'You're not to take anything, mind,' she shouted after him. 'My Les will be back one day and he won't be happy if anyone's been messing about in there.'

Poe walked out of the kitchen and into the back garden. He opened the shed's padlock and stepped inside.

He stared in amazement. The shed was like a museum. Hundreds of maps, documents and photographs were pinned to the walls, some of them aged and yellowing, some of them much newer. Sagging shelves were laden with weird-looking instruments, old uniforms and carefully arranged ROC memorabilia. An old Geiger counter and a hand-operated siren took pride of place in a pine display cabinet. It was a trove of someone else's treasure.

So, Poe thought, this was what obsession looked like.

Day 14

CHAPTER FIFTY-FIVE

Flynn paced the hotel room like a trial lawyer. 'Why the hell did you come back here?' she asked.

Poe was seated on the bed. Bradshaw was at the hotel room's desk. He'd asked how their investigation was going but hadn't got a good response: Bradshaw sulked – her searches still hadn't yielded anything close to a theory on how the blood had been swapped – and Flynn seemed to think that Chloe Bloxwich had disappeared off the face of the earth. Her one small success was that she knew where Chloe's boyfriend, Ned, was. He was backpacking in Asia, wasn't contactable and, even if he was, he'd been out of the country months before all this had begun.

It was three in the morning, and not fifteen minutes earlier Poe had rung Flynn's burner and asked her to meet him in Bradshaw's room. Five minutes before that he'd sneaked up the hotel's fire escape and knocked on Bradshaw's door. Loud enough to wake her, quiet enough to not wake anyone in the adjacent rooms. He should have known better – Bradshaw hadn't been sleeping: she was still working on the blood.

'I assume you have a good reason for dragging me out of bed,' Flynn said. 'And where the hell have you been? You look as though you slept in a fucking car.'

'Sit down, boss,' Poe said with a grimace. 'I have a story to tell and it's not nice.'

Flynn sat.

Bradshaw lifted her head from her screen and faced him.

Poe talked.

Poe told them what he'd learned, that the Observer Corps was a civil defence organisation formed in 1925, tasked with visually identifying, monitoring and reporting on aircraft flying over Britain. They were awarded 'Royal' status after their work during the Battle of Britain phase of the Second World War. In 1955 they were given the additional task of detecting and reporting on nuclear explosions – a necessity of the Cold War.

When their task was that of aircraft tracking, it had been fine for their observation posts to be above ground. They were brick-built with open-topped observation platforms. However, Cold War nuclear bombs were capable of producing blast waves and heat flashes that travelled at 5000 miles per hour. The heat would turn humans into charcoal and the blast would turn them to dust. Anything combustible would melt or explode. Overground observation posts were useless. The government needed structures capable of surviving the explosion and, for a period of at least fourteen days, remaining operational in a post-nuclear attack environment.

So, Poe explained, they did the only thing they could.

They built underground bunkers.

Officially called Royal Observer Corps (ROC) Underground Monitoring Posts, they were deep enough to survive a nuclear explosion while limiting the effects of radiation. They were large enough to house three volunteers and all the equipment needed to relay information on the power, height, distance and spread of a nuclear blast back to a command post.

'The government built hundreds of them,' Poe continued. 'Over fifteen hundred in total, all over Britain. Essentially they were concrete boxes in the ground covered with compacted earth.'

Bradshaw and Flynn listened.

'The original bunkers had a monitoring room, a chemical toilet and a room with bunk beds. They were only accessible via a fifteen-foot shaft.'

'And you know all this how?' Flynn said.

Poe told them what he'd discovered. About how in 1991, with the Cold War finally over, the government had decommissioned the last surviving bunkers. They'd been stripped bare, sealed up and abandoned. Most were left to go derelict, their locations lost.

'But the British are proud of their history and the ROC's work wasn't going to be buried in the annals of history,' he said. 'An organisation cropped up for ex-volunteers: the Royal Observer Corps Association. Its aim was to promote the work of the corps, help with the restoration of old bunkers and provide a benevolence fund for ex-members who'd fallen on hard times. But mainly it was a conduit for ex-corps members to get together with people who'd been through the same experience.

'Morris was a member of the Cumbrian branch of ROCA. He'd never been an ROC volunteer himself – he was a bit too young – so was an associate rather than a full member. Nevertheless, his shed was full of ROC memorabilia.'

He paused for questions but there weren't any.

'I spent an hour reading the material but there was nothing that hinted at a truffle-patch discovery. I was about to give up when I found a membership directory. It was a couple of years old but it did have the name of a fellow ROCA member who lived in the same village as Morris. His name was Harold Hayward-Price and he *had* stood posts with the Royal Observer Corps.'

Poe told them how he'd thanked Mrs Morris, walked across the village and knocked on Harold's door. The man was in his seventies but spry. White hair surrounded a shiny bald dome. He had fingernails like cheese rind. Poe explained why he was there and Harold invited him in. He'd recently lost his wife and seemed starved of company.

He was also an expert on the ROC and the ROCA.

During the hours he and Harold spent together, Poe learned everything there was to know about the corps and the association. Poe told him that Morris had stumbled on truffles somehow, and did he know where that might have been?

To his amazement, Harold did.

Sort of.

And it was nothing to do with any lady-friend that Morris had been trying to keep quiet.

It was something far more interesting.

Harold explained that Morris had always been bothered by his associate status and, to try and elevate his standing in the local branch, he'd taken on a task most members thought was a fool's errand: he began searching for the 'missing' bunker.

The missing bunker was a myth among the Carlisle ROCA branch. It was supposedly one that had been sited in a position immediately deemed unsuitable. One rumour was that it had been too prone to flooding, another was that it didn't have the 360-degree sightlines required. Morris believed it had been filled in with rubble, sealed and buried almost as soon as it had been finished. He became obsessed by the idea and believed finding it was his route to full ROCA membership.

It was no more than a rumour, though. All the Cumbrian bunkers were accounted for. Some had been refurbished and were occasionally opened to the public.

But . . . about a year before he disappeared, Morris began dropping hints that he'd found it. Nothing specific, just the odd comment that he'd soon be a full member, that kind of thing.

Harold thought it possible that while Morris had been searching for the non-existent subterranean bunker, he could have stumbled upon some truffles.

There'd been nothing in the shed to suggest Morris had actually found something, but Harold dismissed that out of hand.

Because ROCA members were in each other's sheds all the time, he said that if Morris had found something relating to the bunker, he wouldn't have left it lying around for anyone to see. He'd have kept it on him at all times.

It was at that point that the *News at Ten*, silently on in the background, had finished, and switched across to the local *Border News*, affectionately known as border-crack-and-deek-aboot. Poe's face was front and centre. He couldn't hear what the anchor was saying, and he could hardly ask Harold to turn up the volume, but the message was clear. The public were being asked to keep an eye out for him. Probably ended with warnings not to approach him but to dial 999. The report had then switched to a shot of the police removing things from his property. One after another, a succession of items in evidence bags were taken from Herdwick Croft and placed in the boot of a CSI Range Rover, probably the only vehicle they had capable of navigating the rough land. It was still raining and the clear plastic evidence bags glistened with raindrops.

He hadn't realised it at the time, but something about the scene had thrown open a door in his mind and began to bother him the way a blinking clock does after a power cut.

After the news had finished, Poe made his excuses. He had nowhere to go but he knew he couldn't stay near Armathwaite. Harold wouldn't be watching any more news tonight but it was possible that Mrs Morris had seen the report and had already called the police.

He'd battled through the opening thrusts of Storm Wendy, slipped out of Armathwaite unseen, and found a secluded lay-by to try and get some rest.

Unsurprisingly, sleep wouldn't come. The rain beating down on the Land Rover's roof sounded like a snare drum. He didn't mind; he had too much to think about anyway.

Although the news about a possible bunker had been

315

interesting, potentially important, it was the evidence bags being placed in the CSI Range Rover that had gnawed at the edge of his memory. Something told him it was this, and not the missing bunker, that he should focus his thoughts on.

He spread himself out in the back of the Land Rover and replayed the events of the evening while he searched the recesses of his mind for what it was he'd seen.

At 2 a.m. he thought he had it. CSI had been using a Range Rover and six years earlier so had Keaton.

But . . . that couldn't have been it. Keaton's vehicle had been seized and subjected to a detailed forensic examination. There'd been nothing linking his car to his daughter's disappearance. If Keaton had used his Range Rover they would have found blood. There was simply too much at the crime scene to avoid forensic transfer, even if he'd wrapped her in bin bags.

Once he'd dismissed the Range Rover connection, he began to think about the evidence bags he'd seen being carried out of Herdwick Croft. They were bugging him but he didn't know why.

He couldn't get there, though. No matter how hard he tried, whatever it was wanted to stay hidden. Instead of what the evidence bags meant, he tried focusing on what they were.

They were plastic.

They were waterproof.

They were completely sealed.

They were see-through.

The ones he'd seen on TV had been dripping with rainwater. Dripping wet.

Just like . . .

He sat bolt upright. Stopped breathing. He didn't want to frighten the thought away. He ran through a recent memory. Someone explaining a process. He hadn't really been listening but it had stuck in there somehow.

The answer, when it came, was both sudden and terrifying.

And the reason he hadn't been able to see it earlier was that it was so awful, so mind-bogglingly depraved, that his mind simply wasn't wired that way.

It wasn't possible . . .

Was it?

He stress-tested it. Every step, hoping to find a fatal flaw in the chain of events as he knew them. He didn't want to be right.

It was disgusting.

It was obscene.

It was unbelievable.

And yet Poe had never been more certain of anything in his life.

CHAPTER FIFTY-SIX

'Why do we use evidence bags, boss?'

'It's five o'clock in the morning, Poe,' Flynn snapped. 'I haven't got time for a fucking quiz!' She was back to pacing the room again. Poe didn't blame her. She was in an impossible position. By not arresting him on sight she was committing an offence – assisting an offender.

'Would you like an energy drink, DI Stephanie Flynn?'

Poe allowed himself a small smile.

'This isn't funny, Poe. And how is any of this relevant anyway?'

'Humour me.'

'I'll do more than bloody humour you,' she muttered.

He repeated his earlier question. 'So, why do we use evidence bags? What is their basic function?'

Flynn threw open her arms in exasperation. 'To provide an incontestable chain of custody.'

'More basic than that.'

Her brow knitted. 'To contain evidence in a sterile and contamination-free environment.'

'Exactly. Once that bag's sealed, the plastic ones at least, nothing gets in and nothing gets out.'

'Get to the point, Poe,' Flynn said.

'Think back six years and imagine you're in the kitchen of Bullace & Sloe. You're Jared Keaton and, for reasons unknown, you've just killed your daughter.'

Flynn stared at him. So did Bradshaw. This was more like it.

'You hadn't planned to kill her, but you're a psychopath so you don't have a normal reaction. Instead of panicking, you start thinking. The way you see it, you have two options: either someone else takes the blame or it all goes away.'

'And without any planning, blaming someone else is dangerous. It's too uncontrolled,' Flynn said.

'Exactly. So you decide to make the problem go away.'

He opened Bradshaw's mini-bar fridge. From top to bottom it was packed with bottles of POW, her preferred choice of energy drink. It was sweetened with fruit and contained natural caffeine extracted from guarana, a climbing plant from Brazil. He unscrewed the cap on one and took a long drink. It was sickly sweet but he immediately felt the caffeine kick. Borrowed energy he'd pay back later with interest.

'Now, spin back two years earlier. You're approached by a man called Les Morris. He has some valuable truffles to sell. You buy some because it's good business. But . . . it would be better business if you could gather them yourself.'

He waited for them to catch up.

'You think Keaton killed Les Morris?'

'I think it's possible. He's certainly not been seen since.'

'I thought you said the bunker didn't exist?'

'I didn't say the bunker didn't exist, Harold did. And Keaton's one of the most persuasive men you're ever likely to meet. It would have been the easiest thing in the world for him to convince Morris to tell him where he'd found the truffles.'

'And while he was there he probably couldn't resist showing his new friend his secret bunker,' Flynn added.

'That's the way I see it,' Poe said.

'So you think he killed him and left him in the bunker?'

'That's exactly what I think. Probably staged it to look like an accident in case Morris *had* told someone. Maybe Keaton shut the hatch lid and left him there to starve, maybe he bashed his head in and threw him down.'

'And Keaton has the truffles to himself,' Flynn said.

'And a hidey hole should he ever need one.'

'OK. He has a deposition site – which potentially overcomes the problem of the ground being too frozen to dig in – but we know he didn't use his car to transport Elizabeth. I've read the forensic report. Nothing incriminating was found.'

'I agree. And there were no other vehicles he could have used.'

'So . . . ?'

'So we come back to the evidence bags.'

Flynn frowned again. 'Stop talking in riddles, Poe. Just tell me what you know.'

'I saw myself on television when I was at Harold's. A succession of evidence bags being taken from my home to the back of the CSI Range Rover. And it was pissing down.'

'I was there,' she reminded him.

'Well, anyway, there was something familiar about those bags. The way they were see-through and dripping wet. They reminded me of something and it kept going round and round in my head. About ten past two this morning I remembered what it was.'

Flynn said nothing.

'It was the sous-vide bags, Steph. The ones coming out of the water baths at Bullace & Sloe . . .'

CHAPTER FIFTY-SEVEN

'That's disgusting, Poe. You're not seriously telling me he ate his daughter?'

'No, of course not.'

'But you *are* saying he cooked her?'

'I'm not.'

'What then?'

'I think he sealed her in those sous-vide bags, washed them off, then drove to this bunker and dropped them inside.'

Flynn stared at him, her mouth open in astonishment. 'That's . . . preposterous, Poe.'

'Is it? As a way of transporting a murder victim, sous-vide bags are absolutely perfect. They're designed to contain meat for hours at a time without letting hot water in or the juices out. There'd be no forensic transfer in the car. None whatsoever.'

'No, that's not right, Poe,' Bradshaw said, shaking her head. 'I saw their vacuum sealer. No way is it big enough to seal a whole body.'

'Not a whole body, no,' Poe replied.

'You're not saying . . . ?' Flynn said.

He nodded. 'What made me look at Keaton in the first place?'

'Timeline discrepancies. *Match of the Day* not being on.'

'And?'

Silence. Poe didn't break it.

The dawn of understanding started with Flynn's eyes. They

widened. Her breathing quickened and she paled. She put her hands to her mouth in shock.

'Oh my God, you're right,' she whispered.

'What else, Poe?' Bradshaw asked. 'What has DI Stephanie Flynn worked out that I haven't?'

'The knives, Tilly,' Poe replied. 'Keaton reordered a set of knives, a butcher's saw and a cleaver.'

'I don't understand.'

'Jared Keaton dismembered his daughter, vacuum-sealed the parts in sous-vide bags and deposited her in the bunker that Les Morris found.'

As horrific as it was, it worked. They talked it through. They looked at it from all angles. They agreed that, as well as his daughter, Keaton would have had to vacuum-pack the clothes he'd been wearing, along with the tools he'd used to cut her into manageable-sized pieces.

If he was right, and he knew he was, somewhere out there was a subterranean bunker containing the body of Les Morris, the dismembered remains of Keaton's daughter and all the evidence they'd need to ensure his conviction at the retrial.

All they had to do now was find it . . .

Find it *and* avoid Cumbria Police, apparently. Flynn disappeared to make a phone call. She didn't say to whom but Poe knew it would be to van Zyl. New information or not, she simply didn't have the authority to ignore an order to arrest him. If van Zyl decided to do things properly, he'd have to accept it. He'd let Flynn and Bradshaw do their jobs. Now they had a definite lead, they'd put everything into that bunker. With or without him, they'd find it. Poe wouldn't risk Flynn's career just to save himself some time on remand.

The chances were he'd be superfluous anyway. Les Morris

hadn't been a walker – if he *had* found the missing bunker it was because he'd followed a paper trail. The location of the original bunker would be on a register or archived somewhere.

Flynn came back in and nodded. Her meaning was obvious: for now at least, he was in the clear.

Things were looking up.

Things were looking down.

It was midday and they'd made no progress. Bradshaw had accessed every public record available to Morris, and some that weren't. The locations of the decommissioned bunkers weren't easily available. There were bits here and there but nothing on any government database.

Bradshaw confirmed that there probably was a missing bunker.

'I've found an anomaly anyway,' she said.

After glugging a whole bottle of POW, she told them what it was. It was the kind of thing only Bradshaw could have found. On a requisition register for the equipment needed to construct the bunkers, she'd noticed that the parts ordered for Cumbria didn't match the number of known bunkers. There was an extra ladder and an extra hatch.

But that was it. Despite all her best efforts, nothing on any database pointed to its location.

And Poe knew why. When Bradshaw had mentioned requisition orders, Poe remembered something else Harold had told him. Something about the government managing the process but local building firms undertaking their construction. He bet that Morris had been through the archives of local building firms until he'd found the one who'd been awarded the contract for the missing bunker.

They'd be able to do the same, of course. And eventually they'd find the building firm and get the location of the bunker that way. He had no doubt about that. Flynn and Bradshaw were too good at their jobs not to succeed.

But it would take time. Time they didn't have.

The sobering reality of the situation caught up with him.

Keaton was out of prison. In a week or so the media would leave his doorstep and he'd be able to slip away and dispose of everything properly. The way he'd almost certainly intended to, had he not been arrested. He'd probably worried about the bunker's discovery every minute of his six-year prison sentence. Dreading the day some kid stumbled across it. Fretting that there was another Les Morris out there, equally obsessed, equally determined to find it.

No way would he leave it for long. He'd be desperate to finish the job he had begun six years ago.

Poe knew everything, yet he could prove nothing. He was no better off than he'd been a week ago.

As far as Wardle was concerned, Elizabeth Keaton was still missing and Jared Keaton had still been subjected to a massive miscarriage of justice. Finding Chloe Bloxwich would help them but not as much as they'd initially thought. Flynn pointed out that Bloxwich would deny it and she would no doubt look different to how she had two weeks earlier anyway. And there was no physical evidence to prove anything otherwise. And, although Rigg and Flick Jakeman would be able to say that Chloe Bloxwich had been impersonating Elizabeth, it wouldn't matter.

Because they couldn't explain how Elizabeth's blood had been drawn during the police interviews. DNA was the gold standard of evidence. In any court in the land Elizabeth Keaton was the girl who'd walked into Alston Library. Scientifically, it couldn't have been anyone else.

Thinking about Chloe Bloxwich reminded Poe that he'd missed a step. He still hadn't worked out how Keaton had made contact with her. Barbara Stephens had told them that Bunney's visits hadn't coincided with Chloe's visits to her dad. They'd never been in the visitors' centre at the same time. Which was odd. Jared Keaton might only need minutes to completely charm someone, but even he'd struggle without a face-to-face meeting.

A crashing sound made him jump.

Bradshaw had thrown an empty bottle of POW against the wall. 'I can't see how she did it!'

'Don't worry, Tilly,' he said, sitting down beside her. 'It was a long shot anyway.'

'This is really bad, isn't it, Poe?'

'It's not great.'

'Are you going to go to prison?'

He'd made a vow never to lie to her and he didn't want to break it now.

'Maybe. If Elizabeth had simply turned up then disappeared again, too many people would have asked questions. Keaton might have gained his freedom but he wouldn't have regained his reputation. But . . . if some bitter detective, humiliated because he'd made a mistake, were to be convicted of her murder . . . well, that would be a different matter entirely. That's a story the whole world gets behind.'

'Oh boo-fucking-hoo, Poe!' Flynn snapped. She'd stepped out to make another phone call but had slipped back in without either of them noticing. 'Will you listen to yourself? The director and I aren't putting our careers on the line for you to give up now.'

'We're not giving up, Steph. But realistically, we don't have enough time to find this bunker.'

'And Poe will get arrested and have to go to prison,' Bradshaw added.

'Oh for God's sake,' Flynn said testily. 'Look, I wasn't going to tell you this yet, but there's a reason I've been a bit tetchy recently.'

'A bit?'

'Yes, Poe, a bit! Just because I'm not bursting into song every ten minutes doesn't mean I'm . . .' She stopped and took a deep breath. Composed herself.

This sounded serious. Poe hoped she wasn't ill. He didn't think he could handle it. The number of people he cared for could be counted on one hand and two of them were in the room with him now.

She bit her lip and said, 'My partner, Zoe, and I have been trying for a baby.'

'You should have asked Poe to be a donor, DI Stephanie Flynn,' Bradshaw said. 'You'd have given DI Flynn some of your sperm, wouldn't you, Poe?'

Poe snorted. You could always rely on Bradshaw to make awkward situations worse.

Flynn smiled. 'We're going through an IVF cycle, Tilly. Zoe wasn't able to get pregnant when she was married to Tim, and I . . . well, let's just say I can't conceive the normal way either.'

Poe placed his hand on Bradshaw's shoulder, looked at her, and shook his head slightly. Hoped she got the message: this is one time it's not OK to ask.

'Anyway, we were prepared to pay privately but we pushed up against a problem that neither of us had expected. Without discussing it, both of us were worried about the career repercussions.'

Poe stayed silent. It wasn't right but discrimination in this area did exist. The NCA was one of the better employers, but it was a fact: women who took maternity leave were statistically disadvantaged. Career breaks were well named: they broke careers. Maternity breaks were the same. In tribunals, employers had admitted that women returning from maternity leave weren't taken as seriously, that it was assumed their priorities lay elsewhere.

'Neither of you wanted to take maternity leave,' he said. He didn't blame them; they both excelled in what they did. Zoe worked in London. Something to do with analysing the price of oil. She was extremely well compensated. Seven-figure salary compensated. Other than the fact she'd been married to a man before deciding she didn't like it, Poe didn't know much else about her. Flynn kept her private life private.

'No, Poe, you have it the wrong way round. We both wanted to be the one to have the baby. We both wanted to protect the other's career.'

Poe didn't respond. He didn't feel he should offer an opinion.

'I wanted to have the baby as Zoe's career is too important.'

'Your career's important too, Steph,' Poe said. What he actually thought was that a detective inspector in SCAS was ten times more important than someone who worked in the City. But he didn't. He was being sensitive. Remarkably, so was Bradshaw.

'So that's why I've been slightly off recently. We've been going through a rough patch.'

'And it's sorted now?' Poe asked.

'It is.'

'And?'

'And what?'

'How *was* it sorted?'

Flynn looked at him and Poe knew that was all he was getting today. She could never be accused of being an over-sharer.

'I'm glad to hear that, Steph. And may I put in an early offer for godfather?'

Flynn smiled. 'If you behave yourself . . . I might show you a photograph of the baby one day.'

Poe smiled back. Mates again.

'What does that have to do with this, though?'

Flynn's jaw hardened. 'My point is this, Poe: until I decided to take the bull by the horns and make a decision, Zoe and I were heading for trouble.'

'So . . . ?'

'So stop feeling fucking sorry for yourself and do something about it!'

'But we've—'

Flynn stopped him with a raised palm. She looked at Bradshaw and said, 'Who do we work for, Tilly?'

'We work for the Serious Crime Analysis Section, DI Stephanie Flynn.'

'And what do we do?'

'We profile people and help the police catch them.'

'Exactly.'

'But there's no one left to profile,' Poe protested.

'Isn't there?'

Poe stopped to think. He ran through everyone involved in the case. Came up with a big fat blank. He shrugged. 'There's no one left.'

'Not a person. A thing,' she replied. 'The paper trail might have gone cold, but we have more than enough to go on.'

Ah. Of course.

Poe smiled. Bradshaw did too.

'Exactly,' Flynn said. 'We're going to profile this missing bunker.'

CHAPTER FIFTY-EIGHT

Flynn took charge. 'Tilly, you work the computer.'

'Duh, what were we going to do, let Poe do it?'

They stared at her in surprise.

'Sorry,' she said.

'Don't worry, we're all exhausted,' Flynn said.

She turned to Poe. 'You say all the Cumbrian bunkers have been accounted for?'

He nodded and checked his notes. 'According to Harold, the local bunkers were in strategic clusters. The local observers reported to the Carlisle Control Group who relayed everything to the western sector's headquarters in Preston. Preston then reported to something called "NATO Strike Command Operations Centre", which was down south somewhere.'

'And you think Morris found the truffles near Bullace & Sloe?'

'Nearer to the Gamekeeper's Kitchen, I suspect. He tried to sell them there first.'

'Could he have been driving home? Found them miles away but he was in the middle of nowhere?'

'I don't think so. The chef at the Gamekeeper's Kitchen said Morris was "grubby" and that the truffles looked fresh out of the ground. And the bunker would have been near an existing one. If it *was* replaced, it was because the specific site was unsuitable, not the general location. If it had gone operational it would have been part of the original cluster.'

Bradshaw brought up a map of the area.

'The nearest existing bunker to the Gamekeeper's Kitchen is here,' Poe said, pointing at the screen. 'On the register it's down as being in Armathwaite, which is where Morris lived, but Harold told me it's actually nearer the village of Aiketgate.'

'I don't suppose that's the bunker we're looking for?' Flynn asked.

Poe shook his head. It was a sensible question and one he'd asked Harold. 'No. This one's intact and well known. And it's in a farmer's field, not a wood.'

'But given that Morris visited restaurants nearby, it's probable that it's the Aiketgate bunker that replaced the missing bunker,' Bradshaw said. 'And if it is, then the missing bunker's going to be nearby.'

'Agreed,' Poe said. 'It's almost certainly in a wood near the village of Aiketgate.'

'OK then,' Flynn said. 'We need a Venn diagram with the needs of black summer truffles in one set and ROC Nuclear Observation Posts requirements in the other. We can then see what they have in common.'

An hour later they had a list.

Flynn summarised for them 'The ROC post had to be in a position that had a 360-degree line of sight.'

Poe nodded. 'Yes, unlike the original aircraft positions that only required a clear view of the sky, the nuclear bunkers also needed unobstructed views of the ground to measure blast waves and flash burns. Almost all of them were in farmers' fields. And because land around here isn't flat it means they had to be in elevated positions.'

'So when it was built it was in a field. But that field's now a wood?'

'Seems so. A new wood.'

'But not so new that the trees aren't mature enough to sustain truffles,' Bradshaw said.

'I'm not sure I understand why a farmer would plant trees,' Flynn said. 'Surely a field's more useful?'

Poe knew the answer to this. Thomas Hume had told him.

'Exposed topsoil on elevated positions becomes eroded. Farmers plant trees to stop the soil becoming barren and rocky. Woods also protect the land downhill by taking some of the water during wet weather. And, as well as creating shelter for animals and crops by providing a natural barrier from the wind, lots of farms in Cumbria now run game shoots, and woods and treelines are the ideal habitat for pheasants and other game birds.'

'OK. So we need trees that grow fast and sustain truffles.'

'Not oak then,' Bradshaw said. 'They're slow-growing. That leaves beech or birch. They're the only ones that grow fast enough, while also having the roots truffles prefer.'

'Probably not beech either,' Poe said. 'A lot of Cumbrians don't accept beech as a native tree. It is down south, but this far north it's seen as a non-native. Farmers round here are traditionalists. Especially when it doesn't cost them money.'

'How do you know this?' Bradshaw seemed amused that he knew trivia she didn't.

Poe shrugged. 'The MP for Kendal was part of a group trying to get its classification changed. It was in the paper a few years back.'

The room went silent.

'You've got to care about something, I suppose,' he added.

Bradshaw said, 'Birch works. It's fast-growing and cheap to buy. The most likely sub-species is the silver birch. They need well-drained soil, which fits with the elevated position we're looking for.'

'So we're looking for a new birch wood on an elevated position near the bunker at Aiketgate village?'

Poe nodded.

Bradshaw did too.

'OK then,' Flynn said. 'Now we find it.'

Poe stared at her blankly.

'And when I say "we", I do of course mean Tilly . . .'

With all the aerial and satellite tools available to Bradshaw, finding a silver-birch wood in a small defined area shouldn't have been too difficult. And if they were in Manchester or Sheffield or Birmingham, it wouldn't have been.

But she was searching Cumbria.

Finding birch woods wasn't difficult; their silver, peeling bark was distinctive.

Finding the *right* birch wood was much harder.

She eventually narrowed it down to nine.

Three of them looked old and weren't just birch. Poe discounted them on the basis that if a farmer was planting a wood from scratch, he'd buy trees in bulk. There'd be no reason to mix and match. Two were close to the River Eden and therefore probably prone to flooding.

That left four.

Bradshaw put the best satellite images in a grid formation on her laptop. The three of them leaned in. For a while no one spoke.

Poe checked their locations on the map. One was an obvious favourite, he decided. It was near the village, it had decent road access and it was close to the existing bunker. Woods two and three were also possible. They didn't have the road access of the first but otherwise they met all their criteria. Poe thought about dismissing the fourth. It was a trek across three fields and two other woods. It wasn't near Aiketgate nor was it near where Les Morris had lived. It was also tangled with undergrowth. In the end he chose to leave it on. Realistically, it could have been any of them, or none of them.

'Do you think Chloe Bloxwich is hiding there?' Flynn asked quietly, her eyes still transfixed to the screen.

He hadn't thought about that. It was as good a place as any, he supposed. Somewhere safe to lie low for a while. Wait for whatever reward Keaton had promised her.

A crash of thunder reminded him of something Harold had told him. He looked over Flynn's shoulder and out of the rain-blurred window. The charcoal sky spewed rain like bullets. The thunder roared with untamed power. Storm Wendy was everything they'd been promised.

'If she is, I hope she's wearing her wellies,' Poe said. 'Those bunkers weren't fitted with drains, only sumps. That's why most of the derelict ones are flooded.'

Bradshaw yelled out without warning: 'DRAINS!'

Without explanation she killed the pictures of the woods and began typing furiously. Her glasses reflected webpage after webpage as she searched for something. 'Omigod, omigod, omigod,' she kept repeating.

After twenty seconds she stopped typing and read what was on her screen. She leaped from her seat and ran over to the printer. She hopped from foot to foot while she waited for the document to crawl out.

Poe and Flynn exchanged glances.

'We're enjoying this awkward silence, Tilly,' Flynn said.

The printing stopped and Bradshaw handed them both a two-page document. She also handed Poe the reading glasses he'd left in Shap Wells. '*This* is how Chloe Bloxwich cheated the blood test.'

Poe glanced at the paper he'd been handed. It was a Wikipedia entry on a Rhodesian-raised Canadian citizen called John Schneeberger. He frowned at Bradshaw in confusion. She nodded for him to read it.

He did.

Before he'd reached the end of the first page he'd stopped breathing.

Because John Schneeberger was the man who'd made the impossible, possible – he'd found a way of having someone else's blood in his body. In 1992, after being accused of rape, he'd twice cheated the court-ordered DNA test and the charges were dropped. It wasn't until his wife reported him to the police for raping her daughter from her first marriage that multiple samples, including mouth swabs and hair follicles, were taken. His DNA this time matched the DNA found on the first rape victim. Poe read how he had managed it. He'd been right – it had been a low-tech solution. Brilliant in its simplicity.

Poe ran Schneeberger's method through their own case, strand after strand, making sure it fitted the facts.

It did.

Everything worked.

Everything was explained.

Realisation dawned on him. He stared at Bradshaw. 'But this means . . .'

'It does, Poe,' Bradshaw said, her face devastated. 'I'm so very sorry.'

CHAPTER FIFTY-NINE

The storm was louder than war.

That was Poe's thought as he stared out of the hotel's fire escape. The rain machine-gunned the ground. The thunder was raw, deafening and continuous, like listening to radio static at full volume. Lightning – not the usual intermittent zigzags he was used to – filled the sky with unrelenting bursts of brilliant light that turned night into day. To Poe it looked more like celestial camera flashes than lightning, as if the gods themselves couldn't resist photographing the swirling maelstrom below them. The trees weren't just swaying – like seaweed in an eddy, the wind was bending and straining them, testing their roots to the limit. Branches littered the car park like torn-off limbs.

It was a night to stay indoors.

Poe fastened his jacket up high, said goodbye to a grim-looking Flynn and a terrified-looking Bradshaw, and stepped outside.

Wardle might have been chasing a padded envelope in Scotland, but not every Cumbrian cop was an idiot. If he were seen, he'd be arrested on sight. So, even using Victoria's Land Rover, Poe was uneasy about using major roads.

He didn't have a choice. To *not* use them would have been too suspicious in this weather. The smaller roads would be impassable, or dangerous enough for traffic cops to be constantly monitoring them.

The M6 it was then.

The one-track lane out of Shap Wells had turned into a fast-moving stream. Poe followed it up the hill, glad he was in the Land Rover and not his hire car. Its thick tyres bit into the mud and debris on the road and kept him going forwards.

Visibility was down to only a few yards. Even on double-speed the wipers couldn't cope with the water battering the windscreen. With luck rather than judgement, he made it to the end of the track. He turned right onto the A6 and put his foot down until he hit a steady thirty. A few minutes later he was on the motorway.

He increased his speed to forty miles per hour as he headed north. Slow enough to manage the buffeting wind and avoid the major debris, fast enough to make progress.

He had one sticky moment. A mile after the Wigton junction he saw the tell-tale blue lights of emergency vehicles. It looked like more than one. If it was a planned operation to stop him they'd got it exactly right. Close enough to the junction for other cops to join in if he fled, far enough away so that he wouldn't spot them until he'd passed the turnoff.

He slowed to thirty.

Then twenty.

He needn't have worried. It was an overturned lorry. It had blocked the hard shoulder and left-hand lane, the driver sitting forlornly in the back of an ambulance while a white-capped traffic cop no doubt gave him a lecture on the folly of driving high-sided vehicles in extreme weather.

Poe breathed a sigh of relief, took the right-hand lane and crawled past the police cars and ambulances. No one gave him a second look.

Half an hour later he was at junction 42. He turned off. Another flash of lightning lit up the River Petteril. The usually languid river was swollen, torrid and so muddy it looked like it was upside down. It was scattered with vortexes and carried along vegetation, uprooted trees and, if Poe wasn't mistaken, what looked like a garden table.

Ten minutes later, he turned right towards Cotehill. Five minutes after that he pulled into the empty car park of Bullace & Sloe . . .

CHAPTER SIXTY

Poe remained in the Land Rover. The car park was empty and the restaurant was bathed in darkness. For a moment he thought he'd got it wrong. That not even the die-hard gourmets were out tonight. It was only when he remembered the Met Office warnings about power cuts that he took a closer look.

There *were* lights on. They were dim and flickering. Bullace & Sloe was using candles.

The restaurant was open.

It was now or never.

Poe opened the driver's door and stepped onto wet gravel. He had to shield his face against the stinging rain. He ran the thirty yards to the front door and paused. The porch gave him a degree of protection from the storm. He peered through the stencilled window.

Jared Keaton sat alone at a table.

He was wearing a pale blue suit. The short, unfolded stand-up collar was buttoned up to his neck. A mandarin collar, Poe thought they were called.

He was sipping from a wine glass and reading what looked like a menu. He glanced up and saw Poe. He didn't look surprised. If anything, he looked happy. He beckoned him inside.

'Ah, Poe,' Keaton said, with a genial smile. 'You've arrived. I was beginning to worry.'

Despite the monsoon, Poe's mouth was bone dry. He tried to clear his throat but it came out as a scratchy cough. He took in his surroundings. A resplendently dressed waiter stood in the corner. Otherwise, it was just the two of them.

'Dining alone tonight, Jared?' His words were croaky. He reached for a bottle of water on a nearby table, flipped the top and raised it to his lips. He took a long swig.

Keaton's smile remained.

'Steady on, old chap.' He pushed an empty wine glass in Poe's direction. 'Have some wine if you're thirsty.'

Poe continued to drink from the bottle.

Keaton raised his hand and the waiter approached. 'Fill Sergeant Poe's glass please, Jason.'

'Yes, Chef Keaton.'

Jason filled the glass with white wine. Poe didn't touch it. Keaton shrugged. He looked at Poe's mud-spattered jeans and his squelching boots, the hair that was plastered to his forehead and the rainwater that dripped from his clothes onto the flagstone floor.

'You seem to be pushing our dress code to the extreme, Sergeant Poe.'

He held Poe's gaze for a moment before cracking a grin. 'Just kidding. It's a private function tonight – that's why I'm alone – you wear what you want.' He gestured at the seat opposite him.

Poe pulled out the seat and sat down. He picked up a cotton napkin and used it to get the worst of the rainwater out of his hair. Keaton watched in bemused silence.

When Poe finished, Keaton beckoned the waiter again.

'Tell chef there will be two for dinner, please.'

'Yes, Chef Keaton.'

The waiter left the room.

'I'm not staying, Keaton,' Poe said.

'You want to speak to me, yes?'

Poe nodded.

'Then you eat with me. I refuse to converse on an empty stomach.'

Poe didn't respond.

'I understand you dined here recently?'

'I did.'

'Well I can assure you, what you ate that day is nothing compared to what you're about to eat now. My old mentor, Chef Jégado, has driven from Paris to cook for me tonight. A special treat after all I've been through.'

Poe frowned. This wasn't going the way he'd expected. 'Fine. Just one dish, though. I'm not sitting through fifteen courses again.'

'It is settled then.' Keaton smiled with what looked like genuine delight.

'Why did you—'

Keaton raised his hand. 'After we've eaten, Sergeant Poe. After we've eaten.'

Poe gave up. Keaton obviously wasn't going to budge on this. Not when he was enjoying himself so much. Instead, he took a sip of wine from the glass Jason had poured. He rarely drank wine so doubted he had the palate to differentiate between a good one and an excellent one. This seemed OK, though. Different from anything he'd had before.

'Where did you get this from?' He may as well get him talking about something.

'My wine merchant procured this from a vineyard in France almost ten years ago. It wasn't cheap, but then the best things in life never are.'

Poe couldn't think of a reply and they fell into an uneasy silence.

Keaton broke it first.

'Do you know what I have missed the most these last six years, Sergeant Poe?'

'Your daughter?'

Keaton smiled and shook his finger in admonishment.

'Freshly cut flowers,' he said. He closed his eyes and breathed in deeply. 'They really do make a room, don't you think?'

Poe looked around the dining room. The eerie glow of the candles had partially hidden them but there *were* a lot of flowers. He didn't remember there being that many when he and Bradshaw had dined there.

'And because of increasingly exploitative child labour laws, they're surprisingly economical,' Keaton added, with a smile. He took another deep breath. 'The perfume of misery. The perfect metaphor for tonight's business, do you not think, Sergeant Poe?'

Before Poe could respond, the kitchen door opened.

'Ah, excellent – here's the first dish.'

The waiter approached carrying two copper serving pots. They were aflame and sizzling.

'I think you'll enjoy this dish. It's a songbird called the ortolan bunting. Chef Jégado brought them over from Paris herself, and not fifteen minutes ago she drowned them in brandy . . .'

CHAPTER SIXTY-ONE

After he had emerged from his napkin, blood and grease dripping from his lips, Poe decided that Keaton was about as off-guard as he was likely to get.

'We've identified the girl claiming to be your daughter, Jared.'

Keaton's smile flickered then recovered.

'Chloe Bloxwich. She's the daughter of a prisoner on your wing in HMP Pentonville.'

'Is that so?'

'And we know where your daughter's body is.'

Keaton opened out his arms. 'And where might that be?'

Poe looked deep into his eyes before he answered. 'An abandoned Royal Observer Corps nuclear observation bunker near the village of Aiketgate.'

There it was!

The flutter of an eyelid. It happened so fast it barely happened at all.

He'd surprised him.

Keaton recovered quickly. The shock faded, the easy charm returned. He looked around in an exaggerated fashion.

'I'm not a simpleton, Poe,' he said. 'You're here on your own, which means that the warrant for your arrest must still be outstanding. So, I'm guessing you're here to what . . . get me to confess to something? Perhaps you are recording this conversation?'

'I don't need a confession, Keaton. You know as well as I do that when we find this bunker – and we will – we will discover

342

the remains of your daughter, and the remains of the man who showed you it.'

Keaton relaxed slightly. 'As it happens, I know a bit about decommissioned ROC bunkers. Even if you'd somehow got a list of their locations, the one you claim to be looking for wouldn't be on it.'

'The so-called "missing bunker".'

'You've been busy, Sergeant Poe.'

'We'll find it.'

'But my understanding is that you will soon be in custody.'

Poe said nothing. It was probably true.

'And by the time your impending legal problems are resolved, I will have been acquitted of the crime you're going to be charged with: the murder of Elizabeth.'

'I don't work in isolation, Keaton. I have a team of analysts to call upon. And we have a double jeopardy law now. You *can* be tried twice for the same crime.'

'How nice for you all. But this missing bunker you talk about is not on any register. The government can't confirm it ever existed, and the experts are sure it didn't. And even if your team persist with looking for it, it's a concrete box that's been buried in the ground for seventy years. In a county this size, a thousand men could search for a thousand years and still not find it. Face it, Poe, there *is* no bunker.'

Poe said nothing for a moment. 'You might be right, Keaton. That bunker might never be found.'

Keaton smiled like a man who held all the aces.

'But on my travels, I met a gentleman who'd served with the ROC.' Poe picked up his glass and drained his wine. 'Very chatty and knowledgeable. Taught me all sorts of things about these bunkers.' Poe paused. 'And he also knew Les Morris.'

Keaton stiffened.

'Do you want to know what he told me?'

343

Keaton nodded.

'He told me that Morris wasn't an outdoors person. His wife said the same thing. So did the chef he first tried to sell those truffles to.'

Annoyance crossed Keaton's face. Poe didn't know if it was because he was getting too close for comfort, or because Bullace & Sloe hadn't been Morris's first choice.

'So, what can we surmise from this?' Poe asked.

'Do tell, Sergeant Poe.'

'Well, we can surmise that there *must* be a paper trail leading to this missing bunker. Mr Morris couldn't have found it without one.'

Keaton relaxed. 'I told you, there are no records . . .' He trailed off. 'I see what you did there, Sergeant Poe. I won't incriminate myself. "Why would he be searching ROC bunkers?" the CPS might say at my retrial.'

'Your confidence in government bureaucracy is well placed, Keaton. They have indeed lost all knowledge of this bunker.'

Keaton shrugged and smiled. 'I told you, Sergeant Poe, a thousand years. That's how long you'd have to look. Do you have a thousand years?'

'But the other thing the ROC gentleman told me is that, although the government oversaw the construction of the bunkers, the actual building work was contracted out to local firms.'

Keaton's smile slipped. It was clear that he hadn't known that.

'And what I think happened is this,' Poe said. 'Mr Morris searched the archives of building firms in the 1950s until he found exactly what he was looking for: the invoice for the "missing bunker".'

The discomfort behind Keaton's eyes increased.

'And first thing tomorrow morning, a team of my analysts will descend on Cumbria County Council's Archive Service. We already have the warrant. If that was how Mr Morris found it, we'll have the location by the end of the day.'

Keaton's eyes lost focus. He seemed to be considering his options. For a minute neither of them spoke.

'It's an interesting story,' he said eventually. 'But alas one we can't continue, I'm afraid. It seems there are others joining us.'

Poe spun in his seat. Rigg and a uniformed cop were at the door. He turned to face Keaton.

'So close.' Keaton beckoned Rigg inside.

Rigg approached the table. 'Sir, could you come with us, please?'

Poe looked round, searching for a way out. The waiter was still in the kitchen with Keaton's French chef so there was no escape through there. The uniformed constable with Rigg had already extended his baton.

'Don't do anything stupid, sir,' Rigg said.

'Too late for that,' Poe snarled. He grabbed the half-full wine bottle by the neck and held it in front of him. The contents sluiced down his still damp shirt.

For a moment, no one moved.

'You have to let me explain!' Poe hissed, his eyes fixed on the uniformed officer's baton.

'You'll get your chance tomorrow,' Rigg said.

The uniformed cop moved to Poe's left. Poe tracked him with the bottle.

The kitchen door opened. The waiter walked out. He was holding a platter of oysters. He saw the scene in front of him and dropped the metal dish. Ice cubes scattered across the flagged floor.

It was all the distraction they needed. The cop went low; Rigg went high. The baton took Poe behind the knees, Rigg's punch caught him squarely on the jaw.

Poe fell to his knees then collapsed onto the floor.

By the time he regained his senses, he was handcuffed to the rear. He tried to struggle but the uniformed cop was kneeling on his back, forcing his head against the floor. The stone tiles felt cold on his cheek.

Everyone but Keaton was breathing heavily.

Rigg stood over him. 'Washington Poe, I'm arresting you on suspicion of murder. You do not have to say anything but it may harm your defence if you do not mention when questioned something that you later rely on in court. Anything you do say may be given in evidence.'

Keaton stood. He drained his glass of wine and walked over. He looked down at Poe.

'But how . . . ?'

'I called them the moment you arrived,' Keaton said. 'I win, Sergeant Poe.'

Poe groaned and shut his eyes.

He couldn't bear to look at Keaton's face for a moment longer.

CHAPTER SIXTY-TWO

The uniformed cop frogmarched Poe to the waiting police car and bundled him into the back. The cop then got into the driver's seat and waited for Rigg, who was clearing things up with Keaton. Keaton was gesticulating theatrically. Rigg was doing his best to placate the angry chef.

Rigg joined his colleague in the front of the car. As soon as he'd closed the door, they pulled away.

The worst of Storm Wendy was over. The lightning, thunder and wind had fizzled out. The rain fell vertically instead of horizontally. The journey out was quicker than the one in.

After a mile the car slowed and then stopped. Rigg turned in his seat. 'We'll send someone to collect your Land Rover tomorrow, Poe.'

Poe rubbed his jaw. It clicked. He could taste blood in his mouth. 'Did you have to hit me so fucking hard?'

'Hey, you said to make it look realistic.' He reached over and unlocked the handcuffs.

Poe flexed his wrists and got the blood circulating again. He looked across at the driver. 'And you, what was with the baton behind the knees? That bloody hurt.'

'Sorry, Sarge. Andy here told me to give you a whack if you picked up a weapon. It's standard practice.'

'Fair point,' Poe conceded.

Rigg's smile dropped. 'Do you think he bought it?'

Poe sighed. 'Fuck knows.'

347

'It must be a laugh a minute managing Poe, DI Flynn,' Rigg said.

They were standing in the wood that Poe had initially dismissed. The fourth wood. The one that was thick with scrub and bushes and miles from anywhere. What had looked wrong earlier had suddenly seemed right. He couldn't put his finger on why.

Sometimes you just had to go with your gut.

Flynn had met them there after his staged arrest. Poe had wanted them to split the four woods between them but one of Rigg's conditions was that he never left his sight. If tonight didn't bring a result then Rigg would arrest him for real. Poe had no choice but to agree. And Flynn had wanted to be with him in case it came to that. She didn't want him going through it on his own.

Cops whom Rigg trusted were staking out the other three woods.

Hours earlier, after Bradshaw had discovered how the blood test could have been cheated, reality had set in. They knew everything, yet they could prove nothing.

Their options were limited.

They could go and see Wardle. Lay out what they knew and hope that he'd put his personal ambitions aside and do what was right. Poe didn't like that option. At this point in the investigation Wardle would be impervious to reason. He had too much to lose.

They could apply for surveillance funding and operate in Cumbria without the chief constable's knowledge. This time it was Flynn who didn't like it. The county had been used as a terrorist training ground in the past and the NCA couldn't afford to alienate the Cumbrian cops – as always, local knowledge was key in intelligence gathering.

Bradshaw wanted Poe to keep hiding at Victoria's while she

and Flynn tried to find the bunker before Keaton found a way to destroy the evidence. Poe hated that idea the most. If he was going down, it wasn't going to be while he cowered in a hole like a failed dictator.

None of the options were pretty.

'Everything's against us,' Poe said. 'We can't win this game. It's rigged.'

Flynn's look changed. It seemed like she was listening to something inside her head. Eventually she said, 'We change the rules then. That's how we win this.'

Poe stared at her.

Change the rules . . .

Of course that was what they should do. They were dealing with the most unconventional criminal they had ever encountered. Normal rules didn't apply.

And they had to go further than that. Simply changing the rules wouldn't be enough. They'd still be playing Keaton's game. He'd still hold the high cards.

But what if they didn't play Keaton's game?

What if they played their own?

And what if that night, their game of choice was misdirection?

So Flynn had called Rigg and asked him to meet her at Shap Wells. Told him it would be worth his while. Wardle was in Scotland chasing Poe's BlackBerry so Rigg had been able to come alone.

When Rigg saw Poe he tried to effect an arrest. Poe let him.

Poe had been right about Rigg. As the case had developed he'd become increasingly uneasy about Keaton's innocence and the way no one seemed to be questioning it. Wardle's direction of travel, and his point-blank refusal to entertain other ideas, had also bothered him, to the point he'd been ready to go above his head.

At the end of the day he was too good a cop not to have his own ideas.

So he'd agreed to listen to what they had to say.

Bradshaw led.

She ran him through the sequence of events: the Bullace & Sloe meal that led them to Jefferson Black; the missing tattoo; the identification of Chloe Bloxwich; the truffles and the bunker; and finally, how the blood test might have been cheated.

Rigg admitted it was compelling. He also confirmed what they already knew: without evidence it was all just a neat theory.

'I assume I'm here because you need something from me?' Rigg asked. 'What is it?'

'You're not going to like it,' Poe said.

He was right.

Rigg didn't.

It was an unusual stakeout. Ordinarily a suspect would be under surveillance from the moment they were identified all the way up to the point of arrest.

Nothing about the Keaton case was ordinary. Air surveillance – the safest way to follow suspects in rural areas – was out of the question. They didn't have the authorisation and even if they had, Storm Wendy had grounded all helicopters and light aircraft.

Ground surveillance was out too. In daylight, if there were enough of them, cars could be used. Even that was risky, though. Rural roads were like rabbit warrens. Some weren't even mapped. Get too close and you were seen by the target. Hang back too much and you lost them. At night it was impossible. With head-lights on, surveillance cars stood out like pepper in salt.

Poe had gambled. Trusted that Bradshaw had identified all the possible woods. Although it was the middle of summer and the days were long, Storm Wendy was helping for once. The rolling clouds were black and low and provided an unseasonal darkness.

Rigg's driver had dropped them off as near as he could but they had half a mile of rough and slippery ground to negotiate before they reached the elevated wood. The wind had died and the silver birches stood ramrod straight. In the pale light the bark seemed to glow.

The wood wasn't large but a ring of vicious gorse bushes guarded it. The birch trees were well spaced and the overhead canopy allowed enough sunlight for the undergrowth to grow thick and heavy. From a distance it had looked impenetrable but up close Poe could see it wasn't. Natural paths, probably made by sheep seeking shelter in winter, had been forged through the brambles and hawthorns.

Poe, with the natural eye of the ex-infantryman, soon found somewhere he was happy with. It was in the middle of a thornless shrub that he couldn't identify. It afforded them decent cover. He began clearing out a patch big enough for the three of them to stand in. When they saw what he was doing, Rigg and Flynn helped.

In less than five minutes they had finished.

Now all they had to do was wait.

Time moved slower than concrete. The British Army saying 'hurry up and wait' sprang to mind.

They'd been in the wood for three hours and, apart from getting drenched, nothing had happened. By the time midnight came and went, the storm had ceased completely. It was hot and still and humid. The earth was damp and the air ionised. Other than the drip-drip of rainwater falling from leaves, and the occasional flutter of unseen wings, it was ominously quiet. The pale light had been replaced by a darkness thick enough to block out silhouettes. It was disorientating and oppressive. The humidity became less and less bearable. Poe wafted his shirt to create a breeze but sweat and rainwater pooled at the base of his spine.

'This is a waste of time,' he whispered. He was jittery. His neck muscles were beginning to spasm. They had no margin of error. If they were staking out the wrong woods, or if Keaton held his nerve, then it was over.

'The only thing we've wasted so far is the Queen's diesel,' Rigg whispered back. 'Give it time; you know these things never work out exactly as planned.'

But an hour later their worst fears were realised.

CHAPTER SIXTY-THREE

Rigg's mobile phone vibrated. He shielded the screen and whispered into it. 'Say again.'

Somehow Poe knew the call was about him.

Rigg's hand dropped and the screen lit up his face. The furrows on his brow had deepened. His eyes were flashing. He ended the call and the wood descended into darkness again.

'That was control. DCI Wardle's driving back from Scotland as we speak. Although we were expecting Keaton to call us when you got to Bullace & Sloe, the control room guy hadn't been briefed and thought it was a real arrest. He logged it on the system. One of Wardle's team was working late, got an alert and called him.'

Poe grimaced.

'He didn't try to call you?' Flynn asked.

'Probably, but I'm on my personal phone tonight. DCI Wardle doesn't have this number and no one will give it to him.'

'Did Wardle have a message?'

'I'm to detain you until he arrives. He wants to arrest you himself.'

Poe shook his head. They were so close . . .

'It gets worse,' Rigg added.

Poe didn't see how it could. He braced himself anyway.

'He's pulled all surveillance. Apart from this wood, none of the others are being watched now.'

FUCK!

Poe wanted to scream but settled for punching a tree. He put his hand to his mouth and sucked his bloody knuckles. Flynn put her hand on his shoulder.

'What are your intentions, DC Rigg?' she asked.

'DCI Wardle's the other side of Dumfries. That means he's at least an hour away. He wants me to detain you but he didn't say where. This place is as good as anywhere, I reckon.'

Poe blew out his cheeks in relief.

They still had a chance.

Poe waited. Time, glacial before the phone call, moved faster than the swollen rivers they'd driven over to get there. He checked his watch again. Ten minutes had passed since he'd last looked a minute ago.

He tried to calculate where Wardle would be. Figured that by the time Rigg had finished briefing them, he could have reached the Dumfries ring road. He saw it in his mind's eye – Wardle, hunched over the steering wheel, glaring at the road as he urged his car to go faster, his hatred of Poe making him ignore the dangerous driving conditions.

Rigg reckoned an hour. Poe thought that was generous. He doubted he had more than forty minutes.

More time passed.

He checked his watch again.

Another ten minutes had gone by.

His heart sank further.

Keaton was going to win.

Rigg's phone rang again. He didn't bother shielding it this time. He showed them the screen. It said, 'Anne'.

'Rigg.'

He listened.

'Say that again, Anne.' He made no effort to keep his voice down. He then covered the mouthpiece and said, 'DC Anne Hawthorne is one of the detectives I assigned to the surveillance

354

posts. She's also my partner so watch what you say to her.' He removed his hand from the mouthpiece. 'Can you please tell DI Flynn and Sergeant Poe what you've just told me, Anne? I'm putting you on speakerphone.'

Her tinny voice was loud in the noiseless wood.

'I'm outside the target's residence as per instructions.'

For Poe and Flynn it was a moment of confusion.

'I thought DCI Wardle had pulled all surveillance, DC Hawthorne,' Flynn said.

'Did he? I didn't get that message. Perhaps my radio is faulty.'

Poe just knew she was grinning. If he came out of this unscathed he would owe Anne Hawthorne a big drink.

'And anyway, even if I had got the message, which I definitely didn't, as soon as DCI Wardle cancelled the op's OT, I went off-duty. He doesn't get to dictate where I spend my free time.'

'And can you repeat what you told me?' Rigg asked.

'Target's on the move. Not thirty seconds before I called you.'

There was a stunned silence.

It was happening.

Right now.

Except . . . except Wardle was going to get there first.

Flynn said that she'd stay behind while Poe went to Carlisle police station with Rigg. 'At least the surveillance won't be compromised.'

It was a good idea and Poe said so.

Rigg agreed. With one small modification. He spoke into the phone, 'Can you ring control, Anne? Tell them I'm taking Poe to Kendal nick, not Carlisle. Oh, and add that my mobile's died so I won't be contactable until I get there.'

'Happy to,' she said, and rang off.

'That'll buy us some time,' Rigg said, his expression grim. 'I'm going nowhere – for better or worse, we're in this together now.'

Poe breathed out slowly. That was the problem with managers

like Wardle who demanded loyalty they hadn't earned: they were only given a superficial version. Cops resented them. The first chance they got to fuck them over, they did. And it was a good solution – by making him drive past Carlisle and all the way down to Kendal, Rigg had added another hour to Wardle's journey. By the time he realised he'd been duped, one way or another, it would all be over.

They'd either picked the right wood or they hadn't.

They heard the car door shutting.

Poe prepared himself. There was any number of reasons why someone might choose to get out of a car in this area, at this time of night, in this weather. A flat tyre, an emergency piss, some enthusiastic dogging.

All possible.

But not really.

Not in this context.

They knew that the car door shutting signalled the beginning of the end.

Someone was coming.

The sound had come from where they'd been dropped off. Made sense. They'd taken the shortest route, whoever was coming was doing the same.

The field they'd walked through to get to the wood was predominantly sheep-grazed, springy grass. And because of the deluge of rain, it was soundless to walk on. For ten minutes they heard nothing.

And then . . . a torch snapped on. It was close and dazzlingly bright. Poe felt Flynn and Rigg tense up. His scalp tightened. He pushed himself further into the groundcover. The others did the same.

The torch cast left and right, navigating the protective gorse bushes.

Then it was shining into the wood. Fractured beams of light cut through the trees like a laser show.

Nearer and nearer.

After twenty yards it stopped and went still. It had been placed on something.

Someone grunted. They couldn't see what was happening but it sounded like mud and leaves were being moved.

The bunker's hatch was being uncovered.

'Now?' Rigg whispered.

'Not yet,' Poe replied. 'Wait until it's open.'

'OK. Your call.'

Poe tried to calculate what was happening not twenty yards away. Tried to figure out how much earth and leaf litter had been used to hide the bunker's entrance. Not much, he imagined. It wouldn't need it. The wood was isolated and virtually impenetrable.

After two minutes there was a metallic creak and a solid clunk. They caught a faint smell of something putrid and sinister.

It was now or never.

Poe stepped out from the shrubbery and turned on his torch. He shone it directly in the face of the person holding a red plastic fuel container. There was a cry of surprise. Rigg and Flynn ran up, handcuffs at the ready. No resistance was offered.

'I so didn't want to be right about this,' Poe said.

The person Rigg and Flynn were holding wasn't Jared Keaton. It was Flick Jakeman, the force medical examiner.

One week later

CHAPTER SIXTY-FOUR

Poe, Flynn and Bradshaw watched a live link of the interview with Jared Keaton. It was a Cumbrian case and it was right that they led on it. They were at Durranhill, Carlisle's Northern Area command building and the largest police station in Cumbria. The interview room was modern and spacious.

The door opened and Superintendent Gamble stepped in. He nodded at Poe. 'What's happening?'

'DC Rigg's just laying the groundwork.'

'Keaton still not spoken yet?'

Poe shook his head.

'He doesn't look worried.'

Poe didn't respond. It was true. Keaton didn't look worried.

'How'd Wardle take your return?'

Gamble smiled. 'Ever seen a headmaster who's just found out one of his teachers is a paedophile?'

'Yep.'

'Like that.'

'How's Chloe Bloxwich doing?'

Gamble's face darkened. 'Still in intensive care. Another three hours and she'd have died, they reckon. The doctors will let us know when she's out of danger. We're asking the CPS to consider charging Keaton with attempted murder as well as everything else.'

When the hatch had opened, and Flick Jakeman had been arrested, Poe lowered himself down to have a look inside the bunker. He wanted to confirm his suspicions. Elizabeth's dismembered remains and the dried-up corpse of Les Morris were down there. He'd also found Chloe Bloxwich. She was half dead and drifting in and out of consciousness.

Poe had made sure Flick Jakeman was forced to wait as the fire and rescue workers lifted Chloe out and the paramedics performed emergency first aid on her. He needed her to see what she'd been a part of.

When she saw Chloe, she collapsed on the ground screaming.

'Chloe talked yet?' Poe asked Gamble.

'Briefly,' he replied. 'She's just a fucked-up kid, though. Went off the rails when her mother died of cancer a few years ago. Seems her dad loved her but couldn't express it. He wanted her to be an accountant, she rebelled and became an actress. Lived off handouts from her mother. When she died, Chloe hooked up with some arsehole and got addicted to heroin. Started self-harming. She didn't know Elizabeth or Keaton. Never met either of them. Just had the misfortune of looking a bit like Elizabeth on a photograph that Keaton found in her dad's cell. She did her bit to camera and was in that bunker before you even got up here.'

Trapped in that bunker, Poe silently amended. The bunker's original ladder hadn't been fitted – it had either been taken away by the building contractors or requisitioned for something else – so Morris had been using a roll-up rock-climbing ladder to get in and out. He'd no doubt fastened it to the iron ring beside the hatch that was specifically there for that purpose. Poe reckoned that after Morris had shown Keaton around, Keaton had climbed out and then switched the anchor point from the iron ring to the underside of the hatch. He'd then closed it, effectively sealing Morris inside. His own bodyweight would have kept it shut. As he was hanging from the very thing he needed to push, the hatch would have been impossible to open.

And even if his body had been discovered, it would simply look like he'd made a terrible mistake. The coroner would have passed a 'death by misadventure' verdict without blinking.

Chloe Bloxwich had found herself in the same predicament – entombed in a bunker with no way of getting out and no way of calling for help. When she recovered, she would spend time in prison for perverting the course of justice. What she really needed was a psychiatrist. 'She spoken to her dad?' Poe asked.

Gamble frowned. 'She has. The prison arranged for a compassionate telephone call. Why?'

'No reason,' Poe said. He went back to watching the monitor.

Rigg was showing Keaton a photograph that had been taken in the bunker . . .

It was the most complex crime scene with which any of them had ever been involved. After Chloe Bloxwich had been rescued, Flynn had resealed the hatch and waited for Rigg to call in the full resources of Cumbria Police. Before long, the wood was lit up like Glastonbury.

The attending forensic pathologist was the same one who'd flip-flopped on the amount of blood spilled in the kitchen of Bullace & Sloe six years earlier. Rigg told him to get lost.

In the end, and as a favour to Poe, Estelle Doyle had driven across from Newcastle to supervise the crime scene. Wearing hazmat suits, it had taken her and her team two days to recover the body of Les Morris, and the dismembered remains of Elizabeth Keaton, from the hellhole that the ROC Nuclear Observation Bunker had become.

Les Morris had been straightforward. Well, as straightforward as it could be in a subterranean bunker with crumbling concrete walls, hazardous biological material on every surface and CSI having to photograph everything they touched or wanted to move. Morris was badly decomposed but his skin had held his bones together and he was lifted from the bunker in one piece and without incident.

Elizabeth's recovery was more complex. She was in forty-three separate sous-vide bags, some of which had burst or were leaking putrid and dangerous fluids. Estelle Doyle handled each one carefully and, while other members of her team vomited and retched, she showed neither disgust nor distaste.

Doyle took both bodies to Newcastle for the post-mortems.

She quickly determined that Les Morris had died of dehydration. He also had a broken ankle, almost certainly from falling down the ladder shaft during a futile attempt to escape the bunker. His post-mortem had taken six hours.

Elizabeth's had taken three days.

Estelle Doyle had to open each sous-vide bag – which was in itself a crime scene and had to be managed as such – before determining which part of the body she was dealing with. Even for an expert in human anatomy, which Doyle undoubtedly was, it would have been a complicated puzzle to put together, but because Elizabeth's flesh had broken down and become liquefied, and her bones and cartilage were soft and spongy, it had bordered on impossible. An ordinary pathologist wouldn't have known where to start.

On the third day she'd called Poe, Flynn, Rigg and the newly reinstated Superintendent Gamble to her mortuary in Newcastle. She had Elizabeth's remains laid out on a stainless steel inspection table.

For an hour, as they stood behind the glass in the viewing area, she had talked them through what had happened.

Elizabeth had died of blood loss caused by a single puncture wound to the heart. At just over three inches, the wound wasn't deep, and Doyle believed a short knife had probably been used. Just like the one they'd recovered from the bunker . . .

After establishing the cause and manner of death, she moved

on to what Keaton had done next. He'd started at Elizabeth's head, which had been cut in two with a butcher's saw then hammered with a meat tenderiser – another of the sealed kitchen tools they'd recovered – until it was flat enough to be vacuum-wrapped.

The rest of the body had been butchered – there was no other way to describe it – in a similar way to how pigs are prepared. Elizabeth's knees, shoulders, elbows, hips and ankles had been jointed. Big and bulky bones like the femur and tibia had then been sawn into smaller pieces so Keaton could fit them in the vacuum machine. Long and thin bones like the fibula and humerus had been cleaved in half.

Poe watched Estelle Doyle's briefing without showing any emotion. It wasn't until Doyle pointed to some putrid flesh on the outside of Elizabeth's smashed-up pelvis that he allowed himself the luxury of a single tear.

With close and careful examination, the outline of the jigsaw tattoo that Jefferson Black had described – the one that interlocked with his own – could be seen. Presumably Keaton had missed it when he dismembered his daughter. Hard to see a red tattoo in all that blood.

Poe smiled at Keaton as he took his seat in the interview room. Keaton stared back without expression. Rigg sat beside Poe. The detective constable had agreed not to speak during this part.

After the formalities were over, David Collingwood, Keaton's brief, tried to boss the interview. He was a fat man with a pouchy face.

'Gentlemen, I think it's about time you told Mr Keaton what evidence you think you have against him. The sooner you do, the sooner we can bring this farce to an end.'

Poe placed a photograph face-down on the table. 'I'm going to tell you what we think happened, Mr Keaton. Then you're going to tell me the few bits we're struggling with.' He looked up and smiled. 'And I assure you, you *will* tell me.'

Keaton's expression changed from neutral to a smirk. He didn't speak.

Poe turned the photograph over.

'The late Les Morris. He died of dehydration approximately eight years ago. His corpse had been moved to the room that would have been the bunker's chemical toilet. Do you want to tell me how you trapped him down there?'

Silence.

'Allow me to continue then.'

Keaton looked at his nails. Buffed them on his shirt.

'As we suspected, Mr Morris had found the bunker by going through the business records of building companies that were around in the 1950s and 1960s. Copies were in the bunker with him. We think he was putting a presentation together.'

Keaton said nothing.

'We're guessing, but we think it was while he was clearing soil and debris as he searched for the top of the bunker that he found the black summer truffles.'

Poe stopped to take a drink.

'And for a while, that worked for you both. He got money to fund his secret restoration project and you got an expensive ingredient at way below market price. But . . . you're a psychopath, Keaton, and that was never going to last. You'll tell me later but here's what I think happened. You used the old Keaton charm on him and persuaded him to let you see this wood of his. And, of course, while you were there he couldn't resist showing off his bunker. You're not interested, but you climb down anyway. And you realise that if Morris were to die in there, he'd never be found. He's told no one where it is, and the only people who might look for him don't believe the bunker even exists. It was probably a spur of the moment decision, but you decide to climb out and trap him down there – subjecting him to the most appalling death.'

The trace of a smile tugged at the corner of Keaton's lips.

'How am I doing?' Poe asked.

Nothing.

He placed another photograph on the table. This was of the car crash in which Lauren Keaton died.

Keaton stirred in his seat.

Poe placed another photograph in front of him. This time of a laptop. Smashed.

'This is your laptop, Mr Keaton. You destroyed it. It was vacuum-packed in a sous-vide bag. We found it in the same room as Mr Morris.'

'If it's destroyed, how can you demonstrate that it belonged to my client?' Collingwood said. 'It's a common make, it could be anyone's.'

'I said destroyed, Mr Collingwood, not destroyed beyond repair,' Poe replied. 'You see, I work with this quite brilliant woman. She does your head in sometimes but what she doesn't know about computers . . . well, you get the point. Within an hour she'd extracted the information from the hard drive and uploaded it to her own laptop.'

Keaton's eyes registered fear for the first time. He hadn't expected that.

'And lo and behold, hadn't someone only gone and researched how to kill someone in a car crash and get away with it. The page you spent the most time on described legitimate reasons to turn off airbags. And also a different page on how to stop them reset-ting after the engine starts again.'

Keaton snorted.

'Shame on you. You killed your wife to keep a Michelin star,' Poe said.

'That's not even circumstantial, Mr Poe,' Collingwood said.

Poe ignored him. 'Long story short, the coroner has changed the verdict on your wife's death from accidental death to unlawful killing. Oh, and in case you were wondering, you *will* be pleading guilty to her murder. To all three in fact. Lauren Keaton, Elizabeth Keaton and Les Morris.'

'Are you threatening my client, Sergeant Poe?'

'Have you heard me threaten your client, Mr Collingwood? No, let's just call it . . . predicting the future.'

Keaton's smirk slipped. He was unnerved.

'With your wife dead, Elizabeth took a greater part in the business. According to my friend Tilly, it was while Elizabeth was using your laptop to check a payroll discrepancy that she stumbled across the same evidence we did: how you murdered her mother.'

Poe stared at the man in front of him. Keaton turned away.

'She challenged you on what she'd found and you murdered her for it.'

CHAPTER SIXTY-FIVE

Keaton's brief asked for a break and PACE dictated that he was allowed one. After they'd all eaten, and Keaton had rested, Poe continued.

'Of course, then you had a problem. You couldn't bury Elizabeth: the ground was too hard to dig and, even if it hadn't been, you couldn't carry her corpse far enough away from Bullace & Sloe for it not to be found. And you knew enough about forensic transfer to know you couldn't use your car without leaving something for us to find.'

Poe glanced at Keaton. He was eerily calm.

'I don't know if you'd been back to the bunker since you locked Les Morris in there, but you knew if you could get Elizabeth's body down there without leaving evidence in your car, we'd never find her.'

He put the next set of photographs on the table. Keaton didn't look at them. Collingwood did and nearly lost his lunch.

'And then the most horrific thing I've ever been involved with. Using your well-honed butchery skills, you dismembered her. Cut, chopped and sawed her into forty-three pieces. You vacuum-packed the body parts in sous-vide bags, then hot-washed the outside to remove any blood or trace evidence. You did the same with the tools you'd used to cut her up, the laptop containing the evidence about your wife's murder, and the clothes you were wearing. With everything nice and clean, you drove it all to your bunker.'

'This is preposterous,' Collingwood said.

Poe ignored him. 'You were thinking ahead, though, and you kept some of her blood. Used a small squeezy-bottle to suck some up, then you hid it under some built-up ice in a freezer in the development kitchen. You probably planned to frame young Jefferson Black when the time was right.'

'Is this all you have, Sergeant Poe?' Collingwood asked. 'Because it's beyond feeble. A first-year lawyer could get this thrown out of court.'

Poe continued to ignore him.

'Let's spin forward six years. Your plan didn't work. You're convicted of Elizabeth's murder and you're in HMP Pentonville. There's a riot in another wing. You get locked in someone else's cell and for the next few hours you have a good old nosey around.'

Rigg handed him a photograph. It was the one Barbara Stephens had found in Richard Bloxwich's cell.

'You see Richard's family snap and you can't believe your eyes. His daughter bears a striking resemblance to your own. She's even the right age.'

Keaton glared at him.

'But how could you use this? She might *look* like Elizabeth, but you can't *prove* she's Elizabeth. You needed a way to introduce the blood evidence. But how?'

Poe waited, but only to annoy Keaton. He'd talk, but not yet.

'And this is when another actor enters the stage,' Poe said. 'Since you were sentenced, every personal officer you've ever had says you were terrified when you were on general population. So much so you'd do anything you could to spend time on the hospital wing. It was there that you met Flick Jakeman. She's an attending doctor from London's University College Hospital and, more for something to do, I suspect, you've been working the Keaton charm on her. You convince her of your innocence. When you mention what you'd seen in Richard Bloxwich's cell, and that you still had access to some of your daughter's blood, she tells you about a man called John Schneeberger, and how he'd been able to fool a DNA test. It was a simple but brilliant plan, but if you were going to have any chance of pulling off something similar, you'd need to get out of the prison for a while so the two of you could speak without being overheard. So, after being shown where by Flick Jakeman, you stabbed yourself. You now have a wound too serious to treat in the prison hospital.'

Poe paused again. Looked Keaton in the eyes.

He handed across a statement.

'Take an hour, gentlemen,' Poe said. 'It's fascinating reading.'

When Jakeman saw the half-dead Chloe Bloxwich being carried out of the crumbling bunker, she'd collapsed in despair.

'Oh my God, what have I done!' she'd screamed.

When she saw that her actions had almost led to the death of Bloxwich, and was shown the photographs of the corpses in the bunker, she realised how much Keaton had exploited her. Although she'd been manipulated, and was in her own words 'a little bit obsessed with him', she wasn't one of those people who refused to believe the things in front of her.

She'd told them everything.

It wasn't an excuse, she'd said, but she had been on medication for depression at the time. Her divorce had been far tougher on her than she'd told Poe when he'd talked to her at her surgery in Ulverston. Before he left, her husband had racked up significant debt in her name. Debt she had no hope of paying off.

She'd met Keaton in the prison hospital wing. She'd been susceptible to promises of a happy ending and, although she knew love was just a chemical imbalance that invariably corrected itself, and that what he was asking of her was illegal, his promise to sort out her finances proved to be too attractive. She was a doctor and that meant she was practical.

They came to an agreement and began planning.

First Jakeman had to recruit Chloe Bloxwich. That hadn't been difficult. Chloe was an aspiring, but as yet unsuccessful, actress. When Jakeman promised her a Debbie McGee-type role on the cookery show that Keaton said he was planning after he was released, she'd jumped at the chance.

Next, Jakeman moved up to Cumbria. It wasn't a hardship. She'd been close to losing her London house anyway, she liked hill walking and visited the Lakes at least once a year. And the county needed doctors. Ensuring that she got on the FME register was even easier – competition for the role wasn't fierce.

According to Jakeman, she and Keaton discussed her progress almost every night on the phone. The prison service had a lot to answer for, Poe thought. They really needed to do much better on curbing the use of illegal mobiles.

The next thing was to recover and repair the blood that Keaton had hidden at Bullace & Sloe. He told her he'd kept it to ensure whoever had murdered his daughter was convicted. If he'd had to plant evidence he would, she said.

It was in a 50-millilitre sauce bottle. One of those that you squeeze and release to fill it. He told her he'd loosened some ice in a freezer in the development kitchen, hidden the bottle, repacked the ice, then sprayed it with water to make sure the seal was seamless. Keaton told her where the spare key was and she let herself in one night and retrieved it.

She had a problem, though. You can't just freeze blood untreated. When it thaws, the walls of the red blood cells are damaged by the ice crystals that have formed. But Jakeman was a doctor and she knew how to fix this. She bought a second-hand centrifuge machine used by laboratories and hospitals to separate blood into red blood cells, white blood cells and platelets. She gently defrosted the blood then removed all the damaged red cells. As red blood cells don't carry DNA, all she had to do was replace them with her own and add a bit of anticoagulant to stop it clotting. She now had blood with Elizabeth's DNA.

And then came the really clever bit, the impossible bit: the trick that had convinced everyone that Chloe was Elizabeth. She put the blood in Chloe's body.

When Poe mentioned the lack of drainage in the bunkers, it had triggered an alarm in Bradshaw's mind and she had remembered the John Schneeberger case. He'd fooled the DNA by inserting a surgical device called a Penrose drain, normally used to remove fluid after surgery, into his own arm. It was full of another man's blood and some anticoagulants to prevent it from clotting. Twice he'd fooled the laboratory technician into taking the sample from the area where the Penrose drain was fitted.

Jakeman had access to more modern equipment and she was able to refine the process. Instead of a Penrose drain, she used an artificial vein with the end blocked with surgical resin. She inserted the blocked end into Chloe's arm. It only needed to go in a couple of inches. Just enough so that it was hidden and Jakeman could find it with her needle. The other end, the end that wasn't in her body, ran up the inside of her arm and into a blood transfer bag that was strapped to her armpit. When they were ready, Jakeman turned the valve on the bag of blood and gravity filled the vein.

The blood was then drawn from her arm despite it never having been in her body. Not even for a second.

It was a low-tech solution from start to finish. Brilliant in its simplicity. If it hadn't been for the black summer truffle proteins attached to the white blood cells, they'd have almost certainly got away with it.

After the blood was taken and the lie had been told, it was essential that Chloe disappeared before anyone who knew Elizabeth had a chance to bump into her. Keaton had already told Jakeman where the bunker was, and that he'd fixed a rock-climbing ladder to the inside of the hatch so anyone inside could climb out. Jakeman hadn't thought to question it. She'd driven Chloe there, helped her climb down, never realising that it had been rigged so it couldn't be opened from the inside. She then covered the hatch with a light covering of leaves and dirt. Chloe was to wait three days then climb out and head home to Birmingham. Keaton would contact her after he was released.

Jakeman also admitted to planting a smear of Elizabeth's blood in Poe's trailer. Keaton had told her that Poe would be exonerated after he'd tracked down the real killer but they needed to explain Chloe's disappearance. She had trekked across to Herdwick Croft before he'd even got up to Cumbria and selected his trailer as the place to leave the evidence.

She knew it was all a lie now. Knew that Chloe had to disappear for good, and someone had to take the blame. Keaton's daughter being murdered by the cop who'd been disgraced by her reappearance was more plausible than her reappearing only to disappear again without explanation.

Keaton also had her make sure Chloe's phone was near Herdwick Croft the night Poe arrived back in Cumbria. A friend of Jakeman's on the force had told her when Gamble had asked Poe to come up.

She'd also called Keaton after Poe had asked her if Elizabeth had a tattoo on her hip. When Keaton confirmed that Elizabeth hadn't, Jakeman had relayed this information to Poe.

Jakeman now understood that Keaton's zero-tolerance attitude towards risk meant that she'd have had to disappear too at some point. She was under no illusions she'd had a lucky escape.

'As soon as we understood how the blood test had been falsified, and that Doctor Jakeman had to have been involved, I decided to speak to your client,' Poe said. 'I convinced him that my team would find the bunker as soon as they were able to hit the archives.'

They were back in the interview room. Keaton still didn't look worried. Poe thought he knew why, but he was happy to wait for Collingwood to officially tell him.

'We knew he wouldn't visit the bunker himself; we might have been watching him. Instead, he convinced Jakeman that the evidence of Chloe Bloxwich's three-day stay down there had to be destroyed. If it wasn't, the whole thing would have been for nothing. That was what she believed she was doing with the fuel anyway. Destroying trace evidence. Of course, what you were really getting her to do was destroy everything: the bodies of Elizabeth and Mr Morris; the presumably dead by then body of Chloe; the laptop and the tools you used. Everything.'

Keaton stared without expression.

'So, we didn't watch you, we watched her. And she led us straight to the bunker.' Poe waited for a reaction. Didn't get one. 'And here we are. Two dead bodies and two live witnesses. We can't wait to hear your side of this.'

Collingwood cleared his throat.

'What a nice story, Sergeant Poe,' he said. 'It is, of course, complete balderdash.'

CHAPTER SIXTY-SIX

A quirk of the British legal system gave the accused a peculiar advantage. Because all evidence against them had to be disclosed, it allowed the defence to explain it away after the fact. That was why all solicitors advised 'no comment' responses until everything was laid out in front of them. They could then start explaining their way through the facts, weaving alternate theories where they could.

'It is true that my client met Doctor Jakeman in the hospital wing and that she visited him in London's University College Hospital after he'd been assaulted,' Collingwood said. 'It is also true that they struck up a brief friendship while he was being treated. She visited him daily and made sure his treatment was going to plan.'

Poe said nothing. He was expecting this. Keaton had been planning his escape for years and, like a chess Grandmaster, he was always thinking ten steps ahead. And he'd never had a problem with sacrificing his pawns . . .

'I'm glad Doctor Jakeman has admitted she is obsessed with my client but it goes deeper than you realise. Long before they met in prison, long before he was stabbed, long before he was wrongly convicted of his daughter's murder, in fact. She told you she visited the Lake District quite often, I see?'

Poe nodded. He didn't really care.

'What she probably hasn't told you is that she ate at his restaurant. Several times, in fact. My client has no recollection of this, obviously, but there's a chef there called Stuart Scott who has already confirmed this.'

Stuart Scott? Almost certainly the 'Scotty' that Jefferson Black believed was responsible for telling Keaton about him and his daughter. The man he beat up badly enough for him to lose his spleen. Black had said Scotty was a careerist. He doubted he'd have a problem with lying for Keaton.

'Please continue,' Poe said.

'We think, in the balance of probability, it was Doctor Jakeman who killed Elizabeth.' Collingwood settled back in his seat.

'Doctor Jakeman killed Elizabeth?' Poe repeated.

'We'll probably never know why. It could be, in her deluded state, she believed she could have him for herself if the daughter wasn't there any more. We further believe that she kept some of Elizabeth's blood and set about the chain of events that you've been investigating this last week or so. We also believe that it was she who arranged for Mr Keaton to be stabbed. As you know, she spent a lot of time on the hospital wing – it wouldn't have been difficult for someone this manipulative to arrange for one prisoner to stab another. And obviously you caught her red-handed trying to kill the only witness who could have proved her guilt.'

'Why wait six years then?' Rigg asked. He looked worried, but he didn't know what Poe knew.

'Not my job to do yours, DC Rigg.'

'How did she find Chloe Bloxwich?'

Collingwood shrugged but didn't answer.

'Your client's prints are on every one of the bags Elizabeth's body was packed in.'

'It's his kitchen, DC Rigg. I imagine his prints will be on most things.'

'And the laptop researching his wife's murder?'

'Who knows why Elizabeth was looking into that? Perhaps it was she who disabled the airbag. We'll likely never know.'

'Oh, I think we will,' Poe said. He stood. 'Interview over.'

Rigg followed him outside and into the viewing room. Gamble, Flynn and a senior member of the Crown Prosecution Service were waiting for him. Bradshaw was on her laptop.

Gamble looked grim.

'What's up, sir?' Rigg said. 'You don't believe that bullshit, do you?'

'Of course not,' Gamble replied. 'But, this man here . . .' He gestured towards the CPS guy.

'I didn't say I believed him,' the CPS guy said, 'but now I know what their defence is, to be honest, it stands a good chance. Doctor Jakeman has already admitted being part of the conspiracy. She's admitted being obsessed with Keaton and she's admitted making contact with Chloe Bloxwich and helping her to try and pervert the course of justice.'

'But Keaton . . .' Rigg said.

'Other than when he was in hospital, there is no evidence tying the two of them together. Prison records will support this.'

'Accessing a mobile in prison's easier than getting a fucking blowjob!' Rigg shouted.

The CPS man nodded. 'And undoubtedly that was how it was done. But we can't prove it. Keaton's team will say she acted alone and we have nothing to suggest otherwise.'

'Chloe Bloxwich will back up Doctor Jakeman.'

'She already has. But she's also admitted that she has never personally spoken to Keaton. All her instructions came from Jakeman.'

They descended into silence. Rigg glared at the CPS guy. So did Gamble.

'Face it, Keaton played Doctor Jakeman perfectly. He almost certainly *is* behind everything but it'll be her who takes the fall.'

Poe had to hand it to Keaton – he was a clever man. It was only his lack of interest in the lives of others that was going to bring him down. The rest of the plan was flawless.

'You're taking this remarkably calmly, Poe,' Gamble said.

'Calm's my middle name, sir.'

'I thought you didn't have a middle name, Poe,' Bradshaw said.

He winked at her and the room went silent again.

His phone beeped. He read the text. 'Ah good, she's here.'

'What *are* you up to, Poe?' Gamble asked.

Poe ignored him. He turned to the CPS man.

'What do you need?'

'Short of a full confession,' he replied, 'I'm struggling to see how anything will help us at this stage.'

Poe smiled. 'A full confession it is then.'

CHAPTER SIXTY-SEVEN

Poe returned to the interview room. This time, instead of Rigg, he had a woman with him. They both took a seat.

'Who's this, Poe?' Keaton sneered.

Collingwood looked satisfied with his morning's work. 'Unless you have some new evidence, Sergeant Poe, I think the next time we speak should be at my client's retrial. We'll put our version of events in front of the jury – you can put yours.'

'If it even gets in front of a jury,' Keaton said.

Poe gave him a polite smile. 'You're right, Mr Keaton, this won't be going in front of a jury.'

Keaton's smile broadened.

'I'd like to talk about someone we've barely mentioned yet, if I may?' Poe said. 'I'd like to talk about Chloe's father, Richard.'

'Him? What can he possibly have to add to this? I barely knew the man.'

'That, Mr Keaton, is abundantly clear.'

Keaton looked indifferent.

'We've allowed Chloe to speak to him. Did you know that?'

He shrugged. 'Why should I care?'

'I just wondered what you thought of him. Between these four walls, we all know you tried to kill his daughter. He'll be out in a few years. Are you not worried he'll seek revenge?'

Keaton snorted. 'Even if this were all true, and I'm not admitting anything, what could Richard Bloxwich possibly do to me?

He's a feeble man. A pen-pushing accountant. What's he going to do, hit me with a calculator?'

Poe nodded. 'You're probably right. He probably doesn't have it in him.'

'Exact—'

'Only, I'm wondering why, in an overcrowded prison, he had a single cell?'

Keaton's smugness slipped. Collingwood looked thoughtful.

'Tell you what, why don't we come back to that? I think it's time I introduced you to Detective Chief Inspector Barbara Stephens.'

Stephens was a slender, confident-looking woman. Her short hair was black and spiky and she wore a pair of red designer glasses. She gave Keaton and Collingwood a little wave. 'Hello.'

Poe turned to Collingwood. 'She has a photograph she'd like to show you, Mr Collingwood. After you've seen it, you'll have a decision to make.'

Keaton frowned. 'What is this, Poe? What trick are you pulling here?'

'No tricks, Mr Keaton. It's just that . . . you should never assume that *you* know everything *I* know.' He looked at the camera in the corner of the ceiling. He gave it a thumbs-up. The green light changed to red. 'We are no longer being recorded, Mr Collingwood. You'll understand why in a second.' He turned to Stephens. 'Over to you, guv.'

Stephens slipped a glossy photograph out of a file. It had been taken at long-range but the two men in the picture were clear. One of them was Richard Bloxwich. The other man Poe knew only by reputation.

'That's Richard Bloxwich on the right. Do you know who the man on the left is?'

Collingwood looked at the photograph and paled. His breathing became quick and laboured. His pallid brow became clammy. He wiped it with a silk handkerchief. He nodded. 'I do.'

'Your firm has had dealings with the organisation he belongs to, have they not?' Stephens said. 'And now it appears you're briefing against them.'

The fat solicitor couldn't tear his eyes away from the photograph.

'Do you want to continue to represent Mr Keaton?' Poe asked.

Collingwood shook his head like a child refusing spinach. He was terrified. He turned to Keaton. 'Tell them everything, Mr Keaton. Omit nothing. Do it now.'

Keaton's smile collapsed so suddenly it looked like someone had severed his facial muscles. 'What's going on, Poe?' he demanded. His affected French accent had disappeared – it was pure Carlisle now. 'Who is that man?'

'The NCA's a broad church, Mr Keaton. My job is to catch people like you. DCI Stephens's is to work on the transnational organised crime taskforce.'

'Transnat—'

'Have you ever heard of an organisation called Entity B?' Stephens asked, clipping his sentence.

Keaton looked blank.

'There's no reason you should have. Your brief has, though. Do you want to explain, Mr Collingwood?'

Collingwood shook his head again.

'No? OK, then allow me,' she said. 'Entity B are the biggest and, therefore by definition, the most dangerous organised crime group operating in Europe today. Human trafficking, cyber crime, drugs obviously, weapons, including smuggling banned items to countries on watch lists – Entity B have their fingers in it all.'

Keaton's jaw developed a tic.

'Most people don't believe they exist. Unfortunately they're wrong. Entity B *do* exist and they are thriving.'

She prodded the photograph with her pen.

'And this man here, the one who appears to be talking to your boy Richard, is one of the organisation's top UK men.'

Poe took over. 'You see, Keaton, people think the power these organisations exert comes from all the horrible things they do, but their real power comes from being able to retain the money they've earned from all these horrible things they do.'

'Last year, Entity B is estimated to have turned over upwards of two billion euros,' Stephens added. 'That's a lot of money to clean.'

Realisation dawned on Keaton.

Poe nodded. 'You see where we're going with this, Keaton? These organisations exist solely because of the anonymous genius of the money launderer. Richard Bloxwich, the "feeble pen-pushing accountant" as you called him, is doing seven years for such a crime. Small-scale stuff, but he had information that could have proved useful to DCI Stephens's unit.'

Poe paused before continuing. 'Did he ever speak to you, guv?'

'No. Not even when we offered him a no-prison deal. Richard's a good boy. Very loyal to his organisation.'

Keaton was drumming a beat with his fingers. He stopped to rub the back of his neck. He didn't utter a sound.

'Chloe has spoken to her dad so he knows what's happened. It's a fair guess he's already called in the favour Entity B owes him,' Poe said. 'The way I see it, you have two choices. You either carry on with this facade and take your chances on the outside, or you give me a written confession now.'

Keaton's eyes were focused elsewhere. Poe wasn't sure he could hear him any more.

Collingwood cleared his throat. 'If my client gives you what you want, can you guarantee his safety?'

Poe shook his head. Stephens did too.

'All his confession buys is the same status afforded to protected witnesses,' Stephens said. 'He'll get a new name and he'll spend his sentence in a CSC.' She turned to Keaton and said, 'A CSC is a closed supervision centre. A prison within a prison, basically. It's the highest security available. And even that might not be enough.'

'You're lying,' Keaton whispered. He wore the forced smile of a hostage.

Poe planted his knuckles on the table, leaned forwards and stared into those baby-blue eyes. 'Oh yeah? Bet your life?'

CHAPTER SIXTY-EIGHT

It was early evening by the time Poe returned to Shap Wells. He collected his mail, said goodnight to Flynn and Bradshaw, and climbed wearily onto his quad. He felt curiously flat.

He hadn't known how long he would be interviewing, so Victoria had agreed to look after Edgar. He'd pick him up in the morning. Flynn and Bradshaw were staying on and they were all going out in Kendal for a curry the following night. Poe planned to invite Victoria as a thank you.

It had taken six hours before the CPS guy was happy that Keaton's confession was watertight.

Richard Bloxwich had never met the guy in the photograph. He was too far down the pecking order. Entity B bosses didn't meet with lowly money launderers. But they *appeared* to when Bradshaw got to work with her photograph manipulation software. And neither Poe nor DCI Stephens had explicitly said they *were* talking in the photograph. They merely suggested the possibility and let Keaton fill in the blanks.

It worked. Keaton admitted everything.

How he'd killed Les Morris. It was as Poe suspected: he'd moved the ladder from the fixed ring to the underside of the hatch. Morris had had no way of getting out. Keaton had returned three months later to put his corpse in the chemical toilet room.

He told them how he'd killed his wife to save his Michelin star, and how he'd killed Elizabeth when she'd found the evidence on his laptop. How he'd used the sous-vide vacuum machine to seal her dismembered corpse before depositing her, and everything else, in the same room of the bunker as Morris.

The blood he'd kept back had been to frame Jefferson Black.

The rest tallied with what they'd heard from Chloe Bloxwich and Flick Jakeman. He'd recruited Jakeman while on the hospital wing then stabbed himself so they could get a bit of time to do some planning – prison officers were required to leave doctors and patients alone in outside hospitals due to confidentiality issues. Keaton admitted that Jakeman wouldn't have known that she was trapping Chloe in the bunker, and that she'd thought she was bringing petrol to the bunker that night to destroy all evidence of her stay down there. She had no idea she would be destroying corpses.

Flick Jakeman and Chloe Bloxwich would both do time. Two more ruined lives to go with the three people Keaton had murdered.

Keaton would be charged with the murder of Les Morris, the murder of his wife and the attempted murder of Chloe Bloxwich. He'd already submitted an early guilty plea for the murder of Elizabeth. The CPS planned to push for a rare 'whole life' sentence. Keaton would never be eligible for parole.

Poe asked if Keaton had tried to frame him because his dad had refused to sell him his property in Kendal. Keaton didn't know what he was talking about. It had been a coincidence, one he was happy to accept for once. Keaton had chosen him for no other reason than he had to choose someone, and Poe was the one who'd refused to be fooled all those years ago.

Before he left Carlisle, Poe had shaken hands with Rigg and Gamble. The two men had come through. Not just for him. They'd ensured the right result for Elizabeth, Les and Lauren. Justice wasn't swift but it had been delivered.

On the drive down the M6 he'd called Jefferson Black and told him the news. Maybe finally knowing what had happened to Elizabeth would give the ex-Para the closure he needed. Poe doubted it, but it was the least he could do. Jefferson Black was the one who'd unwittingly blown the case wide open.

Poe crested the peak and saw his croft. He braked sharply. The lights were on. Not all of them, but some. Someone was inside. He'd already spoken to Victoria and he'd only just left Flynn and Bradshaw.

He didn't know anyone else.

He found his binoculars but couldn't see any movement inside. He revved the quad gently and approached his home cautiously. He parked in his usual place and dismounted. There was still no movement.

He noticed a document in a plastic cover stuck to his door. He ripped it off and read it. It was from the council. He suspected there'd be a corresponding document in the mail he'd just collected. He tore the plastic wallet open with his teeth.

It was an official order to return the property to the condition he'd found it in.

Bastards. Victoria was right: they *were* evicting him.

He checked his mail and saw a letter that stuck out. This one was in a plain manila envelope. His name was printed on the front. It had been hand-delivered to the hotel. He opened it.

It was a blank application to review planning permission for buildings in the Lake District National Park. He turned it over and read the message. It said, 'Fuck you, Poe'. There was a 'W' printed underneath. Wardle, the vindictive prick, had sniffed out Poe's newfound weakness like a rat sniffing out an unguarded turd.

But . . . that didn't explain who was in his home.

He pushed open the door and let his eyes adjust to the gloom. A man was asleep on the sofa. It couldn't be . . . surely?

He peered closely.

It was.

Poe was shocked at how much he'd aged.

He turned on all the lights and the man awoke at once. He squinted in the harsh glare.

'You startled me,' he said.

Poe walked past him and opened the fridge to get a beer. It was heavily stocked with fruit and bottled water. He allowed himself a wry grin. Bradshaw was still trying to look after him. He grabbed two beers, flipped their tops and passed one over.

'I think we need to talk, Washington,' the old man said after he'd taken a sip.

'Tomorrow, Dad,' Poe said. 'We can talk tomorrow.'

ACKNOWLEDGEMENTS

A semi-literate knuckle-dragger like myself invariably needs a team of people behind him to turn an incoherent, random stream of consciousness into a readable novel. And invariably this team likes to be thanked. In order of height they are:

My editor, Krystyna Green, for her unwavering support, unbridled enthusiasm and boundless energy. Thank you for taking a chance and thank you for seeing the wood when all I can see are the trees.

My structural editor, Martin Fletcher, gets special thanks for his expertise and sound advice. We have a shared vision for what Poe and Tilly can achieve, Martin – I think we're getting there.

Howard Watson, my copy editor, for putting my words in the right order and for diligently fact checking. It was Howard who caught that, according to the timeline I'd set up in *The Puppet Show*, Poe would have joined the police when he was eleven . . .

Joan Deitch, my proofreader, for hunting and killing all those stubborn little typos.

Sean Garrehy gets a special mention for another killer cover. I didn't think you'd be able to beat what you did with *The Puppet Show* but you've smashed it out of the park with this one.

Rebecca Sheppard – almost certainly the best desk editor in the universe – for her ability to herd the cats named above. Every team needs someone who can stay calm when everyone else flaps about like lunatics.

And finally from Constable, Beth Wright and Brionee Fenlon –

without publicity and marketing no one would have read anything I've written. So . . . technically this is all your fault.

As is traditional, I've saved the most important person for half-way down the list. David Headley, my agent and friend, you're a force of nature. I'd gnaw my own arm off just to get half your energy and drive – I really don't know how you do it. Thank you for keeping me on the right path, thanks for your friendship, and thanks for getting Poe and Tilly to the widest possible audience.

And while I'm on DHH Literary Agency, the oft-put-upon Emily Glenister should get a shout. She bears the brunt of my insecurities and neuroses and does it all with good humour. Thanks, Em!

There are two people I trust to read my books before I have the courage to send them to David. My two beta readers, Angie Morrison and Stephen Williamson – thank you for taking the time to offer honest and constructive feedback. You're both an integral part of my process and the books wouldn't be what they are without your valued input.

My wife, Joanne, should get a page of dedications all of her own. But, I've checked, she can't have one. So, I'll just say this: none of this would be possible without you, Jo. Your encouragement during the early days, the professional eye you cast during these later ones, all of it is appreciated. I'm that grateful I'm considering telling you where I hide the crisps.

There are a few people who helped with the research for *Black Summer* who I should probably thank (they'll only moan if I don't).

Stuart Wilson, my friend of over forty years and fellow real ale enthusiast, for patiently explaining how a farmer could cut out the middleman and take their lamb and mutton directly to the consumer.

Harold Archer, 22 Group ROCA, for your incredible input on what ROC Nuclear Observation Bunkers were really like, how they were constructed, what it was like to stand a post etc. It added a level of authenticity I couldn't have achieved by surfing the net.

Katie Douglass, my brilliant niece, for helping me work out a solution to a seemingly intractable problem. It was 'Tilly-like' in its ingenuity. Please, Katie, don't ever decide to become an evil genius – you'll be too good at it.

Brian Price gets a big thumbs up for the invaluable scientific advice.

My police advisers, Jude and Greg Kelly. As always, my random questions never failed to amuse but, as always, they never failed to get a reasoned and considered response.

And finally the section you've all been waiting for: the miscellaneous thanks:

Crawford Bunney – for allowing me to say your 'simian arms were pale, hairy and disproportionately long'. Your friendship has been one of the highlights of my life these last twenty years.

To all the bloggers, reviewers and readers – a book isn't a book until the words on the page have been turned into pictures in the mind. Keep doing what you do, guys. I guarantee there isn't an author out there who isn't truly grateful.

Fiona Sharp, from Waterstones Durham, deserves a special mention. Her enthusiasm for *The Puppet Show* was overwhelming. Wherever I went last year authors and publicists would mention your continued promotion of it.

Barbara Stephens gets a shout for her extraordinarily generous donation to the Cumbrian charity Safety Net (UK). It was an honour to name a character after you, Barbara.

Mary Jackson, my mother-in-law, gets a nod for buying a copy of *The Puppet Show* every single time she sees one in a shop. She now has more copies than the Little, Brown warehouse.

Moffat Crime Writers and the Crime & Publishment gang get a cheer for their support, friendship and camaraderie.

Iron Maiden should get a vote of thanks for having a playlist for every writing mood. I grew up a punk but will die a Maiden fan. Up the Irons!

And finally, Bracken: my own version of Edgar. Without you barking to tell me that someone two miles away had just opened their door, this book would have been finished in half the time.

Thanks, everyone. We must do this again sometime.

Mike

P.S. I really have no idea how tall you all are. Except Crawford – he's freakishly lanky.

Enjoyed *Black Summer*? Read on for a special preview of book three in M.W. Craven's Washington Poe series . . .

The Curator

'The player who understands the role of the pawn, who really understands it, can master the game of chess,' the man said. 'They might be the weakest piece on the board but pawns dictate where and when your opponent can attack. They restrict the mobility of the so-called bigger pieces and they determine where the battle squares will be.'

The woman stared at him in confusion. She'd just woken and was feeling groggy.

And sore.

She twisted her head and searched for the source of her pain. It didn't take long.

'What have you done?' she mumbled.

'Beautiful isn't it? It's old-fashioned catgut so the sutures are a bit agricultural, but they're supposed to be. It's not used any more but I needed the "wick effect". That's when infection enters the wound through the suture. It will ensure the scar stays livid and crude. A permanent reminder of what has happened.'

He picked up a pair of heavy-duty rib shears.

'Although not for you, of course.'

The woman thrashed and writhed but it was no use. She was bound tight.

The man admired the exacting lines of the surgical instrument. Turned it so the precision steel caught the light. Saw his face reflected in the larger blade. He looked serious. This wasn't something he particularly enjoyed.

'Please,' the woman begged, fully awake now, 'let me go. I promise you I won't say anything.'

The man walked round and held her left hand. He stroked it affectionately.

1

'I've had to wait for the anaesthetic to wear off so this is going to hurt, I'm afraid. Believe me when I say I wish it didn't have to.'

He placed her ring finger between the blades of the rib shears and squeezed the handles together. There was a crunch as the razor-sharp edges sliced through bone and tendon as if they weren't there.

The woman screamed then passed out. The man stepped away from the spreading pool of blood.

'Where was I?' he said to himself. 'Ah, yes, we were talking about pawns. Beginners think they're worthless, there to be sacrificed – but that's because they don't know when to use them.'

He removed a coil of wire from his pocket. It had toggles at each end. He placed them between the index and middle finger of each hand. In a practised movement he wrapped the wire around the woman's neck.

'Because knowing when to sacrifice your pawns is how the game is won.'

He pulled the garrotte taut, grunting as the cruel wire bit into her skin, severing her trachea, crushing her jugular vein and carotid artery. She was dead in seconds.

He waited an hour then took the other finger he needed.

He carefully arranged it in a small plastic tub, keeping it separate from the others. He looked at his macabre collection with satisfaction.

It could begin now.

The other pawns were in position.

They just didn't know it yet . . .

CHAPTER ONE

Christmas Eve

It was the night before Christmas and all wasn't well.

It had started like it always did. Someone asking, 'Are we doing Secret Santa this year?' and someone else replying, 'I hope not,' both making a pact to avoid mentioning it to the office manager, both secretly planning to mention it as soon as possible.

And before anyone could protest, the decision had been made and the office was doing it again. The fifteenth year in a row. Same rules as last year. Five-quid limit. Anonymous gifts. Nothing rude or offensive. Gifts that no one wanted. A total waste of everyone's time.

At least that's what Craig Hodgkiss thought. He hated Secret Santa.

He hated Christmas too. The yearly reminder that his life was shit. That while the colleagues he outwardly sneered at were going home to spend Christmas with their families and loved ones, he'd be spending it on his own.

But he *really* hated Secret Santa.

Three years ago it had been the source of his greatest humiliation. Setting himself the not unreasonable Christmas target of shagging Hazel, a fellow logistics specialist at John Bull Haulage, he'd wangled it so he was the one who'd bought her Secret Santa gift. He reckoned buying her a pair of lace panties would be the perfect way to let her know he was up for some extracurricular activities while her husband long-hauled across mainland Europe.

His plan worked.

Almost.

It *had* been the perfect way to let her know.

Unfortunately she was happily married and instead of rushing into his bed she'd rushed to her husband, who was between jobs and was having a brew in the depot. The six-foot-five lorry driver had walked into the admin office and broken Craig's nose. He'd told him that if he ever so much as looked at his wife again he'd find himself hogtied in the back of a Russia-bound shipping container. Craig believed him. So much so that, in front of the whole office, he'd lost control of his bladder.

For two years everyone had called him 'swampy'. He couldn't even complain to Human Resources as he was terrified of getting Hazel into trouble.

For two years he hadn't made a dent in the girls in the office.

But eventually Hazel and her brute of a husband had moved on. He took a job driving for Eddie Stobart and she went with him. Craig told everyone that Hazel's husband had left the company because he'd caught up with him and given him a hiding, but no one had believed him.

Actually, one person seemed to.

By Craig's own standards, Barbara Willoughby was a plain girl. Her hair looked like it had been styled in a nursing home, her teeth were blunt and too widely spaced, and she could have done with dropping a couple of pounds. On a scale of one-to-ten Craig reckoned she was a hard six, maybe a seven in the right lighting, and he only ever shagged eights and above.

But there was one thing he did like about her. She hadn't been there when he'd pissed himself.

So he'd asked her out. And to his surprise he found they got on really well. She was fun to be with and she was popular. He liked how she made him feel and she was adventurous in bed. He also liked how she only wanted to do things at the weekends. During the week she would stay in and study for some stupid exams she was taking.

Which suited Craig just fine.

Because, after a few weeks of dating Barbara, he'd got his swagger back. And with it he began carving notches again.

To his amazement he discovered it was actually easier pulling the type of woman he went for when he told them he was in a long-term relationship. He reckoned it was the combination of his boyish good looks and the thought of doing over someone they didn't know. Which gave Craig an idea: if those sort of women enjoyed the thrill of being with someone who cheated, they'd go crazy for someone who had affairs . . .

So Craig Hodgkiss, at the age of twenty-nine, decided he would ask Barbara to marry him. She'd jump at the chance. She was in her early thirties, had some biological clock thing going on (but was unaware he'd had a vasectomy two years earlier) and would almost certainly be left on the shelf if she said no. And then he'd reap the rewards. A faithful doormat keeping his bed warm and a succession of women who'd happily shag a man wearing a wedding band.

And because he wanted everyone in the office to know he was about to become illicit fruit, he'd decided to put past experiences behind him and propose during the office Secret Santa.

Arranging it hadn't been straightforward. He'd got Barbara's ring size by stealing her dead grandmother's eternity ring, the one she only wore on special occasions. While Barbara turned her flat upside down looking for it, he'd been asking a jeweller to make the engagement ring the same size and to recycle the diamonds and gold. The whole thing had only cost him two hundred quid.

The next thing was to think of a cool way of proposing.

Something that would get the office girls talking about how romantic Craig was. A rep like that could only help. He decided on a mug. It was the perfect Secret Santa gift as it met the five-quid limit set by the office manager and, although half the gifts under the cheap fibre optic Christmas tree looked like they were mugs, half the gifts under the tree didn't have 'Will You Marry Me?' printed on the side.

When Barbara read the message and then saw what was inside . . . well, he reckoned she'd burst into tears, shout yes and hug him for all she was worth.

The office floor was strewn with cheap wrapping paper. All reindeer and snowmen and brightly wrapped presents tied with ribbons.

Barbara was next. She picked up her parcel and looked at him strangely.

Did she know?

She couldn't. No one did. Not even the girl he'd persuaded to swap with him so he was the one buying for Barbara.

Tiffany, Barbara's best friend, began recording it on her mobile phone for some reason. That was OK though. Better than OK actually. He'd be able to post it on Twitter and Facebook and keep a copy on his phone. Ready to show girls at the drop of a hat. Look at me. Look how nice I am. Look how *sensitive* I am. You can have some of this . . . but only for one night.

Craig caught Barbara's eye. He winked. She didn't return it. Didn't even smile. Just held his gaze as she lifted the wrapped box from one of his old gift bags.

Something wasn't right. The wrapping paper was thick and white with black pictures; he thought his had been cheap and brightly coloured.

Barbara ripped it off without looking at it. The mug was in a polystyrene box. He'd taped the two halves together to increase the suspense. Barbara ran a pair of scissors down the join before separating them.

She pulled out the mug and Craig's confusion intensified. It wasn't his. He hadn't seen this one before. Something *was* printed on the side but it wasn't proposing marriage. In inch-high black letters it said:

#BSC6

Barbara didn't know she'd opened the wrong parcel though. Without looking inside the mug, she glared at him and upended the mug's contents.

'Cheating fucking bastard,' she said.

Craig didn't protest his innocence. He couldn't. He was unable to tear his eyes away from the things that had fallen on the floor. They were no engagement ring.

He recoiled and gasped in revulsion.

A familiar and unwelcome warmth began spreading from his groin again.

And then the screaming started.

Also by M.W. Craven

Born in a Burial Gown

An Avison Fluke novel

'Deeply layered, fiendishly clever and absorbing'
Matt Hilton, author of the *Joe Hunter* series

The first gritty thriller in the Avison Fluke series by
M.W. Craven, the acclaimed author of *The Puppet Show*.

Detective Inspector Avison Fluke is a man on the edge. He has
committed a crime to get back to work, concealed a debilitating
illness and is about to be made homeless. Just as he thinks
things can't get any worse, the body of a young woman is found
buried on a Cumbrian building site.

Shot once in the back of the head, it is a cold, calculated
execution. When the post-mortem reveals she has gone to
significant expense in disguising her appearance,
Fluke knows this is no ordinary murder.

With the help of a psychotic ex-Para, a gangland leader and a
woman more interested in maggots than people, Fluke must find
out who she was and why she was murdered before he can
even think about finding her killer . . .

Body Breaker

An Avison Fluke novel

'This is high-quality crime writing' A A Dhand

The second dark and twisted thriller in the Avison Fluke series by M.W. Craven, the acclaimed author of *The Puppet Show*.

Investigating how a severed hand ends up on the third green of a Cumbrian golf course is not how Detective Inspector Avison Fluke has planned to spend his Saturday. So, when a secret protection unit from London swoops in quoting national security, he's secretly pleased.

But trouble is never far away. A young woman arrives at his lakeside cabin with a cryptic message: a code known to only a handful of people, and it forces Fluke back into the investigation he's only just been barred from.

In a case that will change his life forever, Fluke immerses himself in a world of New Age travellers, corrupt cops and domestic extremists. Before long he's alienated his entire team, has been arrested under the Terrorism Act – and has made a pact with the Devil himself. But a voice has called out to him from beyond the grave. And Fluke is only getting started . . .

Help us make the next generation of readers

We – both author and publisher – hope you enjoyed this book.
We believe that you can become a reader at any time in your life,
but we'd love your help to give the next generation a head start.

Did you know that 9% of children don't have a book of their
own in their home, rising to 12% in disadvantaged families*?
We'd like to try to change that by asking you to consider the role
you could play in helping to build readers of the future.

We'd love you to think of sharing, borrowing, reading, buying or talking
about a book with a child in your life and spreading the love of reading.
We want to make sure the next generation continue to have access
to books, wherever they come from.

And if you would like to consider donating to charities that help
fund literacy projects, find out more at www.literacytrust.org.uk
and www.booktrust.org.uk.

Thank you.

little, brown
BOOK GROUP

*As reported by the National Literacy Trust

Help us make the next
generation of readers

CRIME AND THRILLER FAN?

CHECK OUT THECRIMEVAULT.COM

The online home of
exceptional crime fiction

KEEP YOURSELF
IN SUSPENSE

Sign up to our newsletter for regular recommendations,
competitions and exclusives at www.thecrimevault.com/connect

Follow us on twitter for all the latest news @TheCrimeVault